#23

The Orange Tree

The Orar

ge Tree

Mildred Walker

Edited and
with an introduction
by Carmen Pearson

UNIVERSITY OF NEBRASKA PRESS • LINCOLN AND LONDON

© 2006 by the American Heritage Center, University of Wyoming ¶ Introduction and Comments on Editing © 2006 by the Board of Regents of the University of Nebraska ¶ All rights reserved ¶ Manufactured in the United States of America ¶ ∞ ¶ Designed and set in Carter & Cone Galliard and Delphin by R. W. Boeche. ¶ Library of Congress Cataloging-in-Publication Data ¶ Walker, Mildred, 1905– ¶ The orange tree / Mildred Walker; edited and with an introduction by Carmen Pearson. ¶ p. cm. ¶ ISBN-13: 978-0-8032-4828-1 (cloth: alk. paper) ¶ ISBN-10: 0-8032-4828-8 (cloth: alk. paper) ¶ ISBN-13: 978-0-8032-9864-4 (pbk: alk. paper) ¶ ISBN-10: 0-8032-9864-1 (pbk: alk. paper) ¶ 1. Married people—Fiction. ¶ 2. Older couples—Fiction. ¶ 3. Marriage—Fiction. ¶ 4. Boston (Mass.)—Fiction. ¶ 5. Domestic fiction. ¶ I. Title. ¶ PS3545. A524073 2006 ¶ 813'.52—dc22

Tuzenbach: "*What trifles, what little things suddenly a' propos of nothing acquire importance in life! You laugh at them as before, think them nonsense, but still you go on and feel that you don't have the power to stop. Let's don't talk about it! I'm happy. I feel as though I were seeing these firs, these maples, these birch trees for the first time in my life, and they all seem to be looking at me with curiosity and waiting. What beautiful trees, and, really, how beautiful life ought to be under them! See, that tree is dead, but it waves in the wind with the others. And so it seems to me that if I die, I'll still be part of life, one way or another.*"

Anton Chekhov, *The Three Sisters*, act 4

Comments on Editing *The Orange Tree*

It did not seem to occur to Mildred Walker to ever stop writing. As Walker's daughter Ripley Hugo puts it, in Walker's life, particularly in her later years, she was "writing for her life." To her last days, Mildred Walker was a novelist—whether or not anyone wanted to publish or even read her work.

When the manuscript for *The Orange Tree* was rejected and returned to Walker by Atheneum and then by Little, Brown and Company in 1976, she wrote in her journal, "Last night I was utterly discouraged. . . . Still it is good to have that 360-page opus that has been on my mind for two years. Yet still I believe it will find a place. . . ."[1] For a number of years, she put the manuscript away after adding that "except for the waste of time and hope and energy and loss of faith in everyone in my ever publishing another I almost don't care that they didn't take it" (Hugo 263). Even as late as 1988 her journals indicate that she continued to work on the manuscript, considering changing the narrative to the first-person and of perhaps having Tiresa "as the central consciousness."

Mention of *The Orange Tree* first appeared in Mildred Walker's journals in the early 1970s, and in 1976 she completed her first version of the novel. Today three versions, sometimes with different renditions of particular scenes, comprising 746 double-spaced typed pages are found in The Mildred Walker Collection at The American Heritage Center in Laramie, Wyoming. From these pages, plus Walker's hand-written journals ("The Orange Tree" as well as personal journals), and numerous helpful observations by Walker's daughter Ripley Hugo, I have constructed a final manuscript of Walker's *The Orange Tree*.

Although one version of the manuscript is entitled "That Odd Word Joy," Walker and her family referred to the text as "The Orange Tree", which seemed to be her final choice of title. Because the actual mention of the orange tree only appears at the beginning and ending of Walker's text, I have inserted it in several scenes. Without this, I felt its significance was diminished and possibly even confusing to readers.

Having read through the pages a number of times, it seemed to me that Walker played with the ordering of the events. In constructing the manuscript, I first created what appeared to be the most logical organization for the novel based on both page numbering and, at times, just common sense. From this, I chose the version that seemed the most polished. After typing the exact words from this version, I then went through the texts of the other versions, at times adding or deleting or melding words and phrases. I only changed or added words or punctuation when there were obvious typos or it seemed necessary for clarity.

Walker seemed to have experimented on a few sections of the novel by presenting the narrative in the first-person, using either Tiresa's or Olive's voice. However, a third-person narrative appears to have been her ultimate choice for the novel. Her decision on this matter is reinforced by comments in her journals.

The most rewritten sections of Walker's manuscripts are found at the beginning and the ending. The version of the beginning that I chose seemed to me to flow most naturally into the rest of the narrative. The ending was extremely problematic for Walker, and she didn't seem to have a definitive version. In creating an ending, I relied on Ripley Hugo's personal reminiscences of her mother's thoughts at the time of the writing and of my working knowledge of the Walker's style and concerns—

as presented in her other novels, and in my own sense of balance and closure appropriate for the material—after the time I have spent with the manuscript.

It is apparent that Mildred Walker was, as always, juggling many concerns in this manuscript. In her journal and scattered throughout the text are various quotes—from such authors as Willa Cather, Arthur Miller, Enid Bagnold, and Lennie Adams—that she must have considered including in the novel. She also had a number of thoughts on the organization of the novel, with suggestions for three, four, and even six separate sections. Because the most consistent text Walker referred to directly in the novel and also used throughout her text was Chekhov's *The Three Sisters*, I chose to present the novel in four sections to parallel the play's four acts.

Beyond the fact that the characters in *The Orange Tree* attend Chekhov's play and then refer to it on a number of occasions, Walker's techniques closely parallel Chekhov's in *The Three Sisters*. For instance, both have characters searching for meaning and happiness in their often-uneventful middle class lives. Walker even has Tiresa and Paulo whisper to each other "tarara-boo-dee-ay," as do the characters in *The Three Sisters*. Chekhov's sisters comment on a green sash; Walker's women discuss a green cape. There are the winter scenes in both works, and the fire in the Russian village seems to parallel Ron's speeding on the New York Thruway. Chekhov employs the metaphor of the migrating birds to illustrate his theme, while Walker uses the orange tree. With these examples, and many more that remain unmentioned, it seemed fitting to organize the novel with the four scenes and four sets of corresponding quotes from *The Three Sisters* instead of offering quotes from the many authors Walker had considered.

In much the same way that Michael Cunningham recently contemporized Virginia Woolf's *Miss Dalloway* in *The Hours*, it might be said that Mildred Walker had contemporized Chekhov's

The Three Sisters in *The Orange Tree*. In doing so, both authors made their own unique and lasting contributions to literature. There are two qualities that distinguish literature from the rest of writing. One is that literature "stands on the shoulders of giants" and two, that its authors "make it new." By this, Ezra Pound surely meant that lasting literature speaks to, relies on, and is enriched by the past, and that a work of literature speaks in the genuine voice of its creator. Both qualities are to be found in *The Orange Tree*. Readers familiar with Mildred Walker's distinctive voice will surely find it here. And some readers may even be inspired enough to find themselves searching for old copies of Chekhov's play.

Note

1. The original manuscript for *The Orange Tree* is housed in "The Mildred Walker Collection" at The American Heritage Center in Laramie, Wyoming in Box 1, Accession Number 1393-01-08-24. Justin White produced the photocopies from which I compiled much of this text.

Introduction
A Brief Discussion of Chekhov's *The Three Sisters*

In all of Mildred Walker's novels, readers will find many elements of drama; she often presented her material as though it were created for the stage or camera. Her novel *The Southwest Corner* was easily and successfully adapted to both Broadway and television. Perhaps more than any other of her previous novels, Mildred Walker's *The Orange Tree* presents readers with a work of fiction whose structure most closely parallels a theatrical production. Not only does this novel read almost as a play—with the setting primarily within the walls of the two families' homes, a structure dependent upon the arrivals and departures of its key figures, and the conventional action almost always "offstage," deliberately giving precedent, instead, to the characters' thoughts and reactions—it, closely and purposely parallels Chekhov's *The Three Sisters* in its structure and thematic concerns.

As there was in Chekhov's play, a plot helps to move the story along and to assist in presenting the authorial concerns. In *The Orange Tree*, Walker allows her readers to discover this plot within the first few pages of her novel. There are three women in *The Orange Tree*, as there are in Chekhov's play. In *The Orange Tree* Tiresa, Olive, and Gumshoe search for meaning and happiness. From almost the start of the novel, readers can sense that Olive will divorce, Tiresa will die, and Gumshoe's means of finding happiness will evolve.

Having presented the plot and characters and a fairly gloomy situation so early on, Walker's challenge as a writer then focuses on maintaining her readers' interest in other ways. Chekhov is able to hold his readers' interest throughout *The Three Sisters*, which he himself described as "an atmosphere more gloomy than gloom itself" and which many critics described as "a play in which nothing happens—a bleakly actionless, plotless and shapeless drama"—by focusing his readers' attention on the characters' voices and feelings that are continuously "counterpointed against each other across various themes"; so too is Walker.[1] These voices, feelings, and themes are presented through a combination of dialogues, internal monologues, journal entries, and letters.

Within the first few pages of her novel, Walker presents her primary characters. Within these presentations, there is immediately a feeling of stasis—as though she has painted a still life of the two families. Paulo and Tiresa Romano are a middle-aged, educated couple. Tiresa has just returned from hospital. It is apparent from the care provided by her husband that her condition is chronic. Next door, in the same Boston apartment house, Olive and Ron Fifer are newlyweds getting settled in their first home. Olive is restless at home, unable to find a job, and somewhat disappointed with her marriage, and Ron seems either oblivious to this fact or purposely evasive of it. Although these two couples seem to have absolutely nothing in common other than proximity, they, in fact, become deeply involved in each other's lives.

From the very start of the text, there is a feeling of isolation. Not only does this completely focus the readers' attention on these two families, it also portrays the often-lonely reality of modern life.

Walker takes great care to present her characters with their many flaws. Tiresa is judgmental and tends to be either manipulative or blatantly controlling. Paulo, from Sicily, seems to carry the scars of his past by often romanticizing life's bare-bone facts—a point that Tiresa criticizes, but at the same time admires. Olive is self-absorbed almost to the point of obsession in her personal search for happiness and meaning in life, and Ron is hopelessly caught in his single-minded struggle for corporate success as he begins his career in the insurance industry. How then—with these characters, can Mildred Walker hope to create readerly sympathy? Walker shares with us these very ordinary lives—filled with job demands and aspirations, family demands and other frustrations, pasts best to be forgotten or to be remembered, dreams, births, and deaths—and reminds us what constitutes most of our lives: quiet dramas of domesticity. As uncomfortable as it is at times, Walker's characters are so human, we begin to sympathize with even their flaws; perhaps hoping that somebody someday will do the same for us.

As is the case in all her fiction, Walker presents many themes in *The Orange Tree*. There is the search for meaning through love and work and friends. Like Chekhov, Walker counterbalances youth with age and interweaves this with her characters' concerns about their own mortality. Laced through such worries are her characters' comments on such topics as women's liberation, marriage, abortion, familial obligations, ties to the past and to ethnic groups, the value of a liberal arts' education, the increasingly superficial nature of a culture driven by commerce, and the meaning of motherhood.

Not coincidentally, Tiresa is an English professor. Through Tiresa, Walker is conveniently able to present and explore what undoubtedly must have been some of her own thoughts on literature. For instance, when the Romanos invite the Fifers up to Vermont to their farm for the weekend, the date falls on the Eve of St. Agnes. Tiresa hopes to read Keats's poem on the Saturday night; however, Ron has brought up his disc player and much to Tiresa's dismay, the couples end up listening to Simon and Garfunkle instead.

It is also, upon Tiresa's insistence, that Paulo and Olive attend the production of Chekhov's *The Three Sisters*. Not surprisingly, Olive is drawn into this melancholy drama, pointing out that she is almost the same age as the sisters and that, metaphorically, she too, will never get to Moscow (the metaphor for happiness).

Because of Tiresa's position as an English professor, not only is Mildred Walker permitted to explore and present her thoughts on literature, she is also able to explore her thoughts on secondary education. Having taught young women in liberal arts colleges for over two decades, her insights into this subject are both engaging and contemporary.

When Tiresa's health deteriorates to the point where she must quit teaching, she continues in her scholarship by working on her book "Memory in Fiction." Tiresa's interest in this subject indicates a further interest of Walker's. For readers familiar with Walker's life, studying the integration of her own memories into her last major work of fiction adds an extra dimension to reading *The Orange Tree*. For instance, Walker draws upon her own trip to Sicily in forming Tiresa's journal entries. She includes details of her Vermont home, her teaching experiences, her own need to write and work even as her own health failed her, and concerns with her mortality. The scenes between Tiresa and Paulo arose from memories Walker had from the evenings she and her husband reviewed each other's writing. The descriptions of Tiresa's death from a heart condition surely were extracted from Walker's memories of her husband's painful death caused by heart complications.

Tiresa's interest in memory also indicates a subtext of *The Orange Tree*. With the possible exception of Ron, who becomes a secondary character relatively early on, Tiresa, Paulo, and Olive are torn by their memories and their pasts. This interest in the relevance of family and community history in the formation of character is a subject that emerges in one form or another in all of Walker's novels. As much as characters try to pull themselves from their roots and re-create themselves, they are inevitably tied to their own histories. For example, Tiresa constantly strives to be urbane, cool, aloof—always rational and under control; however, she continually acts on impulse—only to later rationalize and regret such moments. She remembers her mother's *kaffee klatches* and chats at the family bakery and shudders at the thought of how those women spilled out all their secrets to each other and yet, repugnant as she is of such seemingly low-class behavior, she is most human and likeable when she does the same. Paulo, an immigrant from Sicily, is happy to have made his life and fortune as an eye doctor in the United States and reticent to talk about his past. However, his language and philosophy are laden with his background—a background he is both proud of and tortured by. Olive wants to be the modern woman of the seventies. She is educated and ambitious and almost contemptuous of her traditional suburban mother back in Summit, New Jersey; and yet, like her mother, she is drawn to the secure home, the husband who is the breadwinner, and to early motherhood.

If readers approach *The Orange Tree* hungry for a resolution of all or even any of these conflicts, they will be sadly disappointed—as they would equally be of Chekhov's play. In both works of fiction, the richness comes not in resolution of the tension, but only in its expression by different voices and in its song being heard. It is their struggle, their survival, and their shared experiences that ultimately dignify these otherwise flawed characters.

Chekhov used the metaphor of the forever-migrating birds to elucidate this theme. Mildred Walker used her orange tree.

Note

1. These quotes are from the essay "*Tri sestry* [*The Three Sisters*], 1901" written by John Reid, from the University of West England. His essay is available on-line at www.litencyc.com/php/sworks. php?rec=true&UID=7930.

Vershinin: *"I often think, what if you were to begin life over again, knowing what you're doing! If one life, which has already been lived, were only a rough sketch so to speak, and the second were the final copy! Then, I think every one of us would try before anything else not to repeat himself, anyway he would create a different setting for his life; would have a house like this with plenty of light and masses of flowers . . ."*

Anton Chekhov, *The Three Sisters*, act I

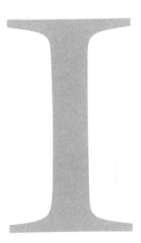

I

When Paulo came with Tiresa's morning coffee, he found her out on the balcony of their apartment. "Here you are! It's good to see you out, but don't stay too long."

"I feel well, Paulo. Really well. And I had to get out."

"This is a glorious October day. Enjoy." He kissed her and was off.

She would enjoy, and the whole Fall and Winter and Spring again, she told herself. To lie here on the chaise and listen to the traffic on the Avenue below and catch a glimpse of the tops of the little white sails on the Charles River was living again and blotted out the two weeks in the hospital. Her coffee might have been a vintage wine, it had such a flavor.

Now the sun had reached farther into the balcony. She spread her hands to it. The small oranges on the little tree that stood in the sun were golden in the sun. She had given the tree to Paolo when it was barely a foot high, the year they came back from Sicily, because Paolo missed the orange groves and the orange trees he had known as a boy in Sicily. The tree had grown at least four feet.

A flash of yellow came past and stopped next to their apartment. Tiresa pulled herself out of the chaise in time to see a young girl emerge from the yellow V-W with a bag of groceries. She was in jeans and a bright blue shirt, and her blond hair hung in a braid down her back. The girl's face was hidden by the leafy top of celery protruding from the brown paper bag she carried, but she must be the young girl who had moved into the next apartment on their floor. "She and her husband are newlyweds," Paulo had told her. "It will be fine to have young people next door," Paulo had said. Paulo, lover of youth, was delighted, of course. "She's quite lovely looking, you might enjoy her Tirese. Fifer's their name."

"How is the husband?" she had asked. Paulo's lips pursed. "Rather typical; young American business man, determined to be a success. We must have them over some time when you feel up to it."

She decided to ask them over that evening. Maybe then Paulo would realize that she really was well.

"Bessie, I'm going to invite the new young couple next door for cocktails tonight," she told the woman who came in at nine every morning to do for them.

Bessie placed Tiresa's breakfast tray on the little table beside her. "If you'll pardon my saying so, Mrs. Romano, I think you're making a big mistake just because you feel a little better. We've done a lot of worrying about you."

"But I'm feeling well again, Bessie. I'm going back to teaching next week. These are young people, so I think we ought to have a little heartier canapés than usual, something broiled . . ."

2

Ron was home. Olive could hear the television when she came to their door, but the minute she called to him, the door flew open.

"Hi, gorgeous." Ron took her bag and kissed her.

"Hi, handsome." It was their ritual greeting.

"Why didn't you wait till I got home so you could take the car?"

"I wanted the walk. It isn't that far. How long have you been home?"

"Just long enough to get a beer and think how empty the apartment is without you in it."

"Now you know how it is all day." But sometimes she liked having it to herself during the day, she thought. "You were sitting here in the dark practically, Ron. Why didn't you turn on a light?"

"Didn't think about it. I was watching the tube." He settled back on the couch.

She switched on the lamp near the front window and moved it so the light would shine out on the balcony. But it wouldn't reach eleven stories to the street; how secret it was living up here in their own world—how far away from everyone else.

"I met the old Roman as I came in tonight," Ron told her at dinner. He said we must come in for a drink; they hadn't asked us before because his wife's been sick, but now she's better."

"I hope they do ask us." It was weird not knowing people who lived right next door. At first she hadn't minded; she and Ron were busy with their own lives, but the days were longish, and if she didn't get a job . . . She had applied at the museum today. "Try again in the Spring," the woman said. That was what they all said. And there was her roommate, Gumshoe, over in Paris, just walking in and landing a job on *Time*.

After dinner they moved over to the couch for their coffee. This, too, had become a ritual. They had been given six after-dinner coffee cups for a wedding present and Olive insisted on using them. "Takes four of 'em to get a decent cup of coffee you know," Ron had grumbled, but he thought it was cute of Ollie to serve them, and the over-size mug at breakfast with "His" inscribed on it made up for the tiny cups at dinner.

Olive carried out the coffee tray and came back to sit in the circle of Ron's arm. She kicked off her sandals and rested her bare feet on the coffee table and prepared to watch T-V with him, but her gaze wandered to the apartment. Nice; it really was. A unit of green modular couch faced the orange butter-fly chair across from the coffee table. The black bean-bag chair she had had in college was great against the white carpet. But it was the painting of the purple iris that really gave the room panache. She and Ron had bought it on their wedding trip, at a show on the common in some Connecticut town. The canvas stood five feet tall and it had been all they could do to get it on top of the V-W. Ron hadn't been sure about it at first.

"You do like the iris now, don't you Ron?"

He had grown so used to it that he hardly saw it any more, but he was emphatic. "I think it's terrific; sort of sexy," he added on the spur of the moment.

"I don't see that. What's sexy about it?"

Ron shrugged. "Just gives me a feeling. I'm quick at the sexy feelings, haven't you noticed?"

"Oh yes, I've noticed." She gave him a quick grin and then

her face sobered. "But isn't it funny, Ron, how many things we do feel alike about?"

"Mhmm. Like pizza and Bloody Marys and Liv Ullman."

Olive bunted him with her shoulder. "I don't mean just the things like that. You know what I mean." She bunted him once more.

"Quit it!" He tightened his arm around her. "I knew the minute I met you on that blind date that you were what I wanted; that's for sure."

"I know what you mean. I felt the same way about you."

"And when I think that we might have broken up. God, I was wiped out. I didn't know what to think when I got your letter." He had told her this before in almost the same words, but they fell freshly in her ears.

"I don't know what got into me," Olive admitted as she had before. "It scares me to think I might have lost you. But it's good in a way, because now I know I couldn't live without you."

"Same here." The lips that had been so apt to speak their lines found each other. The sudden jangle of the telephone seemed to come from some other planet. "Let it ring," Ron murmured. "It'll be your family or mine an' they'll call again."

"I can't ever let a phone ring. You don't know what it might be." Olive was already halfway to the bright yellow phone hanging on the wall of the kitchen.

"That was Mrs. Romano," she announced when she came back, "and she did invite us in for a drink tomorrow evening. I liked her voice—it's real throaty."

"He looks like an interesting old duck," Ron said.

She would wear her hair up tomorrow night, Olive planned as she washed the dishes. Mrs. Romano would be so middle-aged she didn't want to seem too young. He was, too, of course, but there was something dashing about him. It was being Italian, probably. He had a flashing smile that began in his dark eyes, reached his mouth, and spread over his whole face. "You must be our new neighbor, he had said that morning when she got into the elevator with him.

"Ron, do you realize that the Romanos will be the first married couple we've met since we're married? And we've been married two and a half months and four days; I counted it up today. Ron!"

"I'll be darned," Ron said. His eyes were on the screen in front of him.

3

The Fifers came promptly at six.

"Welcome to Casa Romano," Paulo said as he opened the door. "Come in. Mrs. Fifer, I want you to meet Mrs. Romano."

"Oh, call me Olive, please, and my husband is Ronald." That tiresome way the young had of calling everyone by his first name, Tiresa thought. But the girl did have a certain charm. She was still in jeans, but she wore an over-size purple and green blouse and a long gold chain and dangling earrings that gave her a festive air. All that shining blond hair was brushed to one side and held by a gold barrette. The young man was in a proper business suit and Tiresa could understand Paulo's description of him.

"Dr. Romano told me about meeting you and your husband when I was in the hospital, but unfortunately I have been a little under the weather ever since I came home," Tiresa explained.

"I kept hoping I'd meet you in the elevator," the girl said.

As Ronald shook her hand in an over-hearty grip, he said, "Mrs. Romano, I should confess we've been calling you the mystery woman because we never saw you."

How assured he was for one so young. "I'm really quite flattered to be the mystery woman," she told him. "Now if I can just keep up the illusion! Yet all human beings are mysterious enough. Even husbands and wives are often a mystery to each other," she couldn't resist saying, but she doubted whether these two ever had that feeling.

"We're delighted to have young people as our neighbors," Paulo told them.

"You're not afraid we'll play Rock and Roll and dance all night?"

"We'll risk it. The building is altogether too quiet; besides, it has excellent insulation. What may I give you to drink?"

"Ollie will have a little white wine; I'd like a bourbon," Ronald said. "Can I help?" He followed Paulo out into the kitchen.

Why didn't he let his wife speak for herself? Tiresa wondered.

When Paolo came back, he said, "I want to propose a toast to *la Sposina* and her husband. That's the Sicilian word for little bride," he explained. "How long have you two been married?"

"Over two months," Olive said.

Paolo lifted his glass to them. "Long life and joy to you both."

"And may your marriage remain an ever-recurring miracle to you each," Tiresa added, and then wondered if she and Paulo didn't seem a little old-fashioned to them. "You must have married right out of college," she added hurriedly. Annoying the way the young could make you feel so self-conscious.

"Yes, I just graduated in June. Ronnie graduated the year before."

"Ollie was a brain in college and she had all these grand ideas," Ronald said. "She wanted to do graduate work, and then she wanted to go off to Paris with her roommate and get a job. But I persuaded her that I needed her more than Paris did." He beamed as though it had been a proud achievement.

"Paris is very important," Tiresa said.

"Particularly when you're in your twenties," Paulo added. "If it's any help, Olive, when we first looked at it, this apartment building made me think of apartments in Paris.

"Paulo, that's absurd. This building is enormous, is not made of gray stone that catches a magic light, and these balconies have steel netting around them instead of lovely iron filigree."

"But the feeling, Tiresa! The feeling is quite like Paris."

"Avenue Foch, I suppose. Without the chestnut trees, of course!"

He shrugged. "But even the Avenue Foch does not face the Charles River and the Boston skyline. The view from our balconies is more brilliant."

It was irrelevant, but she wanted to show that little girl that you could disagree with your husband now and then, so she said, "But not as brilliant as the view of Mount Etna and the Tyrrhenian Sea from Casa Marguerita's balcony."

"Well no, but that is Sicily; no view can top that, and that is a view that we carry in our hearts always." He turned back to the Fifers. "Tiresa is talking about a villa in Sicily where we once lived. Your name is Olive; I like that."

"I don't. Everyone always says Popeye's' girl-friend," Olive said.

"But I'm not acquainted with Popeye or his girl-friend. The name of Olive makes me think of Sicily and the olive groves."

"We keep that little orange tree over there by the balcony to remind us of the trees in Sicily," Tiresa explained. "You see, Sicily is Paulo's birthplace and also his heart's home."

"Have you folks lived in this apartment building long?" Ron asked with an air of getting back to sensible matters.

"Twelve years," Paulo said. "How did you happen to hear of it?"

"A guy—a man at our office told me about it. I'm with Twentieth Century Insurance." Ron's voice gave weight to the connection. He would be ponderous in middle age, Tiresa decided.

"Ah, you're an insurance man. I had rather guessed you were in a bank," Paulo said.

Ronald had taken a second drink and was telling Paulo about his work. "I guess Twentieth Century selects a new man very carefully, and I didn't think I'd get the job, but luck was with me . . ." Tiresa was amused by his pseudo modesty but she wanted them to go now. Good, the girl was standing up.

"Well, we have had your young couple," Tiresa said at dinner.

"Yes. Did you find them interesting?"

"She's a charming girl. I don't see her as a brain exactly, but she had the good sense to interrupt her husband's expansive talk about his job. I thought he might go on and on."

"They're both very young, of course, although he tells me he's twenty-four. There's a quality I like about her. I can't define it. What would you say it is, Tirese?"

"Youth."

"Yes, but it is more than that; it's a kind of eagerness—a liveliness even when she's quiet. He's more a type, as I told you."

"Oh, Paulo, you're so completely predictable you give me a sense of stability. She's a type too: the American College girl. Less sophisticated than some, but refreshingly."

"She's very natural. She hadn't gotten dressed up to come, and I liked the way her hair framed her face so loosely and was caught up to one side." He was smiling with pleasure as he pictured her.

"You and Ben Johnson!"

> *Give me a look, give me a face*
> *That makes simplicity a grace;*
> *Robes loosely flowing, hair as free*
> *Such sweet neglect more taketh me*
> *Than all th' adulteries of art*

she quoted at him.

"Exactly. But she has a certain style, too; that purple and green business she wore."

"I could have done without the jeans."

"All young girls wear jeans."

"You've observed?"

Tiresa blew out the candles and went over to sit by the fire, watching him fix the coffee. How he enjoyed these little ceremonies of his. He poured some of the coffee essence he made himself into the heated copper pot he had brought from Sicily, and he added the boiling water, measuring it with his eyes, and he brought her a cup. His making the coffee after dinner disoriented guests, but then so did her carving the entrée. "Those old Romanos," they probably said, "of course, they're Italian."

"What a mistake for her not to go to Paris. She married too young," Paulo said.

"Perhaps, but Paulo, let's not get too interested in these young people. They seemed pleased to come tonight, but once they meet some people their own age, they may not have time for older people"

Paulo didn't answer. His face that was always so transparent to her darkened at any reminder of their age, but the next instant brightened. "Curious that her name is Olive, isn't it? It hardly fits her; she's too blond and fair for that name."

Suddenly, Tiresa was tired. They had been living so quietly that even having these children over was exhausting. She could feel her heart skipping. "I think I'll go on to bed and read a little," she said.

"Are you not feeling well tonight, Tiresa?" His voice was always a trifle hostile when he was worried.

"I'm feeling *very* well, but the idea of stretching out appeals to me." She could feel Paulo watching her as she went across the room, and moved more briskly than she wanted.

In their room the light by the bed was on, the bed opened, and her gown and negligee laid out. It was a rite Paulo seldom forgot. He liked selecting exquisite gowns for her, and the monogrammed sheets they slept in. Little luxuries were important to Paulo; a proof, she thought, that he would never again live in the poverty of his first years in America.

She sometimes wished for his sake that she were more slender and lithe lying in those sheets, but she consoled herself with her private idea that Italian men, Sicilian especially, liked slightly maternal figures—or was it a sign of the children they had borne them? She began undressing to break her train of thought.

4

As Ron closed the door of their own apartment, Olive flopped down on the couch. "Aren't they terrific! She's absolutely stunning, and their apartment is something else again!"

"How old do you think he is?"

"Oh, late forties. He's a lot younger than Dad. Isn't he handsome."

"In an Italian sort of way. And he's a lot older than that. He's fifty at least. He's an opthamologist. I guess that's a pretty lucrative specialty. You know there's a big field now in medical insurance, just protecting doctors who're sued. You have to have some legal background, of course."

Now Olive saw Dr. Romano in a darkened room. That shining round thing eye doctors wore on his head. And then he'd take it off and look at you with those deep dark eyes.

"They must have been married for some years, but they seemed really in love."

"Say, what is this! Don't you think people can stay in love for years?"

"Oh Ron, you know I didn't mean . . . but how many middle-aged people do you know who seem really crazy about each other? You know what I mean. It scares me a little."

He reached over and pulled her closer. "Sure I know what you mean, but not us. By the way, Ollie, what are we going to eat tonight?"

Ron moved over to his side of the bed. "I came too fast for you, didn't I?"

"It was all right." Olive's voice was flat.

"Sorry, we'll do better next time." Ron leaned over to kiss her. "G'night beautiful." He patted her rump.

"Goodnight." Olive didn't add the usual "handsome." She felt far away from him. In those marriage lectures she went to, they told you that you could feel let-down after loving—they had a special name for it—but not how alone you could feel.

It was different at noon the other day when Ron came home from lunch unexpectedly. Her eyes had met his across the table and without words at all they had moved over to the couch. It was fantastic; they made love right there with the sun coming in so bright she could feel it on her face. Ron had to hurry off without finishing his lunch. He'd got all the way down to the elevator and then he came back to tell her how terrific she was. And she had lain there after he went, so happy she didn't want to do anything else but just think about him. Maybe that was one of the miracles Tiresa meant.

"Ron," she whispered. She wanted to tell him that. But he was already asleep.

She thought back to their meeting on the blind date. It had seemed so magical; their both coming from New Jersey, only a few miles apart. And she was Taurus and so was he. He was the first boy—man—she ever took home from college who Dad liked right away. Of course, he didn't come right out and say so. He said, "He's an improvement on Weirdo Harold you brought back last year." And then when Dad knew Ron had a job already for himself after college, he was all for him. And Mother smiled in that sappy sentimental way. "My family is nuts about you," Ron told her. And she liked them; they weren't terribly interesting. His father kept calling her "Olivetti" for the typewriter, and thought he was being witty or something, but he was nice enough.

Ron had come to the dorm the next three nights after they

met, and finally she had to tell him she had a paper to do and couldn't see him until the weekend. The whole dorm was pretty impressed.

And the night Gumshoe had got out of their room and Ron came to spend the night. She had thought about it a long time beforehand, but with the new rules the College didn't take any responsibility for your morals any more; you were on your own, and with the pill there wasn't any danger. Ron had wanted to come, and it had seemed stuffy not to let him.

She had taken the pill—pink and round in its small box—one each morning, to be ready, and then they hadn't. She felt terrible about it. But when Ron was actually in her room, she couldn't. He looked so awkward and out of place there with her pictures and the books on the shelf over her desk. The books weren't against it; there were *Marriage and the Family* and *Youth and the New Ideology* and *Women in Love* and *Fear of Flying*—books that made loving seem the natural thing to do, but you had to be caught up by the passion kind of thing—and she wasn't. Maybe Ron wasn't either, really. "If you feel that way about it," Ron had said in a hateful, sarcastic voice.

He'd gone back to sit on Gumshoe's bed and said what was the idea of getting him up there, and she said she hadn't gotten him up there just to—for that; it was because she wanted to be with him. And he'd been horrid and said she certainly put on a strip tease act letting him take off her clothes, and she hadn't answered. And he'd only unbuttoned her blouse. She was uncomfortable just remembering how dreadful it had been. But just before he left, he came over and gave her a little peck on her cheek.

"See you Saturday," he had said. "If you want to, that is." If he had stayed a minute longer, she might have changed her mind, but he wanted to get away, too.

"How was it?" Gummy had asked the next day. And she had said she'd rather not talk about it and looked blissful as though it were something too sacred. Gumshoe said she knew how it was, but of course she didn't.

Ron had made it easy on Saturday. When they were in the car driving to The Lucky Horseshoe, he said, "Well, I guess we flubbed it." And she had said she was sorry.

"No sweat; there'll be another time soon." He pulled her over and kissed her. They hadn't tried it again until they were married, which was pretty square. Now she wasn't using anything—if she got pregnant, well, all right.

But she was absolutely panicked along in May. Everything seemed to be moving too fast. She didn't even want to be graduating, and she certainly didn't want to be married in August. Connie Fox and Gumshoe were going to Paris in June, and they wanted her to go with them. Maybe they'd get a job over there. Gumshoe had an uncle in Belfast. And right in the middle of their getting excited about it, Connie said, "What about Ron?"

They had a class then, but she had hardly heard a word of it. She had slopped out of class before the others and rushed back to the dorm to write him, telling him that she didn't want to marry now; that she was going to Paris, and after that, maybe she'd get a job for a year. She couldn't remember now what all she said. But Ron was mad.

He stirred and reached his arm across her. Very carefully, as though she were playing pick up sticks, she lifted his arm and laid it on the blanket and slid out of bed.

She went out to the kitchen and made herself a cup of coffee. It was like being back in the dorm when she stayed up late studying for an exam. There was nothing to snack with it but some crackers. Ron must have eaten up all the cheese with his beer.

Why hadn't she let him stay mad? And gone to Paris? Connie backed out, but Gumshoe went and was still there. She and Gumshoe would have had a wonderful time.

But she knew very well why. Ron hadn't come to Prom. And she hadn't asked anyone else, just stalked around by herself in jeans and a terrible old top; she and Gumshoe, who never had a man anyway, went over and watched the dancing and made funny remarks about the dates, but all the time she wished Ron were there. She'd thought he might just come up some night and say, "What's this all about, Ollie?" But he didn't even call. She told herself she wouldn't have felt so awful if she didn't really love him. If she never saw him again she didn't think she could stand it. She remembered how sweet he'd been about their not sleeping together—well, considering. Sally Daniels said the time she had that date of hers over night, it was just like rape.

Olive took a gulp of coffee. She had left it standing so long it was cold. She had been afraid that she'd never meet anyone she'd like as well as Ron. She might not even marry. *The Marriage and the Family* said young marriages had the best chances of survival because you grew together and your ways weren't so fixed.

When she broke down and called him—just to test out how she felt about him after not seeing or hearing him for two weeks and a half—she almost hoped he wouldn't be there. But he had been. "I was just going to call you," he said. And she was excited to hear him, she could hardly talk at first.

"Say, what's wrong with your voice?" Ron asked. "Look, why don't I come up? We'll go to The Lucky Horseshoe. You walk out a ways so I don't have to go through all the hoopla of sending up word that I'm there."

She walked a mile at least on the highway before she saw his old V-W tearing around the curve. He parked the car and they both ran toward each other. He lifted her right up off the ground. And they were married in August—August fifteenth.

She felt cold. She poured out the rest of the coffee and went back to bed.

Ron was thinking about Olive as he drove home the next night. She had seemed kind of droopy this morning at breakfast. Of course, she was disappointed about not finding a job right off, and he supposed it did get dull in the apartment all day. Ollie had had a letter from that roommate of hers with the silly name, Gumshoe, that was it, telling her all about the job on *Time* in

Paris. That hadn't helped any. After dinner, he'd take Ollie with him to check out that car wreck Ruskin told him about. Something to do anyway.

"Hi, beautiful," he called into the apartment.

"Hi, handsome." Olive came out from the kitchen with a full-length red apron over her jeans.

"The Chef!" he said, kissing her. "What an outfit. We must be having a standing rib roast of beef at least."

"No we aren't. We're having hash. It's good though, and a smashing dessert, and it's ready, what's more." She was in high spirits.

"You don't care if I have a beer first, do you?" He was learning to catch her mood the minute he came in. Funny, he'd never thought of her as having moods.

"I'll have half a one." She perched on the arm of the chair while he brought her a glass.

"Know what we're going to do tonight? I'm going to drive us over to see a car that was in a wreck. Our man in Auto Insurance told me about it. This is a real buggy—an AMC, only two years old."

"Why on earth should we go and see a car wreck?"

"I thought maybe we could buy it for a song. Get the major repairs done, but I'd work on it myself. My first jalopy was one I fixed up."

The wreck was clearly visible under the lights of the used car lot. From the driver's side the white sports car looked unhurt; the green leather upholstery gleamed. But as they walked around to the front they could see the mass of twisted wires and jammed steel under the bent hood. The right-hand door hung crazily askew. Ron peered anxiously into the engine, knelt down and then slid underneath the car. When he emerged, he said "The axle's bent, and the frame is jammed . . ." He seemed to be talking to himself. "I can see how the girl on the right side was killed."

"Killed!" The unexpected word stabbed her mind. "Ron, I wouldn't want it. I'd always think of that wreck and that girl."

19

"You wouldn't when it's all fixed up. But he sure made a mess of it."

Olive stood silent, hands pushed down in the pockets of her jacket.

"Well . . . it's too close to a total, but we sure could do with a buggy like this."

Olive was so quiet on the way home, he pulled into Friendly's.

"Want one of the seventy-seven varieties, hon?"

"No thanks."

5

Tiresa was barely in the apartment that next Friday afternoon before Bessie announced that she had a phone call. She nodded to the pad on the table and then waited while Tiresa digested her painful handwriting. "That girl next door."

"Oh, you mean Mrs. Fifer."

"She wants you to call her. I told her you was teaching."

"I just wondered if you were sick again because we hadn't seen you. I didn't know you taught school," Olive said.

"Only part-time, I'm sorry to say, but still it's a pleasure. I taught so many years I wouldn't like to give it up altogether."

"I can imagine. I called to ask you over for a cup of coffee."

When Tiresa hesitated, Olive said, "You haven't seen our apartment yet."

"That's so. Well, thank you. I'll just run over for a little bit." Tiresa remembered going with her mother in the middle of the afternoon for a kaffee klatch. She could remember her mother and grandmother in a basement kitchen. She had removed herself from all that. And she mustn't let this young girl take for granted that they were going to run back and forth, or that she was a mother image. Why had she asked the Fifers in the first place—but, of course, it was for Paulo. He loved having people in—young people especially. Reluctantly, Tiresa capped her fountain pen. Yet it was rather touching the way the girl wanted her to see the apartment. After all, it wasn't much to do for that nice child.

"You're my first caller, except for the family," Olive said. She hadn't expected to see Mrs. Romano in slacks and a tailored shirt; she looked younger.

"I'm honored to be your first guest," Tiresa took in at a glance the white shag carpet and the enormous green couch, the long painting of purple iris, and the cups and a plate of doughnuts laid out on the table. "How inviting."

"Maybe you'd like to see the rest of the apartment first."

Since she seemed to want to show it, Tiresa followed her down the hall to the bedroom, past the bathroom that looked crowded by the two large plants hanging above the tub. A low bed without a head or a foot nearly filled one end of the bedroom and on its bright orange spread reclined a stuffed monkey.

"That's Pedro; Ron bought him for me on our wedding trip."

Tiresa paused in the doorway.

"You have to come in to get the full effect," Olive said. "It's a water-bed and simply perfect. Do you have one?" Olive asked.

"No, we've never tried one," Tiresa admitted.

"Well, come and sit on it." Tiresa complied with caution and felt the bed roll slightly beneath her. "A little like being on ship-board," she said, hoping that was adequate praise.

Tiresa moved over to look more closely at the large framed wedding picture of Olive's on Ron's chiffonier. "You were a love-ly bride, my dear."

"Oh thank you. I wore Mother's wedding dress and it makes me look really quaint. I told Ron he better treasure that picture because I'm never going to wear a dress like that again."

On Olive's dresser was a companion picture of Ron. He looked out at her with chin lifted and eyes focused on some dis-tant point. "Isn't Ron photogenic? I tell him he looks like Sir Galahad or Paul Newman or someone heroic. I'm getting a little tired of having the pictures staring at us all the time. Sometimes, they don't seem like us at all; almost like strangers. But Ron likes 'em."

On the wall facing the bed hung a large poster of Biarritz, pasted together with Scotch tape. "Isn't the poster yummy? We had it in our room at college, but since my roommate was going to France and I wasn't, I kept it. You should see it when the sun comes in in the morning and hits that beach. I can lie in bed and think I'm lying on the sand for sure. Ron says he's getting sunburned just looking at it. I got the orange spread to match those tiled roofs in the background."

"That's going to stand you in good stead on a Boston winter morning." Tiresa was looking with amusement at the magazines and paperbacks on the floor under one side of the bed. On the other side were two heavy books, the word "Insurance" on the binding of one of them.

"Don't mind the clothes on the floor in the corner; there just isn't enough room for everything in the closet."

But these two young people were too contained in their room. Tiresa escaped with relief to the more impersonal atmosphere of the living room.

"Sit down and I'll bring the coffee," Olive said. "Do you take Sanka? I know my mother does."

"No," Tiresa said quickly, resisting the category of Olive's mother's generation. "Paulo and I like our coffee black and strong. He makes quite a ceremony of it."

"Oh, we do too. We have after-dinner coffee every evening out here," she said with pride.

By-passing the butter-fly chair, Tiresa sat on the couch. It was almost impossible to realize that except for the fireplace this room was a smaller version of their living room. This was so sparsely furnished. She wondered if theirs wasn't too full. But there was little sign of Ron's and Olive's personal interests; the T-V of course, and a player—the painting of the iris and the Klee print, but that was about it. The whole impression was of imper-

manence, not as if they had settled down to living here—a motel look.

Olive came back with two large mugs of coffee and sat on the
couch beside her.

"You know, the other evening I didn't ask where your home
was," Tiresa said.

"Summit, New Jersey. I lived there all my life. And the first
night we met, Ron and I discovered we were both from New Jersey. He's from Montclair. After that, he figured we'd better marry. We're both Taurus, too."

The coffee was weak; the large sugar doughnuts discouraging. Tiresa crumbled hers and ate a small piece, suddenly taken
back by the sugary fragrance to her father's bakery ship in Chicago.

"I suppose the man you marry is always something of a miracle as you look back. I came from Nebraska and Paulo came from
Sicily and we met in Chicago." Some impulse made her want to
interest this young girl on an ageless level. "He was in a class I
was teaching—"

"I can't get over your teaching," Olive said, "What do you
teach?"

Tiresa gave a little laugh. "It sounds a trifle ponderous, but it
really isn't. I have a seminar on Henry James and George Eliot—
as an introduction to contemporary literature," she added, not
wanting to sound completely nineteenth century. Watching Olive's face, Tiresa felt assigned at once—relegated to the slot of professor. She didn't want that either. "At least teaching one course
makes me feel I'm still on campus. If you liked that life at all, you
miss it, I think. Especially the first year out of college."

"You can say that again." Olive's face changed so swiftly Tiresa was startled. A look of discontent passed over it and then was
gone.

Tiresa advanced tentatively. "You always think that without
classes you will read all the things you didn't have time for, but
you don't."

"I know. I should read some Henry James. I've never read anything of his. But I've been reading a tremendous book, *Against Our Will*. It's about rape."

Of course—the violence in Henry James wouldn't strike her, but she'd like to have her in class and make her see it . . .

"How would you ever get over being raped?" Olive demanded.

Surprised, Tiresa spoke slowly, "You would have to realize that your body and your spirit are quite separate, and your true identity is in the spirit, wouldn't you?" Now she was sounding like a teacher—or a mother, offering a solution too patly.

"I suppose," Olive said slowly, sounding unconvinced.

A little silence spread between them. Then Tiresa stood up. "I have some work that I must do. This has been fun." She reached for the word, feeling that delightful was too formal. Not in the right idiom, but neither was fun. "I like your apartment. Did you paint the iris?"

Olive laughed. "No, we saw it at an art show, and I just had to have it. Ron didn't go for it at first, but now he's crazy for it. I think it gives the room panache—maybe a little like your orange tree."

Tiresa smiled. "It strikes a definite note," she said. "Thank you Mrs. Fif—"

"Oh, please call me Olive."

Tiresa was not fond of this passion for first names, but she said, "Then you must call me Tiresa. And I know Paulo would like to have you call him by his first name."

"I'd like to. That will make us feel we really know some people here."

It was a relief to get back to their own apartment. Tiresa glanced from the Oriental rugs to the books that lined the end of the room. She would regale Paulo tonight with her afternoon adventure. He would chuckle over the thought of themselves swaying gently on the sea of a waterbed.

"All right, that's enough for tonight, Trise." Paulo leaned back in his chair, but she went on reading what he had written.

"'Adherence' sounds awkward, Paulo. Isn't 'connection' closer to what you mean?" This was an old game they played when she helped him with his translations. More than a game; she almost felt she was inside his mind, feeling her way, offering an alternative word tentatively, as if his own mind were suggesting it. "How about 'attachment'?"

"No, Tirese, that it is *not*. 'Attachment' might apply to the normal condition. If you only understood the anatomy of the eye! Or could read Italian!" He was always impatient, emphatic, and slipped easily into despair on finding the right word, or making her understand the sense he wanted. In an odd way she enjoyed his impatience, his unwillingness to accept a word that only partially suited him. But she never doubted that they would find the right word.

"Leave it as I had it, Tirese. It's accurate in meaning even if it does sound awkward." He banged the cover on the volume in front of him. "I don't know why we slave over this. Nobody had ever heard of Colucci outside of Italy. Now if we were translating somebody like Morgagni . . ."

She ignored his plea for reassurance about the value of his translation. When something was started, it was to be finished. When the galley proofs came he was secretly delighted. Finally, after he had convinced himself that the publishers had pushed it aside as unimportant, the translation appeared, and he dismissed it as nothing. It was ironic that Paulo struck his colleagues as arrogant, as he often did. He spoke with authority and was scornful of views he disagreed with, his air of assurance was a mask. He was really a modest man.

Tiresa watched him picking up his papers and dictionaries, folding the card table. Even in little actions she could feel his quick energy.

Paulo came back with two brandies. "We deserve the best brandy after that drudgery."

"It wasn't drudgery, but it was a little flat tonight without any rages," she teased.

Paulo shrugged. "Oh, the man with the corneal transplant is coming along," he said diffidently.

"Good." That was the operation he had been so pessimistic about, and so irritable over when she suggested that it might go better than he thought. His telling her the result was by way of apologizing for his irritation.

He came over and helped her out of her chair. "Thank you, Tirese."

"I always enjoy working on the translations, you know."

Standing there, they were drawn closer irresistibly.

"Come," Paulo said.

"We'll go and dream we're floating on our water-bed." It was absurd the way she couldn't seem to get that young girl out of her mind.

6

Paulo looked up from his journal. "Are you thinking of inviting anyone for Thanksgiving, Trise? Or shall we go out for dinner?"

Poor Paulo, he was trying to be so tactful, but he loved celebrations and he had embraced Thanksgiving and all its customs as though it were a Sicilian feast day. "When did we ever go out for Thanksgiving dinner, Paulo? I thought I'd invite the Shepards and the Chicesters and perhaps that Chinese intern and your resident. How does that strike you?"

"Very good. What do you think of inviting the Fifers? They have no family here, I'm sure."

"Do you mean with or instead of?"

"Oh I mean with . . . Unless that many would tire you."

"Of course, we haven't seen them for a month or more, except in the elevator that time," she reminded him. "Do you think they'll enjoy such a medical group? And that would mean ten so we'd have to do a buffet, I think."

"Not on Thanksgiving, Trise; get someone in to help Bessie. And you'll have to carve the turkey!" Tiresa didn't answer, but she'd do it when the time came. "I'll go ask the Fifers now."

She came back from the phone and gave Paulo the gist of the conversation. "Olive would love to, but she'll have to talk to Ron who had mentioned something about driving back to New Jersey for Thanksgiving."

28

"Oh," said Paulo.

"Well, for one thing, Thanksgiving is a family day. I can't understand why you would want to be with anyone else but the family, especially when Mom is inviting your folks over so we can all be together. I don't see how we could explain our not going."

"Togetherness," Olive said scornfully. "We just saw them all in September. Oh Ron, you know how breathless it will be, and I'll rush out and help your mother until dinner is on, and my folks will come and we'll eat a great big meal and then your Dad and mine and you will go off and watch the game, and I'll help clear and both my mother and yours will tactfully try to find out whether we're ecstatically happy and if I'm pregnant yet, and the next morning we'll drive back. The only good thing about it is that they'll send all the turkey that's left back with us."

Ron's coffee cup made a sharp sound as he set it down on the saucer. The kitchenette seemed too small. Olive jumped up and carried the dishes over to the sink and let the hot water run full blast. "You have to let the water run ten minutes to get it hot enough to wash with," she muttered. Ron went on into the living room and turned on the television. That was the way with Ron, Olive thought. He never wanted to talk anything out. If he didn't agree with something, he'd flee into the tube. She'd rather he get mad. Of course, he was mad now, but he showed it by that zombie-like silence of his. Why didn't he come out and wipe the dishes and *talk* about Thanksgiving like a civilized person?

After she finished the dishes, she took the garbage out to the utility room at the end of the hall, but Ron didn't look up. That was his job at night. She wiped the stove, even polished the chrome on the frig and watered the anemic African violet on the windowsill. She hesitated before going into the living room again.

The sound of the television stopped so suddenly the silence was louder than the roar of the game before.

"Ollie?"

"Yes."

"Hon, what are you doing out there all this time?" She came to the doorway.

"I'm sorry Ollie, but it's just that neither of our families would understand our not *wanting* to come. Yours wouldn't be any better than mine."

She was silent.

"You expected to go until the Romanos asked us there. What would be so special about having dinner with a couple of foreigners we never heard of a few months ago?"

"I happen to enjoy them. I thought you did, too. And we're living our own lives now." That sounded a little weak. She sat down on the couch beside him and picked up the evening paper he had brought.

"I like 'em all right, but not enough to give up Thanksgiving at home."

"And then there'll be Christmas and Easter," Olive said from behind the paper.

"I'm only talking about this Thanksgiving. Most people want to spend that day with their families; go twice as far as we have to go to do it."

Olive folded the paper. "I might as well go and tell Tiresa we can't come."

"Why don't you do that. Or just call her on the phone. They'll understand. Gosh, foreigners make a terrific thing of family feast days, Sicilians especially, I bet." Ron switched on the television. He was watching the picture, but waiting for her to leave before he turned on the sound.

Olive saw his eyes moving with the action on the screen. He was someone she hardly knew. "You don't have to call the Romanos *foreigners* in that patronizing tone of voice," she said. When he didn't answer, didn't even look up, she said, "That's a terrific drive in holiday traffic, you know. And you'll want to stay until Sunday. Then we'll have to come home in all the Sunday jam."

"For God's sake, Ollie, I can't see why you want so much to

go to the Romano's. They're interesting enough, but hell, they're not more than ten years younger than my folks and maybe fifteen than yours."

She remembered now with a chagrin that she had told him once—way back when any least little fact about either of their childhoods was important—that she was the child of her parents' old age. She had even told him that the child of elderly parents was said to be more than ordinarily bright. Like Alexander Pope. And he loved to tease her about it. Ron was born the year after his parents were married. The children of young parents make the best lovers, he had told her. That was back when they kidded about everything and had fun.

"The Romanos happen to be very different from your parents, Ron, or mine. Anyway, age has nothing to do with it. I just think they're interesting. Paulo won't spend the whole afternoon watching a ball game," she added.

"Well, if you think I'm going to miss the game, you're really nuts, Ollie. Even if we did go to the Romano's, I'd come home and watch the game."

"You probably would, and Paulo and Tiresa would think you were a boor."

When Ron turned up the television, Olive pushed the coffee table out of the way and started across the room, expecting Ron to stop her. She went on down the hall, hesitating a minute before she opened the door. Very slowly, she walked the length of the brown carpet to the Romano's. Ron was so sure she'd do what he wanted; it never occurred to him that he might try to see her point of view. If both families weren't mixed up in it, she wouldn't give in. Dr. Romano—Paulo—opened the door.

"Good evening, come in." His obvious pleasure at seeing her felt like soothing lotion on the rough skin of her feelings. "*La Sposina* is here, Tirese."

"How very nice. Bring her in," Tiresa called from the bedroom. "I just came in to bed, Olive, so I would be more comfortable while I read this set of papers."

"I shouldn't have come so late." Tiresa was hardly Olive's idea of a professor, sitting up in bed in her apricot bed jacket with yellow sheets and blanket and yellow roses on the table across the room. But the typewritten pages on her clip-board looked ruthlessly marked with red pencil.

"It's far from late, I'm just fond of being on the horizontal, and I thought if I moved in here, Paulo wouldn't keep talking to me," Tiresa said, her eyes sparkling.

Paulo brought a chair for Olive, and he sat on the side of the bed. It was all as easy and natural as the dorm.

"I just came over to tell you that we can't come for dinner Thanksgiving. I'm so disappointed, but Ron thinks we have to go to New Jersey to have it with our families." Here with the Romanos she minded even more.

"I thought you might be going home, of course, but we asked you just in case you were alone here," Tiresa said.

"I wish we could. We'll spend half the weekend driving there and back. And I don't want to go anyway. We'll eat a great big meal and then my Dad and Ron will disappear into the T-V room to watch the game. And I'll clear the table and help with the dishes and both Mothers will try to find out if we're ecstatically happy and if I'm pregnant yet. And the next morning we'll drive back. It seems so silly to drive all that way when we just saw them. If we go this Thanksgiving I feel we'll be setting up a pattern and we'll have to spend every holiday with them for the rest of our lives." She looked from Paulo to Tiresa with a mournful expression.

"But it means a great deal to your families. I quite understand. We'll ask you on an ordinary day. I hope our invitation didn't make a problem for you and Ron."

Olive looked at Tiresa, wondering how she had guessed. "It isn't that I don't love them but I just feel tied."

Paulo laughed. "Nothing is for the rest of your life, *Sposina*, believe me."

"But I know that feeling," Tiresa said. "If Paulo and I had lived in Sicily when his family were still there, I tremble to think what family gatherings there would have been. You can't imagine how important family is in Sicily."

Paulo listened with a rueful face. "I don't deny it. Family is important. I'm on Ron's side."

"Ron said you'd understand about the family." She stood up to go. Nothing was changed, but she felt better.

"Wait. We have something special to share with you," Paulo said, mysteriously. He came back with marron glacés which he passed as if they were a rare treasure from the Indies. "Do you like marrons?" he asked anxiously.

"I do. They're delicious." She felt like a child given a treat.

"Well, it's about time, Mrs. Fifer," Ron said. "I decided you were staying for a drink."

"We didn't have a drink," Olive said.

"I thought the old Sicilian always had a wine skin bag slung over his shoulder."

"You're so sure you know what everyone is like. I'm not even sure you know me."

"Now you're not going in for that mystery idea of Tiresa's. Did they weep when you told them we had a prior engagement?"

"No. They understood."

"Right. Any sensible person would. You should have told her we were going home for Thanksgiving when she first asked you."

Olive made no answer and went out to the kitchen to make herself a cup of coffee. She heard the snap of the T-V, and the sudden abrupt silence. Ron came out to the kitchen and put his arm around her.

"I'm sorry, Ollie. I like the Romanos all right, but I missed you. I love you, Honey."

"I love you too."

"Make me a cup of coffee, will ya? And we'll watch the ten o'clock movie."

"I see myself in that child—when I was trying to make my own life and not follow the family pattern," Tiresa said.

"You succeeded, but I doubt if Olive will," Paulo said. "That young husband has firm ideas."

Tiresa laughed. "And you had none, I suppose. It's a lucky thing that I didn't marry you when I was in my twenties. There was something a little wistful about her tonight, didn't you think?"

"Far from wistful. She was glowing. And why not? She's just married, she's young and lovely. That's what I find refreshing about her. She wants nothing."

"You've forgotten, Paulo. When you're that age, you want everything."

7

Tiresa left her car at the gas station around the corner from the apartment and was starting to walk home when Ronald Fifer drove in.

"Can I give you a ride home, Tiresa?" he called out.

"It's only a block, Ron. I'm supposed to walk more than I do. But, yes, I'd rather drive," she said on a sudden impulse. He helped her into the little yellow car that she saw so often going past from the balcony.

"We were sorry you couldn't join us for Thanksgiving," Tiresa said. "The other couples we invited couldn't come either so we drove up to the farm we have in Vermont by ourselves."

"Ollie was sure disappointed, but you understood how it was, didn't you? Both Ollie's folks and mine would have been wiped out if we hadn't gone. We're both only children; I guess that makes a difference."

"Of course, Ron. I understood perfectly. Why don't you and Olive come over for a little supper with us tonight. Bessie has made a turkey casserole for us."

"Oh thanks; we came back loaded down with turkey. We've eaten all we could and frozen the rest. I hope Ollie has some honest to goodness beef tonight."

Tiresa laughed but she liked him better than when she had first met him. He was so frank and not trying to be impressive. "I should have known you would come back laden." They drove into the garage under the apartment house and rode up the elevator together.

"Thank you for bringing me home Ron. I hope you have steak for dinner. If you do, you can pity poor Paulo."

"Hamburger anyway, I hope." He grinned back.

Tiresa let herself into the apartment with the pleasure she always felt when Bessie was off and they had the place to themselves. She was thankful that Ron didn't want another meal of turkey. She drew the curtains against the early November dusk and lit the fire Bessie had laid. Tiresa stood a moment listening to the stillness of the apartment, deepened by the subdued sound of the traffic on the avenue below. She was listening too for Paulo, savoring this anticipation of his coming and the evening ahead.

"Tiresa!"

There he was. Always the imperative call, anxious, demanding, so eager that her whole being leaped to answer, but she said calmly, "Yes, Paulo."

He had packages in his hands as he came to kiss her. "Look, Trise, what I have. Strawberries and Brie—just right. And we don't have to have dinner until we want it. No worry about Bessie's getting home."

"Paulo, the price of strawberries! And Brie! You're shocking."

"But why not? For us. Don't we deserve some of the good things of life, at least a few small ones."

"No, but they're pleasant." She delighted in these extravagant gestures of Paulo's.

"Don't fuss around with food yet. Wait till I change and then I'll bring us a drink."

When Paulo came back he was in the light clothes he enjoyed, his shirt open at the neck with the sleeves rolled, his skin always tanned as though it had been burned too brown by the Mediterranean sun ever to lose its color.

"Now for some music," he said.

He was setting the stage. Either his day had gone very well or so badly that he wanted to block it out of his mind.

"Mrs. Jenkins came out with 20-20 vision with her contacts," he said as he came back from the kitchen with the martinis.

"How fine." So he was elated. Then Tiresa saw the corner of a pink envelope protruding from his pocket, and caught the start of an address in a poorly formed hand. He had heard from Cathy, his brother's widow. But it wasn't until he had finished his drink that she said, "You heard from Cathy."

"Yes. You read it while I see what Bessie has fixed us."

She opened the letter, put off as she always was by the pink stationery and the handwriting with the circles over every *i*, knowing beforehand what it would contain. Cathy's letters were apt to follow pretty much the same pattern: they told of a new crisis in her affairs and appealed for money.

> Dear Paulo,
>
> *The damned school won't keep Tony after this week. Partly because I'm behind in my payments, partly he's getting harder to manage. Besides, I've simply got to move. The landlady gets on my nerves, which you know are not good. I know you will help me in this time of need, so if you can take Tony for a couple of weeks till I get settled some place (I have my eye on one, much better than this dump) I'd be obliged. I'll put him on the bus next Friday morning. He will arrive in Boston at four fifteen. I'm sorry to do this without waiting for an answer but don't know what else to do.*
>
> *If you could let me have a couple of hundred dollars for a few months, Paulo, I can pay most of the school bill and an installment down on the apartment.*
>
> Thank you and love,
> Cathy Romano

She wondered if Cathy always signed her name in full to remind them that she was a relative. "I can meet the bus, Friday," Tiresa said when Paulo came back in.

"But Tirese, you've been sick; you can't have him here."

"I'm feeling fine again. I'm sure Cathy doesn't have anyone else to turn to. And I'd like to see Tony."

Paulo's face darkened. "Cathy has no business sending Tony to us without waiting to hear whether it's convenient for us to take him or not. I'm going to call her tonight and tell her that you've been sick, and we can't possibly have him. We'll send money but . . ."

"Oh Paulo, you sound so firm. You don't mean a word of it. Of course we'll take him."

"I do mean it, Trise. He upsets us both for weeks after he's been here."

"Perhaps it's good to have our tranquil existence disturbed. I'm going out to get the strawberries."

Holding the perfect red berries under the water, she thought how it would be with Tony there. He was eleven now and his slowness would bother Paulo even more than the last time he stayed. Paulo would live the whole tragedy over again, and wallow in his sense of guilt.

She bit into a strawberry, letting the sweet juice run down her throat as she used to do when she was a child. It would be good for Tony to be here. A whole school year would be even better. Then Paulo would feel he was really doing something for him besides sending Cathy money. He hadn't spoken of his brothers for a long time, but she knew that he thought of them often. They had been so close growing up. Maybe not Luigi and Paulo: Luigi was ten years older and had gone into a monastery. But Anthony was only eight years older, and Paulo had worshipped him. When Anthony went to America, Paulo made up his mind to follow him as soon as he finished medical school in Italy. He always remembered that Anthony had sent him money—sporadically, of course. Anthony didn't do anything consistently.

"If Cathy would only let me, I might be able to do something for him. At least, I could see that he got proper medical care, and went to the right high school," Paulo burst out as Tiresa brought the strawberries and cheese in. "But she won't; she still holds me responsible for Anthony's death . . . and of course she's right in a way."

"Oh Paulo, don't say that, or keep thinking it. Cathy doesn't really. She was just in shock over his suicide. She had to blame somebody instead of Anthony," Tiresa said. They'd gone over this a dozen times before.

Paulo didn't answer. She wasn't sure he'd heard a word she said. He began eating his strawberries, but without tasting them, or the Brie he was so fond of. Now he was going over all the ugly circumstances of Anthony's death for the hundredth time. Cathy had written to Paulo telling him Anthony was drinking heavily and she worried about him. And then, in one of his drunken rages he knocked little Tony down a long flight of stairs. "He's really all right except for bad bruises on his head," Cathy had written. Paulo went to them at once and tried to talk to Anthony. He tried to persuade him to go some place for treatment. When he wouldn't go, Paulo had been angry. But it wasn't Paulo's anger than pushed Anthony too far, Paulo insisted. It was his telling him that he used to look up to him as a boy. "I shamed him," Paulo had muttered. "And hurt his pride. To a Sicilian that's the worst thing you can do."

That night, Anthony took an over-dose of some drug. He died the next day. Paulo went to pieces. "I'm to blame for his death as much as though I had given him the over-dose. Don't try to excuse me, Tiresa, he kept insisting. Nothing would ever free him from his sense of guilt. Tiresa looked over at him now. His face was expressionless. Even his skin had taken on a shade of dried leather. She began to put the dishes back on the tray.

Finally, he looked up with a sheepish smile. "Well, if you can meet Tony, Trise, I'll try to be back here by the time you get home."

"Fine."

But Tony had been injured. Paulo took him to a doctor there and found that he had some sort of brain injury. Now, at eleven he spoke slowly and sometimes seemed to think slowly. When he stayed, they both tried to watch for signs of improvement. Paulo went to the greatest lengths trying to teach Tony to play games, and he listened to Tony's hesitant speech without any sign of impatience. Nobody could be more gentle. But being with Tony seemed to deepen Paulo's sense of guilt . . . or was that what he wanted?

"Paulo," Tiresa asked, "did you remember to get my prescription refilled?"

8

Paulo was watching Tony over the journal he was reading. Tony and Tiresa played games every evening after dinner. Very simple games, but it was good to see Tony concentrate on them. Paulo thought he should be playing computer games by now. A lock of wavy black hair, like Paulo's, fell over Tony's forehead as he spun the hands of the cardboard dial. He moved his "man," counting the squares in a loud voice.

"Ten. I'm in. I beat, Aunt Treecie!" He jumped up and down on his chair.

"I'm afraid you did," she said ruefully, looking properly downcast. Tony was better though; all he needed was a triumph or two at school to give him confidence.

"Congratulations, Tony," Paulo said. "Your Aunt Treecie is a hard one to beat."

Tony was setting the board for another game. "No, Tony. Not tonight. We'll play another game tomorrow before you leave. Why don't you tell Uncle Paulo where you went today."

All of the animation went out of Tony's face. After a long minute he said in a colorless voice, not looking at Paulo, "We went to the Zoo."

"That's a great place. What all did you see?" Paulo asked.

Again a wait, then Tony said in a low voice, "a monkey."

"I remember I was scared of the first monkey I ever saw. He moved so fast in his cage and made such queer sounds," Paulo said.

Tony looked at Tiresa. "I wasn't scared." He shook his head. "Was I Aunt Treecie?"

"I should say not. You wanted to get closer to him. Where else did we go?"

Tony retreated into himself again and was silent. She should have drawn him out about the monkeys. "What about the Church?" She prompted.

He beamed. "The lantern!"

"Yes," she said. "And the horseback rider?" But Tony was through.

"Could I have a snack, Aunt Treecie? I'm hungry."

"I'm hungry too, Tony. Come on out in the kitchen and we'll see what we can find," Paulo said, as he pushed back his chair. Both of them were glad to be free of the conversation.

Friday afternoon Tiresa was surprised when Paulo left the office in time to go with them to the bus. But she shouldn't have been, of course. Tony meant a great deal to Paulo. He was family, and all he had of his brother. He was sitting beside Paulo in the front seat for this trip to the bus. She studied the backs of their heads. Not unalike, with their dark, slightly curling hair. Both sitting very straight. She had packed the suit and white shirt and tie Tony had worn when he came, now he was wearing jeans and a Rugby shirt and a red jacket she had bought him, and he looked very proud and handsome. She had bought him a book, too, to read on the bus, but she doubted whether he would.

When they came to the station, Tiresa sat in the car while Paulo put Tony on the bus. Paulo gave him a big hug and then stood by his window until the bus started.

He came back to the car and got in without speaking. Now he would brood.

"I told Bessie we would be out for dinner, and I called and made a reservation at Salvatore's," Tiresa said. She didn't want to go home just yet. "We might drive past and see what is showing at the Brattle," she added.

"All right. If you wish," Paulo said without enthusiasm.

They didn't mention Tony until they were near the end of their meal. "It went better than usual, I thought," Tiresa said. "And he definitely shows improvement, Paulo."

Paulo's mouth moved derisively. "He seemed content enough. The glasses may help him. I thought he read a little more easily, but Hoskins says his hearing shows definite impairment. The trouble is Cathy doesn't have him checked regularly." After a minute, he said, "Poor Anthony, if he could see his son."

Tiresa was impatient. "He'd see a fine looking lad." Tony's troubles were all due to Anthony, but there was no use reminding Paulo of that. For a man so beautifully capable of objective judgments and logical conclusions, he was incredible. Sometimes she thought that guilt was easier for him to carry than plain grief. At other times, she wondered if he couldn't bear to admit that one of his own family would commit suicide. Pride, the Sicilian pride. Luigi had stayed in the safe confines of the monastery over in Italy saying prayers for Anthony's soul.

In the movie Tiresa reached over and took Paulo's hand. He was thinking about Anthony and Tony, but his hand tightened on hers. He couldn't bear losing someone in his family. If she should die before he did . . . as of course she would with her heart, he would go to pieces. She put the thought out of her mind and watched the meaningless figures on the screen.

Tony seemed to walk with them as they went out to the car, and Tiresa knew they would feel his presence in the apartment for weeks. Paulo would brood, and until he came out of it, they would be quite separate, with little to say to each other, just as they had been last time he left. All those long silences at meals, and the stricken look of Paulo's face. Except when he came to her in bed; then she would feel his anguish ease. And if her heart bothered her, she knew it would quiet again as she lay close to him.

9

"I won't stay but I hadn't seen you for ages, and I was so blue I had to get out of the apartment," Olive said, sinking into a chair.

"I'm glad to see you," Tiresa said. "It has been a while, but I thought you were busy exploring Boston."

"Oh, I was. I've done all the historical places you're supposed to see—well, the main ones: Faneuil Hall, Old North Church, the Old State House, you name it. I had a wonderful time on those old streets with the yummy eighteenth-century fronts. I just drooled over those. I got a parking ticket there, I stayed so long." For a moment she was animated, then she was silent, playing with an alabaster paper knife.

"Are you getting bored?"

"No, I'm not bored. Perish the thought! It was always being drilled into us at College that the educated woman never lets herself be bored. Isn't that supposed to be one of the aims of a liberal education for women? But sight-seeing isn't like having a real job."

"No. Still you would hate to live here and not get to know the city a bit. When you do find a job, you won't have time." She had never seen Olive in such a down mood. But she was a little impatient. It seemed to her that in Olive's place she would have found something to do by now. Did Olive feel she was too much of a brain to wait tables in one of the myriad of Boston's tea-shops?

Or what about clerking in a boutique? "In the spring there will be more openings," Tiresa said.

"When I applied at the Art Museum, last fall—I majored in Biology but I had a minor in Art History—the woman took my name and said if there were any openings next spring she would let me know. Just filling in, of course." Now Olive was trying to balance the paper knife on one finger. It dropped to the floor and she reached down to pick it up.

"That would be a fascinating place to work." She could see Olive in that ambience. "You would enjoy that, wouldn't you, no matter how small the job to start with?"

"I did get a card today saying there would be a small summer job; to apply in March."

"How fine! The summer job might well turn into a permanent one, you know." Tiresa was growing weary of this fiddling conversation. In another minute she would tell Olive she had to get back to work. "I would think you would be delighted."

Without looking at her, Olive said, "A summer job is too late. I'm having a baby sometime in June."

Her words came out in such a low voice, without expression, Tiresa hardly took them in at first. "Why Olive, how wonderful."

"I wasn't going to tell anyone till it was obvious, but I guess it doesn't matter if you and Paulo know. Ron had to tell the families when we were there at Christmas. They made a big deal out of it, of course. I hate that."

"Then I won't make a big deal out of it," Tiresa said. "But I think it's very thrilling news."

"I don't know whether I even want a baby. Not now anyway."

"Perhaps that's because you have had so little time to think about it. Did you plan to have a child so soon?"

"Not really. I took the pill at first, and then one time I didn't. And after that I didn't bother. It sounds witless, doesn't it?"

Tiresa glanced at her and then away in distaste. Olive looked like a sullen child. At the first chance of being involved in life she wanted to get out of it. Without warning, anger stirred in Tiresa's mind. Olive was a healthy young creature who could have a child with no difficulty, and it meant nothing to her. The anger turned to agitation; Tiresa was having trouble breathing. She tried to put her mind on the sound of the spinning tires down in the street; sometimes she could ease her breathing if she fixed her attention on some object outside herself. The sound began again. The car was really stuck. Tiresa drew a long breath and looked back at the girl sitting there with her feet twisted around the leg of the chair, and then beyond her, out the window.

"I was much older than you when I became pregnant." The words came without her knowing what she was going to say, or that she was going to say anything. "My baby was due in December—the twenty-first. You can imagine how thrilled I was, and Paulo was beside himself." She had to go on now that she had started. "I . . . wanted that child more than, than I had ever wanted anything. But he . . . he was . . ." Her mouth refused to shape itself around the word "dead." She tried again. "He was . . . stillborn," she managed to get out. She pulled herself up out of her chair and went into the bedroom without looking at Olive.

Olive stared at the white paneling of the door. The sound of the spinning tires down in the street began again, racking the stillness of the room. Tiresa had hardly seemed to be talking to her; she hadn't looked at her. Tiresa must think she was scum to say she didn't know whether she wanted a child. But even that wasn't the truth, she only knew she just didn't want a baby right now. She might even have an abortion if Ron would hear of it, but he'd kill her if she suggested it. She had been a dope to let herself get pregnant. She let herself out and went back to their apartment.

Tiresa sat at her dressing table, palms down, in front of her. Her shoulders sagged and she was breathing heavily. Her heart seemed to stop, holding her suspended in panic—then it began again, dragging her back with it. She remembered driving to the hospital in the ambulance with Paulo, holding on to him when the pain tore her apart—enduring, to give birth to their child. And in the hospital, thinking she was dying, never of the baby's dying.

She stared at the gray-faced woman in the mirror above the dressing table. She hadn't known until the next day that the doctor had taken the baby in his hurry, crushing the head with his forceps . . . it was to save her, Paulo kept saying.

Not for years had she let herself go back like this. Even on the anniversary of that day, she kept her mind under control. Why would she tell that shallow young girl about her baby? How had she come to do that? Like some loose-tongued peasant woman pouring out her tale of childbirth as the one drama of her life— "making a big deal out of it." Now Olive would tell Ron about it. Over dinner, doubtless. And they would feel sorry for her! She didn't want their pity.

She sat a long time, trying not to think, forcing her mind to empty itself, feeling her heart slow down. When she could breathe more decently again, she got up from the dressing table and went in and bathed. Afterward, she put on her long red dress and added the heavy gold chain and locket that Paulo had bought her in Florence the summer after she lost the baby. Both chain and locket had been made by an eighteenth-century goldsmith for some woman with the initials *CLS*. She had traced the intricately engraved monogram with her finger a hundred times, until she almost knew CLS through her initials.

The locket was in the form of a book with clasps. Within the covers were three gold pages, paper thin. Paulo's name and hers were engraved on the first page and the date of their marriage, October first, nineteen hundred and sixty. The second gold sheet bore the name Paulo Sebastian Romano, December twenty-first, nineteen hundred and sixty-five. The third page was bare, but the wavy surface showed that engraving had once covered it, as well as the fourth page. *Libro di Donna* the jeweler had called it, to be

47

given to a woman on her marriage and filled with the names and dates of birth of all her children. "Not to make sad, Trise; to make proud," Paulo had said when he gave it to her. She went into the living room to wait for him.

"Are you all right, Trise?" Paulo asked as he bent over to kiss her.

"I'm quite splendid. I've spent most of the day with my feet up. My ankles are as thin as a doe's.

"Look at them and admire."

"Exquisitely svelte, but you look pale, and there's a kind of quietness about you. You were just sitting there by the fire when I came in, brooding."

Always Paulo knew. "I was thinking," she said. "Cultivating the lost art. Your hands are cold, but they feel good." She held them against her face.

"Ah, you're wearing your locket," Paulo said with pleasure.

"What were you brooding about?" He asked when he came in with their drinks.

"I was thinking about Olive. She dropped in this afternoon."

"Is she still exploring Boston?"

"Yes, but she's about to explore another world now. She's going to have a baby."

"A *bambino*." Paulo's face gentled. "*La Sposina* is losing no time in becoming *incinta*."

"In the next breath Olive told me she didn't know whether she wants a child. She wished she had kept on taking the pill."

"She's a little late thinking that. I told you she'd be having a *bambino* and didn't need to worry about a job."

"Oh, Paulo, you are hopeless. She needs to worry about doing something with herself, with her brain. She's incredibly immature and shallow, I'm afraid."

Paulo shook his head and gave a wry smile. "Just young, Tirese. Give her time."

48

Their evening followed the usual pattern. After dinner, Paulo put on some music and opened a medical journal. Tiresa had a book in her hand but she hardly turned a page. She was still writhing at herself. In spite of her carefully developed habit of reticence, she was blood relation to some Slavic great-grandmother who doubtless told her woes over and over and drew some ancient woman-comfort from the telling.

Paulo got up restlessly and went over to the window. "It's still snowing." He opened the glass door and stepped out on the balcony, letting a wave of fresh cold air into the over-heated apartment. Snow powdered his hair and shoulders when he came back in. "I wonder how much snow they're getting in Vermont."

"I'd like to be there," Tiresa said.

"We were just there at Thanksgiving."

"That was in November. I love it then too, but that's a different thing—all brown and bare, with the lemon-colored light on the stone walls and hills. I'd like to see it in early winter before the snowbanks harden." As she spoke, a craving rose in her mind to look out those small-paned windows into a white world, to be able to open a door and with one step stand on the ground. "What about driving up there this weekend, Paulo?"

He shook his head. "The cold air isn't good for you, Tiresa."

"I'd stay inside by the fire. You know how I love a whole day in that house. And you could ski all day." She saw him skiing across the meadow back of the house, making a herring-bone pattern in the snow as he climbed the hill and moved off out of sight, blessedly free from all his worries about patients, or even about her.

"Paulo, let's do it. You know, it's just occurred to me that we might ask Olive and Ron to go with us. I know they ski. Then you'd have someone to ski with, and it might be just what Olive needs at this point."

"I fail to see what magic that will work for the *Sposina*, but they might enjoy it." After a moment, he said, just like Paulo, "Unless something develops, I have nothing to keep me from going away this weekend. I wonder if Ron could get away Friday noon. Of course, it depends on the weather."

49

"Naturally," she said, smiling at him. When did weather prevent Paulo from going anywhere?

But why had she suggested taking the Fifers along? It was going to be awkward seeing Olive after the scene she had made. Of course, she was thinking of Paulo. He would love to have people to ski with . . . or was it, her stubborn mind insisted, that she was afraid she had put that girl off? And why did she care if she had? It was good for Olive to hear about someone who couldn't have a baby, someone who wanted it. That was the trouble with these young creatures, they were so wrapped up in themselves.

Masha: "*I think man ought to have faith or ought to seek a faith, or else his life is empty, empty . . . To live and not understand why cranes fly; why children are born; why there are stars in the sky . . . You've got to know what you're living for or else it's all nonsense and waste.*"

Chekhov, *The Three Sisters*, act 2

I

It was snowing all the way along the turnpike, but Paulo loved
to drive, and the hazard of the snow only added to his enjoy-
ment. He sat back in his seat at ease, his gloved hands resting
lightly on the wheel of the five-year-old Mercedes that he was
so proud of. Ron sat in the front with Paolo. He had offered to
drive up with Olive in the V-W so there would be two cars, but
Paulo rejected the idea. "No, you can drive yourself up another
time, I must take you the first time you go." Once Paulo invited
people he made them royally welcome. Now he would point out
each view, do the distance in two and a half hours exactly, and
take the steep hill at the end with a flourish. They did not invite
many friends to the farm; these two were unaware how favored
they were. But that was typical, Tiresa thought, of young people like these who had grown up taking every privilege as their
birthright from nursery school to college. Still, they were easy
to take along. When Paulo asked them if they could be ready
Friday noon, Ron had said they could be ready at dawn, and
when Paulo was called to the hospital and they hadn't gotten off
until three o'clock, it hadn't bothered them in the least. When
they took their own contemporaries to the country, there was
always so much fuss about what they needed to take along, concern about the weather, and when they would be coming back
that she and Paulo had given up. As Paulo said, there would be
no trouble in entertaining the Fifers; they would be gone skiing all day.

It hadn't been awkward when she saw Olive. She had run into her in the storage room in front of her locker, getting out their ski things.

"Oh Tiresa, I'm so excited about going to the country. To get away from the apartment for a whole weekend will absolutely save my life." Her clear blue eyes had no least trace of pity. "And Ron is in seventh heaven at the thought of skiing. He's really good." Perhaps the girl had more sensitivity than she had thought. Or perhaps it didn't mean that much to her.

The men were talking about skiing as they drove. Ron had skied in Colorado, Paulo had once skied in the Alps. "I usually go cross-country skiing above the farm," Paulo said, "but if you and Olive want to go up to the ski area, Ron, it's quite close, and you can take the car and drive up. We'll have two days if Tiresa is willing to come back late Sunday."

"Thanks," Ron said. "I don't believe Ollie will go; she'll just ski a little around the place. She's not, uh, being too strenuous, but I might run up and have a crack at it. A man at the office was telling me it's really good up there."

"Ron is so sure about what I'll do and won't do," Olive murmured to Tiresa. "I know he'll be awful when I get near term."

Tiresa was amused, but she made no comment. She always felt quiet driving to the farm. That was another thing about contemporaries, you had to keep up a steady stream of conversation. With someone so much younger, she felt no obligation to talk. After an hour or so, she looked over and saw that Olive was asleep, her head on the hood of her ski-jacket. Paulo was right, there was a naturalness about her. If she was sleepy, she slept; if she was down, she showed it. When did you begin to feel you must keep a certain demeanor toward the world?

No one they ever brought was prepared for the steep pitch of narrow road up through the woods to the farmhouse, nor the meanness and simplicity of the house when they got there. Today, the woods on either side of the road were hung with fresh snow; the late afternoon sun made tunnels of light between the trees.

"Gosh, it's pretty," Ron exclaimed. "Ollie, wake up and look."

Olive stared sleepily out at the transformed world. "It's the most beautiful thing I ever saw, absolutely."

"'And God said to Job, "hast thou entered into the treasures of the snow?"'" Tiresa quoted.

"I have right this minute," Olive said.

Paulo beamed with proprietary pleasure.

The road made a final curve and came to an end in the door-yard of an old farmhouse that had once been painted white, but so long ago that the clapboards were more gray than white; the narrow porch at the corner of the house sagged a little toward the woodshed. Behind the house, stood the barn, peering over the roof. It had been painted a sturdy red, but sun and rain and snow—time itself—had bleached the color to what Paulo claimed was Pompeian red. Snow, a foot high, topped the roof of both barn and house.

Tiresa turned the big key in the lock and opened the front door into a box hall barely large enough for four people to stand at once. Out of it opened the long low-ceilinged living room. An almost-comfortable warmth greeted them.

"Our neighbor came up the hill to turn up the heat and build a fire in the kitchen stove, but I warn you the heat doesn't more than take the chill off in the upstairs bedroom. You'll have to depend on electric blankets and each other for warmth," Paulo warned them.

"How nice it is," Olive said, but she was startled by the bareness of the room. It was so different from the Romanos' apartment. A prim horse-hair sofa, three straight chairs, and a rocker, along with one large arm chair by the table made up all the furnishings except for the well-worn braided rugs.

"And this is the kitchen, the real center of the house," Paulo called to them from the next room. He had lighted the fire that had been laid in a fireplace stretching halfway across the end of the room.

"Wow. The real thing, crane and everything," Ron said.

All the light in the room came in through two small-paned windows over the gray soapstone sink; already, the other end of the room was in shadow.

"We bought the farm two years ago," Tiresa said. "Furniture and all. We haven't done anything to the house except for putting in a furnace and two bathrooms. Oh yes, and some bookshelves. The farm had been in one family for four generations and had a pronounced personality of its own, so we've respected that."

"But wouldn't you think they would want to make it cozier, Ron?" Olive said when they were up in their dormer bedroom.

"Yeah. You could do wonders with it," Ron agreed. "I'd damn well put some wall-to-wall carpet over these cold board floors to begin with. I don't wonder that they want to bring people up here with them, it's so isolated. Do you know that they don't even have a T-V!"

But at dinner at the long board table in the kitchen, the room seemed richly furnished by the glow from the four candles on the table and the fire on the hearth. In the close light, their faces changed. Olive's, touched with eye-shadow and lip-stick, took on interesting shadows of its own. The blue eyes turned a deeper hue. Ron's face went through an even more remarkable change; his gray eyes sparkled, the cleft that weakened his chin was smudged over by shadow. Paulo's high forehead gleamed as he bent over the spoon he was dipping in the casserole, and in the firelight Tiresa's face took on a look of glowing health. They leaned a little toward each other in the shadowy light as if they had things to say to each other—important things.

"To our guests," Paulo said, lifting his glass. "Thank you for this wine, Ron."

"I didn't know just what to bring, but I thought it better be an Italian wine," Ron said.

"It was a good selection. Now we should drink to the *bambino* I hear is on the way. Congratulations."

Of course Paulo would do that. It was so Sicilian, Tiresa thought. She glanced at Olive over her raised glass and saw her flush.

"I'll sure drink to that," Ron said.

"The first family who built this house had ten children," Paulo told them. "Probably all born in that room off the kitchen that Tiresa and I have. It was called the borning room."

Olive groaned. "The thought of having ten children exhausts me."

"The idea of educating them does me," Ron said. "I'm going to take out an educational policy straight off, you better believe."

Paulo shrugged. "They seem to have had a good life."

Tiresa laughed. "Oh Paulo, we don't know anything about them. We just want to think they had."

"I feel it in the house, in the way they built it and kept it up." He brought the coffee and poured it into thick blue mugs. Then he set the pot over on the brick hearth and came back to the table.

"I can see how being in an old house makes you want to know more about the owners, doesn't it?" Olive said.

"I suppose you have to have all this wood trucked up here," Ron said, assuming an interest that he didn't feel.

Tiresa was bored. She sipped her wine, casting about for some subject that might be more interesting, and more revealing than these dull remarks. "I've been making a study of the use of memory in fiction," she began. "Let me ask you each for a childhood memory—something that happened that made a deep impression on you. Ron?" She smiled at him as if he were her brightest student.

"Oh, uh, gosh. I guess the first time my Dad took me up in

a plane, when I was about six. He thought I'd be scared, but I wasn't a bit; I cried when I had to get off. It was a business trip really, and a private plane so he could take me into the cock-pit to see the pilot. I'm going to have my own plane one of these days." He had come alive as he told it. Olive's eyes were bright as she looked at him, and Tiresa saw that he had caught Paulo's interest, too.

"Your turn, Paulo," Ron said.

"Ah, now you have turned on me," Paulo said smiling. "Well, I have no trouble recalling my sharpest childhood memory. It's of being taken out of bed at night to watch the eruption of Mount Etna. I was only two years old, but I see that terrible spectacle today sometimes in nightmares. I remember flames shooting into the air—straight up, thousands of feet and red hot lava pouring down the sides of the mountain like rivers of fire, then turning gray as the flow stopped. But the most terrifying thing was the steady roar—as if the whole earth were going to break apart. Every now and then there would be a booming sound, like an explosion . . ."

The volcano seemed to erupt in front of his eyes as he talked, Tiresa thought. But of course he couldn't have remembered all that if he was only one or two. He had never told her it came back to him in nightmares.

"How far away from it were you?" Ron asked.

"Oh, twenty miles as we looked across from our garden, three times that by the road." He smiled suddenly, as though letting the vision go. "What do you remember, Olive?"

"I've been trying to think. I remember one thing I'll never forget. I must have been around four. My grandmother, who hadn't seen me since I was one, was coming, and Mother told me all about her: that I was named for her and had her eyes, and how she'd play with me and we'd be the greatest friends. I could hardly wait to see her. And then she came." Olive paused and looked around the table. "Maybe it was because I'd never been around older people, but she frightened me. She was tall and had gray hair and wore glasses, and her eyes seemed to be looking right through me. She'd read me the longest stories and if I wriggled she'd put me down from her lap and wouldn't read any more. I didn't mind that, but I knew she was cross with me. One time Mother and Dad went out and left me with Grandmother. I must have been asleep, and she came to see if I was all right. Anyway, I woke up and she was standing by my bed in the dark. I was so scared I screamed and wouldn't let her touch me. I guess I settled down eventually, but it was awful. I wanted her to go away and I didn't want to have her name or eyes like hers. I remember I looked in the mirror to see if my eyes did look like hers."

"Poor child," Paulo said. "My grandparents on both sides were such a natural part of my life. In fact, they were a refuge when I wanted to get away from home."

"We must remember that, Hon, and make sure Who's-it spends some time with both sets of grandparents so he knows them."

"Did you ever see her later and grow fond of her?" Tiresa asked. "It must have been a terrible thing for her."

"No. She died the next year. It was so awful because I expected to love her."

Paulo gave his slightest shrug. "Isn't it part of the human experience?"

"Have you ever been disappointed so many times in your life, Paulo?" Tiresa demanded. The next instant, Tiresa wondered if he was thinking of his brother.

"No, fortunately. I was speaking of mankind," Paulo said, gesturing largely.

"Well, then! You sound positively embittered by your disappointments," Tiresa said. "Now my memory is a cheerful one, and I couldn't have been more than four either because my head barely came above the glass case of fresh baked goods in my father's bakery. I remember I had to stand on a stool, and my father was standing beside me, wrapping the bread and currant

59

buns and kohlachies, and then he would give them to me to hand to the customers. 'You're the princess giving out the treasures, Tracy, see! Good smells, good tastes, good nourishment; you give them all that,' he said."

Tiresa could see that Ron and Olive waited for her to go on. But that was all of it. Only Paulo saw any meaning in the memory, bless him. She was sorry she had wasted it on them. "When I was in my teens and didn't like having to work in the bakery afternoons after school and on Saturdays, it helped to remember that I was the princess giving out treasures," she said, trying to make a point for them.

Tiresa's voice seemed to set off some vibration in the low-ceilinged room, Olive thought. She felt it down her back or in her head somewhere.

2

The air was so cold that it stood in their room like a presence. Olive's nose was cold. In the pale light that came in through the high dormer window, the room she had seen only dimly stood completely revealed: the faded brown wallpaper with sprigs of once-pink flowers, the gray board floor covered only by two strips of rag rug, one in the front of the dresser, one beside the bed. The dresser and washstand were painted a dull mustard color, the bed and chairs were dark. Olive's eyes moved from object to object. Like the cold, the stillness seemed to press through the white-curtained window.

"Ron," she raised on one elbow and whispered in his ear, biting the rim of it.

"Cut it out," he said sleepily, without opening his eyes. "Ollie?" He put his arm around her and pulled her closer.

"It's freezing cold. Turn on the blanket."

"Poor little thing. Papa warm," he murmured, kissing her, covering her with his body and making the old bed squeak as they moved.

"Sh, Ron!"

"Doesn't matter. This bed must have squeaked before now if they had all those ten kids." They stifled their laughter against each other.

When they heard the dinner bell rung in the hall below, they had almost fallen asleep.

"*Buon giorno*," Paulo called up the stairs. Ron opened the door to answer, clad in the red nightshirt Olive had given him expressly for this trip. The sound of wood crackling came up to them and a mingled smell of woodsmoke and bacon cooking.

"Good morning," Ron called back down. "We'll be right there."

"What a place!" Ron said as he came back. "They're pretty lively for their age, you know."

"And they're so much more fun than you'd think they would be," Olive said. "You don't even think about their being older." She stood on the braided rug, brushing her hair. She too wore a red flannel nightshirt.

"I'll never understand why you brush your hair before you get your clothes on," Ron said.

"Because it gets in my way, silly."

Tiresa was a little wistful as she watched them go off after breakfast. Olive, in her bright blue ski suit with her hair in two braids, looked still in her teens. She was laughing at something Paulo said to her. Ron hit her with a snowball and she screamed and threw one back. Paulo was getting into it now, feeling as young as Ron, she was sure. They skied off across the meadow, bright figures in a world that was all black and white except for the pale blue sky. Moving so smoothly with an effortless grace they seemed favored creatures to her.

For one tantalizing moment, she let herself think back to their excited hope that she could have heart surgery—and then the decision that it wasn't wise in her case, and the terrible let-down. Yet something remained; she had dreamed of herself miraculously freed from her bondage and she kept some sense of that although physically nothing was changed. She had told Paulo she believed she was better anyway. He looked at her pityingly, but, nevertheless, there was some slight truth in it. "She will go on living precariously," she had overheard the doctor say to Paulo, but even that she could take—except on bad days. Thousands, millions more likely lived that way—pilots and explorers and men who went down in the mines. Didn't everyone really?

She was glad that Paulo was going to take Olive and Ron into the village for lunch. "And don't get back before mid-afternoon," she had told him. "I want the whole day here by myself with no lunch to get." She had said it to make him feel free, but partly for herself, too. And now that the pang of watching them go off was over, and they were out of sight, she was entirely content. Paulo had built up the fire in the big kitchen fireplace and the one in the living room, and left a small pile of logs she could put on.

She liked having the kitchen to herself. She hadn't let Olive help with the dishes because she wanted to do them alone. There weren't many but she wanted to putter. Kneading bread was too strenuous any more, but as she wiped the thick pine counter, she could almost feel the elastic mass of dough under her hands.

She took her time, delighting in the shape of the thick bowls that seemed to soothe her hands, and the look of the big gray stoneware pitcher, and thought herself as the woman in the Vermeer painting. After the dishes were put away, she poured the fruit juices, along with the spices, into the kettle on the crane, and got out the wine, ready to add and heat when the time came. They would bake the potatoes in the fireplace oven, and Paulo would broil the steaks. She would make the salad later—there was nothing more she needed to do about dinner. Now she could go from window to window, repossessing the fields and the stone wall and the very line of the barn roof. Paulo had filled the bird feeders early this morning, but it would take a while for word to get around. Did the birds send out scouts to check?

She stood a moment looking out the window, sending her eyes up the slope to the highest line of trees against the sky. The bare branched deciduous ones were dominant, but not dead black as you'd expect; they were almost purplish when they were massed together like that, and the deep green hemlocks and balsams and pines scattered among them softened the winter bleakness.

It was odd that the white bark of the birches stood out so against the snow. They seemed to have eyes—like potatoes. Well now that was far-fetched, but for a minute . . .

Halfway up, beyond a tumble-down stone wall, was the old cemetery almost buried in the snow; only eighteen or nineteen worn slate markers slanting as though pushed by the winds that had blown against them for the last hundred and seventy or more years. She wished she could walk up there. It was a restful place where peace came dropping slowly. She liked reading the names and the legends and the dates; by now they had lost any sense of tragedy or even sadness. One day last summer she had discovered that Zilpha and Hepzibah and Mercy—with last names that belonged to creeks and roads around here still—had each lost one child or more at birth or in the first year of life. "You and I," she had murmured to Mercy as she touched her stone.

She went in to make their bed in the borning room off the kitchen. The bed should have a Vermont quilt, but the heavy woven coverlet from Italy was a brave burst of color against the faded wallpaper. At the far corner of the house, this room got the full brunt of the wind that swept down from the northeast, and she and Paulo had often lain here in each other's arms, feeling themselves rocked by the wind . . . She threw back the blankets with such energy she had to stand still and lean against the bed until her heart quieted.

Here, by herself, in this small room she could admit that she was worried about her heart. She was so much more conscious of it than she had been. Going across campus to the library last week, she had had to stop and struggle for breath. And that young French instructor came along and saw that she was in trouble. She was glad to lean on him for a few minutes, and then let him get the book she had come for. But she hadn't told Paulo. He would only worry and want her to stop teaching.

"You have these bad times, Tirese," he had said just the other day, "but your general condition is good. You'll live into your seventies if you just follow a sensible regimen and don't overdo."

She had felt as if he had given her—promised her—twenty more years. But did he really believe that?

She walked away from her question back to the living room, and sitting down by the bookcase, began to put the books they had brought up this time on the shelves. Every time they came, they added a few more, building a wall against the wind, she always thought, whether that wind was worry or cold or whatever.

She left out the volume of Keats. Tonight was St. Agnes Eve—January twenty-first. She wanted to read the poem aloud, taking turns the way she and Paulo did one time. It wasn't long.

> St. Agnes Eve—Ah bitter chill it was!
> The owl, for all his feathers, was a-cold;
> The hare limp'd trembling through the frozen grass . . .

She quoted to the empty room, and the familiar words swept her mind clear of anxiety. Olive and Ron might be horrified at the idea of reading poetry aloud, but they would like it once they began. Poetry didn't bore the young; it was their natural language if they didn't have to come to it in a text.

As she sat having a bowl of soup at noon, Tiresa looked around the big kitchen and drew its quiet simplicity into herself. All the human commotion these rooms must have known had been absorbed into the very wood and plaster, leaving a patina of calm. She felt curiously at peace here, and strong. Oh yes, she felt very strong again. If life wasn't to go on very long, so what! She was living it now, wasn't she this minute? How many times did she have to learn that?

She finished a set of papers from her seminar and had a cup of tea in the middle of the afternoon and set the table for dinner. Then there seemed nothing more to do and she went over to look out the window again. Shadows had crept down from the hill and lay across the snow. Paulo and the Fifers must be starting back about now. It was time. She had been alone long enough.

Tiresa pushed the crane over the fire where Paulo's great logs still sent up heat. Wine mulled over burning logs had a richer flavor than any simmered on a burner. Then she went to dress for dinner. She always wore the same long woolen skirt up here on winter weekends, and a deep red blouse Paulo liked.

The fragrance of the wine filled the kitchen by the time Tiresa heard Paulo and the others stacking their skis against the house. Olive opened the door, her face bright with cold and Paulo, behind her, was beaming.

"Oh Tiresa, it was glorious," Olive said. "Mmm, what a heavenly smell."

"Tirese, you weren't lonely?" Paulo asked, kissing her.

"Not until five minutes ago. Where's Ron?"

"He wanted to go to the end of the trail. He'll be along. That wine does smell like ambrosia."

"I hope you had a good lunch?"

"Absolutely fantastic," Olive burbled. She went over to stand by the hearth.

"And you didn't get too tired?" Tiresa looked over at her glowing face and felt her excitement.

"Oh a little—just at the end. But I loved every minute. It was out of this world, absolutely. And it was lovely coming back and seeing the lighted house across the meadow, and opening the door to a fire and you here to greet us."

Paulo and Tiresa laughed over her enthusiasm. "Come and have some mulled wine," Tiresa said. "And then you can go up and take a hot bath and rest before dinner. Paulo, 'taste and see,' as the hymn says, how the wine is."

Olive carried her empty cup over to the sink. "If you don't need me, Tiresa, I think I will go up."

"Is she all right, Paulo?" Tiresa asked when she had gone.

"I'm sure she is. You should have seen her. She was radiant the whole time. And Ron was in his element. He's a regular speed demon. I'd keep up with him for a stretch and then wait for Olive to catch up. If I hadn't been along, Olive would have had a pretty solitary time of it. Tirese, you haven't had any wine yourself." He brought her a cup and leaned against the counter. "How was your day?"

In the face of Olive's excitement, she felt a little deflated now as she thought about it. "Peaceful, quiet; time to think and look out all the windows."

"Too much time, I'm afraid. I worried about you."

"No need. It was just what I craved, but it did get a little longish. I was glad when you got back. I missed you."

"And I you, Tirese."

Olive was glad to get upstairs by herself. She turned on the electric bulb hanging from a cord, but the sudden glare was too harsh and she lit a candle on the dresser and turned out the light. Curious she peered in the mirror at the bright face and the scarlet cheeks, almost expecting to see some new grace of air of joy hovering over it. She slid out of her ski things and got ready for her bath, but instead of hurrying to take it, she climbed on the high bed and wrapped herself in the quilt.

Now she could think about what had happened too fast to take in . . . she had been tired and told Ron and Paulo to go on, that she'd putz along and take her time going home; she'd be fine. And she was for a while. She sat on a wall and rested, but it was gloomy in the woods, with odd rustlings and sighings and queer cracklings. She slogged on, dreading the long trek home.

And then she came down the trail out of the woods and saw Paulo coming across the meadow below her. She was so relieved she waved her pole and called to him.

"I was afraid you were lost," he called back.

What had she called back? She didn't remember; she was so glad to see him. She dug her pole in and pushed off down the hill and he came across to meet her.

When she came to a stop beside him, he put his finger under her chin and kissed her on the lips ever so gently. "You're a child of joy," he said.

She had stood there, smiling stupidly, but feeling different—
feeling joyful. It wasn't just his kissing her—men were always
kissing you, it was the *way* he did it. As though there were something delicate and rare about her, about their meeting there on
the snow.

They hardly said anything, but they didn't need to. And then
they skied back, with Paulo always just behind her or beside her—
not like skiing with Ron. Once when the trail led across a field,
she struck out in a wide arc, Paulo circled the other way and
came in front of her, making a bow as he passed. And then, for
the fun of it, she circled again and he followed her tracks in a
wider arc and then they stood still laughing. "That was like a
dance," he said. She had never known anyone so quick to follow your mood.

The dark came fast, but the snow seemed to grow whiter and
lit up their path. It was snowing steadily. She wished she could
have gone on skiing another hour.

She lay with her eyes closed, still feeling the motion of her
body as she skied. If Paulo were your lover . . . he would be so
gentle and sensitive; you could tell from his eyes how passionate he would be . . .

The kitchen door banged so it shook the house. "That didn't
take me so long, did it?" Ron's voice carried through the thin
floor. Olive hurried into the bathroom to draw her tub.

"Hi," Ron said as she came back into the room. He was stretched
out on the bed. "Wasn't that the greatest!"

"Super. Do you want that bright light on?" She wondered if
all that had happened to her showed in her face.

"I don't care. Turn it off if you want." Olive snapped it off
gratefully.

"Did you get tired, hon? Tiresa was afraid you had."

"Oh, a little maybe. The bath rested me. Hurry and take yours
while there's still some warmth left in that cold room."

Olive dressed slowly, feeling far removed from the disgusting commercial world where the word "joy" was used as the title of a cookbook or the name of a dishwasher detergent to a world where the word "joy" was bequeathed as a tribute. She leaned closer to the mirror as she fastened her earrings, glad she had had her ears pierced last year; it was much more European.

Ron whistled when he came back and saw her. "Baby. I like. I bet that long skirt feels good and warm, but you're not going barefoot, are you?"

She hadn't realized that her feet were icy from the floor.

"Look Ron, why don't you go on down to the fire and have a cup of that hot wine. Gosh, it's good, and Paulo's doing something tricky with hickory chips to give the steaks the right flavor."

"You won't be long. I'll wait." A sudden shyness had come over her. She busied herself with hanging up the ski clothes.

As they came down the stairs into the cold hall, Olive could hear Tiresa and Paulo talking. They always seemed to have so much to say to each other. The kitchen was bright with firelight and smelled both of wine and the steaks Paulo was broiling.

"You must be cold. Come quick to the fire," Tiresa said.

"How charming you look, *Sposina*," Paulo said. "But now you are a grown up young woman, not the child of joy who came skiing out of the woods this afternoon. She was such a rosy-cheeked child, Ron, that I had to kiss her."

Olive blushed painfully. It hadn't meant anything to him then; he just thought of her as a cute red-cheeked child. She managed a laugh.

"Well now! I can see that I should have stayed with you two," Ron joked.

"Oh it was the most chaste of kisses. She was never in safer hands," Paulo said.

Seeing her blush, Tiresa said lightly. "I hope he didn't startle you. Paulo has one failing, he cannot resist youth or beauty."

"And when they are united in one person . . ." Paulo put in.

Tiresa laughed and lifted her hands in a little gesture of

69

hopelessness. "Can you give me a hand here with the salad. The greens are all ready and there are some tomatoes and feta cheese, if you like . . . I envied you this morning, getting up there on the hill."

"It was nice," Olive said.

But this was not the same person who had pronounced it glorious and fantastic earlier, Tiresa observed. She was let down, Tiresa saw. Paulo's telling about it had spoilt it.

"I think I'll go up to Granite tomorrow, Paulo, if you really don't mind my taking your car," Ron said at dinner. "Why don't you come, too?"

"Oh, I think Olive and I will ski cross-country, but a shorter distance," Paulo said.

Olive lifted her head with an over-elaborate look of weariness. The hoop earrings cast shadows on her slender neck. "Perhaps I did overdo today. I think I'll stay around here with you, Tiresa."

"I'd be delighted to have you," Tiresa said quickly. So Paulo had hurt her feelings. "But I think we should start back after an early lunch tomorrow," she added, deciding in that moment. "It's still snowing, and that will slow us down. We don't want to get back late in the dark if we can help it."

"Tiresa! The dark is nothing. How does that line go that you're always quoting from some play? 'The dark is light enough.' I like driving back at night," Paulo protested.

"Wait and see how deep the snow is in the morning," Tiresa said.

The atmosphere had changed from last night, Tiresa thought as she looked around the table. She and Olive had dressed for dinner tonight, and Paulo was looking romantic in his green velvet waistcoat, Ron in his blazer. The dinner was better, too, but neither the candlelight nor firelight seemed to bring them together. Olive was no child of joy tonight, either. She turned to Ron. "Tell me, Ron," she began off the top of her head, "does selling insurance and advising people on insurance make you more cautious yourself or less? I mean . . ."

"Oh, I carry all the insurance I can, I'll tell you. I see people every day who don't begin to buy the protection they need; just take a chance. Of course, there are more without any insurance at all in Europe. Italy, for instance, Paulo. I saw some statistics . . ."

Paulo shrugged. "We're a race of fatalists. *Ca cera cera,*" he said with a laugh. "Insurance costs money! But the things I worry about you can't insure against."

"Like what?" Ron demanded. Yes, Ron would be very good at his job.

"Growing older—death. Man's unconquerable enemies."

"Why those are the very things we insure against, Paulo."

Paulo shook his head. "You can only offer a man material benefits in his older years, or aid his heirs, not give a man back his youth. I'm talking about the things that can't be replaced."

"That's not quite the point, is it, Paulo?"

Tiresa could see that Paulo was growing unreasonable and depressed, and Ron was gathering himself together for an argument. "Paulo, would you bring the fruit and cheese while I take off the dishes," she broke in.

"Here, Tiresa, I'll get the dishes," Ron said.

"Why bless you, Ron." She smiled at him for dropping the subject of insurance.

"I'll take off the dishes; you bring in your player and the discs you brought," Olive said.

"Gosh, yes. Can you beat that, I forgot all about them." Cold air rushed in as he opened the door to the hall and clattered upstairs. Paulo was frowning at his own thoughts. Tiresa had no desire to hear any Rock music, which she knew nothing about. But she could hardly tell him not to play his music since he had brought it way up here.

And then he was back. "Where's an outlet, Tiresa?"

"Ah, we shall have music," Paulo said as he came in with the plate of fruit, the polite host again.

Now, Tiresa thought with annoyance, they wouldn't talk, just sit passively while the music flowed over them. As the music began, she was more conscious of the house than of herself. She felt the old walls being startled by the sounds. The music rising to the cold upstairs through the thin floors would jar the very joists, and the mice in the walls would cower.

But it wasn't as she feared. The voice was beguiling. Paulo was moving his head to the rhythm. Ron, eating a pear, had entered into the music and was smiling in a proprietary fashion, as if it were of his own making. Olive, too, seemed serene. Of course, these young people were used to some sound all the time. Complete stillness put them off. She was hardly hearing the music, but it was a relief after all not to suffer the non-talk or jangling arguments; good not to be so conscious of each mood.

"This one's called 'Sound of Silence'; it's a real old one of Simon and Garfunkle."

"How do you hear silence when you're listening to music," Paulo wanted to know.

Tiresa looked over at Olive and was held by the picture she made leaning on her elbow, holding a cluster of grapes in one hand, picking them off with the other. She was like a figure in some classical statuary. Her face in repose was quite lovely. Paulo was watching Olive, too. Tiresa caught his eye and looked over at Olive. He nodded, smiling. How he did enjoy looking at a pretty young girl.

The music went on—haunting, provocative, drawing them into a different atmosphere. Easy to take, but they could have read the whole of "Eve of St. Agnes." After Ron and Olive had gone up to bed, she would sit here by the fire and read it; the poem had to be read on St. Agnes' Eve. Paulo could go on to bed, or would he sit here with her and let her read it to him? He was patient with her notions.

Paulo brought the coffee from the hearth and refilled their mugs; not hers, she mustn't have any more.

The music came to an end.

"Thank you, Ron," Tiresa said.

"Yeah. You know, if you like that sort of music, they're not bad. Ollie's crazy about them. But I guess all that fresh air and exercise made me sleepy. I'm just about out," Ron said.

"Olive was nodding too, I noticed," Paulo said.

When they were alone, Tiresa lingered by the fire while Paulo brought in a green log.

"And they are gone; aye ages long ago
Those lovers fled away into the storm . . ." she recited.

"And our young lovers fled away upstairs
And to one another's arms shall hie them eagerly," Paulo extemporized.

"This is St. Agnes' Eve, and I wanted us all to read the poem aloud tonight."

Paulo shook his head. "Better you didn't try that, Trise. These children wouldn't go for it. Simon and Garfunkle are more their medium."

"Paulo, maybe you weren't aware of it, but you hurt that girl tonight, telling everyone about your kiss."

"For God's sake, it was just a spontaneous gesture in a beautiful snowy tableau. You don't think for a moment . . ."

"No, I don't, but she thought it was more, I'm sure. I saw her face when she came in. She was all lighted up and then you deflated her by telling us all about it. You noticed how quiet she was at dinner."

Paulo's mouth tightened. He went over to bank the fire.

"It's not like you to be so insensitive. She blew out the candles and for an instant the warm shadowy room held them in silence. "I always hate to leave this room when the fire is still so bright. I meant to sit here and read *Eve of St. Agnes* by myself."

"But not tonight, Tirese."

"No, not tonight."

"Paulo," Tirese said as they lay in bed, "if Olive is a child of joy,

73

and she really did look like that when she first came in, how do you think of me?"

Paulo laughed. "Do I detect stirrings of jealousy? Tirese, my darling, you are my *Donna Simpatica.*"

"Sympathy is a poor thing compared to joy."

"I don't mean that English word. It means—how do I say it?" She let him flounder. "It is understanding, Tirese, complete. You always know how I feel without my telling you. It's—damn it, you know how I am about English words. I couldn't live without you, and you know it." He leaned over and kissed her, lifting his mouth from hers to whisper, "I love you, Tirese. You'll have to be satisfied with that."

"I am," she whispered back.

Tiresa was glad to see that it was still snowing steadily the next morning. Weekends had their own dimensions, and this one had come to its natural end.

". . . ah elfin storm from fairy land
Of haggard seeming, but a boon indeed . . ."

She murmured to herself as she fried the bacon. As if *The Eve of St. Agnes* had lain all night in her brain.

They were quiet on the drive back. The windshield wiper couldn't keep up with the snow and Paulo had his whole mind on the driving. Ron was leaning out to see the shoulder of the road on his side. Olive fell asleep as before. Tiresa watched the snow; it closed them inside in a curious sense of intimacy. And, as always, so fickle in the human mind, all four of them were secretly as glad to leave the country and come back to the city as they had been on the way up to leave the city.

Their waiting apartments seemed luxurious and warm.

Ron turned to the hockey game on television before he took off his ski jacket, and it sounded pleasantly familiar to Olive; even the sound of the refrigerator door and the snap of an opening beer can fell into place in her mind.

"Know what, hon?" Ron asked during the commercial as Olive settled down beside him on the couch. "I'm just as glad we did come back early. I'd had about enough."

"Me, too. It was fun, but I was ready to come home. I'm going to take a bath tonight in a *warm* bathroom."

"I know what you mean, but with your amorous friend there, I was afraid you wanted to ski more with him." Ron grinned at her.

"Don't be a stupe, Ron. He was just kissing a red-cheeked child kind of thing."

"The old lecher. Well, after all, you have to remember that he's Italian–Sicilian, which is worse, so what can you expect? I bet he flirts with all his lady patients."

Olive had started to look at the Sunday paper, but she glanced up to ask, "Why is a Sicilian worse?"

"Ollie, everyone knows that Sicilians are twice as hot blooded as Italians from the rest of Italy. Everything's passion with them—to kill or make love."

"Oh. Doesn't it strike you as odd that Tiresa and Paulo ever married? I mean they're so different. She's sort of—well, she's a teacher type, and he's more a romantic kind."

But Ron was back in his game.

"There's ice cream in the frig, Ron. Butter almond; want some?"

"No thanks, hon. You can bring me another beer."

Olive sat at the kitchen table, curling her tongue around the spoon of ice cream. What a ninny she had been to get such a kick out of Paulo's kissing her. But she went on thinking about him. But wasn't it really more?

In the apartment down the hall, Paulo put a Mozart string quartet on the player and came over to sit in his chair across from Tiresa. "Would you like a fire?"

"No thanks. We had such continuous fires in the country, I feel like a smoked ham. Rather nice to be alone again, isn't it?"

Paulo laughed. "Always. But I think they had a good time.

We'll ask them again, maybe in the spring before she has her babe."

Tiresa went on thinking about Olive and Ron. Were they deeply in love? It was hard to tell with the young—even the ones who were always pawing each other.

3

"I saw Olive and Ron waiting for the elevator with the Eisenharts," Paulo announced. "They're the young couple down on the ninth floor; he's a graduate student in biology, and I gather that she works. I see them going out together in the morning." Paulo was interested in everyone living in the building.

"It's time Ron and Olive found some young people their own age and type," Tiresa said.

"I wouldn't say they're the same type. The Eisenharts are much more intellectual."

Tiresa looked at him with amusement in her eyes. "Would you say we are quite the same type as the Fifers?"

They were having their coffee when Paulo said abruptly. "If we had had children, they would have been about Ron's and Olive's age."

"What a brilliant deduction. Unfortunately, I wasn't very good at bearing a child."

"Tiresa!"

She ignored the reproach in his voice. "While you're having your paternal urges, here's a letter from Tony that came today. I asked him to write and tell me what he wanted for his birthday. He wants an Instamatic camera. His handwriting is improved."

Paulo read the much-erased sheet of paper with irregular lines of hand printing. "Yes, this is quite the letter. In four lines he has only five misspelled words. You send him the camera, and I'll send some money." He got up to answer the doorbell.

Olive stood there in jeans and a shirt, with her hair loose. "No, I won't sit down—well, maybe for just a minute." She perched on the arm of a chair. "I came along to ask you for dinner Saturday night. We've wanted to have you for ever so long. You've never even been in our apartment, Paulo."

"I shall look forward with great pleasure to being in your home."

"And I have some news. You'll never believe it, but I have a job. Isn't that something! Not really a job, but Gerta Eisenhart knew a professor who happened to tell her that he wanted somebody to type the manuscript of a book he's writing, and she told him about me. I went to see him, and I'm to start Monday."

"Splendid," Tiresa said. "How are you at typing?"

"Not bad. I typed one summer in Dad's office, and he's awfully fussy. The man is a marine biologist, Gerta says. I suppose the stuff'll be deadly dull, but I don't care." It occurred to Tiresa that she was as radiant over her job as she had been when she came in from skiing. Well, maybe, not quite . . .

"See you Saturday night, about six-thirty. You'll be our first dinner guests, except for family." She let herself out before Paulo could open the door.

"I'm glad she has something to do," Tiresa said.

"I shall take a bottle of really good Italian wine," Paulo said. "And flowers, don't you think, Tiresa?"

"One or the other would do."

"But a first dinner party—no, I shall take both."

Paulo was so pleased by the invitation he was still smiling, Tiresa noticed. But she was too, rather. Ron and Olive must want to keep in touch in spite of the age difference. What an odd attitude she and Paulo had got into—caring so much about a young couple they had met so casually. There was something a little pathetic about it too.

"Spring flowers, wouldn't you think?" Paulo asked.

Ron greeted them at the door, and Olive came hurrying out of the kitchen. "Welcome to Casa Fifer!" they chorused. "It sounds

78

a little like a swear word," Ron said. "Especially if you run the two words together."

"Or a German party," Tiresa suggested.

"Not at all. It sounds very right and proper," Paulo insisted, proffering his gifts. "Flowers for the hostess, and wine for the host."

The heat from Olive's efforts had given her face a rosy flush, Tiresa noticed, and the loose locks escaping from her high knot hung more carelessly than ever beside her hoop earrings. In a low-necked blouse made of some white cotton stuff that might have been intended for a dishcloth and her long black skirt with the red postage stamp of an apron she could belong to a country square dance group. Ron looked very much the young businessman in his white shirt and dark suit, with his hair shorter than Paulo's.

They went into the living room to background music that Tiresa couldn't identify. The table had been pulled out and carefully set with candles and wedding silver. Olive and Ron both disappeared into the kitchen and Tiresa and Paulo were left to themselves for a minute.

Paulo nodded approvingly. "This room is very light in mood." He was studying the painting of the iris when Olive came back with the flowers in a bowl.

"Just my favorites, Paulo. Japanese iris and freesias."

"Your irises in the painting here are voluptuous beside these," Paulo said. "The fresh ones are more appropriate for our hostess, don't you think, Tiresa?"

"Oh quite," Tiresa agreed, her eyes dancing. He was giving Olive ideas again. She saw her color rise as she went back into the kitchen.

Ron brought out a tray of martinis. "I hope these are somewhere near as sharp as the ones you made, Paulo." They held their glasses, waiting for Olive. "Hon, can you come? We're waiting for our drinks with our tongues hanging out."

"You mean we're waiting for *la Sposina*. Here you are!" He

79

gave her a glass with a little bow. "I want to propose a toast to your first home. The harmony of colors bespeaks a beautiful harmony between you." Paulo beamed, touched to the heart by the moment. This was so natural to him, but he could seem overblown to the young, Tiresa thought. But Olive and Ron were smiling proudly at each other.

"And I'll drink to your new job, Olive," Tiresa said crisply.

"I don't know that I'll drink to that," Ron said. "I don't much like her tackling all that typing now that she's having a baby. You should see the pages of stuff."

"Why Ron, I think its an excellent thing for her to have something to do these next months," Tiresa said.

"Uh, Paulo," Ron began hesitatingly, "what a beautiful bottle of wine you brought, and I wanted to have it tonight, but my wife here insists that we have to have sake because we're having sukiyaki for dinner. She tore all over town today to find some sake cups so you'd be properly impressed."

Olive's eyes flashed. "Nothing like announcing what we're going to have for dinner! I wasn't trying to impress anyone, Ron Fifer, and I got the sake cups yesterday. I just think you have to have sake with sukiyaki."

"Of course," Tiresa said, "the essential taste."

"The wine was for no special occasion, just a little addition to your wine cellar," Paulo said with a little gesture.

"Addition—it'll be the foundation of our wine cellar," Ron said. "I'm going to get one of those racks tomorrow, so it can lie in state. We sure had a great time in Vermont, Paulo. I was telling them down at the office. You couldn't ask for better cross-country skiing."

Paulo nodded. "At . . ." He had been about to say "at my age," but thought better of it, and said instead "I believe I enjoy cross-country most."

"Ron, you forgot to connect the extension." Olive's slightly imperious, housewifely tone amused Tiresa. This gazelle-like creature who skied with such grace almost bustled as she brought in a long-handled copper skillet.

"Now if you'll all come. Tiresa, will you sit here, and Paulo . . ."

Olive lifted the fresh spinach between her chopsticks with a practiced hand and added it to the meat in the skillet. "Cooking at the table takes a little time, but it's lovely for talking, don't you think?" she asked in her hostess voice. Now she was adding mushrooms.

"And the sake is delicious," Paulo said.

"Warm like this, it makes you think of the mulled wine we had at the farm, doesn't it?" Ron said. "God, I'll never forget how good it was when I came in from skiing."

The taste of the bean curd and bamboo shoots was as different in her mouth as these young creatures, Tiresa was thinking. She could see how Paulo was enjoying himself. He passed his plate for another helping.

"I do an Indian dish you must taste some time," Olive said, "I almost did it tonight, but I thought this was more fun."

"This was the right choice. In return, I'll cook you a Sicilian meal," Paulo promised. "And Tiresa will make a cassata for dessert."

"I'd love that, but I'm afraid I broke down when I came to dessert and we're just having a sherbet. I don't go in for pies and stuff, to Ron's sorrow. He keeps hinting."

"I'm thankful you don't," Tiresa said. She liked this girl when she was so ingenuous.

"Ron, if you take off the rest of the dishes, I'll get our elaborate dessert," Olive said. "This was the division of labor we agreed on, but of course Ron has forgotten that he has any responsibility."

"Come on, remember I haven't had too much practice in the domestic routine," Ron said.

"You learn quickly, Ron, I can assure you." Paulo smiled at him. "I'm a completely domesticated product."

Olive brought the coffee in the demitasse cups. "Now if we only had a fire to have our coffee by, but, at least, we can move over to the living room end."

81

"We're all in such a glow, my dear, that we need no fire," Paulo told her.

Olive sank back on the couch, with an air of relaxation, her labors over. "Did you see, Tiresa, that I hung my mirror where you have yours? And if you stand in the exact right place, you can catch a tiny reflection of the river in mine, too."

Tiresa was touched she had noticed so much. "Our mirror doesn't reflect anything very clearly; it's an old mirror Paulo and I brought back from Sicily. It doesn't have plate glass, and the Sicilians don't replace the glass when it becomes clouded, so Paulo insists that we leave it as it is."

"My mother used to say that you see yourself in it as you do when you look in still water, and that's sufficient," Paulo explained.

"It wouldn't do for Ollie," Ron said, suddenly dropping a kiss on the side of her head.

"That's a woman's immemorial right," Paulo said. "I think there must be a whole mystique between a lady and her mirror."

Whether it was the unexpectedness of Ron's gesture or the pretended pout on Olive's face, they were all smiling at her, enjoying the play. Tiresa realized it brought them closer together for a minute.

"You don't watch football, do you Paulo?"

"No, Ron. Since it's the great American passion, I don't like to admit that I don't, but I didn't play as a youngster in Sicily, the way boys do here, and when I got to this country, I didn't know much about the game, or have time to learn."

"Why don't you come over and watch a game some time? I could explain it to you. It's a shame for you to miss out. *Time* said that one in three Americans watched the Super Bowl. Of course, it's too late for football now, but there are some dandy basketball games and hockey games that are worth watching, and then they'll be playing baseball. You don't want to miss those. My Dad wouldn't miss any of the big games.

Tiresa could feel Paulo wince at being in the same category with Ron's father.

"Watch it, Tiresa! You won't be able to get him to go anywhere with you, or even talk when he's watching a game, if he gets the fever," Olive warned.

"I feel disoriented," Tiresa said as they came back to their apartment.

"Ah, that's what being with the young does to you."

"I meant being in their living room. The plan is like ours, and yet the room is so completely different; all that white carpeting and the little horror of a bean bag chair and that painting, for instance. Imagine living with it!"

Paulo brushed aside her remark. "But the evening was delightful. *La Sposina* was bewitching in her domestic role, and I liked Ron. He's not the most gracious individual, but he means well."

"I imagine they're both feeling pretty good about it," Tiresa said. "They have had the Romanos for dinner at last, and the meal was a great success. Now their social debt has been paid and they can relax."

"Tiresa! It wasn't a matter of paying any debt. These young people have become friends of ours."

Tiresa shrugged. "After a fashion, I suppose."

4

"I should think you'd get awfully bored typing all day here at home by yourself," Ron said. "The girls at the office can talk to each other and see everything going on."

But she didn't; she liked having a project, and Professor Halstead's manuscript turned out not to be dull. It had really mindboggling facts: that seventy-one percent of the world is ocean, for example. Human beings, birds, insects, all the flora and fauna of the earth, all the animals and the fish in the ocean depths are crowded into only a small part of the earth's living space. The description of the bottom of the sea was enough to terrify you: pitch black, barely above freezing, with so much pressure it could crush to pulp even a steel object.

Olive became more and more interested in the sea, and one Sunday she made Ron drive to Revere Beach where they could see the ocean. It was a raw, gray kind of day, and the beach was deserted. They walked out to the edge of the sea and stood there looking at it.

"I can't get over the fact that there's more of the earth's surface under the sea than above it," Olive said. "Think of the fish down there."

"Not much can exist very far down." Ron was just being nice and waiting for her to wow him with some new fact she had learned, but she went on anyway.

"They found a crustacean down near the bottom that goes back three hundred and fifty million years—million, Ron. They supposed it had been extinct for centuries. I've seen a picture; it's a cute little round thing called Neopilina."

Ron gave a whistle and grinned at her. "Imagine that!"

"If the baby's a girl, I going to have to name her Neopilina."

"Oh, no you aren't. You know, I don't think it's a good idea to have your mind exposed to all that stuff just now. You might give birth to a mermaid."

Every subject they talked about these days seemed to bring them back to the baby. "Ron, the course on natural childbirth begins next month. They want husbands to come so they won't feel left out. Because you can't have a baby yourself, poor you!"

"Well, since I begat this child, I can't really feel left out."

"But I'm doing all the rest, Mr. Fifer. I can't wait to see you at a class for first-time fathers."

"You may wait quite a while, Mrs. Fifer," he threatened.

It was the next day, while she was typing, that Olive felt a movement in the center of her being—as body-shaking as any earthquake tremor is to the earth. She sat rigid waiting for it to come again. When it didn't come all day, she wondered if she had imagined it. But after they made love that night, she felt the movement again. She laid Ron's hand on her body, just under her heart, and they lay waiting. Then it came.

"Gosh, Ollie!" Ron whispered as though he were afraid the baby might be intimidated. "That was a real flutter-kick. He's swimming around in there."

She had a sudden sense that this sea that the baby swam in was related somehow to that sea that surrounded the earth. "You know what, Ron? I feel absolutely cosmic."

"It's pretty damned spooky all right."

Olive sat in a pool of disorder, typing. Last night's paper sprawled on the floor by the couch where Ron had dropped it, and a beer can adorned the coffee table along with this morning's coffee mugs. She'd forgotten to pick up her shoes last night and they lay abandoned on the white carpet. And above the room floated the acrid odor of burnt toast. It made her faintly ill, but she wasn't going to stop to pick up until noon. She was very serious about finishing her typing before the deadline.

When she spoiled a sheet, she yanked it out of the typewriter and balled it up and threw it on the floor. But typing faster to make up for having to do over the last page, she went right past the margin mark at the bottom and had to discard that sheet too. What was the matter with her! She made herself a cup of coffee; an extra cup couldn't hurt once in a while. But she only drank half a cup and decided to take a break and go down and say good morning to Tiresa. Tiresa's apartment was always in beautiful order, and Tiresa was so calm.

Paulo opened the door. "Come in, Olive. I took Tiresa to the hospital this morning and came back to get some things she wanted."

"Is she—is she very sick?"

"It's a chronic condition with her heart. She has some dyspnea and needs to be in there for a few days. We've hardly seen you for weeks." For the first time he seemed to look at her. "You're the picture of the young mother," he said, smiling.

"Only two months and a half more, I'm beginning to get excited."

"There isn't anything more thrilling." He spoke so solemnly she was startled. "Ron must get you a 'woman's book.' Let me show you Tiresa's." He went into the bedroom and came back with Tiresa's gold locket and chain. "*La Medaglione*, we call it in Sicily. It holds the vital dates of a woman's life."

The locket was heavy in her hands. And why weren't the initials of the monogram Tiresa's?

"Lift that little catch and it opens like a book, you see."

Tiresa's and Paulo's names were engraved on the inside, and the date of their marriage—October first, 1960. On the second thin gold page was the name Paulo Sebastian Romano, December twenty-first, 1965. Just as though he had lived.

"Paulo Sebastian was our son. You didn't know."

"Yes. Tiresa told me about him."

"You may feel honored. I have never known her to mention the tragedy of his death to anyone. She has never really got over it."

Olive fastened the catch of the book and handed it back to him. There didn't seem to be anything to say. He went back to put it away.

She stood there, wondering if she should go. Her eyes fell on the *Della Robia* medallion over the desk. She had only glanced at it before, thinking of it as something Italian, but now she studied it. The baby was closely bound in swaddling bands and laid flat against a deep blue background. But the curved arms and round head were a real baby's. And the wreath of brightly colored fruit was somehow joyous.

"I'll tell Tiresa you were here," Paulo said briskly. "She'll be home Tuesday night if she stays the week. Come over and welcome her; staying in the hospital always depresses her."

"I will. Give her my love."

Back in the apartment Olive couldn't get down to typing. She stood at the window looking across the avenue. It would be so terrible to have your baby born dead—all those months for nothing. "You're a healthy young woman," Dr. Westcott said, but still, you never knew. Things—she didn't know what things—could happen. Olive opened the refrigerator, craving something to eat, then closed it again without taking anything, and came back to type the chapter on the Humboldt Current.

"As the surface waters are swept seaward they are replaced by upwellings from the deep ocean. These waters are not only cold, but also rich in animal materials . . ."

5

Tiresa had waited all day to go home. Her stay that was to be only a couple of days had stretched to a week, but Paulo was coming for her right after office hours. He would be in high spirits at taking her home and there would be fresh flowers in the apartment and Bessie would have a special dinner. "Don't eat another hospital meal, Tiresa. Oh, some soup maybe; I could be late, but we'll have dinner at home no matter how late it is," Paulo had said over the phone. It was going to take more energy than she had to respond to his high mood.

She had dressed after the afternoon's rest, bothered that the mere act of putting on clothes should be such an effort. Everything would be an effort, and Paulo would be too anxious about her, the way he always was, but even that wouldn't matter. She would be docile—but then he would worry about that. Nothing mattered once she was home with Paulo. When her tray came up at five, she drank only a cup of tea. At home there would be wine and decent coffee again.

She heard Paulo, his heels hitting hard on the corridor. He had come early. It made her feel strong just to hear him.

He flung back the door. "Good, Tiresa, you're all ready." He pushed a wheel chair in front of himself, not waiting for a nurse. "I know you don't need it, but you know how fussy they are." She had a sense of being rescued from the hospital by a knight on a spirited steed. Paulo's every act seemed to drop the hospital behind.

His thanks to the nurses—as though he never expected to be back. "No, we won't take the flowers. Give them to someone on the corridor. I have her medicines—no need for those." When she was safely in the car, he leaned over to kiss her. "Oh, Trise, the time's been endless. I'm so thankful to get you home."

As always, the drive home was triumphant; the sweep into the garage in the basement of the apartment house was in itself a homecoming. Had she ever driven in and out of here without thinking about it? Yes, and she would again. Paulo came around to help her and she stepped out eagerly, forgetting how shaky she was, and had to lean on him.

She stood a moment in the doorway of their living room to see it all: a fire in the fireplace, a bowl of great white chrysanthemums on the table, and all the beloved brittle wares of home.

"Oh, Mrs. Romano, I'm glad you're back. The Doctor has been lost without you," Bessie said.

In their bedroom were the yellow roses Paulo always had there to welcome her. He had put on Beethoven's Sixth, turning it a little too high in his exuberance, but let it be, Tiresa thought, her heart lifting.

"Now I can forget you were ever away," Paulo said, as they drank their coffee in front of the fire after dinner.

"Don't speak of it."

Bessie opened the door of the kitchen. "That was the doorbell; I guess you couldn't hear it with the music. Shall I . . ."

"No, I'll get it," Paulo said. The next moment, Tiresa heard him saying, "Olive, come in. Yes, I have her home."

"Tiresa, I just popped in to say welcome back," Olive said, coming over to kiss her. "I'm so glad you're home."

"Thank you, my dear. I'm certainly glad to be back. I was only away a week, but it seemed like a month. I can see that you're fine."

"Getting bulgy," Olive laughed.

"Sit down and have a cup of coffee with us. It's not very long now."

89

"Only two months, if Who's-it comes on time."

Paulo poured her a cup of coffee. "I told Olive Ron must get her a *medaglione*. I showed her yours."

"I've never seen anything like—" Olive began.

Tiresa set her cup and saucer down on the table so hard the china grated. "Paulo! You had no right." Her eyes burned in her pale face "Do you think it doesn't mean any more to me than that?" she demanded in a high, unnatural voice. "You insensitive oaf!" She pulled herself up from the couch.

"But, why should you mind, Tirese? I knew it would mean something to Olive . . ."

"If you don't know why, then you don't understand anything. Don't touch me." She lurched away from him as Paulo took her arm, and went into the bedroom, banging the door behind her.

Olive stood up, too shocked to speak. Paulo shrugged his shoulders and spread out his hands. "That's so bad for her."

The bedroom door opened, and Tiresa set the vase of yellow roses outside in the hall and slammed the door.

"I'll run along," Olive mumbled. Paulo didn't hear her; he went to the bedroom and opened the door.

"Tiresa, what kind of madness is this? It's utter childishness."

"To show my locket to that little chit of a girl who doesn't want her child . . ." she had to stop to cough.

Olive let herself out of the apartment and leaned against the wall to quiet her trembling. "Little chit of a girl . . ." Tiresa had called her, ". . . who doesn't want her child." She would never go near the Romanos again.

"Hi, Ron."

Ron looked up from the screen. "How's Tiresa?"

"She—she didn't seem like herself."

Olive sank down on the couch beside him, eyes on the moving figures in front of her but seeing Tiresa's face, those eyes glaring at Paulo, and her voice when she called Paulo an oaf—she felt she had been plunged into that abyss in the depths of the seas, under terrible pressure, where cold prevailed and fish ate one another.

90

She moved closer to Ron. "I love you, Ron."

"I love you, too, Hon." He switched off the T-V and put his arm around her. "You're so quiet, is something the matter?"

"I was thinking about Tiresa . . ."

Ron nodded. "Paulo told me the other day when we went down in the elevator together that she has something wrong with her heart. That's tricky, you know. We're awfully cautious about taking heart cases as risks."

Olive wanted to tell Ron about Tiresa and Paulo, but she couldn't bear to have him know that Tiresa could be like that. He would think it was because they were foreign. "I guess she's been pretty sick," she finished.

Tiresa sat upright against her pillow and stared across the dark to the gray square of the window opposite. She tried to stifle the nagging cough that Paulo would hear. She heard him go out to the kitchen. He must be getting a drink. He was fixing the fire-screen, turning off the lights. He came into the bathroom that separated the two bedrooms, but he didn't come in.

At first, she was too angry to think, but now she went slowly back over Paulo's perfidy. He knew that the locket was the most precious thing she possessed. She had never opened it for a living soul. Paulo had had the baby's name and birthdate engraved in the locket so she had a visible sign of his birth and identity. And for him to get it out to show to that girl—to let anyone see it—was a betrayal. A sound escaped from her and she buried her face in the pillow, only to have to sit up because of her cough.

Suppose she had told Ron about Paulo's brother, told him that Paulo felt his committing suicide was his fault! He would never forgive her. But he thought nothing of showing her lock-et! She lay back, exhausted by her anger. It was after two when she heard Paulo open his door into the bathroom and saw the streak of light under the door. Paulo opened the door and came over to the bed.

"Tiresa, you didn't take your pill." He held it out to her with a glass of water, and she swallowed it.

"Thank you," she said coldly. He waited a moment, then went out and closed the doors on either side of the bathroom. After a while, she turned on her bed light and took up a book from the bedside table, forcing her eyes over the words on the page until she could sleep.

Paulo brought her coffee in the morning as usual. "Good morning," he said cheerily enough.

"Paulo, I've been thinking. You might as well give the locket and chain to Olive. Ron would have trouble finding one; he'd probably have to have one made and no one in this country could do it. Olive will want one now that she's seen mine, get a kick out of wearing it. But kindly have the engraving taken off before you give it to her. Have the tact and decency to do that."

Paulo didn't answer. He went into the bathroom and she heard him shaving, then the shower. He was dressed when he came back, but he went over to his chest of drawers.

"Did you hear what I said, Paulo?"

"Don't be ridiculous, Tiresa."

"I'm not being; you've spoiled the locket for me. I don't want it any more."

Paulo lifted the marble clock on his dresser and slammed it down so hard the glass top almost cracked. "Damn it, Tirese, that locket is yours, and yours alone. I hunted all over Florence to find it. And the words and names engraved on those pages are there forever."

Tiresa interrupted him in a high, strained voice. "But since it means so little to you that you could take it out of my drawer and show it to a total stranger . . ."

"You know what it means to me too well to make up such childish stuff. Olive is no stranger and I showed it to her to give her a sense of what a woman's birthright and—and pride are. You had already told her about—that we lost our son, and it must have been for the same reason. I was proud of you that you could bring yourself to do that." He stood there scowling. Then he came over and sat down on the bed. "Tirese, my darling, this is so bad for you, and for me, too." She was silent.

"I'm operating this morning so I must go. I won't have time to get breakfast. Bessie will have to get yours when she comes. I'll see you tonight."

He was almost out the door when Tiresa said, "Call me when your operation is over, Paulo."

"Of course," he said.

6

Four people living next door to each other, on the same floor of an apartment house, can hardly avoid seeing each other. Every time Olive went down the hall, or waited for the elevator, or drove into the garage, she was afraid she would run into one or both of the Romanos. She hadn't seen either of them since that night. But Ron had; he said they were all dressed up and Paulo was putting Tiresa in the car as though she were made of glass. They were all smiles. So they must have made some kind of peace. She wondered if Tiresa had apologized.

Olive ran a fresh sheet into the typewriter. "During one or more of the Pleistocene lowerings of the sea level . . ." She broke off to answer the doorbell, and was taken aback to find Tiresa there, smiling as though nothing had happened. "I was going to phone you, and then I heard the clackety-clack of the typewriter as I came by."

"Come in," Olive said a little slowly. "The place is a mess because I thought I'd get at the typing before I cleaned up." She couldn't quite look at Tiresa.

"I'll only stay a minute. We haven't seen you since the evening I came back from the hospital."

"No. I shouldn't have come over—the first evening you got back from the hospital."

"It was pleasant to be welcomed home. I'm fine again, so I'm going to meet my seminar tomorrow afternoon, but I wondered if I could get you to drive me out in my car. It's a V-W like yours. I'm just a little leery of driving myself, for fear I'll be too tired for the seminar."

"Why, I guess I could." Olive stooped down to pick up her eraser that had fallen on the floor.

"The seminar isn't until one thirty. The only bad thing about it is that you would have to wait there three hours for me. But of course, there's the library, and I thought you might enjoy being on a campus . . ."

"I wouldn't mind waiting," Olive heard herself saying.

"Fine. Why don't we start around eleven and have luncheon on the way. There's a pleasant place where I sometimes go. Thank you, my dear."

After Tiresa had gone, Olive sat without typing. How could Tiresa act as if absolutely nothing had happened? Why hadn't she told Tiresa she couldn't take her? That was the only dignified thing to do after Tiresa called her a little chit of a girl. She would be completely reserved with Tiresa; just drive and let her do all the talking.

They sat out on a stone courtyard for luncheon. Masses of forsythia surrounded the small fountain in the center, and warm sun made the April day seem like May. Most of the tables were filled and the place hummed with voices, mostly feminine.

In spite of herself, Olive looked around her with pleasure. "Except for meeting a couple of girls I know in Boston, this is the first womany luncheon I've been to since I was married," she said.

Tiresa laughed her same old laugh. "What a description. But sometimes women's talk has an interesting flavor. Not all the time, Heaven knows, but as contrast. What have you been doing besides your typing?"

"Ron and I have been going to classes in natural childbirth."

Tiresa leaned on the table, her dark eyes alive with interest. "The classes are for husbands, too? I must tell Paulo."

"Oh yes. Ron has to help me with the exercises so he'll know what to do when the baby's born."

"How does he take to the classes?"

"He's used to them now, and he's a real tyrant the way he makes me practice the breathing exercises until I do them just the way the book says."

Tiresa was looking at the forsythia and Olive wondered if she were listening. Maybe it depressed her to hear anything about having a child. Olive felt uneasy.

And then Tiresa looked right at her. "I told you, Olive, about losing my son. I had never told anyone about it before; I always loathed the way women tell each other all the details of child-bearing, and I couldn't understand how I came to do it. Then Paulo showed you my woman's book, I was angrier than I think I have ever been, and I felt utterly betrayed."

Olive tried to look away, but Tiresa's eyes held her.

"I realize now that Paulo wanted to make sure you entered deeply into the tremendous experience you're going through— I suppose it was one of those strange compulsions that rise from some instinct too deep for comprehension, as mine was." She spread her hands and put her head back with a little shrug as though it was possible to understand those compulsions, and gave a quick throaty laugh. "I feel all right about it now."

Olive wanted to tell her how she had dreaded meeting her, how hurt she had been, but before she could say anything, Tiresa was busying herself with the bill. "I'm afraid we don't have time for dessert, but that's just as well for both of us." Tiresa pushed back her chair. "While you drive, I must concentrate on what I'm going to do in the seminar," she said as they got back in the car. "I'm talking about George Eliot today."

Tiresa pointed out the library to Olive. "Maybe you would rather just walk around the campus. Only be here at four thirty, won't you? It will worry Paulo if I'm late. I left him a note, but he'll be outraged with me for coming away. That's all right, anger clears the blood, and I want him to see how vigorous I really am."

Olive watched Tiresa as she went up the walk. She moved slowly but she had a wonderful way of carrying her head. Then she disappeared into the building.

Hardly looking at the students she passed, Olive walked over to the library. They seemed much younger than she, and far removed from her world of child-bearing and strange compulsions. She didn't go into the building; instead she sat on the steps thinking about Tiresa.

Tiresa hadn't apologized, nor even seemed embarrassed. But she hadn't made a sappy emotional scene either. Sometimes Tiresa treated her as a child, but today she just assumed that she'd understand. And she did: really, Tiresa's son's name in the locket was all she had. It was sacred in a way. And she was angry that Paulo would show it to anybody.

What Tiresa said . . . about anger clearing the blood stuck in her mind. She had never seen anyone as angry as Tiresa was, or so hysterical. Her family didn't. But that was nothing to be particularly proud of either.

"I'm exhausted, Olive. I'll just close my eyes and rest on the way home, not try to talk," Tiresa said as she got into the car. Her face had bleached to a grayish white and she was having trouble breathing. Once Olive had to ask directions and Tiresa answered so quickly she couldn't have been asleep. She seemed a little unsteady when she stepped out of the elevator so Olive went with her to her door. The instant she rang, Paulo opened the door.

"Trisa! How could you do a thing like that to me?" He put his arm around her and drew her into the apartment. "That was wicked folly, Trise."

Olive closed the door. She wondered if Paulo even knew she was there.

7

"All right, contract right arm."

Olive lay on the floor of the living room with a pillow under her head, and one under her knees. In her red leotards and black smock, she looked like a circus performer.

"Hon, your left arm is tense."

She tried again and he checked. "You can do better than that. There, that's the stuff. Now contract left arm. Release you left arm . . ."

"You'd make a good sergeant in the army."

"Darn right." He was looking at the book spread open on the couch. "We do the exercises for the third stage of labor tonight. We're getting there, Hon."

"If we were living alone in a cabin, way off somewhere, do you think you could deliver me, Ron? Husbands had to in the pioneer days."

Ron scratched his ear. "I guess you could do anything if you had to. It's going to be hard enough to watch you all through your labor. Take a rest now."

Olive relaxed a big sigh. "I wish the baby would come tonight."

"You don't want to hurry it; that's never good. Didn't the doc say it would be two weeks?" They both contemplated the idea. "Now the contractions and breathing." Ron was consulting the book again. "Contraction begins!" He pressed down above her knee, simulating the beginning of the pain, his eyes on the second hand of his watch.

"We never thought last year at this time that we'd be doing childbirth exercises. It's funny, isn't it?"

"You never know what you're going to be doing a year ahead, let alone ten years," Ron said.

Olive got up ponderously from the floor. "I feel as if I weigh two hundred pounds. I don't want to do any more exercises tonight."

"Okay. You're getting better at synchronizing your breathing with the contractions. I bet if you went into labor tonight you could handle it. Why don't you lie down on the couch. I'll put on a tape." Ron picked up the paper and pulled his chair closer to the couch.

Olive's eyes traced the involutions of the iris blooms on the opposite wall. She was tired of being big and clumsy and marking time until the baby came.

"We're going to be awfully crowded with just one bedroom," she said abruptly.

"Oh, I don't know. These rooms are a pretty decent size, and we decided we could move the crib out into the living room at night, you know. In the daytime you'll be taking the baby out in his carriage, and you can sit in the park good days. I can just see you." He tried to make a picture in his mind, but it was hard to see Ollie.

"Can you? I can't."

"You'll meet other girls with babies, and you'll have a fine time. That's the good thing about having this baby in June; you can get out."

"How boring. We'll discuss whether we nurse our babies or not, and what diapers are softest, like the ads."

Ron glanced at Olive. She was down all right. He tried to think of something cheerful to say.

"You were sure clever to get all that typing finished. You ought to take that whole wad of money and treat yourself to a

99

new trousseau when you get back from the hospital. And we'll get a baby-sitter and go out on the town; go some place where we can dance. Tiresa would love to keep an eye on the baby, I bet. They could both come over and sit for the evening."

"I wouldn't think of asking them. Tiresa lost a baby once."

"She did! Gosh, I never think of their having children. All the more reason why she'd love to take care of Who's-it. It'd be a treat for her."

Olive withered him with a glance.

He gave up trying to cheer her.

Olive let herself go back to what she had been thinking about off and on ever since this morning when Gumshoe's letter came. She took the letter out of her pocket to read again and found the third paragraph.

> *I've been living with Alain for a month now. I wanted to write you right away to tell you I knew now how you felt that time you and Ron spent the night in our room, and you looked so kind of lit up that next morning. But I put off writing because I told myself it was just one of those things; that it wouldn't last. Now I don't see how we can ever live apart. I feel completely different. I guess I'm becoming the way Alain sees me rather than your Stodgy old Gumshoe.*

Gumshoe never gushed, and she didn't have a romantic cell in her whole body, at least not until now. If she felt this way, something really tremendous must have happened to her.

Nothing Gumshoe wrote applied to her. Ron's loving her hadn't changed her in any way. Only once, that time Paulo called her a child of joy, had she felt different; as though there was something in her she hadn't known.

"Want something to eat, Ollie? I'm going to get a beer and some of that cheese. You could have an apple; that wouldn't add any weight."

"No thanks. I'm going on to bed. I had a letter from Gumshoe today."

"Oh yeah. Is she having a great time for herself?"

"She's living with someone called Alain."

"If you'd gone to Paris you might be doing the same. Look what I saved you from! Kept you an honest woman." He stopped to kiss her as he came back in from the kitchen. "I'll be glad when you get through all this."

8

There was some strange power in a calendar—like that of running water—that kept you looking at it. The days went by, one after another, pulled by some current of their own, but the figures that marked the days kept returning: the fifth and the fifteenth and the twenty-fifth, month after month—a Monday and a Thursday and a Sunday again. What would she be doing on all those days?

She had been marking them off since October. Now she had torn off May and was already ten days into June. June fifteenth was circled and decorated with crayon, but you couldn't be sure, of course. Dr. Westcott said the baby would probably come later, since it was her first one. She looked at the sixteenth with qualms. By the twentieth, at least, she would know everything: whether the baby was a girl or a boy, how she had come through childbirth, and whether she didn't feel more love already. Maybe some women weren't natural mothers. She flipped up the page for June, July, on to December. The baby would be six months by then. Underneath December was a calendar for next year, with all the days running past. Your life was just so many calendars before you died.

"Lie still," she said to the baby. He was poking her with what must be a foot. She had got into the way of talking to the baby when she was alone. "Now we'll do the dishes," she would say, or "I'm going to lie down now and you can nap too." If anyone—

Gumshoe, for instance—ever heard her, they'd think she was flaky for sure.

Ron always called around noon, so it was like eating together—sort of. He was late today. She had finished and was ready to go in and lie down when he called.

"Hi, Hon."

"Hi."

"What are you doing?"

"I've just finished lunch, and I'm going to lie down for my everlasting boring afternoon rest."

"Good girl. I wish I could be there with you. Maybe I'd bother you more than young Fifer. Tell him to go to sleep and not wake you up. Say, uh, Rinehart wants me to go with him to some insurance dinner tonight. Someone can't go and he wants me to use the ticket. A man from the office in New York is going to speak and there'll be insurance men from all the major companies in Boston. Rinehart thinks it would be good for me to hear the speech, and also to meet some of them. I told him you were expecting this week, and I was afraid I couldn't make it." Ron paused.

"Well, sure, go ahead, Ron. I haven't had any contractions, and anyway, it's only the tenth. Dr. Westcott says the baby'll probably be late."

"I know, I thought of that, but I don't like you to be alone all evening as well as all day."

"You won't be very late, will you?"

"About ten, I guess." He did want to go; the eagerness got into his voice. "It won't make you nervous not to have me there?"

"No, I'll be fine. Go ahead." But the rest of the afternoon and evening stretched endlessly ahead. When she awoke from her nap she felt groggy. She washed her face in cold water and fixed her hair in two braids—no point in being glamorous. She leaned closer to the mirror. On one cheekbone an infinitesimal blood vessel had spread a cobweb of tiny red lines under her skin, but that would go away when the baby was born. Her whole life seemed balanced precariously on that phrase.

She wondered if Gumshoe looked any different now that she was in love. If she was so happy it must show. She studied her own face, as if love should darken the pupils of her eyes or leave some new expression, but the only difference that she could see was that her face had grown fuller in pregnancy. Maybe she wasn't in love that much.

She went outside with a glass of ice-tea and leaned on the railing, watching the traffic moving up and down the avenue. She wished she were in one of those cars going somewhere. A sudden tight feeling twisted inside of her and she stepped back from the railing. This was a contraction—how funny that you knew when it came. But you could have contractions now and then for a week before the baby was born, the book said. Still, this was a sign.

To make the evening shorter she didn't bother to eat until after the news. Ron always brought home a paper and she missed it tonight. She could pick up the novel by Henry James that Tiresa had loaned her, but it seemed too remote. There was nothing to do but find something on television. Last year she hardly had time to look at it; this year she had watched it until she could recite half the commercials herself. Tonight she listened to the six o'clock news and *Hogan's Heroes* and finally she ate her dinner watching the seven o'clock news. When the same commercials came on again—for Bounty "the quicker picker-upper," and Geritol with that smug, simpering couple boasting how happy they were because they got enough vitamins, she snapped the set into silence and watched the screen fade into a sickly gray surface that faintly reflected her squatting like a pumpkin in front of it, as if it were a drawing of herself inside. She tried jumping up and down to see if she could bring on the contractions and only got out of breath and felt clumsy. The ringing of the phone was a relief. It would be Ron.

"Ollie? We just finished cocktails and are going into dinner so I slipped into a phone booth to call you. Are you all right? Young Fifer sending any signals?"

"I'm fine. Young Fifer's asleep now."

"What are you doing?"

"Watching television."

"This is a pretty big wing-do; must be seventy-five here at least. 'Course the speaker's a really big shot. They're going in now, so I guess I better amble along. 'Bye. I love you."

"'Bye, I love you," she repeated as automatically as the supermarket girl saying, "have a good day now."

That little tweak wasn't worth telling Ron about, and she felt noble that she hadn't. He was dear to call again and she didn't want to worry him. She loved him, only—she wished she didn't feel there ought to be more between them. Like Paulo and Tiresa. Their love seemed deeper in some way. They were older and talked in a different way, of course, but you could feel it in their voices, the way they looked at each other; the way Paulo cried out when Tiresa got back that day.

She had sat down and then undressed and put Ron's bathrobe over her gown, pulling the sleeves around her in an embrace. Then she lay down on top of the bed. When the contraction woke her she almost held her breath for fear it would stop. Ron wasn't back yet. She turned on the light and looked at her watch. It was about ten thirty-five. He'd be here any minute now; he said about ten. But just in case Ron hadn't left yet, she went out to the kitchen and dialed the number he had given her.

"He's at a banquet—an insurance meeting. Can you see if the meeting's over?"

"The dining room is empty."

"Could they—do you think they are having the meeting some place else? It's very urgent. I'm—I'm having a baby."

"Just a minute, Ma'm."

Olive had another contraction before the voice returned. "I'm sorry, the meeting must be over."

Then Ron must be on his way home. She tried to think what she was supposed to do. Then she remembered, she should keep calm and have some tea or jello. She moved around the small kitchen with great care and put on the teakettle. Ron would be impressed that she was so calm. As she sat at the table drinking her tea, the contractions kept up. She dialed Dr. Westcott's number.

"Yes, Mrs. Fifer." She could feel him listening as she told him how long the contractions lasted, how far apart they were.

"I'd like you to come to the hospital and I'll meet you there."

"Ron isn't home yet. Can I wait a little longer?"

"Isn't there a neighbor you can get to bring you? Or call a taxi. I'd like to have you there."

She poured another cup of tea. She must keep very calm. Very calm, after all, it was only a few minutes after eleven. She wanted Ron with her. She finished her tea. Then she called the Romanos.

She dressed and took her bags to the door. What if the pains should stop and she would get there and have to go home again? She leaned against the wall, testing.

"This is a privilege," Paulo said. Tiresa had come with him, in her long Chinese coat. She put her arms around Olive, and suddenly, Olive was clinging to her.

"Ron will come any minute; this is silly to get you out, I know," Olive said.

"I'll leave a note for him to stop in before he goes to the hospital so I can tell him you're fine," Tiresa said.

Olive felt cherished and cared for when Paulo helped her into the car. And he had a way of driving that gave their trip down the avenue a kind of rhythm—like their skiing together. She glanced at him sitting beside her. Then the pain focused all the attention on her own body.

"All right?"

"Yes," she said in a flat voice. "They're harder." But it wasn't time to begin the breathing exercises yet. Ron would get there in time for that. They were so good together. Warm fluid trickled out between her legs—the waters breaking; she knew all about that. Oozing from the sea the baby had been swimming in. "Don't be alarmed," the class director had said. She wasn't; all these things happening to her body didn't seem to have much to do with her.

"We'll take you right up to your room," the nurse said.

"I'll be up," Paulo told her as he saw her to the elevator.

Now she felt herself taken over by the hospital. All she wanted was to get through it. It didn't matter that Ron wasn't there; this is the way it would be for that woman in class who had to do all her breathing exercises by herself.

It was almost twelve when Tiresa heard the elevator and knew Ron had come. She had been waiting with her door ajar. She went to the corridor to meet him. "Olive's fine, Ron. She started to have contractions three minutes apart and the doctor thought she should go to the hospital so Paulo drove her over.

"Why didn't she call me at the hotel?" Ron was belligerent. "I called up and gave her the hotel number. All she had to do was—"

"She did, but the operator couldn't find you. Just one of those—"

"The operator's a damned jackass. They had the lectures in a different room from the banquet. A couple of men got calls in there; I kept watching. Afterwards, I stopped in the bar for a drink with a couple of men from the office—I couldn't have been more than twenty minutes." His face was flushed and he pulled open his collar and his tie. He looked as if he had been running.

"I'm sure she's all right, Ron."

"But she needs me to help her with her breathing!" He stood there as though helpless to move.

"Perhaps you'll still be in time. Hurry, but drive carefully." As if he had been waiting to be told what to do, he went without a word.

Tiresa couldn't think of sleep. She felt close to Olive in her labor. In other circumstances, another time, she might have been the neighbor woman called to help with the birthing. She could have done it; part of the instinctive knowledge of that Czech grandmother of hers. And from the same source of wisdom she had known that day she learned that Paulo Sebastian was dead— that losing the life you carried under your heart so long was also part of women's experience from the beginning of time.

Ron groaned as he drove. To let Ollie down at the most important time of her life, not to share in the birth! She hadn't had any pains and she didn't think it would come for days. He shouldn't have had a drink with Rinehart afterwards, but it was something for the old man to ask him. He shouldn't have stayed so long, but why didn't they page him in the bar?

He parked and ran into the hospital, hardly answering the woman at the desk coherently, and took the elevator to the obstetrical floor, remembering how they had been taken there at the beginning of their course. Ron was breathing hard as though he were doing Olive's exercises.

"If you'll just make yourself comfortable in the lounge, Mr. Fifer—"

"But you don't understand, I have to be with her. We took the course—I know just what to do to help her."

The night supervisor smiled pityingly at him. He hated her on the instant.

"Look, the doctor expects me there with her," he insisted angrily.

"Well, just a minute, Mr. Fifer." She was phoning somebody, turning away from him so he couldn't hear, but he made out the word "frantic." Then she turned back to him. "Mrs. Fifer is getting along very well. Dr. Romano is with her. You can just relax and not worry. They'll call you."

Ron pounded on the desk. "I'm supposed to be there, I tell you. Call Dr. Westcott." He was shouting now.

Tiresa was sitting over a cup of coffee when Paulo came in around five in the morning. "Olive is fine, Tirese, she has a healthy seven pound boy. And she was in labor for only six hours."

"How simple it seems when things go right," Tiresa said. He made no answer, only leaned over to kiss her, and hold her head against him.

"Did Ron get there so he could help her?"

Paulo laughed. "He burst into the room like a madman. Dr. Westcott calmed him down and I slipped out. I was afraid he'd mind my being there. I had a good sleep in the doctors' room until one of the nurses told me the baby was born."

"You should have gone in to see her."

He shook his head. "But she surprised me, Tiresa, she was as sturdy as a peasant woman."

Tiresa waited a minute before she could get over a stab of envy. The peasant women Paulo admired didn't have hearts that couldn't stand the strain. "Good. I'm glad. She can always remember it proudly. Poor Ron, when he came in here, he was like an angry small boy who's afraid he missed the fireworks," Tiresa said lightly.

"I feel as though I had a grandchild born tonight, don't you?"

"No," Tiresa said slowly, thinking about it. "They may be young enough to be children of ours, but I don't think of them that way. I thought of Olive tonight as another woman."

9

Tiresa looked up from the book she was reading but kept her finger in the page. It was annoying to be interrupted just there. Olive had stopped in with the baby in a curious zippered arrangement that she wore in front of her when she carried him outside.

"Don't I look like a mama kangaroo?" She stooped down so Tiresa could see the baby.

"He's beautiful."

"He's a month old tomorrow."

Tiresa watched her with him. In that month Olive had become an expert at taking care of him. Overnight she and Ron had moved from being a young married couple to being a family with one child. She marveled at the ease of the change. And inwardly? Olive seemed happy. Certainly Ron was.

"Tiresa, may I ask you something?"

"Of course."

"Does my bringing Johnny in here bother you? I mean really."

"Not a bit. I'm delighted to see him."

"I'm glad. Well, Jonathan, we'll go home and feed you. Bye Tiresa."

Tiresa put her book down on the table, not bothering to keep the place.

When the baby began to fret at two in the morning, Ron got up and brought him to Olive and then propped himself up on one elbow beside her.

"Thanks Ron, you didn't need to do that. I was going to get up in a couple of minutes."

"Isn't that what a young father is supposed to do? I wasn't there when I was needed; at least let me bring him in for nursing."

"Oh stop it!"

Ron leaned over the baby. "You pulled a fast one, Johnny, didn't you? Thought you'd take a sprint at the end and come in ahead of time, just to make a stupe out of your old man."

Olive closed her eyes. The little tug at her breast was not unpleasant and the baby lay warm in the crook of her arm. After the hot day, the coolness filtered into the apartment. She was drifting off to sleep.

"Ollie, you know what? You're beautiful."

"Thanks."

"It did make a difference, didn't it? You feel I let you down."

Olive shifted the baby to the other breast, "Ron, for heaven's sake, I told you I didn't feel any such thing. I could have told you when you first called that I'd had one contraction, but it wasn't enough to get excited about. When he got started, he just came awfully fast. Anyway, all the time I was in labor I could hear you telling me what to do. If you hadn't practiced the breathing with me every night, I wouldn't have known. I've told you that before, now stop worrying about it."

Ron lay back on the pillow. Olive tried to drowse again. Small sucking sounds mingled with the swish of a car passing on the avenue.

"What is it then?" Ron persisted.

"Is what?" The baby was asleep and she put him back in the crib without waiting for Ron's answer.

"You know what I mean," Ron said as she got back into bed.

"I certainly don't know what you're talking about."

"You're not the same. You're so moody—and kind of withdrawn."

"I guess my mind's on Johnny. I'm just getting used to having him—really."

"If you're trying to make me pay for not showing up on time, you've succeeded, but there's a limit."

"Oh Ron, you're all wrong. How many times do I have to tell you? I never blamed you for not getting there. When I first came back from the hospital, I felt sort of unreal. That's all it is."

"Thank God, Ollie. I felt as if I'd lost you, and I couldn't stand that. I even hated Paulo because he'd driven you over there, and been where I should have been. God, I hated him! You don't know what you mean to me." His mouth pressed down on hers.

"Ollie, you're just the same, only more wonderful, you know that."

Their rapport was still with them the next morning of the hot July day. They smiled at each other at the breakfast table. Ron reached past the box of cereal to hold her hand.

"See you the minute I can get away," he promised as he kissed her goodbye. "I wish I didn't have to go."

"You look handsome. I remember when you came to school wearing that seersucker jacket."

She was happy, she told herself, as she poured another cup of coffee. She loved Ron—maybe not as much as Gumshoe loved her Alain, but . . . She let down the bamboo shades over the windows on the balcony and moved in a striped pattern of shade and light that fell across the carpet. As though drawn in by it, she lay down on the floor and let the pattern fall across her face. This was where she used to lie to do her exercises—ages and ages ago. She lay still, liking the warmth on her bare feet and legs.

Maybe Ron was right. She felt different. She just wasn't satisfied with the way they were together. Maybe it wasn't love—maybe they just had sex. That was the only time they seemed really close. Maybe that was the way married people were. Except Paulo and Tiresa.

Ron spent more time studying his manuals in the evening now, so he didn't watch television all the time; which was fine for her, she'd looked at it so much. She read until he was through. Then they usually talked about Johnny and had a snack, and it was time for bed. They made love—unless she was too tired—sometimes she was, and sometimes she wasn't. And the next day they did the same things all over—even said the same things. It was all fine, she guessed. She watched the barred pattern of light rippling ever so slightly. But it wasn't enough.

By ten thirty, Olive had the baby bathed and fed, and her household chores done. The morning yawned ahead of her. On an impulse, she called Professor Halstead's office. When his secretary answered, she found herself speaking very fast. "I'm Olive Fifer, who typed Professor Halstead's manuscript last spring." The secretary waited. "I wondered if there was more typing that I could do for him here at home?"

"No, Mrs. Fifer, I don't believe so. Professor Halstead has a professional typist now, who is trained in footnotes and copy editing—all that sort of thing. This is his final copy. But I have your name in our files. Should there be anything, I'll let you know."

Olive hung up the phone. They didn't think she was professional; hadn't thought so when she was typing for them. But Professor Halstead had said it was very nice when she took him the last pages. It wasn't that she liked typing so much, but it was doing something.

She picked up Johnny and went down the hall to the Romano's. Tiresa was out on their balcony in the tip-back chair, reading.

"Good morning." Tiresa didn't coo over the baby the way Ron's mother did, or cuddle him on her shoulder, but she really looked at him. "It's a relief to see a completely healthy human being," she said.

"I'm really very fond of him," Olive said a little shyly.

"Did you not expect to?"

"I couldn't really get excited before he was born, and it bothered me. I knew I should be, and I wanted to be."

"Oh, there's no should about it. When did you discover you did love him?" Her tone of voice poked gentle fun at Olive.

"When they laid him on me while the doctor cut the cord," Olive said promptly. "I know it sounds funny, he was all wrinkled and red and sort of wizened, but I suddenly knew he was mine, and I really loved him. I was so relieved."

Olive glanced at Tiresa, afraid she might have made her sad, but the next moment, Tiresa said, "Why don't you let Johnny sleep on my bed and go out by yourself for a couple of hours? We'll get along very well together."

"Do you mean it, Tiresa? He won't bother you?"

"Of course, I mean it. I'm a good baby-sitter. As she followed Olive from the balcony, Tiresa stopped and poured the remnants of her water glass onto the orange tree. "You must bring Johnny in and leave him some night so you and Ron can go out for dinner." She looked up and saw a small smile spread across Olive's face.

"Thanks Tiresa."

Now she had done what she had never intended to do—offer to baby-sit.

10

Did you know that Olive flew home to visit her family?" Paulo asked as he came in one evening a week or so later.

Tiresa looked up startled. "No. I'm surprised that she didn't come in and tell me. She's been dropping in often, but she hasn't been in this week."

"I met Ron in the garage. I asked how Olive and the baby were and he said they'd gone home for a couple of weeks. We must have him over for dinner if he's all alone there."

The night that Ron came, Paulo was held up in the hospital. Ron and Tiresa sat on the balcony with a drink.

"It must have been exciting for Olive to take Johnny home to show her family," Tiresa said.

"I guess so," Ron said. "It's pretty flat to come home and not have him there, I can tell you."

"But I'm sure her mother and father were eager to see him."

"Yeah, I guess."

And then they were silent. She didn't intend to pry but she had the feeling that, like Paulo, if there were something wrong, Ron would feel better talking about it.

"It's amazing to me how quickly you and Olive have adjusted to having a child. Olive seems so much more mature." She heard herself—the voice of the older woman; she must watch it.

"She isn't the way she used to be at all," Ron burst out. "Anything I say—or the fact that I don't say anything—turns out to be the wrong thing. I don't know what struck her to go off like that. We were going to drive back on my vacation, the last two weeks in August, and one night, she suddenly said she was going the next day. She'd called up and made a reservation and was going to pay for it with her typing money. Wouldn't let me do anything about it."

"Perhaps she had a longing to see her family."

"She wasn't that crazy to see them at Thanksgiving," he muttered.

"I imagine, Ron, that she may have felt a little confined with the baby and needed to go some place. If she stayed two weeks that would be the time of your vacation, wouldn't it? Couldn't you drive down and bring them home and make a real trip out of it?"

"That's an idea," he said.

Paulo was no help when he came. "Well, we only have one third of the family tonight," he said.

Tiresa left them on the balcony. The troubles of the young were tiring. They were young and healthy and had so much ahead of them; she felt impatient about problems of their own making. What if Ron were her son, she considered for a moment, come to tell them his troubles about his wife.

"You must feel like a suitor again, writing letters and sending flowers," Paulo said as they came in to dinner.

Ron looked up, "Uh—yeah, sort of."

"Is there something wrong between them, Tiresa?" Paulo asked after Ron had left. "I thought Ron's usual aura of well-being was missing."

"I guess Olive went off very suddenly. They had planned to drive their on their vacation."

"Ah, *la Sposina* is developing independence."

116

II

At first, Olive found it pleasant to be home, back in her old room with her familiar furniture and the painting called *Spring Floral*. Years ago she had discovered a small grinning face in the center of the lily. She found it again. It was exciting to have Johnny in the crib in her room—her crib her mother had saved all these years—and pleasant to show him to friends who stopped in. Ron's family were over and were crazy over him. They brought one of Ron's baby pictures to see whether Johnny looked like him. He didn't really—oh, the forehead, maybe. Johnny hardly seemed to belong to her during the day.

She had called Ron when she got there, but the call hadn't been very satisfactory. She hadn't written, neither had Ron. Her mother noticed the lack of mail. "Everything's all right between you and Ron, isn't it, Olive?"

"Of course, I just thought you'd like to see the baby."

It wasn't easy to say, even to herself, why she had decided to come home. There was that day she felt they had nothing to say to each other. She was panicked. She had got up from the couch after feeding Johnny and walked out to the phone and made a plane reservation. Why shouldn't she do something on her own? She hadn't since she was married, except for going around Boston. That evening she told Ron she was going to make the family a visit. He didn't ask her why, just got cold and distant and said, "Okay, if that's what you want to do. I thought we were going together at the end of August." And then Ron clammed up.

On Thursday, flowers arrived, an arrangement they moved from the dining-room table after each meal to the living-room. The card said only "Missing you and Johnny, Ron." Olive broke off a spray of snapdragon and carried it to her room.

The Hammils beamed. "Isn't that thoughtful of Ron!" her mother said.

Upstairs in her room, Olive burst into tears. Then she called Ron and told him she'd be home on Sunday.

"It's like that time at college, remember?" Ron said as he drove her back from the airport. "The time you wrote that you didn't want to get married, and you were going to Paris instead. And then you called."

"All I care about is now," she said.

"All right. NOW." Ron leaned over to grab a kiss, in spite of the traffic.

The next day she answered Gumshoe's letter, which she hadn't been able to do before. In her last paragraph, she wrote:

> *I've just been home so Mother and Dad could see Johnny. I wish you could see him. Honestly, Gumshoe, he's adorable. It was like being at school again, talking to Ron over the phone, Ron's sending flowers. And I was glad to be back here again in our apartment.*
>
> Love to you—and Alain. He sounds terrific.
> Ollie

But some wistfulness lingered at the bottom of her mind.

12

Tiresa heard the doorbell and was quite sure that must be Olive, but she made no move to answer. She lay in bed, propped against her pillows, exhausted after a bad night. Paulo had been too cheerful, and sung *La Donna e' Mobile* while he was getting breakfast, but he looked worn and depressed. Poor darling. Well, he would be pleased when he came home tonight.

She should have done it earlier, in August. No—last June at the end of the seminar, but she couldn't do it then. There were still ten days before classes began, and classes had been cancelled this late before. Very well, she would write the letter today, and put it where Paulo would see it when he came in.

And when she didn't have that class, she would have no urgency in her days. Her book, of course, but she felt less sure of that. She must put her mind on staying alive, keeping Paulo from worrying about her. People had worked wonders by a strict regimen, doing every little piddling thing they should. Unconsciously she lifted her head and straightened her shoulders. Very slowly she moved her legs to the edge of the bed and stood on the floor, trying not to notice the irregular hammering of her heart. Pulling her robe around her, she walked through the apartment to the balcony and stepped outside.

The river in the middle of the morning was busy with small boats and barges. The air was still fresh, but it was going to be a hot day. No sign of fall except for the tired yellow leaves of the elm trees. She watched a whip-slender scull slice through the water, the shoulders and backs of the rowers gleaming in the sun. The room was dark as she turned back into it.

All right, she would call the turn herself, not wait until she absolutely had to give up. She went to the bedroom, and even with the unmade bed and the feeling of sleep still in the room, sat down at her desk. Taking a sheet of paper from the pigeonhole, she wrote swiftly; the letter had been working itself in her mind for two weeks now. But when she came to the end, she sat still for several minutes. The neat curves of her carefully formed words took her back to the evenings she spent in the back room of the restaurant, struggling to perfect her calligraphy while writing menus for a few extra dollars during graduate school. She sat for a moment more, lost in her thoughts, and then she added, "I deeply regret leaving the Humanities Department, but I shall always value my association with it. Sincerely yours, Tiresa Chesny Romano."

She read it through again and folded it, leaving the envelope unsealed, and propped it up on Paulo's dresser. She mustn't brood about her decision, nor be maudlinly sentimental the way Ella Badgely was about retiring. Feeling brisk, even though she moved slowly, she went in to take her bath.

"I saw that Fifer girl next door when I was in the laundry," Bessie told her. "She said she rang the bell but thought you must have been asleep. She wondered if it would be all right for her to come in and see you this afternoon."

"No," Tiresa said. "Tell her I'm sorry, but I have some work I need to finish. Tomorrow would be better." Now it had begun—the pretense that she was occupied with important work. But she wasn't up to seeing Olive today. What had she to do with heedless health and energy?

But by the time Paulo came that evening, she was herself again. She had dressed carefully in her velveteen slacks and white Italian shirt that she knew was becoming. As she put on her earrings, she noticed that her lips had a purplish tinge. Had they had that before? She covered it with lipstick.

Paulo's face lighted when he saw her. "You look dazzling, Tirese, and fully recovered."

"You're very satisfactory, Paulo, even though you lie through your teeth," she said, smiling at him.

They were having their drink before dinner when Paulo said, "Thank you, Trise. I saw your letter. I know it wasn't easy to write."

"I left it for you to read. After all, it's a rather historic document after twenty-four years of teaching. We should drink to the end of a worthy career, don't you think?" Her voice had a brittle quality that made Paulo lower his eyelids, but he lifted his glass.

"To you, Tirese, in another year, you may teach again, some place else."

"Hardly likely," she said dryly.

"Do you think tonight we could look over that article I'm doing?"

Perversely, she said, "How about tomorrow? I'm a little weary tonight. You must be, too, after being awake half the night with me."

She saw his mouth tighten. He was spreading cheese on his cracker. When he passed it to her, she saw his eyes, flat black, the way they got when he was depressed. "I'm not at all weary," he said, "but maybe it's a good idea to go to bed early. I have a good spy story I want to read."

She felt his awareness of her breathing when she walked over to the dinner table. He was getting ready to tell her he wanted her in the hospital again. She could sense it in his silences, but he was putting it off. He minded her going as much as she did. And then she would come back, and there would be the celebration, and for a few months, she would live normally again.

"You don't seem to have much appetite, Tirese."

"Bessie pampered me; I had bouillon in the middle of the morning, and tea and cookies this afternoon." But it was true she had no appetite; she didn't feel well. She began to cough.

Paulo hurried over to her. The next minute she was coughing up bright red froth. The color frightened her. She tried to hide it in her napkin, but Paulo had seen. He helped her over to the couch. Then he was back with a hypodermic needle, and worry in his face.

She leaned against the pillow. She had never seen blood—or was it sputum—so bright. Almost vermilion. It was a sign of fatality, wasn't it? Keats had that; he wrote about it in his journal. Tears came to her eyes and she rubbed them away quickly so Paulo wouldn't see them. But he had gone in the bedroom and was phoning the hospital.

13

There had come to be something stagy about their after-dinner coffee routine, Olive thought. They were sitting on the couch, as they did every night, listening to the seven o'clock news and drinking their coffee out of the little cups. Maybe she'd skip it tomorrow night and surprise Ron with a big mug.

"Those fat asses down in Washington!" Ron exploded. "You know, they're going to hurt the insurance business if they don't watch it."

"And now turning to sports . . ." Olive started to get up, but Ron stopped her. "Sit still, hon; you don't have to rush. I'll give you a hand with the dishes." He clicked off the T-V, not waiting to hear the sports news.

"An interesting thing happened today. Ben—" He no longer spoke of him as Mr. Rinehart. "uh—called me into his office and we had a long talk. He wants me to train to be a special agent. He thinks I have the personality for it, you know, that I get along well with people."

"What's a special agent? It sounds like the FBI."

"Well, I'd be the link between different agencies and keep 'em in touch with our policies, help them with their problems. It would be a big responsibility."

"You mean you'd travel to these agencies?" Instinctively, Olive felt her world threatened.

"I guess it would mean being away now and then, but I'd make more money. Maybe I could take you and Johnny along on a trip some time. But the thing is, Ollie, it would be a step ahead. Agencies would get to know me as representative of the central office. It's a real opportunity."

"Would we go on living here?"

"No. With the area I'd have eventually, we'd have to live in New York State. Syracuse, maybe."

"When would this be?"

"Uh, Ben suggested that we would be settled by the middle of January. They'd move us, of course." Ron put his arm around her and pulled her closer. "What do you think, Mrs. Fifer?"

"I think it's fine that you've been offered the opportunity, but it takes my breath away to think of picking up and moving," she said a little slowly.

"I was thinking we'd be going home for Christmas, and we could leave Johnny with my folks for a week. You know they'd love it. He'll be six months old in December; you could maybe wean him."

"He'll be weaned by then." The idea rather excited her. "And I can manage him here. I don't suppose we'll ever have an apartment with a balcony and a view like this. And I'll miss the Romanos. We'll never find friends like them."

"I can bear up. I like 'em, sure, but they're heavy going sometimes. But, Ollie, you're willing to make the move?"

"It sounds as though you've already agreed to it."

Ron laughed. "Well, I want to try it, yes. I told Ben I'd have to talk it over with you first. But it won't matter where we live so long as you and Johnny and I are together, will it?"

Olive woke at two in the morning. Johnny no longer had night feedings, but the rhythm had been established, and she still woke sometimes at that hour. She got out of bed and went into the living room. The arc light threw a band of light across the carpet all the way to the big chair at the end of the table. Olive saw each object in a nostalgic haze. The room seemed perfect, never to be duplicated. There would never be such an ideal place for the iris painting; maybe their next living room would have wallpaper that would jar with the greens and purples. It wouldn't open on to a balcony, either. She stepped outside and looked across to the sky-line of the city. She didn't know this city yet. And she was just coming to know Tiresa and Paulo well. She must go over and tell Tiresa in the morning.

But Tiresa had gone to the hospital.

"Just twist it up any way and stick a couple of pins in," she said to the nurse who was looking hopelessly at her long hair. Tiresa watched in the mirror. She looked like a washerwoman but what did it matter? "That's fine." It irritated her to have somebody who had never touched long hair try to pin it up so it would stay.

"There isn't a gray hair on your head," the young nurse said.

"Oh, I imagine if you hunt them, you'll find a few." The nurse must think she was seventy at least. "And will you roll my bed up a little more, please." She wanted to look alert when Paulo came. He always stopped in before he went to the eye hospital.

This morning he came carrying a cup of coffee and the morning newspaper for her, and the English journal from home. Now that she was through teaching, she wouldn't bother to look at it, she decided. As Paulo bent over to kiss her, she breathed in the one strong live aroma of the day, a mixture of clean linen and wool and the scent of shaving soap on clean skin.

"Men's shaving soap is more seductive than women's perfume, I've decided."

"Men's? Why not just mine?" Tiresa looked more rested, but she was still pale, and her lips were bluish. "And you still have a lovely warm fragrance of sleep."

"We're like two dogs smelling each other."

"Why not? Smell is one of the most delightful senses. Ah, good morning," he said to the nurse. "I picked up a cup as I came past some trays out in the hall; do you think I could have some coffee too? Now we can have breakfast together, Tiresa.

I noticed on the chart that you had a good night and that you coughed very little."

"And did the chart tell you what I was thinking, too? I dislike the way every breath your body breathes and everything else it does is spied on and written down."

"I know without any report. You are thinking you should be able to go home tomorrow—if not today."

"And you are thinking 'no, the woman will only go to pieces and have to come back again.'"

"Quite wrong. I am wondering if I can stand it in that apartment without her long enough so she will have a chance to build up her strength."

After Paulo left, Tiresa pushed the table with her breakfast tray down to the foot of the bed and lay back against the pillows, exhausted—from what? That was what frightened her, she tired at nothing. She looked at her hands and saw the pulse beating feebly; hardly more than a quiver under the skin, it seemed. She pushed them down under the spread and closed her eyes to shut out the future.

By mid-afternoon, she was reading the journal Paulo had brought, completely absorbed, underlining, making a comment on the margin. Her door was closed against the sounds of visitors passing back and forth on the floor and the curious eyes that peered into each room they passed, but she heard a light knock on the door. The light beneath the door was blocked in two places where feet stood. The knock was repeated.

"Yes?" Tiresa called.

Olive pushed open the door. "May I come in? Paulo said I might see you for ten minutes. I left Johnny in your apartment with Bessie. I hope that was all right. She seemed glad to keep an eye on him." Her words crowded together in her embarrassment.

"Of course, my dear. How good of you to come way over here to the hospital." But she didn't want Olive here, to see her like this. Why would Paulo think . . . Olive stood there flaunting her youth and her health—slender again, and lovely, wearing a flowered skirt, not jeans. She had brought a pot of pink geraniums. Tiresa pushed helplessly at her hair and sat a little straighter. Olive sat on the edge of the bed by the window. "I went over to see you right after I got home, and again the next day. I began to worry so I called that night and Paulo told me you were here."

"A case of doing too much and paying for my sins is all. Tell me about your trip to New Jersey. Your family must have been happy to see you and Johnny." Why should she have to make idle conversation like this?

"Oh yes, they adored Johnny there. It seemed strange though. I didn't feel I belonged there any more."

Tiresa nodded. It tired her to talk.

"Did you ever feel you had to get away—from Paulo, I mean?" Olive asked abruptly.

"Yes," Tiresa said, breathing heavily. She wished Olive would leave. "You have to be separate sometimes to find yourself," she said with an effort.

"That's it. That's the way I feel."

If she asked one question, Olive would tell her the whole story, wanted to, in fact, but she didn't want to hear.

"I guess I mustn't stay any longer. Paulo wouldn't forgive me if I tired you, and he said ten minutes." She hesitated by the foot of the bed; she had not intended to tell Tiresa they were moving, but Tiresa looked so tired.

Tiresa leaned forward to say good-bye and the pins in her knot loosened, letting the whole rope of hair slip down her back. "The trouble is that my hair wasn't properly brushed and done up this morning. My hair is so heavy that it's hard for me to brush it, and I don't want to bother the little nurse." She wished Olive would leave now.

"Could I brush it for you, Tiresa? I always like to fuss with hair."

Tiresa cringed, but it would be a relief, and she didn't want to look tousled when Paulo came. "You wouldn't mind?"

Tiresa felt her hot, matted hair lifted by the brush, letting air through to the very nerves of her brain. The brush carried her hair away from her forehead with clean sure strokes. She closed her eyes, a child again, having her mother brush her hair in the morning before school, gathering it up to braid in quick, strong hands. Olive was coiling the braids high on her head, not fumbling the way hair-dressers unused to long hair did. She secured the coil with three or four hairpins. Hair-dressers were always sticking in pins as though your head was a pin-cushion.

"There Madam! I've piled it all on top of your head so you won't be lying against the knot."

Tiresa opened her eyes and saw herself in the mirror across the room. "Yes, it looks very well and feels secure. I should have it cut if I'm going to spend half my days in the hospital."

"Don't cut it, Tiresa. It's so beautiful. I thought that the first night I met you."

"Beautiful"—the word let loose a wave of warmth that washed over Tiresa's mind.

"Thank you, my dear—"

"Tiresa, I have an awful thing to tell you," Olive burst out. The news had waited so long to be told, it came out with a rush. "Ron's being transferred to Syracuse, New York, and we have to be moved by the middle of January."

Tiresa was so startled, she was silent for a moment. "I'm sorry you are going. We'll miss you both," she managed. But not until Olive had left did the full weight of Olive's news come down on her mind. She had never really expected the Fifers to stay very long. Hadn't she had a sense of impermanence the first time she went to their apartment? She had told Paulo that. Never think of forming a lasting friendship with the young; they were always on their way to some place else, to new friends. Paulo was going to miss them.

14

October lay like a great tawny cat sunning itself on the bright braided rug thrown across the hills. Yellow and copper and all shades of reds mixed in the braids, and worn in places, black threads showed. The air had a hint of leaf mold under its warm breath, and a drifting smell of smoke from some leaf fire. Tiresa gave a deep sigh and let herself relax, hardly even thinking, as she lay back in her chair. It was good to be back at the farm again.

The screen door banged, and Olive came out carrying Johnny and a blanket to lay him on. Then she sat beside him. "I loved it up here in the winter, but this is something else!"

"It never seemed quite real, but you're content to have it unreal." Their voices took on the languor of the day. Johnny lay awake, making small noises and moving his hands.

"Do you suppose he sees the colors?" Olive leaned back to find a red leaf on the grass, and twirled it over his face until his mouth twitched. She hung over him talking to him as she tickled his nose with the leaf. Tiresa watched them, testing out the thought that had occurred to her on the drive up. Olive had been talking about having Johnny christened when they went home for Thanksgiving.

"I guess we'll do it to please the folks, they're so gung-ho for it, but we've got to think who we'll have for godparents—three of them: two godfathers and one godmother," Olive said.

Well, why not Paulo? He would value the role as few people would, and how it would please his Sicilian soul. At least, he could have a godson. It would be difficult to suggest it, rather outrageous, in fact. Not that that would keep her from doing it. The Fifers were moving away soon, out of their lives; this would be a little tie. Olive might deplore the idea to Ron—"that terrible woman having the nerve to suggest Paulo as Johnny's godfather," but Olive wouldn't say that, and Paulo would never guess she had suggested it.

Tiresa gave a little laugh, making her voice sound amused. "When I saw Paulo sitting in front of the fire last night holding Johnny, Olive, I thought if you're looking for a godfather, you really should consider him. He would adore it, and take his responsibility very seriously. You know Sicilians fairly worship children. Oh, it was just a rather crazy idea. You probably want to select one of your relatives. After all," she added when Olive didn't say anything right away, "Paulo was in on Johnny's birth." Though what did that have to do with it, so was the doctor, she told herself mockingly.

Olive hadn't given prospective godparents more than a fleeting thought. "Why, what a fine idea," she said a little slowly. "No, we don't have to have relatives. I'll have to talk to Ron, but I'd love having Paulo." Ron would probably object, but when she thought of all the Romanos had done for them—they were their closest friends, hers anyway—she liked the idea.

"But we have to have him christened in the church in Summit."

"Your father could stand in Paulo's place and sign the register for him. That's often done," Tiresa said quickly. At least, Olive hadn't rejected the idea or seemed shocked by it. "Why don't you leave Johnny here with me and drive down and play some tennis with Ron? Tell Paulo that I need him. He's played long enough, but don't tell him that!" She knew how Paulo would be playing, his whole belief in his youthful vigor in question. If he could make Ron fight for the game, even if he couldn't beat him, he would be at peace with himself.

Olive left Johnny on the bed in the borning room and was off in a hurry, but Tiresa did not feel deprived to sit alone on such a day. "'Seasons of mists and mellow fruitfulness,'" she quoted aloud.

"'Close bosomed friend of the maturing sun.'" A few Octobers ago she had been reading Keats with a class. She got up and walked the short distance to the barn.

Except in winter, Paulo always opened the doors so the barn looked used. There were birds twittering high up on the rafters as Tiresa stepped inside, and the barn was warm but airy and smelled of sun-cured grass and the grain once stored there, of old wood and mice leavings. Sun poured through the high cobwebbed window and picked out an old scythe, and a sickle next to it, left in a corner; tools that looked well-worked were now useless—like herself. Her eyes traced the rusted curve of the scythe.

No, she was still useful. Paulo needed her. If it hadn't been for her, he would be back in the apartment trying not to show that he was depressed. They had both been ever since her last bout in the hospital. And then the Fifers leaving. "Wouldn't it be pleasant to take Ron and Olive to the farm once more before they go?" she had asked. "And have a baby in that house."

Paulo had been in fine spirits last night, and now he was off playing tennis with Ron. But this would be the last weekend up here at the farm with them. She walked slowly back to the house to see Johnny, trying to block out the sense of loss she felt every time she thought of their going.

Olive could hear the ricochet of the tennis balls before she got to the court, and feel the tenseness of the silence when it stopped. Ron was serving. The ball went out of bounds. She stood still to watch his second serve. He skidded the ball just inside the back line with no bounce. Paulo got it. What a nice backhand he had. The ball went back and forth. Pretty! Ron tried an overhead slam and sent the ball back into the net. He must be on edge. Oh, she hadn't realized it was set point. Ron beat the air with his racket. Paulo laughed. "Well, we're one apiece."

"You're good, you two." Olive said as she came down to the court.

"Hi, hon. You came too soon. We have to play another set. Here you are, Paulo." He sent the balls to him.

"As winner of the last set, I think I ought to have the pleasure of playing with Olive," Paulo said.

"Why don't we play the deciding set first? Ollie would just as soon watch, wouldn't you, hon?" Ron was mopping his face.

She hesitated. "I should think you both need to rest after two sets. What was the score?"

"Seven-five, Paulo's favor. I won the first, eight-six. No, I'd like to finish it up now, wouldn't you, Paulo?"

"But I've already invited the lady to play," Paulo said, smiling at Olive.

"Well—my racket's a little heavy for you, Ollie. You should have brought yours along."

"Yours is okay; I've used it before. Yes, I'd love to play, Paulo. I haven't played since before Johnny was born."

Ron watched for a few minutes, then walked up to the bar at the Inn. Coming in from the sun, he couldn't see much at first; he made out a couple over at one side of the room, and a young fellow back of the bar. And the place was cool. He ordered a gin and tonic.

"I guess it's pretty hot out there on the court," the bar tender volunteered.

"Sure is." Ron took his drink to a table; the kid was a talkative sort.

Paulo, the old fox, knew he couldn't win another set so he asked Ollie to play. Got credit for being gallant and saving his face. The gin and tonic took on more flavor. Paulo didn't have any form, but he was quick—streaking all over the court like an antelope. You wouldn't expect it. Prob'ly have a heart attack if he played another set as hard as the last, and he knew it, so he oozled out of it with Ollie.

Ollie had come down hoping they could play together, and

then after Paulo popped off about wanting the pleasure of playing with her, she couldn't say anything. It didn't occur to her to refuse, of course. You couldn't tell about Ollie any more. She could be very loving, like old times, and the next minute she'd be cool and kinda distant.

"Have a good day now," the bar tender called out as Ron paid for his drink.

"You, too," Ron mumbled as he went back out into the bright, hot afternoon.

He stood watching the two of them. Ollie never whammed them hard enough, but Paulo was pulling his punches, anyway; just volleying back and forth. They might as well be playing ping-pong.

"Your point. Very nice," Paulo said.

Ollie did have a good serve, Ron thought, watching her. She had that nasty little drop on the ball. But Paulo handed it back. That was his whole thing, not his serve. Back and forth, back and forth—gentle as a tea-party. "Wham it, Ollie!" he shouted. But she sent it into the net. Now she was rattled. Yup, the second ball landed outside.

"I have to stop," Olive said. She knew Ron was itching to play. "I left Johnny with Tiresa . . ."

"Thank you, Olive," Paulo said, coming up to the net. "We'll have to finish it another time. Those were good games."

"Fun. I loved it."

"I, too. Your wife plays like a dancer, Ron. She's so light on her feet."

"I don't suppose you feel like another set, do you, Paulo?" Ron asked.

Paulo hesitated only a minute. "Let me get a drink of water, Ron, and I'll take you on."

"I don't want you to do it if you're tired; I mean on my account."

"No, I'm fine."

"You two are absolutely mad to play another set like that last one," Olive said. "Well, I'll drive back and see how Tiresa and Johnny are, and I'll come for you at five thirty."

When Olive drove up the hill to the farm, Tiresa was standing in the dooryard. In a red and orange kaftan with a string of yellow beads around her neck, she seemed part of the fall colors.

"I was just about to go in, but I had to look at it all a little longer. What happened to the men?"

"Oh, they're so stupid, they're going to play another set. They each won one, and Paulo stopped to play with me, then Ron wanted to play another."

"And of course Paulo agreed," Tiresa said.

"I hope he won't be exhausted."

"He will be, but he wouldn't think of admitting it. He is strong, you know. It's hard for him to be saddled with a weak and ailing wife who can't play any sports." But Tiresa smiled as she said it. "I used to wish we had married when we were ten years younger, but I think neither of us might have been ready then. We are strong-willed and very different. Still, we missed some years we might have had."

They walked back into the house. "Sometimes I think I married too young," Olive said, leaning against the kitchen door.

"It takes a certain amount of maturity to realize that," Tiresa said.

"I feel lots older, that's for sure. I wish we'd just lived together first," she said defiantly as though they had been arguing the issue. "Ron wouldn't have gone for that; I don't suppose his firm would have liked it very much."

Tiresa listened, not wanting to interpose any comment. A hard tone had got into Olive's voice, she thought.

"Now you think I'm as hopeless as you did when I said I didn't want the baby," Olive burst out.

"I never thought you were hopeless, Olive. I think you're very honest with yourself."

Olive flushed. "I better take care of Johnny." She rushed out of the room.

Tiresa was washing lettuce when she heard Johnny crying, and turned off the water to listen; the sound must wake echoes in the old house. She opened the door to the stairs and called up to Olive. "Bring Johnny down and I'll hold him for a bit. You ought to go."

"I don't know why he's crying when I just fed him," Olive said. "Would you mind giving him that bottle I put in the frig, Tiresa?"

"That was it, you were hungry," Tiresa told the baby as she sat in the rocker feeding him. When she was finished, she held him against her shoulder. "Who knows, Johnny, you may be Paulo's godson, and that would be very good indeed."

Ron said he had set out his player to bring, but with so many things to pack for the baby, he'd forgotten it. Music might have helped, Tiresa thought as they sat at dinner. Paulo was too exhausted to eat, let alone add any spark to the conversation. It was ridiculous for him to have beaten Ron; he certainly couldn't be better or even the equal of a twenty-four-year-old who had won a tennis cup at college. It was just Paulo's insane will when he set himself to prove something. Did he feel now that he was as young and vigorous as a young man? Tiresa looked down the table at him with scorn in her eyes. Paulo caught her glance and grinned back at her, a little sheepishly.

"Ron will have some more steak, Paulo," Tiresa said. He was too tired even to look after his guests properly.

"I gather your new position will be more diversified, not just claims, Ron?" Paulo roused himself.

"Oh yes, much more. In time, if all goes well, I'll be the liaison between the agencies in four towns and the central office in Boston. I'll get to know these agencies and help them with any difficulty—suggest new opportunities for them; keep in close touch, you know. Some of them are hardly aware of all the services offered. For example, do you know that we sell insurance against cancer, so that the staggering costs—you know, if you should have cancer—are taken care of."

"Against cancer; what a gruesome idea. And people would take it out on the 'I don't think I'll have it, but if I should . . .' attitude?" Tiresa asked.

"I should think the old phrase 'catastrophic illness' would take care of it, without getting down to specific diseases," Paulo grumbled.

"Rather ironic if you developed heart disease instead of cancer and so couldn't qualify for the insurance," Tiresa put it.

"Can you insure against divorce now?" Olive asked.

Ron gave half a laugh. "Well no, I haven't heard of any policy to cover that."

"Maybe you should offer it as a suggestion," Olive said. Ron looked over at her, but she was absorbed in the glass of wine in her hand.

"Man is still a defenseless creature," Paulo said. "Fight as he may, take all the precautions offered, he still has to accept his destiny. Thucycides said it about the Athenians imprisoned in the quarries at Syacusa, 'Man does what he can, and suffers what he must.' I've never forgotten it."

Tiresa looked down at Paulo. What was he saying? It was her destiny to leave Paulo—his to go on; to suffer what they must. Yet there was a kind of strength in the words—or in his voice. But a chill had crept into the room, carrying with it a kind of threat. She went to get the bowl of fruit and cheese.

"Ah, you found mangoes, Tirese!" Paulo exclaimed.

"Bessie did. And persimmons, Paulo, especially for you."

"I don't think I've ever eaten a persimmon," Olive said.

"They're one of the delights of the palate," Paulo told her.

"And look at the size of those grapes," Ron said.

They were like children, Tiresa thought, easily comforted with a sweet—or pretending to be—glad to be distracted from the uneasiness in all their minds. Paulo got up to pour the coffee from the tall pot.

"Say, what was that idiotic crack about insuring against divorce?" Ron demanded when he and Olive were in bed.

"I don't know; it just occurred to me that it wouldn't be a bad idea."

"Meaning what?"

"Why, just what I said. So many couples get divorced, you might propose it."

The silence waited. Ron waited for Olive to say something more, Olive waited for Ron. "I didn't mean . . ." trembled on her lips, but Ron thumped his pillow and turned his back to her.

"G'night. I hope we leave early tomorrow. I'd like to be back by noon," he said.

"Oh, not that early. Sunday afternoon is so flat. Besides, we'll never be back here again."

"I don't see that. They might drive us up in December before we move. I'd like to go skiing up here once more."

There wasn't anything more to say. The silence thickened, yet she could feel Ron lying awake. She wished Johnny would cry so she would have to get up. Ron would ask what was wrong, and they would start talking again, but Johnny slept soundly, and the house was still, except for the wind in the trees outside.

"Ron," Olive said out of the silence.

"Yea." His voice was wide awake, eager almost, but she had something else on her mind.

"Ron, you know your mother wanted us to have Johnny christened when we're there for Thanksgiving."

"Sure, we can do that."

"But we have to get godparents."

"Well, that's no big deal."

"I was just thinking—we ought to have Paulo for one. He's so crazy about Johnny, and—well, they've been our best friends here."

"Oh, Hon, I don't see that. Sure, they're good friends, but . . . Well, for one thing, he's Italian, and probably Catholic."

"What difference does that make?" She sat up in bed. "I can't think of anyone else it would mean as much to."

"Maybe not, but I thought the general idea was who'd mean

the most to Johnny. If you're so set on having the Romanos, why not Tiresa?"

"No," Olive said slowly. "That would be too hard on her after losing her own baby."

"It might be a comfort to her, you know."

"No, I want to have Paulo for one godfather, and then the others can be from the family—families, I mean."

Ron was getting tired; he had that tone in his voice. "You know, Ollie, we'll be leaving here in a little more than two months. We won't see much more of them."

"Of course we will. You'll be coming back to the Boston office all the time."

"Oh hell, Ollie . . ."

"Ron, you know I didn't mean anything by what I said at dinner, don't you? It just popped into my head. I guess I was just trying to be clever."

"Sure, I know, hon. It just seemed such a sour crack."

Tiresa heard the wind and got up. Paulo was too exhausted to wake easily. Through the dark house she made her way by touch, feeling the uneven floor with her feet, and lifted the latch of the wide front door. Leaves were coming down in fitful drafts, with a rustle that sounded like rain. When she stepped outside the shelter of the house, the wind blew her hair across her face and tugged at her gown. She felt herself part of it.

Out here in the wind it was easier to look at the thing she kept hiding from. A couple of years—not much more, maybe not even that. Nobody had said, but she knew. Her shortness of breath was always with her now, and the swelling. But she had known from the bright froth and the stricken look on Paulo's face that time, and his depression. He had been beating devils of despair today when he played tennis, not Ron at all.

The wind gathered strength, bringing down a heavy rain of leaves. There was nothing to do about it. She had had over fifty good years . . . She stood holding her arms around herself and lifted her face to the wind. It was leaving Paulo that she couldn't bear.

She brushed off a leaf that stuck to her wet face and went back into the house. As she crept into bed, Paulo stirred and put his arm over her, then lifted it for fear it was too heavy.

"All right, Trise?"

"I'm all right," she said, moving closer to him.

15

They didn't go to the country again, after all. Once they had planned to go, but Paulo had a patient in the hospital who he couldn't leave. Tiresa had another siege of edema and kept out of the hospital only by agreeing to stay in bed the weekend they might have gone. Paulo offered the place to Ron and Olive, and Bessie agreed to take care of Johnny, but Olive said it would be no fun without them.

After Christmas, when Ron and Olive got back from New Jersey, they came to a farewell dinner. Johnny sat propped up on the couch at the beginning of the evening.

"He's watching the fire," Paulo said.

"I'm not so sure," Ron said. "He has that kind of glassy stare you get after four martinis."

"Don't cast aspersions on my godson," Paulo warned. "And here is his christening gift." Paulo handed Olive a wrapped and ribboned package.

A typical family group, Tiresa thought: the children, the grandchild, and, of course, they looked like the parents. Paulo had been touchingly pleased when they asked him to be the godfather. "I'm amazed, aren't you, Tiresa?" he had asked. "I've found Ron to be—well, truculent, at times. I've never felt at all close to him. Olive, yes."

"But you see—" Tiresa lifted her hands. "You never know how people really feel about you, do you? You should remember that."

Paulo had spent considerable time selecting the sterling silver christening cup. When the clerk told him it would be much less expensive if it were engraved electrically, Paulo was outraged. "I want it engraved by hand, by an engraver who knows his craft. This is for my godson." He wrote out the name, "John Ronald Fifer June tenth, nineteenth hundred and seventy-nine."

"I think I'll put a hundred dollar check in the cup," he told Tiresa.

"That's a little much, Paulo, the cup was expensive in itself. And you'll be remembering every birthday generously from here on, I'm sure."

Paulo was silent, then he said, "After all, Tiresa, I'm his godfather."

Olive was unwrapping the gift. "How beautiful, Paulo," she exclaimed, holding up the shining cup. She handed it to Ron.

"Say, there's an envelope in it." He took out the check. "Paulo, a hundred dollars! That will go into his education fund, I can tell you!"

Paulo looked across at Tiresa, beaming triumphantly.

It was a good evening. Johnny went off to sleep in the study and Ron and Olive stayed on, loath to leave.

"Ron will be coming back to the Boston office, and Johnny and I will ride along to see you," Olive said.

"You must come and stay long enough for us all to drive up to the farm," Paulo said. "Syracuse to Boston is no distance at all."

"Gosh, that would be great."

"I'd love it." Olive hunched her shoulders in pleasure at the thought. "I hate to leave here—you don't know."

"And we're going to be desolate without you next door," Paulo said.

"Indeed we are," Tiresa agreed, but she was tired suddenly.

The day the van came for the Fifer's things, Tiresa dressed early to keep an eye on Johnny. She sat reading, but she heard the furniture being trundled past the door to the freight elevator, and the voices in the corridor. An uneasy atmosphere seeped in under the door.

The movers were through by eleven, and Ron and Olive came to say goodbye and get Johnny. With her hair down her back and in jeans Olive looked exactly as she had when she first saw her, Tiresa thought.

"Paulo was so sorry he couldn't be here to say goodbye," Tiresa said. "He wishes you all good fortune. And Bessie had packed you a little lunch to take along. There are a couple of beef tartare sandwiches, especially for you, Ron."

"These moving guys are really good, you know," Ron said. "I never thought they'd be through before noon. Well, I guess we better push off. Thanks, Tirese, for all you've done for us."

"Oh Tiresa . . ." Olive was crying as she put her arms around Tiresa.

"Goodbye my dear. It's been a great pleasure to know you." The formal words were a defense against her sharp sense of loss. "And Johnny." She pulled his blanket around him a little more closely. "Now remember, Ron, come back and see us whenever you get to Boston, and bring Olive and Johnny with you."

And then they were gone. Very slowly Tiresa walked back to her chair. She felt abandoned, left high and dry. She wanted to ask Olive to write—but why should she write? And what? That they had arrived, were moving into a new life. There was no point. Writing to an older person could come to be a tiresome duty. Oh, there would be a note on Johnny's birthday to thank Paulo for his gift to his godson, and a snapshot of Johnny, and a Christmas card for several years at least, but they had gone out of their lives, really. It irritated her that she minded so much.

Solyny: *"And, restless, seeks the stormy ocean, as though in tempest there were peace."*

quoting lines A. S. Pushkin's poem "Ruslan and Lyudmila" (1820)
Chekhov, *The Three Sisters*, act 4

Chebutykin: *"Tarara-boom-dee-ay . . . It doesn't matter."*

Chekhov, *The Three Sisters*, act 4

I

Tiresa spent her mornings in bed until almost noon. Paulo had elevated her legs at the head of the bed on blocks, and raised the top of the mattress by means of a bolster. He claimed that he had never slept so well as he did on an incline. Why should they be separated before they had to be, each of them thought privately.

This morning, Paulo had brought Tiresa her coffee and was on his way to shower, when she said, "Your stealing forth from my arms so briskly every morning makes me think of that painting of Psyche and Cupid we saw in Europe, remember? She's lying there exhausted—all passion spent—and Cupid goes capering off as fresh as a daisy, with his bow and arrows over his shoulder."

"I'm scarcely Cupid, and I don't caper," Paulo said. "Besides, he's a fat simpering urchin in that painting. I am not fat, Tiresa, or dimpled."

"No. But the idea is the same, you'll admit. I resented his being so full of energy when she looks utterly drained."

"Drained is hardly the word. He had no doubt filled her full of a beautiful child." The bathroom door closed before she could answer back, but he could hear her laugh, and the merriment in it raised his spirits so that he sang "*O sole mio*" from behind the closed door.

When he came in with her breakfast tray and the newspaper, Tiresa said, "Before you go, Paulo, would you bring up from storage that wicker trunk we brought home from Sicily?"

145

"Yes, but why?"

"Oh I thought I'd like to go through some things I've been too lazy to get at." The slightest remark that could be construed as suggesting her poor outlook depressed or infuriated him, so she added quickly, "This is a good chance; by next month, I'll be too busy and won't have time." He was such a realist about everything else; calling things by their right name was part of his morality. Only about her health did he insist on pretending childishly.

After Paulo had gone, Tiresa lay awhile before opening the trunk. It was a pleasure just to look at it standing there in the sun. The wicker had darkened a little. The leather handles, and the corners reinforced with leather, gave it a sturdy look. Something about its shape and workmanship marked it as Italian.

She remembered the shop where they had bought it—on the Corso in Taormina. And Paulo, perching it on his shoulder, had carried it up the seventy-one steps to the villa they had rented. He might have been carrying a hamper of olives or artichokes, like the sunburned, dark-haired Sicilians she saw on the road coming in from the country.

Tiresa unfastened the clasps and threw back the straw top. Of a sunny morning, they often sauntered down the Corso, and Paulo bought things in the little shops they wandered into, just to please the shopkeepers. There were the woven placemats the Sicilian women made as they sat in the doorways of their houses, their backs to the sunny street. She could never understand why they didn't face the door and look out as they worked.

She pulled out a long silk stole that Paulo had bought from a rack that hung out over the sidewalk. A hideous magenta stripe ran down the middle, with a yellow stripe on one side and a green one on the other. She had told him it was garish and shiny and she would never wear it. Besides, she hated magenta. But Paulo insisted that it wasn't magenta, it was cerise, and he always thought of that color with her name, "cerise"—Tirese, so he bought it and put it around her shoulders. "Now you look Sicilian—and beautiful," he said as they went on down the Corso.

And she had felt dowdy but cherished. Even now, she winced at the intensity and harshness of the colors. All kinds of tastes she hadn't been aware of had come out in Paulo on that trip.

There! Her hand came up with the journal she had started on the ship going to Sicily and kept the short time they were there. The red leather cover bore the round stain of a coffee cup across the date, 1963. Three years after they were married, the year Paulo Sebastian . . . She didn't remember all she had written, but she had an uneasy feeling that she didn't want Paulo coming in on it later. The date stopped her for a minute; a pause in her thoughts like the pause that came often now between heartbeats. She didn't need any written record to bring back the whole trip, but always there was that curiosity to find yourself as you were at some earlier time—an odd reluctance, too.

How had she resisted the idea of going to Sicily. But, when Paulo first proposed it, she was still in the hospital and it was the last thing on earth she wanted to do. She wanted only to be still, and not think, not read, and feel as little as possible. Even the doctor had agreed with her and said it would be risky for her to go. But Paulo rode rough-shod over everybody, insisting in that superior tone he could use, that the trip was just what she needed. "I know Tiresa," he had said, "and depression is worse for her than physical illness. She just needs a change of scene." And she had told him he didn't realize what she had been through. Nothing could ever change her interior scene.

She remembered how he tired her with his talk, telling her all she would need to do was sit in the Sicilian sun and let it heal her; that it was gentle in the spring. But, by July it was a beast. He would say it with such obvious glee it irritated her. And he said they would touch Sicilian earth and be invigorated. His excitement had exhausted her and she wouldn't even look at the travel folders he spread out on her bed.

But what if he had taken her at her word when she urged him to go by himself, feeling it would be a relief to have him gone for a bit. And then he had dropped his bombshell. She could still see him, standing at the foot of the bed, telling her he was leaving medical school and taking a position in Boston. She had closed her eyes and not given him the satisfaction of a reaction, until he began telling her about the excellent offer he had received. It had come while she was so sick he hadn't mentioned it before. The enormity of his deciding without consulting her had shocked her to the bone. But he went on telling her how she would enjoy living in Boston, and that it was a distinguished educational center. He was absolutely odious. Finally, when she couldn't stand it a moment longer, she had pulled herself up in bed, glaring at him, and asked him if he expected her to give up her position and run after him like an obedient wife or stay behind and see him on weekends. She told him that her work and profession were as important to her as his could possibly be and she fancied she had done rather well in hers, too. She was so weak she had burst into tears.

She would never forget the way Paulo had cried out, "Tiresa, my darling, you're angry!" As though it was a miracle. All he had wanted was to see her come out of the terrible no-state she had been in. Of course, he hadn't made any decision, and did she have no faith? If she could find no teaching position that she wanted in or around Boston, they didn't have to go, though a year without teaching might not be a bad idea for her; he had tucked that in.

Was it at that moment that she trusted Paulo completely, once and for all? He knew exactly how she felt, the way she saw things—even when he saw them differently. And he had been right. She had revived, slowly but surely, on that trip; her interior world had changed. Only now, he couldn't—wouldn't, she realized, face her dying. She was alone with it. She opened the journal quickly.

March 3, 1963
    After all my protests, it is heaven to be here on shipboard, with nothing to do but sit in the sun and watch the movement of the sea. Paulo does his three miles, how-

ever many laps it is, around the deck, but most of the time he is here with me, reading while I sleep, or reading to me. And he is forever bringing me bouillon or tea, waiting on me. I have learned more about his family and his boyhood than ever before, and I can feel his excitement at going back.

Sicily is different from any place else in the world, he tells me; that I must always remember that it is an island and distinct from Italy. There have been so many different civilizations living there, and each one has left its mark. I wonder if a drop of blood of all those races runs in Paulo's veins.

One day, Paulo said he had always wondered what the Roman soldiers thought the first night they made camp and saw red fire coming out of the top of Etna. It is something you never forget, he says, and I am eager to see it for myself. I have never heard him talk so much about the volcano. Nor did I realize how much Paulo misses Sicily. Tomorrow morning we land at Palermo.

March 4th

The dock at Palermo was a mad house—a frantic jumble of people trying to get off, pushing forward, trying to see relatives; taxi-drivers, baggage men, and beggars all swarming around, and all voluble. I saw an old man weeping as he hugged a middle-aged man, who was just off the ship. Porters were calling out, trying to out-do the shrill cries of little boys begging. Paulo gave money to at least five urchins the minute we got off the ship, and said something to them that made them laugh. He signaled to someone in the crowd in a most imperious manner. "Subito!" he snapped, and instead of a taxi as I expected, a horse-drawn cab appeared, and the driver got down, bowing and scraping, spreading a robe over my knees and calling me Signora every other minute.

Driving along that broad avenue with the beautiful harbor and mountains for a backdrop, and the clip-clop of the horses' hooves sounding through the honking of horns, I felt as if I were in a musical comedy. I looked up the side-streets we passed into a network of lines hung with bright-colored clothes stretching from the balconies on one side of the street to the balconies on the other. Half the women I saw, it seemed to me, had babes in their arms or were sitting on the steps of the horrible tenements nursing them, or shrieking at toddlers playing along the curb. I couldn't help asking Paulo why he had brought me to a place so over-run with motherhood. Paulo looked at me with the tenderest smile in the world and said I understood motherhood.

When I exclaimed at the poverty everywhere, Paulo nodded with a mournful expression, but the next instant he was beaming again. We drove up to the hotel where we will stay for a couple of days, and Paulo talked to everyone—our coachman, the porters who sprang out of the hotel, and even a passer-by. I can see that he delights in using his native tongue again.

Taormina, Paulo's home village, is within easy driving distance, and I thought he would want to get right in the car and go there. But he said no; that this trip was to be very leisurely, that I must rest first, and, anyway, there were things he wanted to show me in Palermo. The trip on the ship was rest enough, but this place is pleasant. And then I wondered if now that he is so near, Paulo has some little reluctance in going back. Since both his mother and father had died, and his brother Luigi is a Benedictine monk, there is no one of his own to come back to. We are alike in this, for I have no family left either.

We had luncheon on our balcony in the sun, looking out at the blue Mediterranean sea. The air is soft, but not as warm as I expected. Paulo has gone off to rent a car.

Later

The car is unbelievable—a Lancia, all white, with red leather upholstery. The showiest car I have ever seen, let alone driven in. Paulo beams over it like a small boy. We went for a drive and I felt horribly conspicuous in that gaudy barouche, but Paulo just laughs and grins. When he was here before, he could only dream of driving a car, so now I suppose it pleases him to have such a magnificent one.

We drove past the medical school where Paulo went, and the rabbit warren, as he calls it, where he lived. He tried to go home every weekend because his father was ill. He could take his father a piece of fresh veal, if he could get any—veal was the only meat the doctor said his father could eat. If he could manage some ice, it got there in fair condition, but the flies always buzzed around the package. He says the meat was all right when it was broiled. When Paulo tells you something, he puts in all the details. I treasure these little glimpses I'm getting of Paulo and his family.

I knew that Palermo is a stronghold of the Mafia, but as we drove around in the late afternoon, it seemed peaceful enough, with nothing sinister about it except the terrible poverty. But just as we drove past the dock, we saw two men circling each other, and a little crowd gathering to watch. The sun flashed on a knife one of them held; then I saw they both had knives. Paulo stopped the car.

One of the men shouted something at the other, and he yelled back. An eerie stillness held the whole dock. I told Paulo to drive on quickly, and asked him where the police were. He didn't even seem to hear me, and he got out of the car and went a little closer. It frightened me— he looked so much like some of the men in the crowd, and just as intent.

The crowd kept growing. I couldn't watch any more, but when a tremendous shout went up, I looked in time to see one of the men on the ground, and the crowd closing in. Paulo got back in the car and we drove away. He fairly vibrated.

"How barbarous," I said. Paulo just shrugged. It didn't seem to bother him. He acted as if I had an inferior mind and a knife fight was so far beyond my comprehension there was no use talking about it. What I really meant was that Paulo's interest in it was barbarous. I had always thought him so civilized.

"Now you have seen one side of Palermo," he said with a kind of disgusting satisfaction. I thought I knew Paulo, but I certainly don't know this Sicilian side of him that can enjoy a knife fight. I'm not sure that I want to. Tonight, I called him a mafioso, and instead of objecting, he grinned at me and said the word with a small "m" is a compliment and means brave, honorable, proud, not that he is a criminal or connected with any Mafia organization. I always knew that Paulo was complicated, but I guess that Sicily is, too, and the language. I wonder if the new country I have come to see isn't Paulo.

March 5th

Today, we drove out to Monreale to see the Grand Duomo. Paulo dropped to his knees so naturally I wondered if he had used to come here as a young medical student.

The mosaics are beyond belief. It is incredible that such profound human expressions are possible with tiny blocks of marble. The piercing dark eyes of Christ reach you wherever you stand, Paulo says, as though he had felt them.

I can see the influences of those different civilizations

Paulo was talking about in architecture. Turkish domes and lemon-colored walls mix with the sturdy Roman arches, and yet they achieve an effect of beauty and harmony.

Again and again, I had to exclaim at the poverty in the streets, and the dreadful hovels in the city, tier upon tier, that human beings live in. But it was the women, completely dressed in black, who really got to me. They can't all be in mourning, I said to Paulo; some of them have such young faces under their black shawls. Paulo said they probably all lost someone in the family. And infant mortality is high. His eyes held mine for a long minute, and I knew he was saying, "You see, you are not alone in losing your child." "If I were a Sicilian woman, I would be dressed in mourning," I told him. Paulo said I had clothed my soul in mourning as it was; whether he meant it as a rebuke or not, I don't know. He also said that Sicilians have a natural born capacity for sorrow and suffering, but that they have an even greater one for joy. I have that, too, he said, but I don't always make full use of it. I can't see that at all.

Tiresa looked up from her reading and remembered that Paulo had called Olive a child of joy.

March 6th

Yesterday, we did know only joy. We were on our way to Taormina on a glorious blue-skied day. The sun shone on every knob and screw of our white chariot, and when we stopped for cappuccino *in a little village, small boys collected around the car; even the shopkeepers stepped out to look it over. In a second, Paulo was in the midst of a lively conversation in Sicilian. I heard the word* Americano *several times. I told him he should tell them he didn't own the car, but he just shrugged.*

This shrugging has become more frequent since we came here; it seems natural to him, and I notice that he carries his coat over one shoulder the way the men do here.

We bought cheese and a bottle of wine, a long loaf of crusty bread and oranges in a dark little store with a pungent smell of earthy vegetables and spices mixed with a fishy odor. But not until we were high up above the sea would Paulo stop to eat. Below us hung a delicate pinkish white cloud—the orange trees in bloom. And the grass, more wildflowers than I have ever seen at once. Paulo picked me a bouquet of asphodels and anemones and white narcissus. Purple and white iris grew wild under the trees. To make the picture completely bucolic there was a flock of sheep and a shepherd with a staff a little distance away.

Paulo peeled an orange and offered it to me on the palm of his hand as a rare gift. It was deep red. Sanguino, he called it, a blood orange. "You see, the blood of life and red wine are mixed even in the fruit on this island," he said.

We had finished, we lingered, not wanting to leave that spot. I asked Paulo how he ever decided to go away from this lovely island. He smiled and said he had to go to find me. I think the sadness—the wistfulness is a better word—that I sometimes feel in Paulo must come from his missing this island where he was born.

Sicily was known to the ancients as the mythical Garden of Hesperides, Paulo says. And they thought the golden oranges and paler gold lemons were those golden apples in the myth. He is full of legends of the country. It isn't hard to imagine Persephone out on that very hillside picking flowers while Paulo was telling her myth, and to shudder at the thought of her being abducted by Pluto. "Now she is allowed to come back to the world of the sun every spring," Paulo said, as if it were the very *truth and he had seen her with his own eyes. I can't help thinking what wonderful stories he would have told Paulo Sebastian.*

When I passed the bottle of wine to Paulo to finish, he said he wanted to save the rest for the sheepherder. I watched him running across the pink and blue and yellow field and marveled that he had come out of this enchanted land into my life.

By mid-afternoon the sun had disappeared and it began to rain, drumming on the glass window in the car roof. I felt a change in Paulo's gay mood, too. He began to prepare me for Taormina. It was always filled with tourists, he said. The English come early in the winter, and the Scandinavians, but by Easter, there is a regular influx of Germans. He used to put up the sign "Deutsch Sprechen Hier" in the window of his father's shop.

I knew Paulo's father owned farm land outside the village that was worked by peasant farmers, but I hadn't know he had a shop. Then I remembered that once when we were buying gloves Paulo said that his father had been in the leather business. His shop was destroyed by a bomb during the war. He never talks about that time, but I know it was terrible for him.

And he warned me that his old home will be rundown; that I won't get much idea of how it used to be. He said he wasn't sure that he wants to see it. But that I will be enchanted by the town; it has the most beautiful location in all the world—high up on the cliff above the sea, and in sight of Mount Etna. And then we drove a long way in silence, and I felt Paulo was back in his boyhood.

We had a villa waiting for us. Paulo wrote an old friend of his who sublet the villa from an American artist who will be away for three months. Paulo, of course, knew right where it is, but he won't tell me anything about it. The cook and the gardener who work for the artist go with the villa. Could anything be more perfect? I wish we could stay the whole three months now that we are here, but Paulo says it gets very hot, and, of course, we want to go on to Florence and Paris, and Rome. We will be moving to Boston at the end of August.

March 7th

What an arrival! Something went wrong in the beautiful engine and we were held up for two hours in the rain in a place that consisted only of a bright red gasoline pump, a tiny store, and a handful of stucco houses huddled together as though there were not an inch of room to spare on that whole bare cliff. A young Sicilian and Paulo fixed the car, but it was close to eleven o'clock, and black as the river Styx, when we drove up the steep curving road to Taormina. After we came to the town, we continued to climb. We got out in the rain on a dark street and went down a steep flight of stone steps between two walls onto a little terrace. I held my big handbag over my head, but got soaked through. Paulo didn't have a key, and the door hadn't been left unlocked as Paulo was sure it would be. Nor was there any light inside the house.

Paulo swore under his breath and went running back up all those stairs while I leaned against the wall of the house to get what shelter I could from the overhanging roof. I heard him call out "Carmela," the cook's name, and, unbelievably, a woman's voice answered back almost at once. He came back out of the dark with a buxom Sicilian woman who kept exclaiming and calling on the Saints. She unlocked the door and switched on a sickly electric bulb.

The long room felt damp and chilly, but it was a relief to get out of the rain. That was all there was, just one room about thirty feet long, with a stunning tiled floor. At the rear of the room stood an ancient gas stove and an iron sink with only one faucet. The front of the room must serve as grand foyer and dining room combined, I decided. From a carved newel post of regal proportions, tiled stairs that might grace a baronial hall go up to the second floor, which consists of a studio and bathroom. A large iron bed, trimmed with brass curlicues and brass knobs, and a massive chest of drawers mark off one end as bedroom. At the front end are floor-length windows, but the shutters were closed over them. A bare easel stands in one corner and empty hooks protrude from the twenty foot high plaster walls. I have been imagining the canvases that might have hung on those hooks. I see them very clearly, and I can change them every day. But I shall find out what kind of things the artist who lives here paints.

A long couch, three chairs and a carved table, all grouped on a thread-bare Oriental rug make up the rest of the furnishings. The effect is sparse, to say the least. In the center of the long wall is a small plaster fireplace that smokes.

Paulo stepped down into the bathroom and let out a thundering Sicilian oath. The floor was two inches deep in water. He claims it was a wonder that he wasn't electrocuted, for he had just taken his hand off the switch.

Carmela came running upstairs and began to lament and raise her hands, then she went running back down and we could hear her outside in the dark calling "Alfio, Alfio," as though the house were on fire at least. Alfio turned out to be her husband. She came back up with some sticks of wood and paper to build a fire, all the time casting her eyes up to the ceiling and saying "Signora," and not getting on very fast with the fire. So Paulo built it. Then he turned up his trousers above his *knees and waded through the water to find the leak. By the time Alfio had carried out most of the water, Paulo had discovered that the leak came from the bidet and he felt absolutely triumphant. "I should have been a plumber, Tiresa, I have the gift," he said, and I realized that he was really having a wonderful time.*

The bathroom has the most handsome cobalt blue tile floor I ever saw, and there is an impressive step-down bathtub, but I wonder if the room will ever be warm enough to take a bath with any comfort.

When we went downstairs, the amazing Carmela had spaghetti boiling in a kettle and our places laid on the table. Paulo had told her we'd had no dinner. Alfio produced vino di casa, *and we actually sat down to eat. Of course, Paulo was in high spirits by that time, and poured a glass for Carmela and Alfio and we drank a toast to Casa Margherita, as the villa is called. "May she hang together while we are under her roof," Paulo said in English.*

It was close to two in the morning by the time Carmela and Alfio had gone, and Paulo and I went up to bed. We warmed the sheets by the fire before we dared to sleep in them. The bed was far from soft, but we were glad to get there.

Bessie brought in the mail with a letter from Olive. A thoughtful child to write so promptly, Tiresa thought approvingly.

January 5th
Dear Tiresa and Paulo,

We are all moved in. Our house is in a new development so all the houses in the neighborhood are pretty much alike, only painted different colors with some little differences in plans. Ours is in two shades of green and looks like a green salad. If the front door were painted red, you would think it was a tomato in a bowl of lettuce. The house has two bedrooms, which is groovy, and a fireplace. I'll think of yours every time I light it—ours is gas. We are two miles from the shopping center, and more to any place else. When Ron is away with the car, I feel marooned out here. But I guess we were lucky to get the house. Someone who bought it couldn't keep up his payments so is subletting to us.

Thank you for taking care of Johnny while we were moving, Tiresa, and for the lovely farewell dinner—and everything. *I miss being just down the hall more than I can ever tell you.*

love,
Olive

P.S. Paulo, your godson is flourishing and will soon be drinking milk out of his gorgeous silver cup.

The letter sounded a little hurried—and dutiful; a little wistful at the end, perhaps, but she may have added that just for them. Did Olive sound happy? She would probably never know how Ron and Olive worked out their little difficulties. Olive had written them her thank-you note, now they would only hear from them at Christmas—perhaps—and have a note on Johnny's birthday. How ridiculous Paulo had been to give Johnny that big check! But, of course, he loved doing it.

Tiresa bathed and dressed, and put the Sicilian stole around her shoulders.

That evening, Paulo saw at once the Sicilian stole Tiresa wore around her shoulders. "Ah, *la bella dama di Sicilia*," he said. "It's good to see it on you again. You must have found it in the hamper."

"Yes, but before we start talking about Sicily, Paulo, there's a note from Olive that came today."

"How splendid," Paulo said, smiling with pleasure, but

when he finished, his face had sobered. "Is she going to be happy there, Tiresa? It sounds dreadful. A house in two shades of green with a gas fireplace."

"She'll get used to all that, and they can use another bedroom, but it sounds isolated for her when Ron is away. I suppose there will be other young wives living there . . ."

"I miss them; I wish they were back here."

They went on talking about Olive and Ron over dinner. "Well, they have to work out their own problems," Tiresa said finally. "It doesn't do any good for us to worry over them. And they probably don't feel they have any problems."

"But what kind of life will Olive have there?" Paulo demanded.

"Whatever kind of life she makes, I imagine. It will be up to her and Ron." Tiresa was tired of thinking about them. "Let's have our coffee and talk about Sicily. Looking over that hamper made me think of Casa Margherita, of course, and I remembered the first night we spent there."

Paulo groaned. "That was a disaster. When I wanted everything to be so perfect for you."

"But I remember the next morning," Tiresa said. "You got up and threw open the shutters with a terrible racket and light flooded the room. And then I saw! I went out on the balcony in my gown, and there was Etna—so exactly like the postcards I had seen of it, it hardly looked real. But is was so close, it made me catch my breath. All I could think of was the title of that novel of Malcolm Lowry's, *Under the Volcano*, and your growing up under one."

Paulo shrugged, and his face took on that expression that always separated him from her. She had never fathomed it completely; it came from his absurdly romantic sense of fatalism. She laughed at him for it, and he never denied or defended his attitude. Ever since they were in Taormina, she had felt it must come from his growing up under Etna.

"That was a wonderful time," she said quickly. "And with all its cold and inconveniences, I wouldn't have missed living in

Casa Margherita for anything. Leaning over the balcony watching those little cars with their silly beep-beeps, and hearing a donkey braying, women calling their children, roosters crowing—I felt so close to it all, I might have been Sicilian myself."

Paulo was smiling again, and his eyes glowed. "Remember the time we went to see Luigi at the Monastery? You wore a black shawl over your head, and Luigi said, "Why Paulo, you married a beautiful Sicilian woman even if you did go to America to find her."

"I remember his giving us his blessing."

Paulo nodded.

The next morning, Tiresa took up the journal again.

March 7th

"Come," Paulo said after breakfast, "we'll go and see what is left of Casa Romano."

We walked down the stairs to the road—street, I suppose, really, that goes to town, but instead of following it, we cut down another flight of stone steps to a lower curve of the winding street. Paulo used to run up and down all these steps as a boy and I think it must be hard for him to walk down so slowly with me. He came to a stop in front of a yellow plaster house, three of four steps down from the street, and separated from it by a scraggly hedge of oleander bushes. The house stood three stories high with four long windows across the lower floor, but some variation on the second floor. A flourish of wood or plaster topped each window and I knew how Paulo must have prized that bit of ornamentation.

Silently, we went down the steps to the walk that led to the front door. I remembered Paulo telling me once that there was a handsome door on their home in Sicily. It was tall and had an ornate iron doorknocker held up by two iron cherubs. Once the door had been painted blue, but most of it was faded to gray. Still, I saw how it must have looked to Paulo as a boy. I admit the house was less pretentious than I had expected. I don't know what I had visualized—something only a little less than the palace in Gattopardo, the novel of Sicily Paulo gave me to read on the ship. Not that Paulo ever suggested that he lived in a palace, it was his tone of voice when he talked about his home that always conjured up a place of dignity.

"I told you it would be badly run down," Paulo said. And he pointed out that the flowerbeds around the front of the house used to be full of white iris and daffodils, and the tree by the corner of the house was always covered with almond blossoms this time of year. I felt so sorry for him; the tree had only a few blossoms and the beds were full of weeds. "And right there by the corner of the house used to be a wonderful filigree of wisteria," he said sadly.

Paulo doesn't know who lives in the house now. We walked around to a grass-grown brick patio that looked straight across at Etna, and, of course, the sea—if you guide your eyes carefully past the double clothesline, heavily strung with dilapidated washing. "What a magnificent view to grow up with, Paulo," I said. I didn't add that Etna made it a little awesome, too.

Paulo decided to talk to the people who live there now, so I sat on a bench by the wall to wait for him. I could hear his voice and a woman's, then the door closed behind them.

I was just sitting there, resting, thinking of Paulo living in that house as a small boy, when I was aware of a movement in the bush beside the wall, and realized a child was hiding there.

"Buon giorno," I said. "Come out and see me."

A boy, not more than six, crawled out. He seemed more curious than shy. He was smiling and his black

eyes might have been Paulo's: dark and alive. With a
quick duck of his head, he made me a kind of bow, and
rubbed one bare foot against the other. Above his ragged
shorts, his straight lean little body was sunburned to an
even copper color. He gave me another quick smile and
then looked down at the ground.

It was good that I was by myself, I was so shaken.
Paulo Sebastian would look like that at six—if he had
lived. I put out my hand to try to bring him closer; I
wanted just to touch him. But he held his ground. "Do
you live here?" I asked, pointing to the house, and I could
see by his eyes that he understood me, even before he said
"Si." I pointed at the mountain and said "Etna"? just
to be talking to him. He nodded and beamed as if he
owned it—just as Paulo would. "Si," he said. He might
have been Paulo at that age, too. Then a woman's shrill
voice called out, "Giuseppe," and with another duck of
his head, and that flashing smile, he ran off toward the
back of the house. I sat here, feeling as if I had had a
vision. I had seen my little son—alive, and I had seen
Paulo as a child. After this, Paulo will always be my
child to mother as well as my husband to love.

As she read the entry, it sounded maudlin. It would never do
to let Paulo come on that. Poor Tiresa, he would think, she never could accept her childlessness. He might also cast back over
their lives and imagine instances of her mothering him. No, the
journal was written for her eyes alone. There were only a few
more pages.

When Paulo came out of the house, he said, "It
doesn't look much like the home I described to you, does
it?" I assured him that I could see how it must have
been. He said he had only gone as far as the front hall-
way, and that it was dark and shabby and smelled of

garlic, but at least he had put his hand on the carved newel-post once more.

"When I was a child, I used to think the woman carved on the post was Persephone. She was in the dark underworld when the front door was closed and the hall dark, but when the room was light, especially when the front door was open in the spring, she was back on earth." (I try to write it down as Paulo said it, because his face was so lighted up as he described the contrast.) Now, Paulo says, there are three generations and at least two families living in the house. He seemed depressed all the way back to our villa, but I felt more alive than I had for months.

March 11th

I haven't written in this journal for several days. We have been caught up in a regular social whirl. Friends of Paulo's who still live here have entertained us. Paulo is in his element, touched that they remember him so well—as if anyone could ever forget him! All of his friends, or almost all, speak excellent English, and I am enjoying them, too.

Our hostess last night I liked especially. She has a richness of coloring, and of spirit, as well as sophistication that appeal to me. She told me she was very much in love with Paulo when she was nineteen and he was twenty-one and in medical school. "And then he was spirited off to America and forgot me, the wretch," she said with a laugh, flinging out her beringed hands dramatically. Her name is Asunta and she is married to an attractive banker. She and Paulo had a lively give-and-take over their young romance.

Twice we have dined on patios out under the stars, with that glow at the top of Etna which for me gives an ominous overtone to the laughter or most casual re-

mark. I wonder if I could ever feel relaxed in the presence of that volcano.

March 15th

There is quite a large group here that Paulo describes as being in the tradition of Hadrian. One of them is a doctor who was in medical school with Paulo. He had a dinner-party for us and was a most charming host. Two of the men at dinner were English and retired from the BBC; witty individuals, both of them. All of this group, and a quite clearly defined one it is, seem to live well here, as though there is room under Etna for all kinds of temperaments and mores. I like the live-and-let-live atmosphere.

Tonight we went to a most handsome villa. Paulo pulled a brass ring set in a bright green garden door, and almost at once a smiling young Sicilian in livery flung it open, bowing and calling us Signor *and* Signora Romano.

We climbed a flight of stone steps bordered by flowers and vines and came out into a magic garden. Lanterns lighted our way and threw interesting shadows on the wall of the house. When we reached the entrance, a butler opened the door and showed us into a spacious room with a vaulted ceiling, and furnished with rare treasures. What is more to the point, there was a delicious warmth of central heat! I must admit that Casa Margherita continues to be damp and chilly. It is almost always warmer outside, even at night.

I hardly had time to appreciate the statue in a niche of the wall, when we were led into the presence of the host, Carlo, a man in his late eighties, and confined to a wheel chair. I felt his bright black eyes looking me over.

"Ah, you traitor," he said to Paulo, "Well, you have come back to show her to us. How you snared him, I'll

never understand," he said to me, which was hardly complimentary. "I trusted Paulo never to succumb to marriage," he added.

I expected some quick retort from Paulo, but he merely smiled and I felt the pressure of his hand on my arm, moving me on toward eight or nine other guests.

The villa was where the German high command stayed during the occupation, a woman told me. Many of the new art treasures were packed away, but the Germans managed to take some things with them. Perhaps it was because of that, but an ominous feeling seemed to linger, in spite of the roaring fire in the magnificent carved fireplace.

The couple of hours we spent there were pleasant enough. I was amused by the companion of the old man, who seemed equally proud of his lineage and his small feet, both of which he happened to mention in passing. He had been on the London stage until he retired and came to Sicily to live with Carlo. He would have been perfect in an eighteenth-century English comedy— Congreve, for example. But I was glad to leave and saunter back to out simple chilly little villa. I told Paulo I had found the place depressing and he agreed; he didn't go on, so I didn't either.

I learned one amazing thing tonight. We were talking about the volcano, and after telling me horrible tales of its eruptions, and how it left the long slope and the whole green valley around it covered with black lava, one of the men said there was nothing more fertile than that lava soil. It seems incredible, a phoenix rising from the ashes kind of thing. He described the grapes that grow there. I told Paulo I'd like my ashes scattered on the slope of Etna. Tonight the crown of Etna is hidden under a sultry cloudy sky. I find it a relief.

March 17th

Paulo went off by himself yesterday afternoon. He said he'd like to wander around and hunt up some old acquaintances if they were still here. "Do you mind?" he asked. "Of course not," I told him. I knew instinctively that he was going to see Asunta.

I had to do something with myself so I wandered down the Corso and loitered in the bookstore; a very good one, with books in French, German and even Greek, as well as Italian and English. I bought a couple of books about Sicily.

And I looked into the shops—wide open to the street, and having all manner of things for sale. Bought a pair of sandals that hung outside the store, standing first on one foot and then the other to try them on, right there on the street. And then, on some bizarre impulse, I bought a straight black skirt, a black shirtwaist, and a black wool shawl, the costume that most of the peasant women my age seem to wear, and not just peasant women. It suits me in an odd way. Paulo's only comment was that he wouldn't like to see it on me often.

March 20th

Today we were invited to have dinner at the villa where D. H. Lawrence and Freda lived some stormy and no doubt ecstatic years. I can hear myself in class next fall, saying, "When I was in Sicily, I went to a house where D. H. Lawrence had lived. There is a sharp contrast between that mining town where he was born and of which he wrote so vividly and the beautiful little Sicilian town across from the volcano. But these towns have one vital thing in common that suggests what was vital to him in his life and his writing . . ." pausing significantly, of course. I would go on, "coal, the means of fire, and fire itself lie deep in the earth of each . . ." How didactic can you be about human passion that was part of living human beings! Contemptible. I had no difficulty in feeling those personalities as I sat in their onetime house.

But the evening was memorable for a different reason. Asunta and her husband were over there. When we got up from dinner and went out on the terrace, Asunta came over to me and said a remarkable thing; remarkable that she would say it, I mean. She said, "I can see, Signora Romano, that you are the right one for Paulo, after all. I have never felt such contentment in him. He used to be difficult in his twenties, very restless." She was generous to tell me that, but I know I am the right one for Paulo.

March 22nd

Paulo got a cable today from Cathy. Poor Tony was knocked down by a car, and had his leg broken. Cathy wants Paulo to come home. I do not understand how a two and a half year-old would get out into the street if his mother had her mind on him. Nor do I see why we should cut our trip short for a broken leg. I do not feel charitable today.

March 24th

Well, we have decided to leave here tomorrow and go on to Perugia to see Luigi at the Benedictine monastery. We both hate to leave Taormina; I think I am even more reluctant to go than Paulo. He is eager to see his brother. We'll come back soon again, Paulo says, especially since Sicily and I are so simpatico. But I wonder how soon he will be able to get away.

This afternoon, we went to the Greek theater. Graeco-Roman, really, because when the Romans took over Taormina, they remodeled the stage to fit their ideas. I wish it were still just as the Greeks had constructed it.

I had caught a glimpse of it from some distance, but not until we walked up to it did I feel its grandeur. Perhaps it was partly because the afternoon was perfect, there were no tourists prowling about, for I do not consider Paulo and me tourists, and partly that we had the great amphitheater to ourselves that it seemed so impressive. But what theater enclosed in walls and ceilings could be as lofty as those few pillars rising under open sky? Beyond the stage, the blue sea rolling gently into its scalloped bays, and Etna above it all offer the most breathtaking backdrop any theater ever had.

"I believe these are our seats," Paulo said, ushering me to one of the tiers of rock-hewn benches. We sat there in silence at first, almost hearing the cadence of the great dramatic utterances of centuries long ago.

Suddenly, Paulo ran down to the front, and standing with his back to one of the pillars, his arms clasped around it as if his hands were chained there, cried out some lines in Greek. His voice reverberated against the ruins and soared out gloriously toward Etna. From his stance and a word or two that I could understand, I realized that he was Prometheus, chained to a rock by Zeus for stealing fire and giving it to man. Paulo looked noble against his pillar, and his deep voice thrilled by its very being. It must have wakened echoes in those ancient ruins, too, hungry for live words. Lines from the Greek plays spoken by great actors are broadcast there certain nights during tourist season, but they couldn't be as stirring.

Paulo couldn't remember any more so he made an elaborate bow and came back to where I was sitting. He laughed at himself and said he had always wanted to do that, but never had the courage before. I'll remember those moments to my dying day, and the way Paulo looked standing there.

Grand Hotel Brufani
Perugia
March 26th

I felt Paulo's tension—uncertainty perhaps, as we set off for the Monastery. On an impulse, I wore my black peasant outfit and the black lace mantilla over my head. I think Paulo was a little startled, but he only smiled. I was nervous, too; this meeting could mean so much to Paulo, or be disappointing and only serve to deepen his loneliness.

There was this other-worldliness about the Monastery as we walked up to the entrance; a quiet about it. Paulo rang the bell, and as we waited I read the name and the date carved into the stone and almost worn away. "Abbatia S. Petri nine hundred sixty-four."

We were led into a small cool room with only a bare table and benches against the wall. A crucifix carved of dark wood hung high on the wall and dominated the room. Then we heard footsteps coming down the long corridor and Luigi was coming toward us.

Luigi opened his arms and Paulo ran to him. They embraced as I have never seen two men do, as though they could never part. I tried to make myself not there; their meeting after so many years seemed private.

"I am glad to meet you," he said when Paulo introduced me to him, and looked deep into my eyes. "You married a beautiful Sicilian woman, after all, even if you found her in America," he said to Paulo.

It is an effort for Luigi—Dom Anselm his name is here, to talk in English, so they spoke in Sicilian. I was content to sit there listening to their voices, watching their faces. Luigi bears a striking resemblance to Paulo, but is ten years older, of course. His head is tonsured but has the same noble Roman lines Paulo's has. And he has the same deep black eyes. They look so much alike but Luigi's face doesn't have the quick play of expression Paulo's has. His is sterner—maybe resigned is the word. I would guess he would be more patient that Paulo. When he talks to you his eyes gaze at you steadily. It was good to see them laugh together once.

Paulo was telling him about Anthony and then there was a long silence I heard Paulo say "Cathy" and "Tony," and then Luigi spoke for several minutes.

When we were about to leave Paulo drew me down and we both knelt for Luigi's blessing. I never felt a blessing so deeply. We didn't speak all the way back to the car. I was thinking how sad it is that Paulo and Luigi never see each other.

When we were driving back to Perugia, I asked Paulo how Luigi happened to go into the Monastery so young. He has been there for over forty years. Paulo said he thought their mother intended him for the Church from the beginning, but that the war had a great deal to do with the decision. When Luigi wrote that he was taking his final vows, Paulo felt he had lost him. "I feel closer to him now that I have seen him and talked with him," Paulo said.

We came back to our hotel in Perugia, and after dinner sat out on our balcony. All the lights of the city were spread out below us, but I found myself actually missing Etna! Then Paulo told me that Luigi thought we should go home to see about Cathy and Tony. "We know Tony is all right," I said, "and it seems terrible to cut short any of our brief time abroad," but I could see that Paulo had made up his mind. Luigi would be more comfort to Cathy, why didn't he get a dispensation or whatever you have to get, and come to America? I don't like Paulo doing this because Luigi says he should, either. But Paulo put his hands on mine and said, "Can you bear it, Tiresa, carissima?" And, of course, I gave in. So—we are leaving this enchanted place on Friday, shortening our time in Rome and Paris and then flying home instead of sailing.

And I think I know Paulo better now that I have seen where he grew up. There will always be mysteries in his nature, but how dull to be married to someone who was completely predictable. He is exciting to live with.

Nor do I harrow myself as I did over the cruel loss of our child. So it is, and I accept it. At least, having that glimpse of Paulo as he might have looked as a child—as our little son could have been—gives me an odd comfort that I am taking away with me. I can't explain it.

Tiresa laid her hand on the page a moment, then she took out the snapshots that had been tucked in the back of the journal. One was of Paulo in lederhosen leaning against the railing of their balcony in Taormina, laughing. How fragile the grillwork looked compared with the railing and steel netting on the balcony here! Behind him loomed Etna, sending up a smudge of smoke that was barely visible . . . but always there. On the back she had written, "Paulo under his volcano." The other snapshot Paulo took of her that afternoon. The big straw hat they had bought on the Corso tied under her chin because the sun was so hot. She had to smile at her own image, she looked positively glowing with health. That had been a wonderful time for them even if they had to leave so abruptly.

And they had gone back to Chicago to find the letter offering her a temporary appointment teaching Medieval Literature at Boston University to fill the place of someone who had been taken ill. Now someone was taking her place because she was ill. What tedious circles life made.

Tiresa put the journal in her drawer instead of back in the straw trunk. She would burn it some day, but not just yet.

2

When Olive rushed out to throw her arms around Gumshoe that afternoon in late July their excited cries met in the air. "Ollie, you doll!"

"Gummie, I didn't think you'd leave Paris for years. Come in quick. I left Johnny standing by the couch when I saw you drive up."

Now at a year old, Johnny was on the move. He had managed to stagger as far as the façade of the television set and collapsed in a surprised heap.

"You don't mean that that half-grown child is Johnny! I brought him a hand-embroidered suit from Paris this big," Gumshoe wailed. "Well, you can save it for the next one."

"Not immediately, thanks." She could see that Gumshoe thought she was completely absorbed in domesticity. "You're so thin, Gumshoe!"

"You walk up five flights of stairs a day for a year and see what it does to you."

Only now, and in an instant, did Olive feel the full blaze of this new Gumshoe. Her short red hair had grown and was twisted smoothly up on her head, her freckles that used to be so brown and conspicuous were now a subtle accent of color. The round face had thinned, showing the bone structure beneath it, and the mouth with that strange cinnamon shade of lipstick shaped and reshaped itself as she talked. Olive felt a rush of affection.

"How's Ron?" Gumshoe asked.

"Fine. He's away a lot of the time. He won't be back till to-morrow night."

"Good, we'll have a chance to get caught up first. I'm anxious to see him. Remember how he used to think I was always under-foot—in spite of the fact that I got out of my room for him! He thought I had a baleful influence on you."

Johnny toppled over at that convenient moment and Olive swooped him up. "Let me show you your room, and you've got to stay a week at least."

"A guest room, no less! I offered a corner of my floor to my guests."

"Rather more than your floor to Alain, I gather." Olive was feeling Johnny's rear with a practiced hand, but she glanced at Gumshoe in time to feel her own her color rise. "I've got to change Johnny," she said.

"How come you haven't house-trained this paragon of a child by now?" Gumshoe demanded.

"He's halfway there, but I can't spend all my time training him, for Pete's sake." She roughened her voice consciously.

"Art yet!" Gumshoe said later, smoking a cigarette as she con-templated the iris painting.

"We bought it on our wedding trip at an art show on the vil-lage green kind of thing. I had to have it—you know. Gosh, that seems a long time ago. It really did something for our apartment in Boston—gave it panache, as you used to say; but it doesn't come off here, does it? Do you think it's garish?"

"No, it's just—" Gumshoe's shrug was familiar, but she had refined it. "It's just that the room is so bright. I'm used to more shadows."

"There's a regular glare out in this new development; every-thing's exposed," Olive said. "And when Ron's away, I'm simply marooned, of course."

Gumshoe fingered her heavy chain as the sharpest impres-sion she had yet had of Ollie came to her. Ollie wasn't as blissfully happy as she had thought, and it hurt her. She had held Ollie and Ron up to Alain as the completely secure marriage. He had scoffed and she had said he should meet them.

"You look terrific, Gummie," Olive said.

Gumshoe laughed. "Jeans and all! Jeans are good in Paris."

"But it's the shirt." Olive looked at the soft green stuff of Gumshoe's blouse that gathered low on her neck, marveling at it. Gumshoe had always worn shirts with collars, preferably button-down. She had never noticed what a pretty neck Gummie had.

"Which reminds me, I brought you something from Paris, honey child." Gumshoe dived into the room where she had left her bag.

The three strands of blue beads, joined at intervals by a silver band and ending in a deeper blue stone burned Olive's hand as she held it. It was the Paris adventure that she had missed, in all its moods and shifting lights—nothing glaring or unsubtle.

"It's divine, G."

"I thought it was your blue. I got it in an antique shop right on the *Rue de la Castiglione*."

The very sounds and scents of the unknown street came to Olive now as she slipped the necklace over her head.

Gumshoe fed Johnny his supper, talking to him with such animation that his round eyes watched her face and he was hardly aware of the spoonfuls of indistinguishable vegetables he was swallowing.

"You're doing fine," Olive said as she went past.

"Alain said once that he could see me happily wiping the noses of five children," Gumshoe said.

"How is Alain?"

There was a barely perceptible hesitation before she said, with a shrug, "All right, I guess. I hadn't seen him for a month when I left Paris. There you are, Johnny O!" Gumshoe said. "You tell your Mommie you ate it all up."

Olive came to take Johnny. "Super. I never thought of you as maternal, G."

Gumshoe shrugged. "Maybe you can't get away from it if you're female—like menstruating and having breasts and bigger hips." Her voice had a sharp edge.

"This is like being at Heine's, only better," Gumshoe said when they sat out on the tiny patio, drinking a beer.

"Is it better?"

"Sure it is. We don't have some paper to write for tomorrow. We know some of the things we wondered about then—men, for instance. Maybe you didn't. I did. Mostly because none of 'em looked at me, I suppose." Gumshoe was never very specific about things. Olive had an urge to confess how that night with Ron had really been. She watched Bill Oberholtz get out of his car in front of the house next door, as he did practically every evening at seven fifteen. The Winters who both worked were already home on the other side. These were the only people she knew in the neighborhood.

"Are you going back to Paris, or get a job, or what?" Olive asked.

"I'm going back some day, for sure, but I'm going to Columbia in the fall. I just heard."

"You are! What are you going to take?"

"I'm going to medical school."

Olive couldn't believe it. The old Gumshoe, yes. But not this new feminine-looking creature. "What made you decide to do that?" It was too dark to see her face clearly, but Olive heard her shift in her chair.

"No great noble reason. I've always been interested; it's something to get my teeth into."

Olive remembered the prom when Gumshoe had immured herself in the library, claiming she had to work on her history paper. It had won the award that year, but when she congratulated her on it, G. had got red in the face and said, "Shut up, will you!" She kept still now.

Olive had planned their favorite dinner: steak, baked potato and salad, topped off by a chocolate sundae, but the new Gumshoe hardly touched her potato and wouldn't have any dessert. She laughed, "I really did have to work hard to get my weight down to a hundred and fifteen. It took a bit more than just climbing stairs . . ."

"A hundred and fifteen! I weigh a hundred and twenty-two." It depressed Olive to weigh more than Gumshoe. She never had before.

Silence fell over their coffee. Olive hoped Gumshoe would say something about Alain. Gumshoe wanted to hear about Ron. Meanwhile, they shared all the bits and pieces about any of their classmates. "Sal and Betsy have shacked up together in New York, I hear," Gumshoe said. "I mean really," she added after a pause. "Betsy's doing something for Women's Lib. Sal has a publishing job."

"Mmhmm. Remember those awful fights they used to have in college? And then the great reconciliations," Olive said. But all this was filler; their minds were on themselves and each other.

"You liked it better in Boston, I gather," Gumshoe began tentatively.

"Much. I wish you could have seen our apartment—up eleven stories, with a balcony, and overlooking the Charles River. It was neat. And there was the most exciting couple next door; he was Sicilian—an eye doctor, and she used to teach in college. She had a foreign background, too."

"What made them so exciting?"

"Oh—the way they were together, I guess. They're so much more vital to each other than most couples, you know what I mean? If I hadn't known them, I'd never have had any idea that marriage could be that way."

"You don't exactly need a model, for God's sake. You never did have much imagination," Gumshoe grumbled.

"But I mean, how do you know unless you actually see people who matter that way to each other? My Mother and Dad aren't like that, and Ron and I aren't, I'm afraid. I can't explain it." She lapsed into silence.

"And you had a job?"

"Not really; just typing for a professor, but I liked it. I ordered his book when it came out. I'll show it to you—about underwater life. I wish I could get something to do here."

Olive changed the subject. "What was Alain like?"

"Fascinating," Gumshoe said promptly. "I never met anyone like him. We worked together on the mag, you know. Funny, he saw me right away. One day he came by my desk and said, "I want to know you." And we went to dinner that night. And afterwards we talked and talked about—things I've never talked with anyone before—like why we're in this world, and not getting caught in the gyres—you know."

But they had talked about the same things in college, maybe not the gyres but . . . didn't Gumshoe remember?

"Alain's really a photographer; he takes things nobody else sees. Do you know who his idol is? Agee. Alain thinks *Let Us Now Praise Famous Men* is the greatest, and he's doing the same kind of a book, only in France; writing and taking pictures both."

"How long did you know him before you began living together?"

"That first night I went out with him, Alain asked if I wasn't going to ask him up, but I said no. I didn't let him make love to me for a month. By that time, I loved him so much I wanted him to. And at Christmas we began living together in his apartment."

Gumshoe might have been reporting a list of figures, her voice was so colorless. Olive wondered how they had ever split up, but she wouldn't ask that.

"Alain's got pictures that are whole novels in themselves. He has a photograph of an old woman looking at her own naked body that would break your heart." Gumshoe laughed. "You should see the pictures he took of me; you wouldn't believe them. I didn't recognize myself. He said I was photogenic—who'd a thunk it? Say, I'm falling asleep on the wine; I got up at six, so . . ."

There was something too quick about her switch from Alain, but Olive agreed that she was tired, too, though she could have talked all night. Ron was away so many nights, and she just sat there and fell asleep in front of the television. It was a relief to have someone to really talk to.

Even in the purple nightshirt, with her hair pulled back in a braid, Gumshoe looked different from the way she had at college. She stood watching Olive take Johnny to the john.

"What good does that do when he's sound asleep?"

"Oh, it establishes a pattern. There!" Olive exclaimed in triumph at the sound of the small tinkle. "Good boy," she told him, carrying him back to his crib.

Gumshoe was sitting on the end of her bed.

"Have a beer or something?" Olive asked.

"Sure, why not?"

When Olive carried the two glasses back into her bedroom, Gumshoe buried her face in the pillow.

"Gummie!"

Gumshoe sat up quickly. "I hate myself when I let go like this. I decided to do it, and there's no use weeping about it. I had an abortion last month, just before I left Paris; it gets to me now and then."

"That's tough," Olive murmured. It scared her to think of it. She looked away from Gumshoe's face.

"I came out of the clinic afterwards and Alain wasn't there. He was going to pick me up. So I sat down on a bench to wait. And then I saw him coming toward me. He was putting away his camera; he'd been taking a picture of me. 'Women Bereft'— or something. I hated him."

Olive hesitated to say anything.

"Oh well, I'm making too much of it. If you're trying to photograph the whole human comedy, of course, you take everything, and if a woman has just got rid of her child, there's a unique poignance to the shot. You see her as you never had before. Voila!" Gumshoe flung out her empty hands. "So I left him."

"Oh, Gummie," Olive said gently.

Gumshoe got up from the bed. "The whole incident *is* a little

179

gummy, isn't it? I'm through with that name, by the way; call me Jane, will you." She went on into the bathroom.

Olive undressed slowly. She was thinking so hard about Gumshoe that she forgot to drink her beer. Maybe Alain just wanted a picture of her with the light shining on her in a certain way—maybe he wasn't thinking about the abortion at all. She should have talked to him about it; not broken up like that.

"You don't really know what Alain was thinking," Olive said when Gumshoe came back. "Maybe it didn't have anything to do with the . . ."

"It did though. I know him very well. It's hard to explain, Ollie. I don't want a man who's always seeing 'Woman' in me; I want him to see me. If there were other things . . . Don't worry about it. As I said, it was just a rather gummy incident—the kind I seem to let myself in for. G'night." She went into her room and closed the door.

The phone range, and Olive knew it was Ron.

"Hello, Ron?"

"Ollie, you'll never guess where I am. I'm at Paulo's and Tiresa's."

"You are!" How could he be there without her?

"Yes. Rinehart called me in Binghamton and wanted to see me, so I drove right on up to Boston. I called Tiresa—just to say hello, and they asked me up, so I'm spending the night. I wish you were here. Tiresa and Paulo want to say hello."

"Hello, my dear." Tiresa's rich, low voice seemed to belong to another world.

"I wish I were there," was all she could answer.

"We do, too. You must come soon, you and Johnny. I hear you have a flourishing flower bed."

Like a sulky child, Olive said, "It isn't flourishing; there's too much sun."

"But you and Johnny are fine?"

"Oh yes; we're all right."

"*Sposina!*" Paulo had taken the phone. "We're glad to have this young man, but we won't let him come again unless he brings you."

"Oh Paulo—I hope not. It's—it's wonderful to hear you." There was so much to tell, and she wanted to keep talking to him and Tiresa. "Paulo, your godson has two teeth, did Ron tell you? And he's practically toilet trained . . ." Why would she tell him that? How wrapped up in domesticity she must sound.

"I'm not surprised. My godson is precocious. Our love to you, Olive. Ron is getting impatient so I'll give the phone back to him."

But not yet. She wanted to talk to Tiresa again—

"Ollie? I feel better about being here since Gumshoe's there with you. I bet you two are talking a mile a minute."

She had forgotten that Gumshoe was there. "Will you be here tomorrow night in time for dinner?"

"You better believe I will. Two nights away is a long time. Goodnight, Hon. Give my love to you and Johnny."

She hung up the receiver that had suddenly gone dead in her hand. She did think that if Ron had to go to Boston, he could have had dinner with Rinehart and stayed in a motel. He could have waited to go to the Romanos' until she was along. Ron had never seemed that fond of them.

Gumshoe came out in the hall between the two bedrooms. "Nothing's wrong?"

"No. That was Ron. He always called when he's away over night."

"Nice," Gumshoe said. "G'night, again."

3

Once Ron turned off the Massachusetts Turnpike onto the New York Thruway, he felt he was practically home. He'd made these quick trips three times now, but he was going to quit. He'd never meant to get started—it wasn't his kind of thing, really, but he could see how guys got involved.

He pressed the accelerator to pass the oil truck ahead of him and caught sight of the State Patrol car behind him. He had been making time, now he was up to seventy. He checked his speed, but he was out in the left lane by then—better to go ahead and pass. Nobody would stay behind a truck like that and take all those fumes in the face. Damn truck was going seventy; he had to get up to seventy-five to pass him. He took his foot from the accelerator, watching the needle of the speedometer fall back— 70—65—55. He couldn't see—then he heard it, that shrill, jeering siren shriek. Hell! As he started to pull over, the truck shot around him. The truck driver was the one; why did the cop let him get away with it?

Ron watched the trooper park behind him. Now he was walking toward him. Automatically, Ron pulled out his driver's license. It would cost him twenty-five bucks, prob'ly.

"Yes, sir," Ron said, managing a faint smile as the gloved hand touched the door beside him. "I guess you saw that oil truck ahead of me. I stood those gas fumes coming at me as long as I could. Then when I started to go around him, he pushed it up to seventy . . ." he handed over his license.

"If you'll just step back into my car while I fill out this warrant." The trooper had steely blue eyes; hadn't listened to a word he'd said. Ron got out and followed him back.

"What about the truck, Officer? What can you do in a case like that except pass it?"

"Now if you'll just fill this in . . ." The trooper handed him his pen.

"I've got my own rights here." His pen that he used just yesterday to write a good fat policy felt good in his cold fingers. His hands always got sweaty like that, every examination he'd ever taken. Ollie said hers did too.

"If you want to contest this claim . . ."

Ron hesitated, remembering all the stories he'd heard. He looked straight at the steely blue eyes in that expressionless mug. "Will it do me any good if I do?" He gave his words what he felt was the right ironic inflection. "And meanwhile the truck driver goes free!" Sudden rage rose in him so sharply he didn't know whether the cop answered or not. He put his pen back in his pocket and folded the piece of paper, slipping it into his wallet as carefully as if it were a love letter. He got out of the car with what he hoped was dignity. Back in his own car, he watched the cop shoot past him down the highway, doing sixty, already.

The good feeling he'd had as he started out from Paulo's was gone under a wash of anger and chagrin. He leaned his head back a second, and moved his shoulders to try to relax. He'd been tense since he started this morning, and he'd been pushing it. Now that he had decided to tell Ollie, he wanted to get it over with.

He wished to Hell that Gumshoe wasn't there; he'd have to wait till she left to talk to Ollie. He had never understood what Ollie saw in her. Her trying to get Ollie to go to Paris instead of getting married. He watched three cars pass him, doing seventy at least, but they were safe enough; the cop was miles ahead by now. He was sweating again, working himself into a lather. He unbuttoned his collar and pulled his tie off. He didn't need to worry. Ollie would understand. He'd remind her of the way she almost smashed up everything between then that time, and then came back to him. Same kind of thing. She admitted that she didn't know what got into her. And then she said maybe it was a good thing, because now she knew she couldn't live without him. That was the way he felt about her. And this would make our marriage all the stronger, he would tell her. It was the truth.

He saw the first Syracuse turn-off. He'd called Betsy from there that first time. She was a lot easier to talk to on the phone than Ollie; always sounded crazy to see him. He could never tell about Ollie. Sometimes, she sounded as flat as a pancake, or abused that she was home all alone. He wondered if she was as fond of Johnny as other mothers were. His mother said she'd be contented after the baby came. He'd told her she was right, that Ollie was, but he wasn't all that sure.

Ollie had sounded sunk when he said he was at Tiresa's, but when he told her how he happened to go there—he was going to play it straight with Ollie, she'd be proud of him. There had been that time with Tiresa this morning after Paulo had left. He'd almost talked to her about Ollie. He had an idea she knew a lot—about life. Being married to that old Sicilian couldn't be that easy. You couldn't tell him that Paulo didn't have a roving eye. And Tiresa seemed to understand Ollie. But it was just as well he kept his mouth shut. He stopped at the supermarket where he often took Ollie to get groceries and bought a quart of butter pecan ice cream; that was their favorite. He felt pretty much in control of his life, even a little noble as he swung into their drive.

"Anybody home?" he called through the screen door. Then he heard them out on the little square of cement in the back.

"Oh Ron!" Olive came running in. I didn't think you'd get back this early."

"Surprised you." He gave her a real kiss. "I sure missed you at Tiresa's. They send their love. How's Johnny?" He felt himself talking too fast.

"He's fine. And Jane's here, you know."

"Jane?"

"She doesn't want to be called Gumshoe any more." The single remark made them conspirators.

"Well, Jane. Good to see you," he said, going over to shake her hand. He'd almost forgotten how she looked, but he could see she'd changed. She was feeding Johnny.

"Hello, Ron," she said in a cool voice. Nothing warm about her.

"Hello, fellow. Can't you stop feeding long enough to say hello to your old dad?" Because of this roommate of Ollie's, his voice took on a bluff note, a little louder than usual.

"She's simply wonderful with Johnny," Olive said. "He eats every bit of his supper when she feeds him."

All of a sudden, Ron wanted to be feeding Johnny as he often did when he got home. Instead, he said, "Oh, hon, I brought some ice cream; I've got to put it in the frig. Jane, can I make you a drink?"

"Thanks, Ron, but I'm in no hurry. Let's wait until Olive is free."

He resented her taking charge like that. As if he didn't think of Ollie.

"No, you and Ron have a drink; I'll be free here in a few minutes," Olive said.

"All right, vodka and tonic, please Ron."

They didn't have any vodka. Mostly, they drank beer, but he'd got in the gin because Ollie said Gumshoe liked it. "Can't give you vodka; I can give you a gin and tonic." As he made the drinks, he wondered what brought her back from Paris if she had such a good job and was living so blissfully with some Frenchman as Ollie said. Why didn't she stay there? But she sure was better looking than he remembered. He took out the drinks and sat down across from her.

"What do you think of Johnny?" he asked as an opener, and liked her better when she sounded genuinely enthusiastic. "How was Paris?" he asked next.

"Rather interesting," she said, and for a moment he was deceived

185

into thinking she wasn't so crazy about it, but then he got it. This was her new way of talking—offhand.

"But I'm glad to be back," Gumshoe added.

"Excuse me. I'll just run up and interview my son before Ollie pops him into bed. I have to be away so darn much I miss out on him." A sense of important pressures suffused his voice as he ran up the six stairs to the bedroom level of the house.

Gumshoe sipped her drink and looked out past the clotheslines and similar patios of the row of houses. She was getting it right between the eyes, the happily married life. It looked pretty sweet, except Ollie didn't seem all that thrilled. She wouldn't take it in exchange for what she had had, except she'd like having Johnny. Ron was too much the heavy father figure. Ridiculous to remember that he had once seemed such a romantic figure of passion to her in college, and Juliet had nothing on Olive. Once this afternoon Ollie'd been about ready to say something, and then fooled around with Johnny instead. Now that Ron was home there wouldn't be any more time to talk. She'd leave in the morning, and from here on out she and Ollie would grow farther apart. It was sad when you thought how close they'd been once. She rather wished she hadn't told Ollie so much about herself.

Olive came out with her drink and sat down. "Ron is so crazy about the baby he's disappointed if there isn't time to play with him before dinner, so I just wait. This tastes good. Usually, Ron has a beer when he gets home. I don't bother with it, besides, if I had a beer every night, I really would gain weight."

Now, oddly, Gumshoe felt her saying something else—something more.

"You don't need to worry the way you buzz around all day. You never seem to settle down; you know what I mean?" She was saying, something's on your mind—tell me. If you want to, that is. I told you . . .

Ron came downstairs with Johnny on his shoulder. "This young man has no thought of going to bed. He wants to go for a walk with his Dad first. Okay, Ollie?"

186

"Sure. We're having casserole."

The two girls watched him from across the strip of yard. He let Johnny put his hands on the cross support of the clothesline posts. "Hang on." Ron held him around the waist and let his legs dangle a couple of seconds. "See that! See our son, Gumshoe."

"Precocious!" Gumshoe called back, and Olive remembered Paulo saying that over the phone.

"If we were back in the apartment in Boston, I'd invite the Romanos for dinner tonight. I'd love to have you meet them. They're—well, honestly, you've never seen a middle-aged couple live so . . . deeply. You could feel it in the way they talked and the way they looked at each other. Oh, I've heard them furious at each other, but it didn't seem to matter."

Across the yard, Ron was singing *Yankee Doodle* to Johnny as he carried him past the row of patios.

"Alain and I lived deeply," Gumshoe said. "Maybe too deeply. That was why—" She broke off, leaning her head back to slide the cube of ice from her glass into her mouth.

"I don't think Ron and I do," Olive said in a small dry voice. "We love each other, of course, and Ron's doing well, and we both adore Johnny, but sometimes I feel it—our marriage, I mean, doesn't go deep enough. Or maybe it doesn't have anything to do with our marriage; maybe it's just me."

Ron came running back, bouncing Johnny into ecstatic screams, and landed him in Olive's lap. "There you are, Mama. I thought it was just about time to make Jane another drink and I certainly need one. Want a refill, hon?"

"No thanks. Ron, you got Johnny all sweaty, just when I had him ready for bed," she said in mock complaint.

"Couldn't be helped. We men have to have our little play," Ron said cheerfully.

"Well, it must have been pretty interesting," Ron said after Gumshoe had been telling about her job in Paris. "Ollie and I hope to get to Europe one of these days, but it will have to wait a while.

Right now, I'm having an exciting time with my job. It's opened up considerably since I've started working." He felt good as he said it. He saw himself, devoted to his family, working hard. "And Ollie does her share. Here, Ollie, I'll take the dishes off." He felt at ease, too, with this old roommate.

"How come you changed you name from Gumshoe?" he asked. "I always got a kick out of that. You must have lost it in Paris."

"Oh, I decided it was a trifle juvenile."

"Well, Jane, I've forgiven you, but there was a time when you almost wrecked our marriage, trying to take Ollie off to Paris with you." His second drink had warmed him, but not as much as the memory of Ollie turning Gumshoe down.

"I tried hard, but I guess she was too much in love." There, that would satisfy him, the pompous ass. Maybe Ollie had been in love with love more than with him. "Thank you, I really can't eat any dessert," she said as Ron set a dish in front of her.

"Not even Gilbert's Butter Pecan—ninety-nine-and-a-half percent pure?" Ron demanded. "Leave it here, Ollie and I can divide it." But he noticed that Olive was only playing with hers; afraid of gaining weight, of course. Well, Gumshoe was too skinny for his taste. She kept watching him the way she used to when he'd go up to see Ollie at college. He remembered how she turned beet red the first time he saw her after she had moved out of the room that time. He supposed he had, too. They were kids then.

"It's too buggy outside; we better have our coffee in the house," Olive said, bringing in three little coffee cups on a tray.

"No rush, I'll push off after Ron goes. I don't want to slow him up," Gumshoe had said the night before. Now she and Olive lingered at the breakfast table over still another cup of coffee, but they didn't have much to say. They had met and the meeting had brought them closer together, but each had said more than she intended, and the realization made them both a little uncomfortable—yet relieved, too, from the pressure of loneliness.

"Golly, it's after ten. I've got to go," Gumshoe said finally.

"It's been wonderful to have you here, G." Olive said.

"You know how it's been for me. Just had to check in on you."

"You've got to come up in the fall—some long weekend."

"Try anyway," Gumshoe said, knowing that she wouldn't, not that soon. "It won't be easy going back to school," her voice trailed off. "Don't forget your Aunt Gummy," she said to Johnny, sitting in his high-chair. "Take care," she gave Olive a quick kiss.

"You too." Already they were moving into their separate lives. From here on, they would only get together to report.

4

"I've told you all there is to tell. As I said, I met Betsy at Rineharts' one time when I stopped by with some stuff, and they asked me in for a drink. She's Ben's sister-in-law. I didn't go out hunting someone, for God's sake." He wished now that he had waited to tell her all this in bed, in the dark, instead of sitting here in the living room, with Ollie staring at him across the whole length of the coffee table. "We just seemed to click—the way you do with some people."

"Before we moved here?" She tried to place herself back in that time. It was more real than this moment. She had thought they were—happy. Well, what everyone seemed to think was being happy. And all that time they were living together and making love, Ron was making love to this girl. She wanted to scream at him, to burst out the way Tiresa had. She tried. "You oaf!" She screwed up her face as she said it, but it didn't come out right; it wasn't loud enough, and she had never used that word before. She felt foolish, miserable.

Ron was frowning, not looking at her. "That was when you were so moody, you know."

"I wasn't being moody. I was busy with Johnny and thinking about moving; it wasn't easy . . ."

"I know, hon. It wasn't an easy time for either of us. But we're over that now. I feel just the way you felt back in school: I couldn't stand the thought of losing you. 'Member you said maybe it was good in a way; now you knew you couldn't live without me. That's the way I feel about you."

"When did you have this great awakening?" She looked at him as coldly as if she had never seen him before.

"I wasn't happy about it, even all the time I was seeing Betsy, but we just seemed drawn together. And that day, I felt I had to see her once more, but when I got to Boston, I realized I couldn't break it off if I went to see her. So I called the Romanos and went there instead. That wasn't so damn easy, either. I drove out there and looked up at the balcony of our old apartment, I thought how you had always loved it, and I could almost see you there . . ." If Ollie would say something it would be easier.

"And the next day, as soon as I'd been to the office, I drove straight home. It didn't help to have Gumshoe here going on about Paris and you drinking up every word of it."

Olive's eyes followed the lines of the iris to the point where they disappeared into the white background.

"Ollie."

"What?"

"Can't you see how it happened?"

She didn't answer.

"I didn't need to tell you any of this, you know. Most men—" Olive's eyes moved back to him. "You didn't see anything wrong when your roommate went off and lived with some guy for a year or so. You were dazzled and thought she was really living it up."

"She wasn't doing it in secret, and she didn't happen to be married to someone else."

"Oh, come off it, Ollie. Our marriage will be all the stronger, if you'll let it."

"I'm not so sure. You must have thought you loved her—Betsy." She pronounced the name delicately. "You can't forget her just like that. I don't want to talk about it any more tonight. Okay?"

Olive went out to the kitchen and found innumerable things

to do. She made up a quart of powdered milk and a pitcher of orange juice—both tasks she always left for morning. She saw Johnny's finger prints on the lower half of the refrigerator door and wiped them off.

Ron stood in the doorway. "Ollie."

"Yes."

"Don't be like that. It's you I love. I didn't feel the same way about Betsy."

"I said I didn't want to talk about it any more tonight." Why did she retreat like that? Why didn't she fight it out. "Anger clears the blood," Tiresa had said. But she couldn't.

"But I have to go to Binghamton tomorrow. I'll be away all day and tomorrow night."

"I'm used to that. Anyway, I need time to think."

Ron got himself a beer, but instead of opening it he set it down on the counter and went over and put his hands on Olive's arms, turning her toward him. "Ollie, what the Hell are we doing? We love each other. Don't throw away what we have." He tried to pull her close, but she held herself stiffly.

"The terrible thing, Ron, is that I . . . don't feel worse than I do about you . . . having this affair. I don't think our marriage ever went very deep," she said, barely above a whisper.

"You know that isn't true, Ollie. The trouble with you is that you think you're Meryl Streep making a big scene. He flipped the ring on the beer can until it gave way with a sharp snap.

After Ron drove off the next morning, the day hung slack. Olive took Johnny out to the communal sand box and sat on one corner of it, filling his pail with sand and pouring it over his feet until he laughed. The girl two houses down brought her little girl over to play with him. Olive and the girl talked about the way prices were rising.

"Could you keep an eye on Johnny for a few minutes?" Olive asked. The mothers often took turns going into their houses, to transfer the clothes from the washer to the dryer, or take the rollers out of their hair, or just to have a change.

But the house hardly belonged to her this morning. Olive looked out the window at the house directly across from theirs— exactly the same except that the top was brown and the bottom tan. Ron had called it the brown derby when they first saw it, and she had thought how clever he was. He was already going to see Betsy then. She lowered the Venetian blinds so that a shadow fell across the iris. It was too bright; Gumshoe was right. Professor Halstead's book lay on the table and she leafed through it, ignoring the introduction and the first two chapters. She had begun typing at chapter three. She read a couple of pages feeling almost as if she had written them.

"In the greatest abysses, as much as three fathoms in depth, we find absolute darkness, freezing temperatures and terrible pressures. Fish at this level often eat each other . . ." She closed the book and went back out into the sun.

"Thank you. I'll be here for the next half hour. If you want to leave Jill, go ahead." The children were playing contentedly. All she had to do was sit here in the sun.

Olive was feeding Johnny when the mail came. She heard it fall through the slot in the door, but let it lie there until she was through. A letter from Ron's mother, probably, she was a great letter-writer, or from hers, an appeal for money from her college or Ron's, or a bill—nothing exciting. After Johnny was in bed, she picked it up. One envelope, addressed to her, had something foreign about the handwriting—a matter of the "f" and an extra flourish on the capitals. On the other side was Paulo's office address.

Dear Olive,
 I write to tell you that Tiresa is in the hospital again. She is wretched. I believe it might lift her spirits to hear from you, if you can find time to write. She had missed you so much. Please do not mention her being ill in the

hospital or that I have written you. It would be better if you found some little pretext for writing, or some new happening to tell her about.

With affectionate greetings to all,
Paulo

Olive sat on the couch rereading it. She spent most of the afternoon composing a letter.

August 5th, 1976
Dear Tiresa,

I still haven't forgiven Ron for being at your apartment when I wasn't. But it was so good to talk to both of you. I've been going to write to you ever since.

My college roommate visited me this week. She had just returned from Paris and that was exciting. She is going into medical school in the fall. Needless to say, she is very cerebral. We talked our heads off. I did wish you were just down the hall so she could meet you. We talked about living deeply, and I said you and Paulo did more than any two people I knew.

Do you remember the time in the country when we talked about marriage? I wish I could talk to you now. Our marriage is in a state of crisis at the moment. I feel like someone in one of those horrible soap operas that run on the daytime on T-V.

Ron has been having an affair with some girl in Boston—the sister-in-law of his boss, but decided—on his own—that he was going to break it off. That's why he called you that night and stayed there so he wouldn't go and see the girl again. He came home and told me all about it. He didn't need to; I had no idea that he was seeing somebody. He says it makes our marriage all the stronger because he knows now he could never live without me. But the trouble is, I believe I could live without him—that maybe I want to. Not just because of this little affair; I know this sort of thing happens all the time, but because of the way I feel.

I don't really care if Ron has been seeing this girl. If I weren't married and didn't have Johnny, I would leave him, I think. I may anyway. He's a nice guy and I was thrilled about him in the beginning, but it seems as if we never got any further. We don't really have too much to say to each other any more. Sex is our best thing.

I hope you aren't shocked, but I don't think things do shock you. Do you think I'm shallow that I don't feel more about Ron?

I hope all is fine with you. Johnny is growing and walks hanging onto my finger.

Love to you and Paulo,
Olive

She got Professor Halstead's book and settled down on the couch to read. The underwater world was a relief from her own today.

5

His visit to the hospital last night hadn't gone well, Paulo thought
as he ate his breakfast. Perhaps he had looked anxious; he must
watch that. Tiresa had been pleased with the violets he brought,
but sometimes when he took flowers, he felt too sharply how
soon his Persephone would leave the land of the sun and growing things.

Tiresa was discouraged. He had never seen her give up so completely. It bothered him that she was willing to wear hospital jack-
ets; always before she had insisted on wearing her own gowns.
And she was letting the nurse brush her hair and put it in a braid.
"What difference does it make?" she had asked when he wanted
to have someone from the beauty shop come in. It didn't do any
good to tell her how much she was improving. She didn't believe
him. He carried his unfinished breakfast over to the sink.

At least, this morning he had Olive's letter to take. It would
make him late, but he wanted Tiresa to have it. He was grateful
for Olive writing so promptly after his note.

"Olive is turning into quite a correspondent," Paulo said as
he gave Tiresa the letter.

"Yes, isn't it surprising? Aren't you going to wait and read it?"

"I haven't time. I'll read it when I come in this evening."

Tiresa read the letter before her bath and thought about it
all through the tiresome ablutions. Amused as she did it, she
fastened the letter to her clipboard now and started to reread it

with a pencil in hand, but with a tenderness she had never felt for the many themes that had been clipped to that board over the years. Her pencil made a faint check in the margin by the first paragraph. That visit of her roommate must have had something to do with Olive's reaction. Olive had been wistful about not going to Paris that very first night at the apartment, hadn't she?

Tiresa's eyes lingered on the sentence about living deeply, touched that Olive should feel that way about Paulo and herself. They did live deeply together, and now, at the end, she mustn't spoil it because they were facing separation; mustn't let Paulo try to pretend that they weren't, either.

Olive's writing her about the crisis in their lives was touching, but a little incredible. She wrote so coldly. That time in Sicily with Asunta, she had brooded over Paulo's half-rueful, half-blithe attitude when he came back, but she wouldn't have dreamed of telling another woman about it.

She remembered how silent they had been as they ate their late dinner on the balcony that night. And after they heard Carmela's feet running down the stairs, and the villa was theirs, they went on sitting in silence, watching the lights of the cars coming down the curving road. As it grew darker, they could see the red fire of Etna. "Always there," Paulo had said. "When you think it's gone cold."

She had understood well enough what he was trying to say, but she didn't help him. And he had gone on about the fools who continued to live at the foot of Etna. "I suppose living there is their life," she had said—something like that. She had known so clearly that Paulo was her life, whatever. And she his.

Tiresa lifted the glass on her tray and drew the water up to her lips through the angled plastic tube until sudden weak tears that stung her eyes had time to be absorbed. Olive wouldn't have any idea what the words meant . . . that Ron was her life. It shocked her that she said so flatly—how did she say it? Tiresa went back to the letter. "I believe I could live without him."

What an ironic contrast Olive's life was to her own. She had wanted her child more than anything in the world—excepting always Paulo, and at first Olive hadn't wanted hers. And now that all she wanted was to have more years with Paulo, here Olive was saying that she could live without Ron. Leave him by all means if you could do it so easily, she would like to write her, but she wouldn't.

When he came in that evening, Paulo was cheered to find Tiresa sitting up in her bed, her clipboard on the table in front of her. He had something else to bring her, too, better than flowers. "Tiresa, wonder of wonders, the galleys of the Colucci article."

"Very nice. Now you must follow it up right away with that report of your four hundred cases."

"Blessed be cruel and white womankind!" Paulo groaned, grinning at her.

"You must though, Paulo. Or it'll come back to haunt you." For a second her eyes held his, but he moved out from under them. "Tell me about Olive's letter." He sat down on the bed to read it, taking a long time at it. Her tray was brought in while he was reading and she ate more than usual.

Once he laughed. "What an anticlimax for poor Ron to come home to pour out his guilt and remorse, expecting anger, threats of leaving him, maybe, but never indifference."

Now he was scowling. "Don't you think her reaction was strange, Tiresa?"

"Honest, anyway."

"But if she loved him in the beginning, I don't see . . ." It was too much for him.

"What do those two young things know about love, after all?"

"One just knows about love. Remember how radiant she was, Tiresa, that night we first met her. They were just back from their wedding trip."

"Radiant over the idea of love, perhaps, and the experience of sex. That remark of hers—"

"'Sex is our best thing'," Paulo read from the letter. "That seems a little crude to me for *la Sposina*.

"Why? There is nothing sacrosanct about sex to the young."

"The young—I give up." He tossed the letter over to her. "The American young," he added. "I think in Sicily they are still the same. But she will feel differently. You must write her Tiresa, and tell her so. Poor child! I must confess though that I feel for Ron. He must have been in the throes of this thing when he was here, do you realize that?"

She nodded. "Without knowing it, we were keeping him from further sinning. If it weren't tragic for them, it would seem like a scene from a French comedy."

Paulo was thinking that Tiresa was more like herself than she had been in weeks—completely absorbed in the troubles of these children. He had been inspired to ask Olive to write, but he hadn't expected such an outpouring.

"All I dare do is to tell her that we don't think she is shallow, and we are sure that she will know what is best."

Paulo waved her remark aside. "No, Tirese, *donna savia che sei!* You must tell her about life; tell her to forgive Ron and love him. Think of Johnny. You must tell her to keep her marriage; that is crucial. Perhaps you can come home tomorrow, you seem so much better. Saturday, anyway."

"Certainly I can come home tomorrow! And Paulo, no celebration this time. These trips are coming too often. Just let me slip in and begin living again." But she thought, as she listened to his heels on the corridor, he would pay no attention. Paulo always had to celebrate.

Dear Olive,

To get your letter was like having you run down the hall and drop in. [No need to tell her that she was in the hospital.] *I was touched by your writing so frankly about* [she hesitated and then used Olive's phrase]— *the crisis in your marriage. That crisis will cause you both to go to a deeper understanding of each other, if you let it.* [She stopped in dissatisfaction. Her tone was too

199

Olympian, as if she knew all the answers, or worse, were running a love-lorn column. But this was only a rough draft, just to get her ideas down on paper.] *Don't make any decisions quickly, and, however difficult, try to talk frankly with each other.* [Now she sounded like one of those marriage counselors whom she had always looked on with a dubious eye. She crossed out the sentence.] *As we all do, you will find yourselves guilty of many sins against each other—infidelities and failures of the minds and heart as well as any of the body, and they are often the more grievous ones.* [Would Olive know what she was talking about? Still, leave it for a minute and put it another way.] *And you must think what it would be like to live without Ron, and the difference it would make to Johnny. I remember you came back sooner than you had planned the time you went off to New Jersey by yourself.*

As I reread your letter again, I see that you really do not ask me for all these comments, but only one question: whether or not I think you are shallow because you do not at this moment feel a deeper attachment to Ron. To that I can answer an emphatic no. Perhaps you cannot judge how much or how little you feel for Ron just now. Give yourself time.

I won't try to say any more, for I don't want to get in the way of your own honest thinking.

My love to you,
Tiresa

It was true; she felt a deep affection for that girl. The letter wouldn't do as it was, but she wouldn't write it over tonight.

Paulo stopped by the nurses' station the next morning to see Tiresa's chart and read: Patient was writing until eleven o'clock, and seemed alert and cheerful.

6

It's odd that we haven't heard from Olive, don't you think, Tiresa?" Paulo asked. "You wrote to her over a month ago."

"Maybe she's too much involved in her own problems, which would be a good sign. Or maybe she's sorry she wrote me so frankly. And, of course, my letter may have put her off." She and Paulo were sitting on the balcony after dinner. Olive and Ron's troubles had been far from her mind; she had been thinking of the leaves starting to turn at the farm. Now in late September there would be a flag of color here and there on the green hill back of the house.

"They moved here two years ago this month," Paulo said.

"I was sick when they moved in, I remember; you told me about them."

All evening she had tried to think that she felt better than she did. At least, she had dressed in slacks and a shirt for the first time in days, and been up when Paulo came home. She had too little energy to talk.

"Yes," she said when he suggested a brandy, and was glad to have a glass in her hand and the sip of fire trickling down her throat.

"I had Stebbins pull out those records on the glaucoma cases today," Paulo said after a long silence. "The comparison of those treated with . . ."

Her mind wandered as he talked about them. That frightened

her. Was she losing the power to concentrate, too? What had he just said? The little glass fell in her lap. She must have drowsed for an instant. Paulo stopped talking.

"Wouldn't you like to go into bed, Tirese?"

"I guess so. I seem . . ." Her voice trailed off. Paulo was helping her out of the chair. She felt beaten, yet it was good to have Paulo lifting her up on her bed, slipping off her clothes, kissing her gently. She moved onto the pillow, closing her eyes. "Just tired tonight . . ."

"I know, Tiresa darling."

"Coming soon?"

"Pretty soon." He turned out the light and went back out to the balcony.

7

The game on the television was only in the first quarter when Olive came into the living room, but Ron turned it off.

"Don't you want to watch the game?" Olive asked. They were very polite with each other these days.

"I'll get the score later. Come sit here."

Olive sat down at the other end of the couch. "Ron, I don't like to go off and leave the house as it is. Are you sure you want to stay here?"

"You may want to come back. When you get to your folks' you may feel the way you did the other time."

"No. This is different. We've gone through all this. I'm really not coming back."

"I can pack up and put the stuff in storage if it gets too lonesome here for me."

She resisted the plea. "It means leaving you with the whole thing."

"No sweat. I'll be coming down in a couple of weeks to see you and Johnny anyway. We can talk about it then. It's funny how fast things change, isn't it? A year ago you'd never have believed we'd be doing this sort of damn thing, would you?"

She didn't answer.

"You sure you don't want me to drive you out to Summit tomorrow? Rinehart said anything he could do to help, or if I needed some time, he'd—"

203

"No thank you," she cut in. "And I don't like you talking over our private affairs with your boss."

Ron went out to the kitchen to get a beer. "Want a beer, Ollie?" he called back as though it were any ordinary night.

"No thanks."

This whole thing was Ollie's doing, Ron told himself. He never would have broken up their marriage. Hadn't he given up Betsy, and that wasn't easy. Now Ollie said it wasn't because of Betsy; that she was even grateful to Betsy for making her realize they just didn't mean enough to each other. But she was plain nuts—if Ollie didn't mean a hell of a lot to him, he wouldn't have bothered to tell her about Betsy in the first place. Couldn't she get that through her head? He hadn't really believed she would walk out when it came right down to it; he didn't yet. He carried his beer back to the living room.

Olive jumped up from the couch. "I guess I'll make a cup of coffee."

When she came back, she sat in the chair across from Ron. "You know how sorry I am about everything." She took a quick swallow.

"Sure, I know. I just think we're giving Johnny a raw deal. I never thought of my son growing up in a broken home."

That bothered her, and she didn't answer at first. "I know that," she said finally, "and I hate it for him, but I think it's better to find out now how we feel than go on this way for the rest of our lives. Better for Johnny, too, as he grows up. It's my fault mostly, I guess."

"Let's just say it's both our faults. Okay? A lot of it is all this women's lib business that got you stirred up. A guy at the office was saying that's the reason a lot of marriages have cracked up."

"Oh Ron, it hasn't anything at all to do with it."

But he didn't want to argue tonight. "Gosh, Ollie, when you think how crazy we were about each other; we couldn't wait to get married . . ."

"It's no use going back over everything. We've done that." She was close to tears, but it didn't make her feel any different.

"I know, but we haven't changed that much, Ollie; we can't have."

They sat silent. Olive set her cup down, not looking at him.

"Ollie," Ron's voice had altered; a different note had come into it. "Ollie, couldn't we make love just once? You know how we are together. It wouldn't mean—Ollie . . ." His voice broke.

It got to her for a minute, and the way he said Ollie. She had to look away from him. Her eyes caught on the iris painting. Ron could have it if he wanted, or he could throw it out. She wondered how she had ever thought she had to have it.

8

Tiresa turned over the postcard that Bessie had brought her. It was from Olive, postmarked New Jersey.

> February 28
>
> *Dear Tiresa, I should have written you to let you know that Ron and I are separated, and Johnny and I are living at home with my family. I planned to get a part-time job, but Mother came down with the flu and it hasn't worked out, so I'm pretty much running the house and doing this and that around here.*
>
> Love to you and Paulo from Johnny and me. Write me sometime. I miss you.

The last sentence was written around the edge of the card. How like Olive, Tiresa thought, to announce such a momentous step so tersely on a postcard. Obviously, her letter to Olive had made little impression since she had never bothered to answer it. In a way, Tiresa felt dismissed by this card. Didn't it say, You see, I have come to my own decision and planned out my life? She must have thought of them suddenly and felt guilty and fired off this card. Well, it would be interesting to see whether they went back together or were divorced. Olive was like so many students she had had. She knew a chapter or two in their lives, but never the whole story.

9

Sometimes it seemed to Olive that she had never been away from Summit, New Jersey, nor gone to college, nor been married and had a child; her way of life was so much as it used to be before all that. A return to the womb, she told herself. Some of her friends at Chelmsford School for Girls had married and moved away, but Maggie Burwell and Mary Chase were still there, and Louise Fennell—Louise hadn't married but had a good job in a real estate office. Maggie's and Mary's husbands were part of the old crowd. Now and then Olive was invited to dinner opposite an eligible young man, but she looked at him with cool detachment, and saw him looking at her with curiosity for, of course, he would have been told that she was getting her divorce, that she had a young child, and was really so brave. No one knew what the trouble had been . . . she had never discussed it outside the family.

They were getting a divorce on the basis of "irretrievable breakdown of the marriage." She mouthed the words to herself. It was true; they couldn't possibly build it up again.

"When you know that he was having an affair with that woman, Olive, I don't see why it wasn't his fault entirely," her mother protested.

"You don't understand, Mother. Just take my word for it, will you? It was mostly my fault," Olive said, and her mother had gone away with pursed lips, bewildered that a daughter of hers could be involved in divorce.

Mother and Dad were marvelous, as Olive told the girls, and so eager to see her getting back into things at Summit that they were almost always glad to baby-sit. She kept busy enough: she had been head of the book sale the YW put on in November, and one afternoon a week she told stories to children at the library. She did marketing and planned the meals, but none of those things was like having a job and earning your own money. Before she fell asleep at night, she let her mind run over possible careers, lulling herself to sleep with glamorous possibilities, but in the morning she returned to the plain fact that so far she had found no job. She had another idea that she kept rejecting, and then coming back to. She'd like to go to graduate school and take marine biology . . . It was wild, of course.

"Olive is quieter than she used to be," Olive's mother fretted. "Even at meals, don't you notice it, Bill? She never used to be like that."

Mr. Hamill frowned at the newspaper he was reading. "Well, yes, she does seem a little quiet sometimes, but that's natural, I guess, considering what she's gone through."

When the time came for their annual winter cruise, the Hamills were worried about leaving Olive and Johnny alone. "Why don't you ask Louise Fennel to stay with you nights, dear?" Mrs. Hamill suggested, but Olive was firm.

"I don't want anyone. After all, I stayed alone when Ron was away. I *am* a grown woman, you know, Mother. You'll only be gone for a month, for Pete's sake." The scornful tone of her voice kept Mrs. Hamill from further protest.

But the house in Summit, filled with all the familiar things she had known all her life, was far more depressing to Olive when she was there alone than in the split-level house in the development. After her parents had left for their usual mid-winter cruise, she felt abandoned. This morning she escaped under the pretense to herself of having to go for groceries.

She parked the family's car in back of the super-market and carried Johnny into the enormous structure whose doors opened to all without even the push of a hand. Soothing music floated over the heads of the shoppers, drowning out the constant beeps of the cash registers. In the shifting air-currents, red, green, and orange pennants fluttered their colossal bargain values, and bright neon lights glared down without relief on the crowded aisles. Olive settled Johnny at one end of the metal cart and joined the slow procession of human beings pushing their carts through the maze of produce—boxed, canned, or green.

Olive had little to buy, but today she began at aisle one and wheeled her way slowly up and down each corridor, one more woman-with-child in the dilatory progression. She was in no hurry to get back home, picking up baby food and canned peaches, passing up the array of detergents. What was she doing trailing up and down the aisles of a super-market with nothing on her mind but killing time? Rushing in with your head full of what you were going to do next was one thing, but wandering around just to be doing something out of the house was the absolute pits. She felt an avocado and resisted it, considered the apples and remembered she still had four; she'd forgotten to bring her list, but there were only a couple of things on it. Johnny was staring at a pyramid of golden oranges, and reached out to a cluster of bananas hanging from a hook. When Olive moved the cart closer to get some bananas, he reached out and seized one of the orange balls, toppling them down around him and frightening him into hysterical screams.

"Oh Johnny," Olive wailed under her breath, not looking at the staring faces around her, ignoring the laughter. She took him up in her arms, trying to comfort him, but he was inconsolable.

"You gotta watch kids every minute in the store," a woman told her. "I always told my kids, 'you can't touch or you can't go.'"

When a store employee appeared and started picking up the oranges, she managed to get a dollar out of her bag to give him. "I'm so sorry . . ."

"We're paid to clean up the messes the customers make all the time, lady, we ain't allowed to take tips."

She bought a box of animal crackers and gave Johnny two in each fist before the sobs ended, then she wheeled swiftly to the meat counter and picked up two chicken breasts. Then she remembered Ron saying, "Gosh, Ollie, we've had chicken two days running, what do you say to a steak?" She put back the chicken breasts and found a small strip steak instead. Well, why not? She was living, too, wasn't she? She felt a little reckless after the ordeal with the oranges. Stimulated by the thought of the steak, she added a bottle of domestic wine and some seedless grapes. They had grapes that time at the farm with Tiresa and Paulo—not little green pellets like these, big ones. She pushed her cart toward the check-out counter and spread out her purchases, watching the items appear in red figures on the machine in front of the clerk. $13.97. How had they added up to so much?

As she came in, carrying Johnny in one arm, a bag of groceries in the other, the house closed around them again. She knew they were lucky to have it to come to, but it felt like a tomb today. Hurriedly, she turned on the small kitchen radio and talked to Johnny in an animated voice while she got his lunch ready.

When he was in bed for his nap, she came slowly downstairs. She remembered falling down these stairs when she was four or five, seeing the world upside down through the banisters, and knocking out a tooth. The sight of her own bloody face in the mirror at the foot of the stairs had terrified her.

She had thrown her wedding bouquet from these stairs, and she and Ron had come down them when they left. She had been rather pleased that she was the first of their class at college to be married; now she must be the first to be divorced.

Across from the hall, in the living room she could see the piano at which she had spent hours practicing exercises and playing pieces. She never thought of playing now. Standing there in all its polished silence the piano mocked her. Didn't anything she started ever turn out? Or was she a born loser? The only thing she had ever done that took guts was to break up their marriage. But if this was all she was going to do with her life, she might as well have stayed married.

It was snowing again. After Johnny woke, they would take a walk in the snow. If they were back in Cambridge now, in the apartment, the Romanos might ask them to go to the farm this weekend. She wished she could see Tiresa and Paulo—she could talk to Tiresa. She hadn't really talked to anyone since she'd been home.

Tiresa said to come and see them any time. She could take a bus, she and Johnny. That would be cheaper than a plane. Why didn't she? Next week after the folks got back, maybe. She went to the phone and called the bus company and found out departure and arrival times.

She would write and ask Tiresa. Surely she would tell her to come—unless Tiresa was back in the hospital. She should have written her more often.

Olive ran upstairs to get the postcard she had bought at the Metropolitan Museum because it reminded her of the Hancock and Prudential towers across from their old balcony—a painting of Klee's, called *City of Towers*, in wonderful colors, with all kinds of depth and lights and shadows. Tiresa would love it; she might even guess why she chose that card.

10

Tiresa has been writing so steadily she hadn't seen the snow begin, and then, between one word and the next, a wave of fatigue overwhelmed her. That was what happened to her these days. She let her pen lie on her bed-table and watched the snow. She might not live to finish the book, but she would keep working at it, she had told herself, and ever since she had felt stronger, or imagined she was. This looked like a real snowstorm, and miraculous as always. Flakes large enough to show their intricate shapes whirled against the window, turning the buildings across the river into faint gray shadows on a lighter gray Japanese screen. Her eyes lost themselves in the delicate brush strokes.

The morning had begun badly. She had seen for herself that the discouraging swelling had crept higher, and the dull ache was steady, but at this moment a feeling of happiness filled her. She got out of bed carefully, not because of her heaviness, nor the irregular beating of her heart, but to try to hold this rare lighthearted feeling an instant longer. And when she got across the room and stood by the window, the lift of spirit was still there. "Why am I so happy?" she said aloud. Was it the snow?

As she settled herself back in bed, she remembered the snow coming down outside the window when she was sick—as she was every winter as a child. Her mother would fuss over her and give her honey from a silver spoon brought from Vienna, and read to her from the big book of *Don Quixote* with illustrations. She always thought of the knight riding through the snow.

The first time Paulo ever really looked at her was bound up with the snow. She was teaching the class in English literature that Wednesday night, and less than half the class were there because of the storm. It was cold in the room and the old radiators banged under the pressure of steam. She saw the handsome Italian student in the last row laughing at the competition and shouted above the banging, "Never mind the racket, listen! I'm reading Keats."

> *Spite of despondence, of the inhuman death*
> *Of noble natures, of gloomy day*
> *Of all the unhealthy and o'er darkened ways*
> *Made for our searching; yes, in spite of all,*
> *Some shape of Beauty moves away the pall*
> *From our dark spirits.*

When she lifted her eyes from the page, she found him staring at her. After class he came up and asked her to have a cup of coffee with him. "Or maybe we make it wine," he said. As they went down the street, the snow became for her the shape that Beauty took. She must remind Paulo of that time.

Now the snow had given up painting Japanese screens; it was falling straight down. Driving would be bad if it kept on. But if they had planned to go to Vermont, it wouldn't keep Paulo from starting out.

It was snowing like this the first time they took Ron and Olive to the farm. And the next day the three of them went skiing and she had the house and the day to herself. She would like one more day in the country like that one. Maybe she would have it!

She wondered what Olive remembered of that day. She remembered Olive and Paulo coming back to the house before Ron, and Olive standing over on the hearth, red-cheeked and radiant. And when she came down for dinner, all dressed up,

Paulo told her she was lovely or charming or something, but she didn't look like the child of joy she had been that afternoon in the snow. Olive would remember Paulo's kissing her, but perhaps she had forgotten his remark. "Memory is highly selective and often attempts to shape the facts to a more pleasing form, and fiction makes skillful use of that trick," she had written just this morning. Tiresa leaned back against the pillows to think about the idea. She made herself remember things as they were, but Paulo remembered things a little better or more tragic than they had really been. Her eyes closed.

"You had a good sleep," Bessie said. "I'm sorry I brought in the mail and wakened you. There was only this postcard and a magazine."

"I wasn't really sleeping." Tiresa disliked dozing off like that.

The card was from Olive and surprised her even more than the first one that announced that she was leaving Ron. They had had a card at Christmas, inscribed, "love, Olive and Johnny" and no other message. "Then she didn't go back to Ron," Paulo had said sadly when he read it. He was always as much disturbed by any separation, or failure of love, as he would have been by some treachery in the solar system. They mentioned Olive and Ron infrequently now, and Paulo only spoke occasionally of his godson. Tiresa thought of Olive from time to time with a kind of tenderness, marveling at how close she and Paulo had been to those two young people for a few months.

What a lovely card: a picture of Klee's *City of Towers*. Olive must be missing the towers across the river. The terse message on the postcard went straight to the point.

> *Dear Tiresa, you once said to come any time I could. This is awful to ask, but could Johnny and I come down and stay overnight next weekend? Maybe Friday? We could take the bus and be there by five-thirty. If you're not feeling well, or if you think Johnny would be too much, please say so. I'd adore to see you. Love, Olive.*

"How amazing!" Tiresa shoved aside the papers on her table and reread the card. She sounded wistful. It would be a good time for her to come, actually; she had felt stronger the last few days in spite of the swelling. And if Olive were here, Paulo would feel free to go to his medical meeting. She reached for the phone and dialed information for Olive's number.

"Hello?" Olive's voice had lost the eager tone Tiresa remembered.

"Hello, my dear, this is—"

"Tiresa! How wonderful to hear you. Were you shocked to have me ask right out like that if I could come and see you? I've felt guilty ever since I wrote that card. How are you?" Her sentences crowded each other in her excitement.

"I was delighted to hear from you, and I'm feeling much better. Of course we want you to come."

"Johnny's all over the place; you don't think he'll tire you too much? He's pretty good though," the voice pled.

"I'm sure Johnny won't be any trouble. His godfather will be enchanted to see him. How are you, Olive?"

"Bored to death. I made Mother and Dad go on the cruise they'd planned before they knew I was coming home, so Johnny and I have been here alone for a month. They're coming back tomorrow, and—if it really is all right, Tiresa—we could come Friday."

"You must plan to stay longer than overnight; give us a few days," Tiresa said. But as she hung up the phone, she wondered how strenuous Johnny would be. Perhaps she should have let them come for overnight first—but it would be fine. That poor lonesome child. They must do something gay for her—go out to dinner and the theater; just the theater would be safer. Tiresa picked up the morning paper and studied the theater section. The Chekhov play would be better than something uncertain, even though Paulo always found it depressing.

She waited until they finished dinner before she told Paulo. "So they're coming Friday by bus, and they'll stay three or four days." She smiled brightly at him.

He was slow in answering. Tiresa had seemed in better spirits lately, but she looked gaunt. The bluish tinge of her lips bothered him. "Why not wait until you're stronger, Tirese?"

"But I am stronger; I've been up and dressed all afternoon and evening. I would be up in the morning; except that you encourage me to be lazy. Olive needs to get away; she sounded a little pathetic. You know you'll enjoy having them, Paulo. Johnny must have grown amazingly. And it will be a relief to me to have Olive to talk to while you're away all day, and—" She brought it in at the end as if it were not part of her reason for having them, "then you can go to your medical meeting without worrying about me."

"I wish you hadn't asked them for several days, Tirese. A couple of days—overnight, perhaps. I've left things in that closet in the guest room, and some papers; the place is full of my stuff." He didn't want to make too much of her not being well enough.

"But I'm much better and I'm sleeping like a child at night. You're not going to sleep in the guest room any more. Bessie will do up the room and put your things where they belong."

"I called the janitor's office, just in case, and they have a crib in the storeroom, and even a high chair. Wasn't I inspired to ask!"

He was cheered to hear the energetic note in her voice.

"I'm sure it will do Olive good to get away from her family for a few days. You can see that the separation is going to be permanent," Tiresa said.

"I don't see that at all. Perhaps coming here and being next door to the apartment where she and Ron were so happy will make her want to go back to him. They certainly seemed happy until they left here."

Tiresa's ring flashed as she threw out her hands. "How do we know? I'm not so sure."

"You must stay in bed in the mornings, and rest after lunch—"

"Olive will expect that. Bessie will be here to keep an eye on

Johnny so Olive can go off by herself, and that might be just what she craves."

He laughed at her. "You've got it all worked out, haven't you?" He looked at Tiresa and saw her face in the firelight, pale with faint lines he hadn't noticed before. Her dark eyes seemed sunk a little under the lovely arch of her brows, but they were dancing at having got their own way. Yet what did it matter if she had Olive and Johnny here? She missed people, missed her work and her students. In spite of her writing, the days must drag. And Tirese had great wisdom. Perhaps she knew best what her soul needed. "Anything that raises her spirits and keeps her from getting depressed is good," Dr. Stiles had said. "So long as it doesn't tire her."

II

Tiresa heard the first touch on the doorknob, then the key in the lock, and Paulo laughing. "Look what I found, Tiresa! This Botticelli angel with a cherub on her back." They burst into the room before she had time to pull herself up from the couch. Olive in jeans and a blue ski jacket, her face alight with eagerness, almost overwhelmed her with her vitality as she stooped to kiss her.

"Tiresa, it's so good to see you!"

"Good to see you, my dear, and Johnny."

Paulo was carrying Johnny on his shoulder and brought him over to her. "Isn't he a splendid godson! He fell asleep on the way home." It struck Tiresa that she hadn't seen Paulo's face so beaming with delight all winter. He must have been a little daunted when Olive stepped off the bus with Johnny in a pack on her back. But, no, she would make him think of Sicilian mothers.

"He is handsome," she told Olive. She was on her feet now, and felt more equal to the occasion. "Come, let me show you how well equipped we are for Johnny."

Paulo was smiling as Tiresa came back. "She's just the same bubbling child."

"Not quite a child. She seems older to me."

"Johnny cuddled down in his crib as easily as though he were home," Olive said as she joined them. "He's practically out cold already."

"Well, he is home. And that speaks well for your training," Paulo said.

"No, I'm tired of him by night, so I'm very firm about his going to bed."

Paulo winced at her remark, "We must have a drink to celebrate your being here," he said hurriedly.

"Oh, Tiresa, you don't know how wonderful it is to be here again," Olive leaned her head against the back of the chair. "Everything's just the same."

It wasn't, of course, Tiresa thought. Her being ill had changed everything. She felt sometimes that even the room had a subdued look in spite of the fresh flowers Paulo kept there. The room saw too few people, heard too little talk. "It's lovely for me to have you and Johnny here. I've been in so much this winter that I'm fast growing into a vegetable."

"Well, I've been so bored I could spit," Olive said. "'Daughter with child comes home to parents!' Do you know anything more pathetic? They've been perfectly wonderful about it. Dad keeps telling me how good it is to have me home and all that, but still—. That's why I made them go on their cruise just as they planned. But, Tiresa, you'll approve; I've never read so much in my life."

"We were sorry to hear you decided to leave Ron. That couldn't have been easy," Tiresa said gently. The subject had been in their minds all through dinner—better to speak of it. Paulo added a log to the fire and came back to sit on the couch across from Olive, frowning a little.

"It wasn't, believe me! But I know it was right to do it. I mean, we weren't going any place with our marriage, and I'm sure Ron will be happier with—someone else. I'm glad he had his little affair; I might have just gone on as we were even though I was uncomfortable with him."

"Uncomfortable" was a strange word to use, Tiresa thought. She had often not been "comfortable" with Paulo, only to find him her only comfort at another time. Human relations weren't always comfortable. And Olive was too young to be thinking of comfort. She could see that Paulo was uncomfortable himself at the turn the conversation had taken. And then Bessie came in to light the candles and announce dinner. "It's good to see you again, Mrs. Fifer."

"Thank you, Bessie, I'm glad to see you," Olive said. But she turned back to Tiresa and Paulo, not waiting for Bessie to leave the room. "I might as well tell you that I'm getting a divorce." Olive's face was flushed; she brought out the remark defiantly, as though wanting there to be no misunderstanding. "On the grounds of—the lawyer calls it 'irretrievable breakdown of the marriage.'" Her eyes sought Tiresa's, seeking reassurance. "Our marriage just didn't mean enough."

"But you've been married so short a time, how could you know? A marriage grows," Paulo objected. Poor Paulo, Tiresa thought, he wanted his *Sposina* to stay married.

Olive shook her head. "No, Ron has his good points, but we're too different."

"Tiresa and I are hardly alike," Paulo began. Olive saw their eyes meet as if they had a private joke.

"I'm getting the divorce here in Massachusetts because it only takes six months. Can you believe it, we've been separated almost nine. So I may see you again when I come up for the final decree."

"Of course, you must come right here," Tiresa said.

Tiresa wondered as they sat down to the table if Olive were remembering their first meal here, when she and Paulo had drunk to their marriage. She set herself to talk of other things through the meal.

"Is our apartment rented?" Olive asked abruptly.

"Yes, a middle-aged couple are in there now, I believe he's at Brandeis in some non-academic capacity," Paulo said. "Rather too old and sober for us," he added with a quick grin.

"I'm glad. I'd hate to have them know you the way we did, and maybe go to the country with you."

By the time they had finished their coffee, Tiresa was too tired to go on talking. "I've been going to bed early and reading a while so I'll say goodnight, my dear. Feel at home and don't try to be quiet or keep Johnny quiet on my account. He'll be one person in the household who doesn't know that I've been sick, and we won't tell him. Did you notice that big bag of blocks in the corner of your room, Olive? Paulo brought it home the other day for Johnny. You and Paulo have a good visit and I'll catch up tomorrow."

"How is Tiresa, Paulo?" Olive asked. Paulo's face lost all its animation and became closed. "She's not good," he said almost soundlessly. His eyes seemed hardly to see her.

"Should I be here, I mean with Johnny? Won't we tire her?"

Paulo shrugged. "She wanted you to come. She gets lonely here all day, I know. We'll just have to see how it goes."

"You'll be sure and tell me if—you know, if I should leave."

"I will do that," Paulo said solemnly. And when Olive said she should unpack, that she was really tired so she thought she would go to bed, Paulo didn't delay her.

But in the guest room, Olive collapsed on the bed with no will to unpack. Did Paulo mean that Tiresa might not get well?—ever—that she might die? She had never had to think about anyone dying—not anyone she knew.

Tiresa did look bad. When she first saw Tiresa tonight Olive had glanced away lest her face show how shocked she was. But at dinner, when Tiresa was talking or laughing, she seemed like herself again. Olive almost wished she hadn't come.

She wished she were back in her own apartment. And then she was thinking about Ron, unable to stop herself. She remembered how comfortable it was sitting on the couch together watching television, and Ron would put his arm around her. And maybe bed before they'd have a snack, and she would take sips of Ron's beer and it was all easy and relaxed. And then they'd go to bed. But there were those other times, too, when they didn't have anything to talk about. And when she thought of living her whole life with Ron . . . At least, Tiresa had been happy all her life with Paulo.

"Tirese, couldn't we let Ron know she's here? He could just happen to drop in," Paulo said as they lay in bed.

Tiresa chuckled. "Oh, Paulo, you are absurdly romantic. We don't even know where he's living."

"Through his Boston office, I'm sure—"

"They're not children even though they sound like children, and it's no good trying to interfere. You can see that Olive has made up her mind."

"But Ron might be able to convince her that she can't live without him after all. If I were he—"

"I'm sure you would, but Ron isn't you, nor is Olive me, perpetually forgiving you and taking you back!"

"Tiresa! Has it been as bad as that?"

"Paulo." She reached over and brought his face to hers.

"It's such a pity to break up their marriage like that," he said.

But the morning was different. Even before Johnny was awake, Olive heard Paulo singing. His voice filled the apartment.

> *L'amor ama gli effluvi*
> *Del vin, de la cucina . . .*

"*Buon giorno*, Olive, *buon giorna*, young man," Paulo said when she and Johnny appeared. He swung Johnny up in the high chair. "If you had waited one more minute I would have brought you a cup of coffee. I've taken Tirese her tray. It saves her energy to have her breakfast in bed. Do you think you can put up with having breakfast with me here in the kitchen?"

"Tiresa must be feeling well this morning."

"She is. That's what you and Johnny did for her." Paulo was in a high mood. Olive watched him as she fed Johnny. Paulo moved so quickly that breakfast seemed to arrive on the table by some sleight of hand.

"How lovely the table looks in the sun. Yellow mats and that yellow rose."

"Tiresa sent the rose from her room. She is always the hand behind everything. I just carry out her orders. Johnny, let's see if you would like to explore the cupboard." Paulo set him down on the floor in front of an open cupboard filled with pans. "My mother used to entertain us that way."

"Won't the clatter bother—"

"No, she'll enjoy the din. We need two of them, Johnny." Paulo sprang up and held out a second cover to him, helping him clash them together. "There! Perhaps you'll play the cymbals in the Boston Symphony some day."

It was all so gay and easy that Olive felt she must have been wrong about Tiresa. She was sick, but she would get well. Johnny banged his lids together and a look of pleasure spread over his round face.

Paulo poured Olive another cup of coffee. "I must be off. Why don't you have your second cup with Tiresa? I'll carry Johnny in there." They made a procession into Tiresa's room, Johnny sitting on Paulo's shoulders, waving his pot-lids in the air.

"I'll leave you in good hands, Tirese," Paulo said as he kissed her goodbye. "Goodbye, Olive."

"Good luck with the operation," Tiresa called after him. "Now we can relax over our coffee. Mornings when Paulo operates he moves through here like a whirlwind."

"I'm so glad you feel well this morning."

"Yes, I do. I'm sure it's all this life around me."

As if to act his role, Johnny threw down his cymbals and began creeping back toward the kitchen with Olive in pursuit.

"You must use this week here as a time to get off on your own a bit; get down to town perhaps," Tiresa said. "I remember watching from the balcony before we knew you. Paulo said you walked as though you loved swinging along."

"I guess I do." She was pleased.

"By the way, I hope you won't mind too much, but Paulo is going to be away for a couple of days. Since you are here, he agreed to go off to a medical meeting in Chicago that I know he wants very much to attend. I'm so glad he's going; he needs to get away from me for a change."

"Of course." But what if Tiresa had a heart attack or something?

"We'll have a fine womany time. I always like it for a day and a night and then I can't wait for Paulo to be back," Tiresa went on.

"Ron was away a lot after we moved to Syracuse and he took on that new job. I hated his being away. I'd give myself a treat with Stouffer's frozen lobster or something glamorous, and an avocado salad and not cook at all. And then I'd splurge and buy a steak for dinner when he came home. But—I often felt let down when he did come. You can be lonely even when you aren't alone. More lonely; I discovered that."

"Oh yes," Tiresa agreed. She could see Olive eating her Stouffer's dinner, feeling a little abused. She waited for her to go on if she wanted to, but Olive got up.

"If you don't mind, Tiresa, I think I will take Johnny and go for a quick walk along the Drive. I won't be long."

"Leave Johnny here. Bessie will be coming any minute. Go for a real swinging walk by yourself."

Olive was gone as quickly as she could slip into her jacket. In her mind, Tiresa went with her, smelling the cold air, crossing over to walk on the river side, feeling the rush of the moving traffic and her own strength. Johnny sat on the floor still playing with one pot cover. She had a chance to look at him. He was a beautiful child. The morning sun caught in his light hair and made his blue eyes squint a little. Her eyes lingered on the healthy color of his skin.

"Hello," she said.

The child looked up at her in the high bed. Then he pulled himself up so he could crawl and moved like a crab toward the open door into the hall.

"Johnny! Here, Johnny!"

He continued out to the living room. Tiresa slid out of bed. He was too heavy for her to lift; she could only follow him. He hesitated, looking up at her. How big she must seem to him. Now he was looking at her feet and swollen ankles. Just then, the clock on the mantel struck ten silvery strokes. He looked over toward the sound.

"Hear the clock, Johnny. Hickory, dickory, dock, The mouse ran up the clock, The clock struck ten, The mouse ran down . . ." She had to stop for breath. "Hickory, dickory, dock," she finished. He seemed to be listening. She repeated the rhyme again, softly accenting the rhyming words, gesturing as the mouse ran up, clapping her hands as the clock struck ten. Johnny gave a little squeal. She laughed—first a simulated laugh, and then a spontaneous one.

"See the gold balls, Johnny!" She went over to the mantel and lifting down the clock that had stood there ever since they moved here, set it on the coffee table. "Come see." Tiresa sat down on the couch in front of it, breathing heavily.

Johnny considered, then began to crawl toward her. He pulled himself up by taking hold of her knees and stood watching the moving balls inside the glass walls. The sun shone through the glass, polishing the intricate brass works.

"Listen!" Tiresa whispered. "Hear the tick." "It's going to strike again." They were both still, and then that trick of mind that forever gets in the way, made her see herself caught inside time with this small human being. He gave a delighted little shout.

"That's right Johnny, you laugh at time. You have years and years of it ahead." Now he leaned against her, watching the turning pendulum with wide eyes. She put her arm around the sturdy little body. "Listen—it's going to strike again." Together they waited for the chime that would mark the quarter hour. It had been a long time since she had wanted to hurry the minutes along, Tiresa thought.

Bessie let herself in while they were listening. "That's just what I was afraid of, Mrs. Romano; you'd be baby-sitting and over-doing. You'll catch your death a-cold out here in your nightgown."

"Shh!" Tiresa put up her finger just as the tinkling chime sounded through the rounded glass walls of the clock. Johnny was standing so close to the sound he gave another squeal and jumped up and down, looking at Tiresa as though she had caused it. "Johnny and I were waiting for the chime," Tiresa explained.

Bessie, who measured time in her own way, paid no attention. "I thought that was her as I got off the bus. Of course, I don't know the whys and wherefores, but it does seem a pity those young folks can't patch up their troubles and all. If you was to have a good stiff talk with her, Mrs. Romano, maybe you could—you know what I mean." She broke off. "You get back in bed and I'll take care of him. And I'll bring some hot bouillon."

"No thanks, Bessie. I'm going to bathe and dress. And I don't want any bouillon; we can have it for lunch."

Olive walked farther than she intended, and came back feeling guilty. "I'm sorry I was gone so long, Tiresa. I just seemed to keep going."

Tiresa was sitting at the desk in the living room. "You could have stayed longer. Johnny and I had a fine time and now Bessie has him with her in the kitchen."

Relieved, Olive sat down on the couch and leaned her head back. She had a delicious sense of freedom. It wasn't like this at home; her mother sometimes seemed to make such a thing of taking care of Johnny and she felt guilty if she left him with her too long.

"You remember I told you I was doing a study of memory in fiction," Tiresa said without turning around. "Remember, we each told a childhood memory at the farm? I always wanted to do a seminar on memory, but since that isn't possible, I'm writing about it. We're all so conditioned by memory—"

"I don't want to remember the last two years," Olive said suddenly.

"You can't do that though. It's a part of you. You're a different person because of those years. You're as bad as Paulo. He claims that he doesn't like to look back. I had to go to Sicily and see where he grew up, and meet people he used to know in order to understand something of his background; I learned very little from Paulo."

Olive reached for the *New Yorker* on the table and turned the pages idly, seeing a woman in a fur coat, a man in a sleek black car, and a young couple at a table in some posh restaurant lifting their wine glasses to each other—all of them living luxuriously in the present.

"Go back farther and think about your childhood. What was it like growing up in Summit, New Jersey?"

"Oh," Olive shrugged, "Pleasant. I went to Chelmsford School; everyone I knew did. We were all College Prep. I remember the day we heard whether we were accepted by the colleges we wanted—we went wild. Mother and Dad were so proud I got early acceptance. There were four of us who went around together—I'd never really been alone until I was married."

"This study that I'm amusing myself with will show," Tiresa went on, "how much the writers I'm examining depend on their characters' memories to give them depth, to define them."

Olive stared at a cartoon in the magazine, not really getting the point. The room was quiet in the winter sun. The tick of the clock, the fire, and the movement of Tiresa's pen were the only sounds, except for Bessie talking now and then to Johnny in the kitchen. She should go get him, but she was in no hurry.

"You know, I can hardly even remember what it was like being married to Ron."

Tiresa didn't look up. "But you don't want to forget any time of joy, or sorrow, or disillusionment—the great sin is not to feel deeply. You don't want to be afraid to look right at what has just happened."

Olive laid the *New Yorker* back on the table. If Tiresa was going to lecture, she would be as boring as Mother.

Tiresa turned from around from her desk. "You mustn't mind me, Olive. I'm talking to myself as well as you. I'm trying to make myself look at the fact of dying."

Olive glanced at her in embarrassment. Tiresa was making a wry face.

"It's not easy, but I don't want to have death creep up on me without really facing it. These unpleasant situations have their illuminations, I imagine." Tiresa laughed. "We both have our problems to come to terms with, don't we? Well, tonight we're going to a play and we can watch other people struggle with their problems. We have tickets for Chekhov's *Three Sisters*.

"Tiresa, how super! But you mustn't feel you have to entertain me. I love just being here."

"We'll all enjoy it, even though Paulo claims he doesn't like the play. He says the characters are half Sicilian, and have the same fatalism and inertia Sicilians do.

"But Paulo isn't like that."

Tiresa lifted her hands and let them fall. "He is fatalistic. And if things ever went too badly for him, he could sink into a kind of inertia." Her face was sober as if she saw him in that state. "But he also loves living; maybe that will sustain him," she said quickly.

They had lunch in front of the fire, but Tiresa seemed tired, and the conversation lagged. Tiresa went in to rest while Johnny was taking a nap and Olive was left to herself. She felt uneasy being a houseguest. If she turned on the television, it would disturb Tiresa, and she couldn't go and leave Johnny to Bessie again. She settled down to write a letter to Gumshoe.

> Dear Gumshoe,
>
> *I'm back in Cambridge, visiting the Romanos. They're the middle-aged couple I told you about; the ones who lived next door to us. After a month alone with Johnny while Mother and Dad were on a cruise I was stir crazy and had to get away, so I came on the spur of*

the moment. (*I love that phrase; I was certainly spurred.*)
*It's good to be here, and not so good. It's a wonderful
change, but Tiresa is sick and I can see that Paulo is worried. Today she said she was trying to look at the fact of
death—imagine! But I don't think she's really that sick.
Anyway, she says it does her good to have Johnny and me
around, and says we cheer her. I don't know why. I don't
feel too cheery myself, particularly this afternoon.*

*At the moment, Tiresa is lying down. Johnny is
asleep, and I hope to goodness he'll sleep a full hour.
I'm here in the living room. I used to think this was the
warmest, loveliest room I knew, but today it seems shut-
in, almost stuffy. I suppose I've seldom been in it alone—
never, I guess, always with Tiresa or both of them and
they give their own atmosphere.*

*Every now and then, Tiresa gives out with ye femme
sage sayings, or a piece of philosophy. Maybe she is trying to get me to go back to Ron, but there isn't a chance.
Even being right next door to our old apartment where
we were happy at first, doesn't make me want to try it
again. And that's a test, I think. Our apartment seems
like cast-off skin—to be lurid about it. I can't explain
what it is, but I just feel it.*

*Tonight, we're going to a play, which will be fun.
Their housekeeper will take care of Johnny. But—I don't
feel I'm really living here any more than I did at home.
Just making time in limbo. Maybe it will be different
after I get my divorce.*

Take care and don't work too hard.
Love, Ollie

When Olive came back from taking Johnny out, Tiresa's door
was still closed. "Does Mrs. Romano often sleep so long in the
afternoon?" she asked Bessie.

"Since she was sick this last time you can't tell a thing about
her. She does one thing one time and something different the

next. Used to be when she went out teaching, you could tell time by her. And I tell you . . ." Bessie's voice sank to a noisy whisper, "When she sleeps so long, I begin to wonder and my heart turns over. I'll put on another log and light the lights. As soon as it gets the least dark, she wants everything lit up."

When Tiresa finally came out, she seemed to hesitate in the doorway. She was still in her Chinese coat she wore for a dressing-gown, and her heavy black hair hung down her back.

"Hello," Olive said. "You had a long sleep."

"I couldn't get to sleep."

"Could I do your hair up for you, Tiresa? Remember you let me once."

"Will you, Olive? It's seems such an effort."

"You'll want it up high, won't you, for the play?"

"I'm not going to the play. But I want you and Paulo to go."

"Oh no, Tiresa. If you aren't going, we won't either. That wouldn't be any fun."

"But you must. We've hardly gone any place all winter and it will be good for Paulo. Don't you see, he has you to go with so I don't have to make the effort. Please, don't make a fuss about going, Olive. He'll go for your sake, and you go for his, and you'll both enjoy it when you get there."

Tiresa was silent while Olive brushed and arranged her hair. She braided Tiresa's hair and fastened it high on her head. "There, I'll get your mirror so you can see the magnificent coiffeur you have."

But Tiresa barely glanced at it and nodded. "It feels good and tight, but I don't much like looking at myself these days. Show Johnny himself in the mirror. But, thank you, that was a great help."

Johnny was caught by the bright shine of the mirror and reached for it but turned away after a moment.

"At the beginning and end of our lives, we're not interested in seeing our own image." Tiresa said. "But heaven knows we make up for it by the tender attention we give our face in be-

230

tween. My dear, forgive me; I sound like a tragedy queen in a small town stock company." She laughed, but a melancholy note still hung in the room. Olive was relieved when Paulo came.

"Roses for my true love, and spring flowers for you, Olive." He presented the paper bundles with a flourish. "To remind you both of me the three days I'm away. And I have a brown bear with a yellow hat for you, Johnny. Tirese, you aren't dressed; aren't you feeling well?" He stood in front of her, still holding the bear.

"I'm quite all right, but I decided I didn't want to go out in the cold. How did the operation go? You didn't call."

"I did, Tirese, but you were asleep. The operation was more or less routine. It went very well and he should get a good result," he said without interest. "Here, Olive, will you take care of the flowers. Now tell me, Trise, how do you really feel?"

"I'm just a little tired, so I'm doing what you're always wanting me to do." Paulo took Tiresa's pulse, and put his hand on her swollen ankles. Then he bent over and kissed her.

"There's no point in any of us going to the play, Tirese, if you're not going. It's not that important."

"Please, Paulo, don't spoil the evening. Take Olive and I'll stay here by the fire. If you don't, I'll demonstrate."

His face relaxed at her old threat. "I'll go get us a martini and we can talk about it."

"Here's to the patient." Tiresa lifted her glass. "You know, Olive, we often drink to Paulo's patients. Wouldn't they be surprised to know they were toasted in—" She broke off in a fit of coughing.

"Don't talk so much," Paulo said, the worried look back on his face.

Tiresa took a swallow from her glass. "I'm all right now. I just needed this martini."

Olive carried Johnny off to bed, holding the bear Paulo had brought him. But after Johnny was in his crib, she lingered. She felt in the way; Paulo's face had become so serious. Tiresa must be very sick. She would leave in the morning. But five minutes later, she heard music from the living room and Paulo laughing. When she went back in, they were talking about the play.

"You read your own ideas into it, you know, Paulo. It becomes more your play than Chekhov's."

Paulo shrugged. "Isn't that the way with any work of art? Tonight we'll get Olive's reaction and see what she makes of it. Don't expect the people in this play to be like upstanding Americans with great ambition and drive, Olive."

"Stop it, Paulo. Don't give her ideas before she sees it. They are human beings, and Moscow is—"

"Now who's giving her ideas!" Paulo teased as he seated Tiresa at the table. All through the meal they talked about the play.

As Olive went to get her coat, Tiresa said, "I have a cape that would look well on you, Olive. Paulo, get that green one we bought in Edinburgh."

Paulo put the cape around Olive's shoulders. "Very becoming," he pronounced.

Olive went out to the hall mirror to see herself. "It's stunning, Tiresa. I've always wanted to wear a cape."

"Then the cape is yours, my dear," Tiresa said. "Now go and enjoy the play. Don't feel sorry for me; it's a luxury to stay home tonight, and I'll read *The Three Sisters* while you're seeing it," she said briskly.

"So!" Paulo said as they drove away from the apartment house.

"You don't really want to go, do you, Paulo?"

"No, but it would upset Tirese if we didn't."

They were almost there, when Olive said, "Is she worse, Paulo?"

"She has her ups and downs—each time a little longer down. She has a rheumatic heart, and she's used it hard all her life. It's playing out."

Olive stared at the frozen banks of snow that bordered the street. She shouldn't have asked such a question.

"It's difficult to park so I'll let you out in front of the theater."

"No, park first. I don't mind walking."

"I'm afraid we're going to miss the curtain," he said when he finally found a parking space. "Let's make a run for it." They raced down the block; people stepped aside to let them go. Olive was a little ahead and looked back over her shoulder laughing. He caught up with her, freed for a moment of his depression. They had to be guided to their seats by an usher with a flashlight just as the curtain went up. Three young women were on stage, one pacing up and down, the second, dressed in black, sat reading, the third stood idly looking off into space. Without a word, they created a tension that spread over the audience. Then one of them spoke, "Father died just a year ago today on the fifth of May, your birthday, Irina. I remember it was very cold and it was snowing . . ."

The voice hushed into silence the slight sounds of an audience settling itself. Paulo laid Olive's cape on the back of the seat, but she was oblivious. The voice seemed to be speaking to her alone.

What a dreary way to begin a play, Paulo thought, talking about death. He crossed his legs and tried to relax as he set himself to sit through the evening. The play was depressing. None of the characters got anywhere. He couldn't understand why Tirese liked it. But she didn't know as many Sicilians as he did, who were always talking of plans they never carried out. When he came to the United States to establish himself in his profession, he had thought he was different from those others—he carried out his plans. But what was the use of any of it without Tirese? He glanced over at Olive, acutely conscious of her glowing young skin; Tiresa's had bothered him tonight. He leaned over to say how comic old Tuzenbach was, but she was listening so intently, he kept his remark to himself. Too bad Tiresa couldn't see her. She would like Olive's absorption.

Now that she had given Olive her cape, Tiresa wondered why she had done it. With a sharp pang of possessiveness, she wanted

233

it back. She used to stride across the campus, knowing that she was striking in it. Just to have Paulo put it around her shoulders now would make her feel vigorous and healthy. Why had she given it so impetuously? Why hadn't she just loaned it? "I want you to wear this tonight, Olive," she could have said, not "Then it's yours." It was a sudden compulsion—like the time she told her about losing the baby. Wasn't she in control of her own mind?

"Goodnight, Mrs. Romano. You sure you don't want me to stay till the Doctor and her come back?"

Bessie's concern touched her. "Thank you Bessie, I'll be fine."

"I mean, if Johnny should cry and you'd have to do for him."

"I shall let him cry. But he won't. He hasn't since he's been here."

Bessie was so anxious about her because she thought she wasn't as well—it was obvious to everyone, of course. "Poor Mrs. Romano, she's in a bad way," Bessie must say to that friend of hers whom she was always quoting. "I don't know how much longer I'll have my job unless the Doctor would want me to stay on and keep house for him. But he'll marry again, likely enough; he's such a handsome man, and full of fun, he used to be before Mrs. Romano took sick. There wasn't any husband more devoted, but you know how men are." Ever since she could remember, Tiresa had made up imaginary conversations for people. She used to think she might write a novel some day, for her own amusement—all dialogue, in the manner of Ivy Compton-Burnett. But now there might not be time even to finish the book on memory.

Tiresa reached over on the table for the battered little volume of Chekhov's plays she had had as a student. It was heavily underlined, and almost indiscernible comments straggled over the margins. The scrawled sentence on the last page with an exclamation mark at the end caught her eye. "Thank God for Chekhov.

He faces up to the way people are." She had written. Today a student would say, "he tells it like it is." The remark amused her. She didn't remember writing it, or even thinking at nineteen that she knew so well how people were. But she could have made a worse comment.

Well, she was facing up—trying to—to the way she was. She was not getting any better. She couldn't hope to live through the year. If she made it through the summer she would do well. If she couldn't tell for herself, she had seen it in Paulo's eyes tonight, and even Olive's. Next year at this time—

> Cold in the earth—and the deep snow piled above thee
> Far, far removed, cold in the dreary grave—

That was the way, play with the idea of death and call it by name. Not her own; Death with a capital *D*. She could think of a dozen poems on death right now.

> . . . for many a time
> I have been half in love with easeful Death,
> Called him soft names in many a mused rhyme,
> To take into the air my quiet breath;
> Now more than ever seems it rich to die,
> To cease upon the midnight with no pain . . .

> Golden lads and girls all must
> As chimney sweepers, come to dust.

She was on a poetry jag now.

> Death be not proud, though some have called thee
> Mighty and dreadful, for thou art not so.

What would English poets do without Death for a subject? But no honeyed lines could make her feel it was rich to die.

> Do not go gentle into that good night,
> Rage, rage against the dying of the light.

No, she wouldn't rage against the dying of the light, or go kicking and screaming. She could never have managed a natural childbirth; maybe she could manage a natural death. Her heart began to race, missed a beat, leaving her hanging in space—she lay still, frightened for a few moments out of thought. The beat began again, banging against her breast, and settled into a pattern. She might as well die as live this way—if it weren't for leaving Paulo.

She could see him coming home to an empty apartment and sinking into one of his depressions. He was watching her yesterday when he thought she was asleep, and his face was so sad she could have wept for him. Ever since she came back from the hospital this last time, he had been depressed and edgy, boringly solicitous. Tonight he had tried hard not to seem concerned because she was staying home, and worked up quite an argument over Chekhov. Olive doubtless thought they were in high spirits and having a real argument over the play.

Tiresa read the entire second act of the play before putting it down, but she could hardly have told what she read. She heard the click of the door. Paulo and Olive were being quiet in case she had gone on to bed.

"Ah Tirese, you waited up for us," Paulo said. When he kissed her, she wanted to reach up and hold him—tell him about the megrim she had had, but she only laid her hand on his face for a moment to feel the cold.

"How was it?"

He shrugged, "Chekhov."

Olive came in, still wearing her cape. "Oh, Tiresa, that was a horrible play. Nothing turns out right. The three sisters want so desperately to go to Moscow and they never do. It was heartbreaking."

"We needed you, Tirese, to explain the play to us at intermission," Paulo said. "You'll have to offer some fancy interpretations to reconcile Olive to it. But I will say I have never seen it better acted. I'll hang up your cape, Olive, while you pour out your rage at the play on Tirese."

"I loved my cape, Tiresa. It was so warm and I felt simply regal sweeping down the aisle. Thank you so much for it."

The word "my" fell sharply on Tiresa's ears. Her heart was bothering her again, and she didn't try to answer. Inside the wide sleeves of her Chinese coat, her cold hands clasped each other.

"The actors were superb for their parts. Old Tuzenbach— Baron Tuzenbach, Krone Alschauer—" Paulo mimicked his manner, "was a real comic and poor Audrey was Sicilian to the bone. Except that he let his wife browbeat him as I trust no Sicilian husband would do."

"What about the women?" Tiresa managed to ask, not wanting Paulo to notice she was having trouble breathing.

"They were tragic," Olive said. "Do you realize that those sisters were just about my age? They had a few moments of happiness, I suppose, but nothing that lasted, and you knew they were just going to go on and on and grow old and bitter in a place they hated."

"Olive, exquisite happiness usually comes in moments. You can't expect constant thrilling happiness every day of your life. They might not have been any happier in Moscow," Paulo said, more sternly than he meant. He flung out his hands helplessly. "You explain what I mean, Tirese. I'll see what I can find for an after-theater supper."

"I must go and see Johnny. Was he quiet all evening, Tiresa?" Olive's face was flushed.

"I didn't hear a sound," Tiresa was glad when they had both gone. She leaned back, resting.

Paulo opened the door from the kitchen. "What would taste good to you, Tirese?"

"There's smoked salmon, I think, and some Greek olives, and some of that cheese you brought home from Sage's. I'll just have a glass of wine and a slice of Melba toast," she added. "Maybe a little cheese."

"There's a bottle of Pouilly Fuisse, I know," Paulo said, disappearing behind the swinging door. Nothing was too much effort for him if he was in the mood.

She followed him by the sounds he made in the kitchen. He was filling the teakettle; he was making coffee, of course. Maybe she would have some, after all. She heard the clink of glasses and the opening of the refrigerator door. He was usually in high spirits after the theater—often when they came back, Paulo would take on the manner of some character; she might, too. What delicious times they had.

"Tarara-boom-di-ay" came from the kitchen. "I'm sitting on a tomb-di-ay . . ." He stopped abruptly, but in a minute, he brought a tray with a flourish and put it down beside her.

Tiresa took up the song, moving her head to the tune. "I'm sitting on a tomb-di-ay," she tried to sing softly, but it made her cough.

Olive came back into the room. "If I'd seen that play alone and then gone home to bed, I'd have been so sunk I'd have had nightmares. Do you remember that Colonel who used to live in Moscow and knew the sisters when—"

"Vershinen," Paulo put in.

"He actually said happiness doesn't exist, we only long for it. I couldn't live if I believed that."

"The trouble is you want to be *la Sposina* all your life, Olive," Paulo said. "All the anticipation and joy. That isn't the way life is."

Tiresa saw the startled look on Olive's face and then tears that filled her eyes. So did Paulo, and he was stricken at making her cry. He looked helplessly over at Tiresa. "Olive, forgive me. I'm not criticizing . . ." No one's voice could be more tender, Tiresa thought. "But the important thing is to be a child of joy first, then you are strong for whatever unhappiness comes." He put his finger under Olive's chin, "I am sure you are going to be very happy in your life."

"I'm sorry, it's just that I've been so unhappy. Everyone thinks I'm wrong about leaving Ron, that I'm childish, and not being fair to Johnny . . ." Olive hid her face against Paulo's shoulder.

"Tiresa and I think you've shown great honesty and—and independence." He smoothed her hair as his eyes sought Tiresa's again. Then Olive rushed out of the room.

"I didn't mean to drive her to tears, but I do think . . ." Paulo began.

Tiresa sipped her wine without answering. The three of them were like characters in a Chekhov play: Paulo repentant over making Olive cry, Olive rushing off in tears, and she, herself, sitting here, a little removed. "She'll be all right; it was good for her to cry. She's been pretty taut ever since she came."

Olive came back smiling. She had washed her face and the hair around her forehead was damp, like a child's. "I'm sorry. Putting on a scene like that will make you sure that I'm a child. All right, so there *isn't* any real happiness that lasts more than a minute, and you have no right to expect it. Great! You just take whatever comes." She helped herself to a slice of cheese, taking pains to fit it on her cracker.

"It's not that bad, *Sposina*. Tiresa and I have found a great deal of joy—far more than sorrow."

"So much more," Tiresa agreed on cue. "And you remember at the end of the play Vershinen says life seems black and hopeless, but it looks as though the time were not far off when it will be full of happiness."

"In hundreds of years, he means. That's no comfort. And Vershinen goes out and gets himself killed in a stupid duel. But the saddest line in the play was when Irina said it wasn't within her power to be in love." Olive was tracing a design on the chair arm. "I wondered if that's my trouble. Maybe I'm like that."

Paulo laughed. "Believe me, Olive, you are *not* like that." He was looking into her face, his eyes on hers. "You haven't yet found the man to whom you can respond with your whole heart. I suspect that you have just become a woman; when you married you were still a child."

As she saw them there across from her, it was suddenly clear to Tiresa that Olive might easily fall in love with Paulo. And if he were left alone, when he was in one of those terrible depressions after her death, might turn to Olive.

Tiresa was so quiet that Paulo looked over at her and caught the expression on her face, as if she were not really listening. "Trise, would you like to go on to bed?"

"I think I would. Don't come; you stay and talk to Olive." But Paulo took her arm.

"Oh Tiresa, you must think I'm a stupid little fool." Olive came over and kissed her.

Tiresa shook her head. "Don't worry," she said, smiling faintly.

Paulo took off the spread and opened the bed. Tiresa stood in front of the dresser, taking down her hair. Her heart had begun to pound so she couldn't hold her hands steady. Paulo came behind her, putting his arms around her.

"All right, darling? We tired you with all the talk."

"Just at the end. Go talk to Olive. I—I'm not up to it."

"I had no idea the play upset her so." An amused smile touched his mouth. "Ah, youth! I'll try to cheer her up a bit and then I'll be along. Imagine that lovely vibrant young creature, just made for loving, fearing it isn't in her power to love! You know that has elements of humor."

Tiresa leaned against the bed to quiet her heart, fending off the thoughts churning in her mind. Slowly she went through the motions of getting ready for bed. She creamed her face, looking at it curiously in the mirror, comforted an instant by its familiarity.

Paulo came back to help her into bed. "Thank you for waiting up for us. I missed you at the play."

After she was in bed, her heart still raced, then stopped—that seeming eternity—then began again. It took a long time for the heartbeat to settle into a comfortable rhythm, but when it had, the same thoughts were in her mind.

The idea was ridiculous. Olive was still a child. She touched and amused Paulo, that was all. And how could Olive ever understand Paulo in all his moods. She was too concerned about her own happiness to worry about his. They were twenty—more than that, twenty-three years, and a world apart.

It was seeing Olive bury her face in Paulo's shoulder—but that was like a child with her father. And Paulo was concerned, as he would be over a daughter he had made cry. He had looked over Olive's head to her, begging her to help.

"Well, I think *la Sposina* is a little more reconciled to the Universe," Paulo said when he came in to bed.

"Mhmm." Tiresa opened her eyes sleepily and let them close again.

"I pronounced more clichés of philosophical wisdom, Trise, than you ever heard me utter. I told her than happiness wasn't the whole aim of human life, that it was a lucky by-product, and that happiness was part of life and didn't mean the end of existence. A little clumsy, maybe, but she cheered up and we had another glass of wine and drank to life. You would have laughed at me. Goodnight, Darling." He leaned over and kissed her. "You'll have to take her on from there."

"No, I think you've covered the ground admirably!"

"Her anguishing over that play makes you realize how much older we are. Youth protests angrily, middle age takes it in its stride even if it doesn't quite accept. Profound? I'm wound up. Now I'll stop talking. Goodnight *Carissima*."

"Goodnight, Paulo."

He settled himself, his hand just touching her. She tried to sleep, but she was too wide awake. She wouldn't ask Olive here again; it tired her too much to have someone staying with them. And all the rest of her life she wanted to be alone with Paulo. He would be away till Saturday; she would have to get through that time. It would be boring. She couldn't go on with all that talk about love and happiness . . . The wretched dry cough began. It seemed to come for no reason. Tiresa pulled herself up higher against her pillows, but she disturbed Paulo.

He laid his fingers on her wrist. Now he was bringing her a pill. She drank the cold water after it, hearing her own swallows in the stillness. She shook her head at the hopelessness of the cough, her eyes on Paulo's. But he smiled back. "You'll be all right now." He rearranged her pillows and turned out the light. "*Ti amo, carissima.*" He lay down beside her.

Slowly, his relaxed body against hers relaxed her own. An involuntary sigh sifted through her and was a relief.

12

When Paulo was ready to leave the next morning, he came out to the living room where Tiresa and Olive waited to see him off.

"I came to be inspected," he explained to Olive.

"A haberdashery model, but you'll pass," Tiresa said. "You might have worn that green tie instead of the brown one."

"Well, this will do. I'll call you tonight."

Olive was aware of the way their eyes met and held. She stooped down to play with Johnny on the floor as they said goodbye.

"Keep rested, Trise, or I'll demonstrate when I get back," Paulo warned.

"And you feel free as the air, with no worries, Paulo, do you hear? I'll be fine. Olive and I are going to live it up. As a matter of fact, it will be a relief not to see your long face and your glowering eyes."

"Tiresa!"

"That's right."

"Well, I'm off. Keep an eye on Tiresa, Olive. Goodbye, Johnny. I'll be back before you know it."

Last night Paulo had given Olive the phone number of the doctor to call if Tiresa seemed to have trouble breathing—or anything. "She knows when she needs someone; she would tell you." But even so, the responsibility frightened Olive. She would be thankful when Paulo got back.

Paulo fastened his seat belt, thrust his legs out in front of him, feet resting on his brief-case, in the automatic movements of the plane traveler, and turned toward the window, oblivious of the man and woman in the two adjoining seats, or the stewardess demonstrating the oxygen mask. The plane rose up above the human tracks covering Boston, above the Prudential Center and the dark mirrors of the John Hancock building. All he could see were winter clouds. He closed his eyes. He needed this. Yesterday he had forgotten an appointment for a consultation, and was half an hour late, and he snapped at the new nurse on the floor over nothing, really. He pushed his head into the chair-back and moved it slightly from side to side to ease the tightness of his neck muscles.

Tiresa knew he had to get away. She always knew, but he wouldn't leave her again. She was losing ground. He couldn't hide it from her; she knew him too well. He'd always thought he knew how she felt—what she was thinking, without any words. Now he wasn't sure. Some days she seemed to have retreated into her illness. Was she frightened, dreading death—keeping it to herself? That worried him.

But she was brave. She had always been stronger than he. She had been his strength when Anthony . . . He remembered her saying, "You're building up this sense of guilt to keep you from feeling his death." It hadn't helped then, but it had later. Trise was wise.

Some evenings as he sat across from her, he felt he had already lost her, but then she would seem like herself—as she was last night, talking about the play. At least, until she got tired there at the end. It had helped to have Olive here.

For these next three days he wouldn't have to guard his face or his tone of voice, or try to think of something amusing to tell her. Maybe he could get hold of himself before he came back so he wouldn't let Tiresa see his worry. Last week he had sat at his desk while a patient waited in the other room, and written Luigi about Tiresa. "Pray for her and for me," he had ended.

Outside the small square of window, half obscured by the curtains, small white clouds stretched beneath the plane—like so many cobblestones on a street in Sicily. They shut off the earth below, leaving the plane free in the endless blue sky. He closed his eyes and tried hopelessly to sleep until he heard the stewardess. "Scotch," he answered, grateful for the interruption.

If Trise could have come along, they would have stayed at the Drake for old times' sake, and they would drive past the Greenwood Avenue apartment where they had lived for ten years, and eat at Jacques's again, and down the steps from the street in the Petit Gourmet where he had asked Trise to marry him. She had said no so promptly he had been knocked off his balance. Then she had added, "I don't know you well enough."

He had told her he didn't care how well she knew him or how little. He only wanted to know if she loved him. "How did anyone know anyone?" she had asked. Trise was always like that, trying to let her head control everything. He had sat in stony silence while Trise ate her dessert. And then he had looked up and seen her eyes laughing the way they could, and he had known she loved him.

He thought of the day he got his appointment as instructor at Michael Reese, and his calling Tiresa to meet him at the usual place—the top of the stairs in front of the El Greco at the Art Museum. He was held up and raced the two blocks from the car and up the stairs to find her there.

He hadn't raced like that since—until the other night with Olive. He and Trise had always lived such a sedentary life.

She had come into the living room this morning to show him how well she was. Her face was pale, poor darling; she had always had such high clear color. Unconsciously, he shook his head. He reached down to get his brief-case so abruptly that he knocked the elbow of the women next to him off the arm rest and had to apologize. Then he concentrated his whole attention on the poorly Xeroxed copy of Turnball's paper he was to discuss.

13

"But Tiresa, why don't you wait until Paulo comes back. You haven't been out in the car since I've been here and I—"

"I've already made the appointment, Olive, and I'll be perfectly all right. I wouldn't suggest going if I didn't feel equal to it."

"Did you tell Paulo you were going to cut your hair?"

"Heavens no. He would have gone up in blue smoke. You have never seen him when he gets really excited. He becomes Sicilian!"

"Well, if he won't like it . . ."

"Oh, he will when he sees it. In the hospital my hair was a burden and a nuisance, and I've had to ask you to do it for me twice since you've been here. I think we should go down, the taxi will be there."

Bessie added her pleas to Olive's. "It's taking a big chance, Mrs. Romano, Dr. Romano would blame us if we let you go and you had a heart attack or something."

"If I drop dead, it won't be either of your faults." Tiresa smiled at them. Bundled up in her fur jacket and slacks that covered the swelling in her legs and ankles, she tied a bright scarf around her neck and thrust her hands in her pockets in a gesture of bravado. Going down the corridor—a little slowly, beside a silent and uncomfortable Olive, getting into the elevator, and astonishing Carl at the desk all delighted her.

"Tiresa, are you sure you want to do this?" Olive asked as they went into the mauve and blue anteroom of Henri's.

She nodded and managed to get out the word "quite."

Tiresa could see herself all too clearly as she sat in front of the wall-size mirror. She was a sick-looking wreck. Henri gathered her hair up in his hand, holding it close to her head. "There is no trouble when the hair is heavy; yours is very heavy. And there is wave. You remember I suggested you cut it a long time ago."

Tiresa closed her eyes. The sound of the shears seemed to cut across her nerves, but when the heavy mass was severed, she felt a curious lightness. She wouldn't look until he was through.

"Voila!" Henri said. "The shape of your head shows now, and this is good. Very *distingué*." Tiresa opened her eyes and took the long-handled mirror from him. Yes, Paulo would like it. "I had your hair put in a cellophane bag. You may want to have it made into a hair piece to make a chignon?"

Tiresa glanced at the dark mass lying in the bag. "No," she said. "I'm through with it," along with so much else, she thought, wryly.

"Tiresa, you're absolutely stunning," Olive said, "And you look so much younger."

Why did the young always think you craved to look young? Of course, Paulo . . . Her slight store of energy had run out. She had meant to take Olive out to luncheon, but she couldn't make it. She sat down to wait for the taxi, not having enough strength to even talk. She was right; she couldn't have gone to the theater the other night.

Olive was frightened by Tiresa's color and her silence, the way her eyes kept closing. She shouldn't have done this. She didn't understand her.

But by evening, Tiresa had revived, and she and Olive had dinner on trays in her room. "I feel light-headed with my hair cut," Tiresa laughed. "I have to keep feeling my head."

The phone rang while they were eating. "Maybe that's Paulo calling again," Tiresa said, eager as a young girl. But she handed the phone to Olive. "It's for you."

"Hello."

"Ollie?"

It took Olive a minute to find her voice. "Ron?"

"Your mother told me you were there so I—uh, thought I'd call. Say hello to Tiresa and Paulo for me. Gives you a funny feeling to be right there next door to where we used to live, doesn't it?"

"I try not to think about it."

"Well, what I called about is that Mother's going to be with me for a few days and she'd like to see Johnny. I mean, after all, he is her only grandchild, you know."

"Well sure," Olive said in a voice not quite her own. "But we won't be back in Summit till Saturday or Sunday night."

"I know, but I'm going to be in Boston and I thought I could pick Johnny up there."

"When would you come for him?"

"Well, I thought tomorrow, if that's all right with you."

"In the morning?"

"I couldn't get up there till late in the afternoon; I'm here in Syracuse. Oh, I'd say five o'clock."

"And then you'd stay overnight in Boston?"

"Well, yes. It'd be easier on Johnny. I'd take him to a motel."

"Why don't you wait and get him in the morning?"

There was a pause. "Well, you know, Ollie, I'm kind of anxious to see him."

"All right. I'll have him ready tomorrow about five."

"Thanks, Ollie, take care."

"And of course, Betsy will be at the motel, and act as if Johnny is hers," Olive grumbled. "I hate him moving back and forth like this."

"I know," Tiresa said. "And it won't get any easier."

"He'll be here around five tomorrow."

"It's too bad Paulo won't be back by then. He's always good at situations . . . it's odd, too. He's often abrupt and blunders in human relations because he's not tactful—with men, never with women," Tiresa added with a laugh. "Women always feel his Sicilian charm."

They had moved now from Ron to Paulo. But Olive was not to be diverted. "Ron must be coming to Boston to see Betsy—she's the woman."

"But he does have to come to the central office on business, doesn't he? I'm sure you don't need to worry about Johnny when he's with Ron. Ron has always seemed to me most devoted to him. But you're not really worrying about Johnny; you're feeling fiercely possessive; you want him all to yourself. We're all like that. I am myself."

"And they'll sleep together—with Johnny there."

Tiresa laughed. "I don't think Johnny is going to receive some deep psychic wound that will bother him all his life, if that's what you're worried about."

Olive ignored her amusement. "Why do people always say sleep together when they mean make love? I hate covering up things."

"Poets often speak of loving as dying, you know." She hadn't meant to say that. Her mind seemed to ferret out the word on every occasion and hold it up to remind her. "'We die and rise the same and prove Mysterious by this love,'" she quoted quickly. "'The dying of self in the act of love.'"

Olive frowned. "If you have an orgasm, you mean. Of course, you'll be the same afterward and it can be an awful let-down. Anyway, I don't like losing myself."

Olive had all the terms, but little experience of any ecstasy. Paulo would be appalled if he could hear her. "How long will Ron have Johnny? I'm going to miss him around here," Tiresa said to move the subject to safer ground.

"Oh, just the weekend. I didn't think to ask him, but that ought to be enough. He'll bring him back to Summit." Olive's eyes could pale or darken with her thoughts. They were almost gray as she looked over at Tiresa. "I don't think we were ever very much in love. You and Paulo made me feel that. In a way, I guess you're part of the reason I didn't want to go on being married to Ron."

"Paulo and I! Why Olive, what do you mean?" Tiresa's voice chilled at the thought of Olive's bringing them into it.

"I remember the very first night we came here to your apartment—you asked us for a drink, remember? There was something between you. Paulo would look at you and you would smile back at him—I don't know; I could feel it. And you always seem to have so much to talk about together. Ron and I weren't that way when we were alone. And then that time you were so angry at Paulo for showing me the locket, but the next time I saw you together, it hadn't made any difference. I hate that word togetherness, but boy, you and Paulo have it. At least, I have an idea of what it could be like."

Tiresa was irritated, but touched. "Olive, you and Ron belong to another generation, you have another idiom, that's all. Of course, your relationship would be different. You don't want to judge yours by that of anyone's else." She was too tired to go on talking. "I'm sorry to give you such a dull evening, Olive, but after my spree this morning, I think I'd better call it a day."

"Oh, that's fine. I was going to wash my hair anyway," Olive said.

Tiresa thought wryly of her saying they would have a womany time.

"Maybe I shouldn't be here when Ron comes," Olive said the next afternoon. "I could have Johnny all ready except for his snowsuit and you could see Ron."

"Wouldn't that make the situation more awkward? Ron will be coming to get Johnny often over the years."

Olive had devoted herself to Johnny all afternoon. Now of a sudden, she swooped down and picked him up, holding him on her lap. "Don't be too good, Johnny. You keep Daddy awake in the night, d'you hear? So he'll be sick of you. It won't be any fun traveling home without you along."

Olive, holding Johnny, was not a traditional mother figure, but an authentic one, Tiresa thought. Her hair fell like a shawl on either side of her face that was alight as she talked to Johnny.

"Want to walk, Johnny?" Olive set him on his feet and took his hand. "Show Mommy how far you can walk."

He was a strong little boy and stepped out in jerky steps across to the table, but when she withdrew her hand he took two more steps and plopped down, beaming at the praise from his audience.

"How long ago was it that you wondered if you would love him?"

"Wasn't I an idiot! But I learn fast!"

It might have been three years ago, Tiresa thought, as Ron and Olive sat there. They might have just come down the hall from their apartment. But how different their moods were. Ron was elaborately casual, Olive was painfully taut. Johnny sat on Ron's knees.

"I've written out what Johnny eats, and I put some jars of baby food to get you started," Olive said. "If your mother has any questions, she can call me."

"Thanks, Ollie. That will be a help."

"Will you have a drink with us?" Tiresa asked. "I'm sorry that Paulo won't get back until tomorrow."

"I'd sure like to, Tiresa, but I think I better push on with Johnny. I feel quite the responsibility tonight, you can see." When he smiled, he was quite engaging, Tiresa thought. He stood up. "I'm going to miss Paulo, you tell him hello from me, but it's good to see you looking so well. I like your hair short."

"Thank you. Olive took me to the hairdresser yesterday. Paulo hasn't seen it yet."

"You didn't get the fever and have yours cut, Ollie, I see." Oh yes, he was quite at ease.

Olive was putting Johnny into his snowsuit. "I'll be in Summit Sunday night, Ron. When will you bring Johnny back?"

"Gosh, Ollie, let us have him three or four days. Mother's dying to get to know him a bit, I'll tell you. I'll call you Sunday night. We can decide then."

Johnny looked dubious as Ron picked him up. "Here we go, Johnny boy." Ron moved him to his shoulder. "Wave good-bye to Mommy." He waved Johnny's hand for him. "Thanks, Tiresa, and Ollie. See you."

Olive followed them out to the door. The apartment was very quiet when she came back to the fire. Tiresa lay against the pillows on the couch. "Ron was here twenty-seven minutes," Olive said.

"It wouldn't have been any easier if he stayed longer."

Olive sat down across from Tiresa. "I hate it," she said vaguely. She picked up the *New Yorker* and looked at the same advertisements and cartoons she had looked at before.

Paulo had stopped to say a word to Carl, downstairs at the office, when Ron and Johnny came out of the elevator.

"Ron!" Paulo said in amazement. "It looks as though you're taking my godson away with you."

"That's right, Paulo. He has to spend some time with his father. I'm glad I didn't miss you. I thought Tiresa said you wouldn't be back till tomorrow."

"I didn't expect to, but I came a day early." Paulo's face was grave. "Ron, this is an incredible situation—you and Olive."

"I think so, too, but it's what Ollie wants," Ron said cheerfully.

Paulo was scowling. "Are you sure of that, Ron?"

"Yes, I am. You ask her."

"Well, good luck to you." Paulo decided that he liked Ron less than he had thought. "Goodbye Johnny. We became good friends, didn't we? And I see you've got your bear."

Paulo watched Ron cross the parking lot, saw the right hand door open and Ron hand Johnny in to someone in the car. All the way up in the elevator, Paulo thought of Olive crying about the lack of happiness in life. If Ron had seen her, he couldn't have let her go.

"Relax, Ron," Betsy said after they had driven a few blocks in silence. "You don't have to spend the night, you know, if you'd feel better alone with Johnny."

"After I've driven all this way? I came to see you, too, you know. I want you and Johnny to know each other." He felt grateful. "I guess I was pretty uptight." He gave a laugh. "You knew it right away, didn't you?"

"I'd be dumb if I didn't. Johnny's a darling, Ron. I love him already."

Ron reached over for her hand. She understood him better than Olive ever had. But, all the same, it hadn't been easy seeing Olive.

14

"You're a free woman then in June," Gumshoe said. "That's only six months."

"That's right. I'll have to appear when the decree is granted and that's all there is to it." Olive traced the pattern of the placemat with one finger. She and Gumshoe were having lunch in New York at Stouffers'.

"I'm amazed you can do it that fast."

"It isn't so fast if you've been waiting for it. Once you know you're really through and you want out, your marriage weighs on you." By a curious turnabout Olive had become the more experienced.

"You must have moments when—" Gumshoe began.

"Not really. I simply saw that Ron and I didn't have any future together, so—" Their conversation came in fits and starts and broken off sentences, and may not have been very different from the conversations going on over the other tables at Stouffers'.

Gumshoe added more coffee to her cup. "I wonder if a relationship between a man and a woman needs to have a future. You just want it to be something you can count on. What do you mean by future?"

Olive spread her hands vaguely. "You want it to keep growing and feel closer; an ever-recurring miracle." But the phrase sounded queer on her lips. "We got so we lived in little routines. I knew what Ron was going to say if I said something. He probably knew what I would. That can get dull. He'd tell me little gobbits about his work, and I'd tell him about Johnny, and then when we were through and watched TV and had a beer, and then we'd go to bed and make love."

"Doesn't sound too bad to me." Gumshoe gave a little laugh. "You were probably both tired at the end of the day. I don't know what you expect. At least you weren't lonely. He'd be lying there beside you. Just having Alain in the apartment made everything different for me. I hate this celibate life."

They were silent, each thinking over her own experience.

"No dessert," they both told the waitress.

"Remember at college, splurging and having a chocolate fudge nut sundae? After you met Ron you started to watch your diet. You don't have any trouble keeping thin now, do you?"

"Sure, I keep my mind on it. Women do when they're getting a divorce—their world is so upset, you know. I read this book about women and divorce. I catch myself having something to eat after the family have gone to bed. Just to be doing something, not because I'm hungry. And then I go to bed and read for a couple of hours. You wouldn't know me; I'm getting positively cerebral."

"You always thought those Romanos had such a great marriage. Do you still think so after being there this time?"

"Tiresa is sick, but you can feel how close they are—not in any stuffy way. You feel they know what life is all about. We had a terrific discussion one night after Paulo took me to see *The Three Sisters*. It's by Chekhov."

"Thanks, kiddy. I read it in French 315. Chekhov was a doctor so I guess he'd seen plenty of life."

But they weren't really interested in Chekhov and relapsed into silence. Olive played with her spoon.

"I've got to get into something pretty soon or I'll disintegrate," Olive burst out.

"I know what you mean. I felt that way in Paris. That's why I came back home and went to medical school. What do you think you'll do?"

"Well, I can't get a job—anything real. A liberal arts B.A. is for the birds, it seems. I'm thinking of going to graduate school."

"And take what?"

"You'll think I'm out of my mind."

"I thought that when you got married to Ron so fast."

"Well, I'm going to see if I can take Marine Biology." She waited for Gumshoe's reaction.

"Why not? You were interested in that man's stuff you were typing, and you were good in Biology 412. I can see you coming up out of the deep in a diver's suit. So feminine, too."

But Olive was serious. "I wonder if they let women do that. I'd like to get a look down there once." At least Gumshoe hadn't hooted at her.

"Get going on it, Kiddie, maybe you could get a grant or something. What about Johnny?"

"I'll manage." She had a sudden feeling of confidence as she picked up the check. "I suggested this so I should take you."

"Let's stick to Dutch. Neither of us is rolling."

As they waited at the cash register, Olive said, "I haven't even asked you how med school is going. Hard, I bet."

"I can cope—just, but it keeps me pumping. You don't know what a spree this is for me."

"Me, too. I'm not exactly living the glamour life."

As Olive waited for the bus back to Summit, she bought a postcard and sat down on a bench to write.

Feb. 17, 1977
Dear Tiresa,
Thank you for letting me come. I was so low and bored—maybe even a little scared about what I'm going to do with my life, and being with you and Paulo gave me a terrific lift. I even feel some days that I might get

to Moscow!!! But, if I don't, I'll remember Paulo saying with that shrug of his, "Happiness comes in moments." I mean to get as many of those as I can.

My love to you both,
Olive

P.S. I just heard that my hearing is coming up in late June. I'll see you then, and I'd love to stay overnight with you if that's convenient. Mother will take care of Johnny while I'm gone, so I'll be alone.

"At least we taught her to think in terms of metaphor," Tiresa said. "That will help her."

"She was meant to be happy; it's such a shame." Paulo shook his head.

"Aren't we all?" Tiresa asked, making a face at him.

"We are." Paulo's eyes met hers.

"Even now, Paulo," Tiresa said, smiling at him.

Tuzenbach: *"Not only in two or three hundred years but in a million years life will be just the same; it doesn't change, it remains stationary, following its own laws which we have nothing to do with or which, anyway, we'll never find out. Migratory birds, cranes for instance, fly backwards and forwards, and whatever ideas, great or small, stray through their minds, they still go on flying just the same without knowing where or why. They fly and will continue to fly, however philosophic they become; and it doesn't matter how philosophical they are so long as they go on flying . . . When we are dead, men will fly balloons, change the fashion of their coats, will discover a sixth sense, perhaps, and develop it, but life will remain just the same, difficult, full of mysteries and happiness. In a thousand years man will sigh just the same, "Ah, how hard life is," and yet just as now he will be afraid of death and not want it."*

Chekhov, *The Three Sisters*, acts 2 and 4

I

The June sun poured into the living room of the apartment, polished the purple plums of the Della Robia wreath and swung in a dazzle of radiance on the golden balls moving perpetually back and forth within the glass walls of the clock on the mantel. The windows on the balcony stood open, letting in the lively sounds of the Avenue below, but they served only to deepen the quiet inside the room.

Tiresa lay on the couch, a clipboard on her lap, her fountain pen lost in the folds of the afghan, her hands idle. Two new books she had ordered lay on the table beside her, but she had no urge to open them. Bessie had the afternoon and evening off, and Paulo wouldn't be back until late afternoon. She could lie here and do nothing. "Relax more, Mrs. Romano. Be content to be a vegetable for a few weeks," Dr. Stiles had said after her last bout in the hospital.

"Trisa Chesny, you're special," Papa used to say. "Yes sir, you're a winner, isn't she, Mama?" A little flame of excitement would rise in her, and she would believe him. The last time he said it was when he came to see her get her doctorate degree. But she wasn't anything special; she was an inert female lying here, only half alive, listening to the clock tick and her heart beat and there was no excitement in her.

She had been like this ever since she came back from the hospital last week, too miserable to be anything else. Paulo had taken to watching television in the study sometimes of an evening, coming out to see her during commercials, teasing her about being too high-brow to watch, but knowing she didn't have the energy to concentrate on the remote antics on the television screen. It was easier to listen to music, eyes closed, not really knowing whether she was asleep or half awake. That was her secret terror—that she was coming to the point where she couldn't think, that the heart wouldn't pump the blood to her brain fast enough. She tried to sound alert when she talked with Paulo and Dr. Stiles, and listened to herself, testing.

Her slow progress on the book discouraged her. Yesterday when she re-read the last ten pages she had written, they seemed all flat statements and stupid generalities. She might as well give it up and say so, but it was something to look preoccupied with when she was too tired to cerebrate. Paulo didn't try to talk if he saw her writing, even if at that moment she was merely sitting with her pen in her hand. Perhaps he was relieved that he didn't have to try to say something cheerful.

Paulo had grown more silent, too. Maybe he felt there was nothing he could say to her—and yet they had so little time left. She saw him looking at her, his eyes growing clinical, seeing that she would never be any better. He didn't try to pretend that she was improving. And this morning she had seen that his face was changing, becoming more like the picture of his mother when she was old—patient, resigned, infinitely sad. Of all peoples, surely Sicilians showed sadness most clearly in their faces. As if all the races that had mingled in their blood-stream had each brought its own experience of sorrow. Did that make sense? She knew what she meant, but she had the feeling that her sentences came out confused.

Her illness had changed them both. Not in their love; that was always there, but they seemed to be drawing into themselves. She had things to think of by herself. It was too hard for Paulo to have her talk to him about dying, but she was coming to look at it with her new mind of winter. She poured herself a glass of chilled orange juice from the thermos Bessie had left on her table, trying not to think, to be a vegetable, but it was no use.

Underneath her thoughts about herself, she worried about Paulo. He had gone to pieces when his brother died, but she had been there to put him together again. He was so apt to give way to self-pity and bitterness, and be morose and withdrawn, except with patients. His practice would help, but coming home to dinner and the long evenings would be hard on him. They had lived too closely together—she should have seen that Paulo went away with his friends, the way men did. But he only went away to medical meetings. He might even throw up his practice and go back to Sicily.

She moved her mind quickly from the picture it conjured up of Paulo sitting on the Corso at mid-morning, drinking Campari and soda, and staring moodily at passers-by. She had seen men sitting there like that. His old friends would rally round, but they had too little in common after all these years; and Paulo could withdraw too deep into himself for anyone to reach. And Asunta—she doubted if she would be interested in him in that kind of mood, or if Paulo would turn to her.

Luigi would help him. Perhaps he could get him into charity work. She could suggest that to Paulo. "After I'm gone, Paulo," she would say. He would only let her get that far, but she would insist. "No, listen to me. Go away for a little; go back to Sicily. Maybe you could work in one of those free clinics for a while. There must be hundreds of Sicilians in those poverty-stricken tenements who needed their eyes cared for." She tried to remember seeing people in Sicily wearing glasses, but she could recall only people with wonderful bright black eyes. Paulo was deeply compassionate; he did plenty of charity work in his own practice, but—a quiver of laughter crossed her mind, she could imagine Paulo's incredulity at the future she had planned for him. "But Trise, I'm no St. Francis," he would say. She could see the face he would make.

And then, as though she had been delaying and now crossed the room and opened the door to someone she had kept waiting there, her mind moved to Olive. Olive might be able to keep Paulo from loneliness and depression. If she came to love him enough, Olive could make a whole new life for him. Tiresa looked at the idea quite calmly, coldly almost.

But Olive was so young—Paulo so much older. If she didn't love him enough, she could hurt him—she didn't understand anything about love. And he would feel remorseful at letting Olive take her place. But, of course, Olive could never do that. No one could. She sat a long time thinking what it would be like for her if she were alone without Paulo. Tiresa picked up her pen and made lines on the half-covered sheet of paper on the clipboard—firm, straight lines. She would want no one else ever; but Paulo was different. All that he remembered would make him sad; he didn't know how to draw joy out of what he had had, he was too rooted in this day, this moment.

What he would feel for Olive would be no transplanted love—her mind drove ruthlessly ahead, screening out what she could not bear to think of, picturing them together. He would feel a tender pride in Olive's youth; they would play tennis and go swimming and go up to the farm in the winter and ski—all those things she had never been able to do with him. He would feel great gratitude.

The phone rang and she knew it was Paulo. He always called about this time in the late afternoon. She took a breath to make her voice sound hearty.

"Hello."

"Trise, you sound fine. What are you doing?"

"Sitting here, thinking." She could feel Paulo hesitate.

"What about?"

"Memory."

"Oh, your book." He was relieved.

"Don't hurry. I'm fine."

"Aren't you anxious to see me?"

"What do you think? I've waited all day for you; I just don't want you to feel hurried."

"Things look pretty good here. I've got three more patients, then I'll be home. My love, Tirese."

"And mine."

But as she hung up the phone, the thought of not being here to answer Paulo's call suddenly stabbed her, and all her strength disappeared. "I can't stand it." Her mouth shaped the words without making a sound.

When Paulo came home, she was in bed. "I felt unusually well today, and then, suddenly, I was tired, so I had a glass of yogurt and came to bed. Do you mind, Paulo?"

"Of course not; that was the wise thing to do. I'll make you some dinner that will taste good to you. First, I'll bring you a drink." But he wondered. Her voice was less strong than it had been over the phone. Something not quite right about it. Usually she made an effort to sit up for dinner with him. When he carried their drinks into the bedroom, Tiresa was already asleep, so he carried them back out.

He had been lonely as a young man in Chicago. "'Loneliness and discontent prove our separateness from dumb animals,'" he had read somewhere and copied it down. He had tried to make a virtue of them until he met Tiresa, and there was no longer any need. But tonight they were in the taste of the lamb chop he ate mechanically, and even in the wine he drank with it.

He saw clearly that Trise was slipping; she seemed a little removed and it bothered him. He must talk with Stiles tomorrow, ask him to drop by. If there was any way possible, he wanted to avoid another hospitalization just now. He looked down the dreary months ahead.

For fear of disturbing Tiresa, he slept in the study, but he went to her room twice during the night. Toward morning, he woke, hearing some sound. When he got to her door, he realized she was crying. Tiresa never cried.

"*Carissima?*"

265

"Oh, Paulo, I had a dream." She shook her head, not able to go on talking.

He put his arm around her, supporting her while he waited for her heart to quiet. "It was because I wasn't sleeping here beside you. What were you dreaming?"

"I dreamed that after I was gone, you married—and had a child and you gave my *medaglione* to your—wife, and put her name and the child's . . ." She was crying again.

"Tirese, dear foolish Trise. I'll never marry again, and I will never show your locket to anyone. Put your heart at rest, my darling." He made her more comfortable against the pillows. "Now try to sleep and don't dream any more. I'm going to be right here." He sat down beside her, with his head on the edge of the bed. "All right, Tiresa?" For an answer he felt her lay her hand on his head.

He fell asleep for a few minutes. When he lifted his head, she whispered, "Yes, Paulo, you must marry again. It won't be like our marriage."

"Trise, no other marriage ever was or could be, you know that."

"None," she said aloud, and her voice was strong.

2

The next evening, Tiresa was sitting up on the couch in her green housecoat waiting for Paulo. She wore earrings and the purplish tinge of her lips was covered with lipstick. Her mind was preoccupied with her plan. Paulo felt the difference in her the moment he came in.

"Tiresa, how elegant you look!"

"I stayed in bed all day so I'd be less droopy for you this evening. I was such a total loss last night."

"Never a loss, Tirese. Even in sleep, you're my gain!"

Tiresa wrinkled her brows. "Now that's too extravagant, Paulo, even for you."

But Tiresa ate hardly anything at dinner, and her face looked gaunt in the candlelight. He had difficulty thinking of interesting happenings in his day to tell her about.

"I've been expecting to hear from Olive. You know she's coming back to Boston for the final hearing this month," Tiresa said.

"That's right. She'll call one of these days, or send one of her famous postcards. What was that word she used for the cause of her divorce?"

"'Irretrievable breakdown of the marriage.'"

Paulo shook his head. "The whole thing is a childish absurdity. Nothing is irretrievable."

"Paulo, how fallacious! Plenty of things are—my health, for one thing."

"All right, all right. *Basta!* But their marriage should be retrievable, if each of them gave a little."

"I don't agree with you, and I think I understand them better than you do—Olive, at least. I'm thinking of asking Olive to stay on with us for a few days as she did the last time. You know, she's coming by herself this time."

Paulo was slow in answering. "It will be fine to see her, but that's not a good idea, Trise. You got pretty tired the last time she was here. By the way, I sent off a little check to Johnny this week for his birthday. I just happened to think of it at the office."

Tiresa was startled that he hadn't talked to her about it, and put it away in her mind as evidence that he depended less on her. "I'd like to have Olive stay for a few days, Paulo. I'm really terribly isolated all day," she said more firmly.

Paulo's face clouded. "I realize that, and it bothers me. As a matter if fact, I talked to Lingelman—he's that bright young man in the Opthamology service. He's interested in getting out into private practice and he wouldn't mind being at the office in the afternoon. It would give him a taste of what it's like and he'd make some extra money. I'd have all my afternoons with you."

Tiresa was silent while Bessie brought the coffee, and they moved over to the couch. "Not yet, Paulo. You know you'd be bored doing nothing but taking care of me."

Paulo filled their cups. "I don't feel that way about it. You don't seem to realize that you matter more to me than anybody or anything in the world, Tiresa. Besides, I'd put you to work on glaucoma cases."

She began coughing and had to lean against his shoulder. "I hate being like this," she said, hardly above a whisper.

"I know, my darling, I know," Paulo murmured. "I hate having you—" He didn't add his usual reassurance that she would get stronger, and they sat there, helpless in the face of their mortality. When Paulo started to get up, Tiresa said, "You wouldn't really mind if Olive stayed a little, would you? I'd like to have her once more."

Paulo winced at the 'once more.' "She has to work out her own life, you know. And I don't think having her up here. Oh,

Trise, let us be by ourselves; selfishly, I don't want anybody else around."

She resisted his appeal. "I'm not up to being alone day after day, either." The remark came out more pettishly than she meant, but she went on, "I'd like to have someone young around for a few days."

Paulo was silent. This wanting someone with them was new. They had always begrudged sharing their life with another person for more than a day or two. Trise needed to rest, and she had her books and her writing—he was here every minute that he could be. He was not sure how pleasant it would be for Olive, either. Tiresa didn't realize how their life revolved around her illness—the very thing she would be so quick to see if she were herself.

"Poor Paulo! The whims of an invalid wife are unpredictable and a trial."

He was surprised that she realized that; she had seemed oblivious of so many things lately. But, of course, she was always aware of everything. Now he was chagrined at being so obtuse himself. "Well, she's going to be here overnight, anyway. Ask her to stay one more day, if you want."

"Paulo, you'll go with her to the hearing, won't you? It's too bleak for her to go alone. And it would be nice if you took her to luncheon afterwards, if the hearing comes in the morning."

"We'll see when the hearing is; it all depends on my schedule," he said a little stiffly.

"Don't be irritated, Paulo, and give me a little more coffee." She was smiling at him.

It took Tiresa a long time the next afternoon to write her letter to Olive. She must let Olive feel that she was needed, that this was no ordinary visit—as indeed it wasn't. In all her life, she had never had anything so difficult to write.

June 8, 1978
Dear Olive,
When you come for your hearing, won't you plan to stay with us longer than just overnight? Paulo needs a

rest from having me constantly on his mind, and I [she held her pen a long time without finishing the sentence, hunting the right word, rejecting one after another. How to say enough and not too much?] *am here alone all day, except for Bessie, and need someone I can talk to.* [When had she ever needed that with Paulo here in the morning and evening, and her books and her writing? But she must make a real plea.] *Paulo is thinking of taking time away from the office to be with me more.* [Now the words were even harder to find.] *But no one knows how long I shall go on existing this way. Sometimes, I feel it will not be very long, but I could drag on, and Paulo must not give up his work. It will be a refuge to him when I am gone.* [She read over what she had written with cold eyes, she hated writing so personally, but she must begin to talk to her. There was so much she needed to say to her, and so little time.]

The thought of coming to an invalid household is not very appealing, I realize—and that is what it has become. Do you think you can stand it? I have my ups and downs, and make pretty dull company when my head feels as though it is filled with cotton, I warn you. But there are other times when I am quite normal and need some—companionship. [Again, she sat hunting for words, then she ended quite simply.] *I would be deeply grateful if you can stay a week with us. We need to have a "child of joy" with us for a bit.*

Tiresa.

She rather thought the name Paulo had given her that day meant something to Olive; she wouldn't have forgotten it. She folded the sheet and slipped it into its envelope. But after Bessie had taken the letter, her mind kept raising questions. What if they came to realize that she . . . But they never would. And she was only bringing them together at a crucial time—no more than that.

Nor had she just made up the idea. There they had stood in front of her, the possibility so clear it had shattered her.

She must make Olive feel that Paulo needed her—would need her—until she found herself loving him. It was quite clear and simple in Tiresa's mind. Olive would come to love Paulo at first; it would take Paulo more time, but Olive would keep him from the loneliness and depression that were more than he could stand. She would seem touching to him in her youth, just as she had that night after the play in her longing for happiness, and he would turn to her more and more.

She was tired of thinking, and lying here in bed. Very slowly, trying to ignore her shortness of breath, she crossed the distance from the bed to the door, then along the hall to the living room. Each trip she made now she compared with her last one. Her legs bothered her more today, and her breathing . . . She sank gratefully into the chair by the balcony windows. She felt like some great unwieldy freight boat landing in the harbor. Her heart was racing, stopping until she lost touch with existence, then beating her into awareness again. She leaned back, closing her eyes. The sun felt good on her cold hands. She spread her fingers as though to rest them from holding too tightly onto something.

She must have slept. Suddenly bright sun was striking her full in the face, blinding her; she had to close her eyes against the dazzle. But she was content to sit there, neither quite asleep nor fully awake. The sun moved away from her face and hands. When she opened her eyes, it had concentrated all its radiance in a wide circle of light on the floor just in front of her, "I saw Eternity the other night like a ring of pure and endless light," she murmured sleepily, hardly thinking what she said, or where it was from. The words spoke themselves, triggered by the ring of light at her feet. Then the meaning began to register on her brain. She stared at the radiant beam until she felt drawn into it, out of herself—beyond wanting or needing.

3

Olive saw Paulo as the bus drove in under the shed of the station. She seldom thought of him as Sicilian, but today in the crowd he stood out clearly as foreign, with his black hair and eyes and the deep tan of his skin. His expression was stern, but when he saw her come out on the platform of the bus, a wide smile transformed his face.

"Welcome back, Olive," he said as he kissed her.

On the way to the car, he asked about Johnny. "I'd like to see him, but I'm glad you didn't bring him in this time. Tiresa has lost ground, and it might have been too much for her to have him." Paulo didn't start the motor at once, but sat looking down the street, his hands resting on the wheel. "She was in the hospital just last week; she really should be there still, but she objects so bitterly, I brought her home again. She's . . ." He lifted his hand from the wheel and dropped it again in a gesture of hopelessness. "I don't know how long she can live this way." His voice broke.

Olive swallowed. "Is it all right for me to come? I can perfectly well stay in a hotel, you know."

"She's looking forward to seeing you. As sick as she was, and a little confused some of the time, she hasn't forgotten that you're coming." It bothered him that Olive's arrival seemed to be one of the reasons she insisted on coming home. "But I wanted to warn you that you'll find her—changed. She's up very little; the least thing she does exhausts her, even talking, sometimes. And she's more withdrawn. She knows her condition, and she seems to accept it; she's very strong. It's I who cannot." He started the motor.

"I'm so sorry," Olive said, feeling inadequate.

"I'm afraid the atmosphere of the apartment is too much like a hospital to be a very pleasant place," Paulo said as they were driving. "A nurse comes in once a day; Tiresa won't hear of having one any more than that."

"I'm just glad I can see her. And I'll leave tomorrow; it certainly is no help to have another person around."

"No. Tiresa wants you to stay a little longer than that, Olive. Perhaps it will do her good to have you. It's hard to tell."

They drove the rest of the way without talking. Olive thought of the time when Paulo drove her to the hospital to have Johnny, but he was too worried to remind him of that. She saw the apartment house up ahead and looked quickly to find their balcony.

Paulo went softly down the hall and looked into their bedroom before he beckoned Olive to come. "Here she is, Tiresa."

"It's so wonderful to see you, Tiresa."

"We're glad to have you here, my dear."

She was very sick, but she wasn't as changed as Paulo had made her think. Her voice was just the same—that warm low way of speaking that made what she said seem important.

Paulo laid his hand against Tiresa's face and kissed her, and she lifted her face up to him, smiling. Reassured, Olive leaned over to smell the yellow roses on the table by Tiresa's bed. She noticed that a couch stood where Tiresa's desk used to be.

Olive felt instantly that Bessie disapproved of her coming. She had carried Olive's bag into the guest room and was waiting for her. "I don't know whether you realize it, Mrs. Fifer, but we've got a terribly sick lady here," she said sorrowfully. "I'm here all day now; we just don't know . . ."

"She seems more mature, doesn't she?" Tiresa said.

Paulo shrugged. "I didn't notice. I expected to see somebody in jeans with a knapsack get off the bus instead of this smart-looking young woman in a dark dress and a proper handbag."

Tiresa nodded. "She's dressed for her appearance in court. You're going to manage to go with her tomorrow, aren't you?"

Paulo smiled. "Yes, Tirese, for you I will manage it, but it's not easy." He went out of the room, but was back in a minute. "The table is set for two out there. Aren't we eating on trays in here with you?"

"No. I really don't want very much tonight, and Bessie brought me a tray earlier. You'll have a better meal if you eat at the table."

Paulo was scowling. "Tirese, I don't like this. Since I eat my dinners with you, wherever you are, every night, I don't see—"

"Don't fuss, Paulo. You can both eat in here tomorrow night. Go make us a drink and we'll have that together in here."

"To your being with us again, Olive," Tiresa said, lifting her glass.

"I can drink to that, too," Olive said. "It seems ages since last February." Tiresa seemed so like herself, Olive was beginning to relax.

"And I'll drink to my godson." Paulo touched his glass to Tiresa's.

"I'm disappointed not to see him. You must bring him in the next time you come," Tiresa said, smiling brightly at them.

"Ron can bring him over some time. He's back in Boston now. He's going to be married this summer," Olive announced without any inflection in her voice; she might have been reporting on the weather.

4

Well, that wasn't so bad," Paulo said as he and Olive sat at lunch after the hearing.

"I thought it was ghastly. I hated everything about it; I felt as if I were going to be tried for a murder."

"You just let your imagination run away with you."

"I thought once it was over, I'd feel relieved and—free, but I just feel let-down and horrid. If you hadn't been there, Paulo, I couldn't have stood it."

"You looked very sober, but beautifully poised, I thought." In spite of his irritation over having to change his schedule of patients, and postpone his rounds at the hospital, he was glad he had been there. When he came into the courtroom, Olive was standing in front of the judge, pale and tense. He had thought she would take it more . . . *accidentalmente.* Tirese said she wouldn't mind it, but she was taking it hard.

"At least, I didn't have to meet Ron. My lawyer impressed it on me that I had to be there. Maybe if you're the one getting the divorce, you're supposed to be present. Why do you suppose Ron didn't come, Paulo?" She was looking in her bag for something.

Paulo's mouth gathered itself together in doubt, then smoothed into a slight smile. "It's a more or less unpleasant procedure, and I imagine Ron doesn't like to be made uncomfortable or embarrassed. And Olive, I'm very sure he feels bad about losing you; that he's still fond of you."

"I'll always care what happens to him, but I couldn't go back to living with him." She chose her words carefully.

"You're both fortunate that the divorce is settled without any bitterness." Paulo laid his hand over hers. "And it's all over now. Try to forget it."

Olive looked at him with a solemn face. "Trisa says you must remember everything that happens to you; that it's the only way to live deeply."

Paulo wished fervently that Tiresa were there. "Yes, I know, Tiresa believes that. She's braver than I am. But I do know that you keep the memory in its proper place, and you don't hug it to you like a hair shirt. What happened, happened, and it may hurt, or make you feel guilty even." He was using both hands now. The wedding ring on his finger caught the light. "But you don't remember just to make yourself suffer." He felt he wasn't doing very well. He was trying to repeat what Tirese had said to him once. "Olive, you have a long lovely life ahead of you in which to get to Moscow." She looked up quickly and met his flashing smile.

He picked up the menu. "Now," he said with relief, "we must have something very good to eat, and an excellent Italian wine." As Tiresa had known he would, he was setting himself to make the meal a special occasion, if not a celebration.

When Olive got back to the apartment, Tiresa's door was closed, and Bessie reported that she had been very quiet all morning. "Hardly said a word, even when the nurse was here. Mostly just laid there. It makes me sad to see her. This is my afternoon off, but I waited until you got back."

"Oh, I'm sorry. I didn't know."

"She wouldn't tell you. She says she's all right alone, but I'm not leaving her. I told you she could go off any time. I asked the Doctor, right out. And he admitted she could. 'We all could, Bessie,' he said. I don't know what he meant by that; that's just his way. If you'll come out to the kitchen, I'll show you about din-

ner tonight. The Doctor does for himself, but since you're here, I guess you could fix it. And your ex-husband called. I left the number with Mrs. Romano."

Olive changed into slacks and a shirt; she felt stiff, as though she had sat all morning in one position. Ron could call back; she wasn't going to call him if he couldn't even bother to get to the hearing.

She went out on the balcony and looked almost shyly over at their old apartment. A middle-aged woman was sitting there, reading a newspaper. Where her geraniums used to be, stood a tall tropical plant. Olive's eyes moved away, hunting the seventh floor apartment that used to have an orange chair by the window that no one ever seemed to sit in, and found it. The chair was still empty. Down on the ground in front of the apartment building, two women about her age sat watching their children play. If Johnny were here, she would take him for a walk along the river, and show him the boats. Maybe when Ron was married, he wouldn't have to have him so often.

"John Ronald Fifer, minor, shall reside with his mother, and his father shall have the right to visit him at all reasonable times and places."

She had the words by heart. But Johnny was mostly hers, she felt. She went indoors and heard Tiresa stirring.

"Come in," Tiresa said when she knocked. She was just getting back in bed.

"Trisa, should you get out of bed?"

"Yes, that's my one freedom I guard jealously." She was short of breath but she looked better, and her voice was natural. "Well my dear, that ordeal is behind you. Paulo called and said you were completely in command."

"Oh, Tiresa, I couldn't have got through it without Paulo. And afterwards he took me to lunch, you know, and it was such a help to talk to him. He was absolutely wonderful."

"Paulo has great understanding . . ." She mustn't say too much, but Olive was listening. Her hair fell over the side of her

277

face, but she could see Olive's mouth and the way she sat. "Oddly, Paulo is no good at helping himself. He needs someone to turn to." Tiresa took a sip of water. She was silent again, but she must say some things that Olive would remember later. "That worries me about leaving him. I'm afraid he won't do well alone. Even now, if I'm not here when he gets home at the end of the day, he can be melancholy." Olive was looking across the room.

Tiresa lifted her head to get more air. "That's why I wanted you to be here for a few days with us. My being sick is hard on Paulo. He gets depressed."

Now Olive was looking right at her. "When I die, Olive, try to come to him—he shouldn't be alone." She wanted to soften that, to explain, to be even a little wry, but she had to stop. Maybe she had said too much as it was.

When Olive found her voice, she said, "I'll try to."

Tiresa picked up the note on her table about Ron's call. "This is for you."

"I'm going to let him call me. I don't know how he knew I was still here."

"Better get it over with. Go call him in the study."

Ron answered at once.

"Ron?"

"I was sure you'd be at the Romanos'. I—uh—couldn't get to the hearing. Technically, of course, the lawyer said I didn't need to be there."

She waited.

"I just wanted to call to say I'm sorry things worked out this way."

"Yes," she said crisply. "I guess it's just one more marriage down the drain. I guess we're not unique."

"I can't help but think the Romanos had something to do with it."

"I don't see how you can say that."

"I always felt you were different when you'd come home from there. I don't know, lots of little things. She had a mother com-

plex and filled you full of advice. I bet you'd never have thought of getting a divorce if you hadn't known them. And, of course, I couldn't compete with the Sicilian lover."

"That's a stupid damn remark, Ron Fifer, and you know it. I was certainly grateful to Paulo today. He interrupted his practice to be there at the hearing."

"Oh, he's good at that; he's always Johnny-on-the-spot. He was on hand to take you to the hospital, too, I remember."

She was too angry to answer.

"Well, Ollie, I'll be talking to you again. Did you get everything you want out of the stuff? I sent everything you had on the list."

"If I think of anything, I'll let you know. Everything you sent is in the basement at the folks'. I haven't looked at it since it came."

"You're sure you don't want the iris?"

"No thanks, it's too sexy for me."

Ron gave a weak laugh. "You never forget anything, do you? How's Johnny?"

"He's fine. He's with the folks."

"Gosh, I want to see him. I haven't seen him for over two months. It's kind of unhandy getting down to New Jersey, now that I'm living back here, but I was thinking, maybe I could go down this weekend and take him to Mother's for a few days."

"I suppose."

"Plan on it then—okay?"

"Okay. When are you getting married, Ron?"

"Uh—the first week in August, I think it is. Yeah—the seventh."

"I see."

"Ollie, I just want to say—in fact, that's why I called. There aren't any hard feelings between us."

"Not on my side."

"That's good. I'll always think a lot of you, you know."

She didn't answer.

279

"So take care, and good luck."

"You too, Ron. I mean it," she added, warming suddenly. She hung up the receiver. Ron had really called about getting Johnny. She went back in to Tiresa.

"How did it all go?"

"Oh, all right, I guess. It's all so unpleasant and stupid. What's the worst about it is that I thought I was really in love, and then I wasn't. That scares me. What if I made the same mistake again some day? If you see me showing any signs of being in love for a long, long time, Trisa, stop me."

"No, I won't have to do that. You'll know next time. I have an idea that you'll find yourself in love with quite a different sort of person—someone more mature."

After a few moments, Olive said, "I guess I'll call the folks and tell them I'm divorced. And I want to say hello to Johnny."

Had she been too obvious? Tiresa wondered. Paulo was sometimes immature, himself. But not often—Olive would find such an understanding and tenderness as she had never known.

When Paulo came home, he would have none of their eating without Tiresa. "We'll all eat on trays in the living room." He carried Tiresa out to the couch over her protests. "This night we must all be together."

They were drinking their coffee when Olive said, "Ron's going to take Johnny this weekend."

"Stay the weekend then," Tiresa said.

"Oh I . . ."

"It depends on whether all this excitement is too much for you, Trise," Paulo said, catching Olive's eye. But he had to admit that Tiresa seemed more interested in things since Olive came—more alert.

"It's the best thing that could happen," Tiresa said, smiling. "I want very much to have you stay, Olive."

5

Do your hair up on your head some time, Olive, will you? I miss so much having mine long," Tiresa said the next morning when Olive was sitting in her room.

"I'll go put I it up right now. Maybe I should anyway. Do you realize that I'm twenty-five!"

"A tremendous age. Don't wear it up all the time, but I'd like to see it up again."

Tiresa had a real thing about hair. Olive coiled her hair into a knot on the top of her head and went back to show Tiresa.

She did look older, Tiresa noted with satisfaction. She was aware of everything about Olive now, watching her, seeing her as Paulo would.

"I'm so glad you came, Olive. Do you know that we haven't had a guest for dinner since you were here way back in the winter. Oh yes, Cathy, Paulo's sister-in-law and her new husband, and Tony, the nephew you met, came one Sunday. Paulo had told Cathy that I was too sick to have Tony for his usual visit and Cathy had drawn her own conclusions so they came to make a death-bed visit. They stood around my bed and looked at me so pityingly that I was ready to scream. I thanked her for coming and Cathy said, "Well, my goodness, we thought it was the least we could do." Tiresa's voice took on Cathy's intonations. She gave a thin little laugh that was swallowed by her labored breathing.

Olive listened uncomfortably. How could Tiresa laugh?

"The visit was really rather amusing in a grim sort of way, and Paulo and I laughed off the grimness after they left—well, almost. So you see we needed you to come and cheer us up."

"Coming here always cheers me," Olive said. "This hasn't been a very good winter for me; in fact, it's been the worst winter of my whole life. But next year will be better. Johnny's over two, at last, and I can take him to day-care next fall. We've gone to see it, and it's a fine place." She watched Tiresa's face. "And I'm going to graduate school—wait till you hear, I'm going to take Marine Biology. Isn't that a panic?"

"I think it's fine," Tiresa said slowly. She could take courses here in Boston, of course, if her heart were set on it. Paulo wouldn't mind, if . . . Tiresa touched the switch that raised the back of her bed and went back to what she had been thinking about ever since she knew Olive was coming, and then recoiled from the idea. But it was a way of giving Olive a younger image of Paulo, and a feeling for his background. Would she think it odd—bad taste even? It was too late to worry about that. Anything queer she did, Olive would just think it was part of her deteriorating state. She waited to feel calmer, but when her heart didn't quiet, she tried speaking in a low voice.

"Since I've mentioned Sicily so often to you, Olive—" she sounded as if she were being confidential when she wanted to sound casual, but she couldn't help it. "—I wondered if you might be interested in a journal I kept of our trip; I came across it the other day. You might see how much Sicily means to Paulo. Of course, you may find it boring—" She was having trouble breathing because she was nervous. "It may seem a little personal here and there, but you can skip over those places. Just read it with an—an understanding eye." She hadn't meant to make such a pathetic plea; how disgusting.

"Why I, of course, I'd be terribly interested," Olive said. Tiresa was breathing so hard. "Are you all right, Trisa?"

Tiresa nodded. "In my bottom drawer . . ."

Olive opened the drawer, thinking Tiresa wanted some medicine. Instead, she saw a red leather notebook with the stain of a coffee cup on the cover. Tiresa nodded, and Olive took it over to her.

"You can see if it interests you. If it's boring, just bring it back. You can read it while the nurse is here." She closed her eyes in dismissal, but she opened them again. "Olive, read it in your room; don't leave it lying around."

Why would Tiresa want her to read her journal? She said to skip the personal parts, but, great Cow! It was all personal, and it all ran together. There wasn't too much of it—twenty pages, maybe, but closely written in Tiresa's neat handwriting. As she flipped through it, two snapshots fell out. Paulo in lederhosen. Behind him was a mountain. He looked so young standing there, and handsome; his hair hadn't started to recede. She would like to have known him when he was younger—but he wouldn't be very different. On the other side, Tiresa had written, "Paulo under his volcano."

In the other snapshot, Tiresa was smiling under a big straw hat. How slender she was then—that must have been fifteen years ago; how could you grow middle-aged looking in so short a time? It kind of scared you. Olive tucked the snapshots in the back of the journal and began reading.

"After all my protests, it is heavenly to be here on shipboard with nothing to do but sit in the sun and watch the movement of the sea." Tiresa must have been nuts not to want to go to Italy. If she and Ron could have gone to Europe—maybe it would have made a difference.

Why did Tiresa think it was so barbarous to get excited about a knife fight? Ron said everything was passionate with Sicilians—to kill or make love. What did Tiresa expect?

The word "joy" stopped her. She read the sentence again. "Sicilians have a natural born capacity for sorrow and suffering, he said, but they have as great a one for joy . . ." Paulo had called her a child of joy—that was a laugh; he couldn't think that now. It was funny the way the word "joy" didn't seem to come up in most people's conversations. It wasn't a thing you talked about, but with Paulo and Tiresa it seemed as natural as a word like sex or money—though she'd never heard them talk about those.

"I sat there feeling as though I had had a vision. I had seen my little son alive, and I had seen Paulo as a child. After this, Paulo will always be my child to mother as well as my husband to love."

Yech! She had never felt motherly about Ron. Not even when his mother showed her all those cute pictures of him as a little boy. Mothering your son after he was grown and married was psycho, let alone mothering your husband. Tiresa didn't seem the sloppy kind that would, either. Olive thought back, hunting signs of this strange propensity. Tiresa did understand Paulo awfully well, but that wasn't mothering. Of course, she had lost her baby when she wrote that; subconsciously she was substituting—only it couldn't have been subconscious when you wrote about it in a journal.

As soon as Olive had taken the journal, Tiresa began to feel uneasy. Once she reached for the bell to ask Bessie to call her back. She would simply tell Olive that she had decided it was too personal, and it wouldn't mean anything to anyone else. She would laugh and say she'd forgotten how much there was about her own reactions than about Sicily. After all, it was written over fifteen years ago.

She put the bell down. No, there were things in there that she wanted Olive to learn about: how much in Paulo went back to his Sicilian background. How else could she understand that side of him and come to love it? And the journal would make her think of him as younger. Olive had never seen him as lighthearted as he was on that picnic running across the field to share their bottle of wine with the sheepherder, or thought of him as a medical student, let alone as a small boy. It would take an imagination to understand Paulo. Olive hadn't the faintest idea of loving a man so that his childhood and adolescence, and his insecurities—even his weaknesses were hers too in a way. It wouldn't hurt her to read about Asunta either. Except that she would just think of Ron and that girl he was going to marry. She wouldn't understand that Paulo's affair with Asunta was quite different. Asunta was Sicily to him, in a sense, and his youth.

When Olive had been gone more than an hour, Tiresa began to wonder. It was taking her a long time to read those few pages. At least she wasn't skimming them. Perhaps she had been so embarrassed by the journal that she wanted to put off bringing it back.

Olive returned it just before lunch. "Oh Tiresa, thank you for letting me read this. I just loved it; it's more fascinating than any novel."

"It's hardly a novel. Just drop it back in the drawer where you found it, will you?" Anger washed over her mind, quickening her heart beat.

Olive had saved out the picture of Tiresa. "I adore this picture of you with your hat tied under your chin. You're so cute standing there against the hill. Could you bear to part with it? I'd love to have it."

"Oh, that period piece. Isn't there one of Paulo, too? Yes," she said when Olive produced it, "I always rather liked that one of him."

"I do, too. He looks so young and handsome."

"Doesn't he look athletic? You two ought to play some tennis while you're here. I guess there's no point in my keeping the snapshots, Olive. Take them both, if you like."

Olive leaned over and kissed the side of Tiresa's head. "Thank you, Trisa, I'll love having them."

Tiresa made no answer. That sleazy use of "love" in every other sentence jarred on her nerves, and she didn't care for her sudden demonstrativeness—a kiss for the poor old wreck.

"What a wonderful time you had on that trip. It was thrilling to read about it. I felt as if I'd been to Sicily myself."

Olive's remarks were flat, *jejune*—rather forced. What a fool she had been to show the journal to her. Tiresa felt demeaned, as if she had exposed her own body with the edema swelling her legs and abdomen. Exposed Paulo, too,

"And I just howled over your first night in that villa!" Olive went on. "You were wonderful the way you took everything in your stride."

Tiresa turned her head away and closed her eyes over the tears that burned on her eyelids.

Bessie came in with her tray. "I guess you'll want to eat here, too," she said to Olive.

"Yes, I'd like to, thank you, Bessie."

"It's too good a day to be shut up in here," Tiresa said. "Take your tray out on the balcony, Olive. Imagine you are in Sicily."

Olive hesitated. "I'd rather be here with you, Tiresa, and hear more about being there."

"I can't talk any more just now," Tiresa said. "If you want to go out, there's a key on my dresser. Keep it while you're here."

But what had she wanted Olive to say about the journal? At least not to gush over it, and her. If Olive had said she could see how much Sicily meant to Paulo or how hard it must have been for him to go back and see his old home run down and full of strangers—anything to show that she had some empathy, some imagination. Or if she had to be effusive, why didn't she speak of the miracle of that little boy appearing right outside Paulo's home. But to say it was more fascinating than a novel! Tiresa's mouth twisted in distaste. She was getting too agitated. She leaned against the pillows trying to get her breath, but her brain ground on.

She had been a fool to think that Olive could be someone for Paulo—whom he might marry in time. Olive was too young and insensitive; too shallow and self-centered for Paulo. She had been trying to make sure Paulo would be all right after she was gone, but it was no use. That was what death was—having to let go, not being able to do anything about the future. Or else planning something like this that turned out to be farcical.

Bessie came for her tray and Tiresa kept her eyes closed. Bessie would tell Paulo tonight how badly she was breathing in her sleep.

Slowly, her anger ran out. Olive couldn't be completely shallow or she wouldn't have wanted her marriage to mean more, or worried about loving her child enough. Olive had so few words to say what she felt—like so many college girls: "fascinating," "thrilling"—"love." That was the trouble. Now her heart was quieting and she could breath easily again. She drifted off.

But could Olive come to love Paulo enough? As though the question had roused her, she was wide awake. Paulo was demanding, and if he were angry or depressed, he could be silent and morose for a day or more. If he became ill—whenever any indisposition struck Paulo, he was depressed that it should happen and always convinced that it was a sign of something fatal and had to be laughed back into rationality.

But if she were sick or depressed herself, or worried about Johnny, there was no one like Paulo. Olive had wanted a marriage that meant more, hadn't she? Tiresa pulled herself up a little higher against her pillows. Her eyes flashed.

Why should she worry about Olive's happiness with Paulo? All she, herself, wanted was to have a little more time with him. A few more mornings to wake beside him, a few more times to have him call from the office—all their little jokes. Olive would learn what it was to die in love. A dry sob wrenched through her. She was losing all that. The wild bird in her breast beat with frantic wings against the cage of her chest, and its sharp beak tore at the bars.

She lay as though she had been dropped on some beach, too weak to move, able only to watch the waves of sun seeping in between the slightly moving curtains. What had she been thinking? It didn't matter. Her limp body seemed to move with the waves.

6

Olive went back out on the balcony. The afternoon dragged. After lunch she had taken a walk, but only a short one. She wanted to be here when Tiresa woke. It had been a mistake to stay over. She felt in the way. This morning Tiresa said it was good to have her here, but she hadn't wanted to have lunch with her. It wasn't that she just wanted to sleep, she was annoyed at something. But what? It couldn't be anything about the journal; she had told Tiresa that she loved reading it. She was different this time.

It was almost four thirty. Surely Tiresa wouldn't sleep all this time. Olive tapped lightly on her door. When there was no sound, she opened it a crack. Tiresa was lying back against the pillows, wide awake.

"Good. You're awake, Tiresa."

"Wha—?" Tiresa said in an odd, thin voice.

Olive pulled open the curtains. "It's a lovely afternoon." When she turned from the window, she was startled by Tiresa's face. It was gray and without expression.

Tiresa tried to sit up. "I think I'll go . . ." She seemed to lose her thought. Olive lowered the bed and took her arm as she walked a little unsteadily across the room to the bathroom. By the time she was back in bed, Tiresa was breathing hard. She hadn't spoken a word.

"I'll get you some juice," Olive said.

Tiresa drank only a swallow and gave back the glass. The phone rang in the study.

"I'll get it," Olive said, but Tiresa looked for the extension that was disconnected on the floor by the bed. Olive plugged it in and handed the phone to her. The receiver slipped out of Tiresa's hand, and Olive rescued it for her.

"Hello, Paulo," Tiresa said into the mouthpiece, still in that odd thin voice. "Are you coming home?" There was another pause. Paulo was saying something. Olive could hear the crackle of Paulo's voice, but Tiresa didn't seem to be answering. He was saying something else. Tiresa let the receiver drop out of her hand.

"Can I help, Tiresa?" She picked up the receiver, but no one was on the other end.

"Will you brush my hair, Olive, before Paulo comes? Up high on my head."

Olive looked at her quickly. "I'd love to if it won't tire you. I have to do something—I'll be right back." Something was wrong with Tiresa; it frightened her. In the study she dialed Paulo's number that was written by the phone. His secretary answered.

"Dr. Romano was called out of the office on an emergency," the secretary began. Olive didn't wait for her to say more.

"I'm calling from his home. Mrs. Romano doesn't seem well."

"Yes, Dr. Romano is on his way home," the secretary said.

When Olive went back into the room, Tiresa lay quietly, her bright eyes in her pale face. She was all right, Olive told herself. Maybe she hadn't been quite awake. Maybe that was why she thought her hair was still long.

"If you turn your head to the side, Tiresa, you can lie against the pillow while I'm brushing." She began to move the brush gently over the short hair that was thick and live, and black as coal.

"It gets matted," Tiresa said slowly.

Olive tried to brush as though she were lifting long hair. "Now I'll do the other side, Tiresa, if you'll turn your head just a little." She glanced quickly at Tiresa's face as she went around to the other side of the bed. Her eyes seemed to be on the sun streaming through the light curtains.

"Is the sun too bright? Shall I pull the curtains a little?"

"I like sun," Tiresa said slowly.

To have Tiresa, who always spoke quickly speak so slowly made Olive uneasy. "I sat out on the balcony this afternoon while you were sleeping and kept thinking about you and Paulo in Sicily, Tiresa," she began. It was better to keep talking. "I loved the time you went to the old Greek theater."

"Greco-Roman," Tiresa said.

"Greco-Roman," Olive repeated, reassured by Tiresa's correction. "And you sat on the top tier and Paulo ran down to the front and stood against a pillar and recited in Greek. I don't wonder you were thrilled." Tiresa's eyes were closed. Olive wondered if she had fallen asleep again.

"He was Prometheus," Tiresa said, pronouncing the syllables carefully, in the same light expressionless voice. Still, she must be all right if she could remember about the theater, and the part Paulo took.

Olive swept her hand gently over the back of Tiresa's head and fumbled with the short hair as if she were twisting it into a knot. Tiresa didn't seem to notice that she wasn't putting in any hairpins. "I'm going to get to Sicily one of these days, and I'll remember all the places where you and Paulo went," Olive chattered nervously, hoping Tiresa would say something.

"There, Trisa!" Olive held the brush still. But Tiresa had dozed off again. Olive leaned over so she could see her face. Her skin was that gray color it had been ever since Olive came. Her lips were bluish. Only her black brows arching above her closed eyelids and the black hair waving back from her forehead looked right. She put her hand on Tiresa's; it was no colder than it often was, but something was different.

"Tiresa," she whispered. She touched her hair. It felt . . . too light, as though, as though it were on the head of a mannequin. Then she saw the lace of Tiresa's gown moving with her breathing. Relief flooded through her. Tiresa was just sleeping, that was all. She was so weak she kept falling off.

Olive went over to the dresser, but sudden fear seized her. "Tiresa!" she cried out, her voice sharp. The name sounded as if she were calling it in an empty room—as if Tiresa weren't there. She went back to the bed. "Tiresa." She lay without stirring.

Yet how could Tiresa be breathing and not be there? She had talked to her just a few minutes ago—corrected her about the theater. Olive looked around at the room to try to stop her own trembling. She looked at the sun moving against the wall, at the dresser where she had laid the brush. She could hear faraway sounds on the avenue and the near sound of the electric beater in the kitchen, but none of these seemed real. She swallowed against the tightness of her throat and sat down on the chair beside Tiresa's bed to wait for Paulo.

When she heard him she went out to the hall.

"How is Tiresa? She didn't quite sound like herself," Paulo said.

Olive shook her head. "I'm afraid she's gone, Paulo."

Paulo gave a startled look and brushed past Olive. She followed him to the doorway.

"She's just sleeping. Her breathing is a little shallow, but . . ."

Olive watched him lay his hand against Tiresa's face. He seemed to look at one side and then the other. He raised one eyelid. Now he was pressing her neck with his fingers. "Call the hospital, Olive." He gave her the number, and she knelt on the floor by the bed, dialing, and then handed him the phone. Paulo was ordering an ambulance, calling Dr. Stiles. Couldn't he see that Tiresa wasn't really there?

"If you'll help me put on Tiresa's robe, Olive, we won't bother with anything more." He brought her red Chinese coat and they slipped it on without her opening her eyes. Paulo laid her back against the pillows. His face was nearly as pale as Tiresa's.

Olive saw Bessie beckon from the doorway and went out.

"What happened? Is she gone?" Bessie asked in a frightened whisper.

"She's still breathing."

"I don't think she'll be coming back, poor soul," Bessie said when she and Olive were alone in the apartment. "Didn't I tell you she could go off like that!" She snapped her fingers. "I never thought Dr. Romano realized how bad she was. After all, he's an eye doctor and he wouldn't know all about the insides." Bessie looked nervously at Olive. She was just sitting there on the couch as if she'd had a shock herself. Some people couldn't take death, and she was so young, she'd probably never seen anyone die.

"Why don't you and me have our supper together out in the kitchen? It'll cheer us up to have someone to talk to," Bessie said. "I guess you'll want to stay here overnight, won't you? I can sleep in the study."

"Oh, no, you don't need to do that," Olive said.

"Well, I just thought—folks might . . . you know. The Doctor'll be staying on here, don't you think?"

"I don't know." Olive looked through the doorway into the living room. How could Paulo stand it here without Tiresa?

"Well, I'll be going then," Bessie said when she was through in the kitchen. She hesitated. "You feel all right not having another women here?"

"Yes, I'll be fine," Olive said, but when the door clicked behind Bessie, the emptiness of the apartment drove her out to the balcony.

Lights were beginning to come on in both wings of the apartment house, and people were sitting on their balconies. An occasional laugh or voice drifted up to her, or the whiff of a cigarette—just as they had that September when she and Ron moved here. She hadn't known a soul, and then Tiresa had called and invited them over.

7

It was nearly ten when Olive heard Bessie open the door of the apartment. "Tiresa went into a coma and died early this morning," Bessie said, eyeing Olive, still curled up on the couch. "I thought I should come let you know. The Doctor'll be back here later, after he's made the arrangements. I thought I should go to the store and get some things ready for him. Can I get you anything before I go? Coffee?"

"No. Thank you, Bessie."

"You sure?"

"Yes." Olive pulled the throw that had always hung on the end of the couch for Tiresa tighter around her neck.

"I'll be back soon." Olive listened to Bessie's footsteps in the hall.

The stillness of the apartment was so loud she could hear it, and she could feel the emptiness. She lay without moving until the clock striking ten broke through the silence.

Yesterday morning, Tiresa was in the room across the hall. Then, Olive was going back over the whole day, as if it lay in her mind in pieces that she had to fit together. She took each happening, everything Tiresa had said, to see where it fitted, what meaning it had. She came again to the moment when she knew Tiresa wasn't there. But this time it wasn't fear that seized her mind— it was strangeness. She struggled with the mystery; never before had she wondered about two worlds of being. Why hadn't Paulo felt that Tiresa was gone? She hadn't imagined it—she had never known anything more surely.

Olive fled her own questions out through the living room to her bedroom. She dressed quickly and let her hair go with a quick brush. Bessie and Paulo would be back soon, and she had to get out before that. When she left the apartment, she thought how strange it was that Tiresa had given her the key just yesterday.

As she went by the desk at the entrance, Carl looked up. "I'm sure sorry about Mrs. Romano. She was as fine a lady as ever lived here. And so young to die—I hear she was only fifty-four."

"Yes," Olive said. She hurried out of the building to the Drive and crossed to the river side.

A boy came by jogging, and after he had gone a block ahead of her, Olive started to jog. There weren't many pedestrians on the walk, but the stream of traffic was steady. She was running abreast of a blue car, and sprinted, trying for an idiotic moment to keep up with it. The car gained on her and slipped past, but there was a black car, and then a white one . . . She was running too fast, her chest hurt and she was breathing hard. She settled back into a slower pace, no longer watching the cars moving past; the easy rhythm of her pounding feet sounded inside her head and carried her with them.

"Atlantis!" a man called out as he came toward her on the walk. She laughed and ran on, a flash of blue with light hair bouncing on her back.

Paulo ought to try jogging, she must tell him how good it made you feel. Without breaking her rhythm she circled around and was running back, so naturally now it seemed effortless. When she sank down on one of the benches above the river, heat suffused her and she broke out into a sweat, but her body glowed, taking over her mind. A breeze from the river cooled her flushed face. Idly her eyes followed the skyline across the river, and came back to watch the white sails maneuvering in the basin, and a wind-surfer in the tow of a boat, but seeming to fly through the water on his great white wings; she never looked up at the apartment house across the drive. The morning was nearly gone when she went back.

"Oh," Bessie said with a hint of reproach in her voice. "You've been exercising from the looks of your face."

"I just went for a walk." She felt a little foolish in Bessie's eyes. On her way to her room, she passed Tiresa's. The door was open, and the hospital bed was stripped and framed in all its angularity of steel mechanism. Bright sun filled the room. Olive hadn't looked in this room since yesterday. Now she stepped in a little timidly, but no least shadow of fear lingered in it, or any sense of desolation. Tiresa had left, that was all. She was through with it and didn't have to lie on that bed any more, or struggle for breath. She was free from all that. Olive felt a sense of relief.

As she turned to go, Bessie came by. "It makes you feel queer, don't it, a room where someone's died?"

"No," Olive said. "Tiresa's room doesn't."

Paulo came for lunch. When Olive saw his haggard face, she remembered what Tiresa had said about his giving up when he knew something was hopeless.

"How did your arrangements go?" she asked.

He nodded. "It went well. I've closed the office for the next few days, and I have someone looking after my patients in the hospital, but it might be better to keep busy," he added with a hopeless shake of his head.

"Paulo, would it be easier if you were alone? Or is it all right if I wait for the—funeral? When will that be?"

Her question seemed to bring him out of his thoughts. "I wish you would stay, Olive. There will be a private service tomorrow at two. Funerals didn't mean much to Tiresa. The only thing I remember her saying about a funeral was once in Sicily. She said she would like to have her ashes scattered on the slopes under Etna." The trace of a smile twisted his mouth. "She was being facetious, of course, but if I were in Sicily, I would do it."

After a few minutes he said, "Olive, I didn't ask if you would like to go and see Tirese. I don't think she would like to be looked at after her death. I didn't feel it was Tirese, lying there."

"I know," Olive said eagerly. "Even before you got here, yesterday, I felt Tiresa wasn't there."

Paulo's eyes met Olive's. "No, that couldn't be. She was with me in the ambulance." Then they were silent again, each confused by a mystery beyond their understanding.

Paulo smiled gently. "I took the gold locket down and put it around her neck."

"She would like that," Olive said in a low voice.

"Yes, I think she would."

As they got up from the table, the maintenance men came to take down the hospital bed, "Good," Paulo said briskly. "Tirese would want to get it out of the way."

The clang of metal as one bed rail hit against the other, the men's voices, and their heavy steps down the hall were a relief. Paulo went to direct them.

Olive stood uneasily in front of the windows to the balcony. She would like to go out—anywhere. To the Natatorium, maybe; she had never got there. But she felt she should be here. The time till the funeral tomorrow seemed endless—and sad. And she was no help to Paulo. What had Tiresa thought she could do for him?

"Look, Olive." Paulo came to the doorway of the living room. "The bedroom is as it used to be, just as if Tirese would come back to it from college, only I must get some yellow roses for her."

Olive's mind writhed in embarrassment. There was something so sentimental or something so—getting flowers for an empty room. But she followed him down the hall.

The big mahogany bed with the low-carved head- and footboard was already made up with its tailored green spread. Tiresa's desk was back in the corner, the front down and her books on it. Olive thought of the first night she had sat in this room. They had had a drink here the night after she got her divorce—Tuesday night, only three nights ago.

"It's good to see everything just as it was," she said. But the realization that nothing was the same, that Tiresa would never be back in this room, struck them at the same minute and they went out silently.

"I thought I'd drive down to the florist's," Paulo said. "Would you like to go along? It will get us out of the apartment."

It was no easier to talk in the car. When he came out with the wrapped bouquet of yellow roses, Paulo said, "We might drive a few miles. Would you like to, Olive?"

"Yes," Olive said, and then because it seemed too brief an answer, she said, "It helps to be moving. This morning, I jogged along the drive. You should try jogging, Paulo."

"Perhaps I will." It was a momentary relief to think of himself jogging. "I've been getting so little exercise."

Olive stole a look at Paulo's stern, closed face and ached to help him. She wished they could go to a movie, but, maybe you didn't do that after a death in the family. She remembered Tiresa talking about feeling sad over the loss of her baby. She said there was nothing to be afraid of in sadness. But it was awful just sitting here, suffering. How would Paulo ever stand it?

They were out in the country now. Paulo was driving faster. "I wish I could have got Tirese up to the farm this spring," he said.

"She loved it there, didn't she?"

"In a special way—she felt she had put roots down there." He took his eyes from the road an instant to look at Olive. "Do you know, Olive, I believe Tirese would like her ashes buried in that little cemetery up above the farm. She used to go up there and read the old tombstones, and enjoy the peace and beauty of the view. I'll go up Sunday and find out about it." His eyes were on the road, and his voice had lost its flatness. "I'll have a stone—as much like one of those old slate ones as I can get, Tirese used to be amused by the old Puritan names; hers will bring a whole new note to the cemetery. Tiresa," he pronounced softly, sounding each syllable. "There won't be another Tiresa."

They had a martini out on the balcony before dinner. Paulo

raised his glass. "To Tiresa, who gave my life whatever grace it possessed, its dignity—its joy." They touched their glasses. His voice was uncertain after the last word.

Dinner passed in the same uncomfortable way lunch had, with long pauses in the conversation, their few comments irrelevant to what each of them was thinking.

"Tirese wouldn't like our sitting here so solemnly, hardly talking," Paulo said. "Tomorrow night, we will go out. There's a little Italian place we sometimes went to, especially when I was depressed. Tirese thought the Italian atmosphere was good for me. In fact, the owner is Sicilian." He smiled. "Tirese had her own ideas about what was good for me, some of them completely absurd, but most of the time, I let her keep them. One was that it was good for me to be with young people." He stopped and seemed to lose himself in his own thoughts. "You know, Olive, I wonder if she didn't ask you to stay longer with us not so much for herself—though she was looking forward to having you—but because—" He had a sip of wine and held the glass for a moment, watching the candlelight reflected in it. "—because she felt herself near the end and didn't want me to be alone. That sounds fantastic, but she could have, you know."

And as suddenly, Olive knew that it was true.

He looked at Olive. "I'm afraid it has been hard on you."

"But how could she know she was so close to—"

"Dying?" Paulo shook his head. "There was no explaining Tirese. She had a kind of mystical sense—and great wisdom."

298

8

Olive waited for Paulo outside the funeral home. She was glad to be out in the sun after the air-conditioned chill and the hush of the gray curtained room. The service was over so quickly that she hadn't had time to enter into it, or think about the words that flowed over her in a well-modulated voice; they seemed so far-removed from Tiresa. Only the music was a help, as Paulo had said it would be.

"This will be a little different from the funerals that you are used to," he said on the way over.

"I've never been to a funeral," Olive said. "I just never happened to."

Paulo was aghast. "Why Olive, you poor child. I'm sorry. I grew up with them. I was an acolyte at *Chiesa Madre* in Taormina when I was six or seven." A faint smile lightened his face. "I wore a scarlet cotta and a lace surplice and was on hand for every funeral that came along. And weddings—I got in on those too." For an instant, Olive could see him as that little boy Tiresa had written about in her journal.

"I would have preferred a mass at St. Peters, of course, but Tirese wouldn't want that. She was a skeptic, but, as she used to say, not an irreligious one." Paulo seemed to lose himself in his own thoughts, his eyes down on the street. Then he said, "This was what Tirese would call civilized and quite brief. But they did play Beethoven's last quartet, number sixteen that Tirese so loved. That helped."

When they got back in the car, Paulo laid his hand on Olive's. "Are you all right, Olive?"

"Yes. It didn't seem very real. I feel as if we were going back now to tell Tiresa all about it—like the night we went to see *The Three Sisters*—" she broke off in embarrassment.

"I know," Paulo said.

They were silent the rest of the way home. Paulo stopped the car in front of the apartment and came around to let Olive out. "I'll be home in an hour or so," he said vaguely, and got back in the car as if he was in a hurry to be off.

It was hard going into the empty apartment. Bessie had shut the windows and turned off the air-conditioner; the room was as closed as Paulo's face on the drive home. Olive went about opening the windows on the balcony and in the bedroom, not letting herself quite look at any of the familiar things. As though it were an automatic reaction, she hurried to change into shorts and a shirt and went barefoot out to the kitchen to get a Coke. With it she drifted out on the balcony. Tiresa used to sit there in the tilt-back chair, reading the *Times* and cutting out clippings for Paulo. He would miss that.

When she finished her Coke, she went in to pack her bag. The bus would be leaving at eight. They'd have an early breakfast and Paulo would drive her to the station. She'd feel bad going off and leaving him alone, but she had been here when Tiresa died—that was what Tiresa had wanted.

She couldn't think of anything else to do, so she wandered back into the living room that was airier now, but the emptiness and stillness still hovered. Without Tiresa it was as ghastly as the funeral parlor.

She looked around the room that had seemed so warm and glowing—at the tapestry on the wall and the glass clock, the books from floor to ceiling on the far wall and the rich red Oriental rug in front of the fireplace. Her glance moved to the long refectory table, and was held there. She thought of the three of them sitting at the table, with the candle-light shining on the tall-stemmed wine glasses. She could see Tiresa leaning back in her chair, laughing the way she did. Now Tiresa had gone, without a word.

The next minute, the shadowy face of the Sicilian mirror reflected a figure—girl or woman—crying against the arm of the couch. Whether out of her own sense of loss, or for Tiresa, Olive herself could hardly know.

Paulo called to her as he came to the apartment.

"Here I am, Paulo—on the balcony." She looked at his face and looked away.

"I was grateful not to come back to an empty apartment," he said as he sat down with her. "I was thinking as I came up the elevator how many years I've called Tirese about this time of day." He shook his head. "It's going to be like that—remembering all the time." He made an effort to come back to Olive. "Did you get along all right?"

"Oh yes, I was fine."

"You look very cool and collected."

"I just took a shower and got dressed. I wasn't sure what time we were going to dinner."

"I couldn't get back sooner." It was true, he thought. He couldn't make himself come back to the apartment. He had gone to his closed office and sat at his desk, merely sat there. He looked at the snapshot of Tiresa he kept under the glass top of his desk, and then got up and went out of the office. On the way home, he had dropped into St. Peters and knelt there in the empty cathedral. Words he had learned in Latin as a boy came easily to his lips. He would have a mass said for Tirese. The idea might have amused her, but she would have understood.

"Shall we have a martini before we go." He sprang up as though glad to have something to do.

In spite of herself, Olive was excited about going out to dinner. It was a relief to get out of the apartment and drive through the city. Her spirits lifted.

"I think you'll like Da Salvatore's. It's *amichevole—allegro.*" He waved his hands. "Friendly and light-hearted. Salvatore Coppolo runs it. He's the son; the old man just walks around and beams, but he's always there. Both of them are very fond of Tiresa."

As they went to the door of the restaurant, Paulo said, "This green door always reminded Tiresa of a garden door in Taormina."

"I know. Where you went for cocktails, and they had central heating and a big fireplace and the house was full of art treasures," Olive said.

Paulo stood still in amazement. "How did you know that? Did Tirese tell you about it?"

Olive flushed uncomfortably. Shouldn't she have mentioned the journal? "Tiresa gave me her journal that she kept in Sicily to read." Maybe Tiresa wouldn't have wanted Paulo to read all those things she wrote about him. She tried to think which parts he might mind. But the door opened and Salvatore Coppolo stood in the doorway.

"Ah, Dr. Romano, *va—non c'e. Che piacere vederla!*"

"Olive, this is a fellow countryman from Sicily. Salvatore, meet *Signora* Fifer."

"*Signora* Fifer, welcome to Salvatore's." He made a deep bow. His skin was the color of Paulo's, and he had a wide smile and black eyes, but he was shorter and heavier. "The table you always like is waiting for you." He showed them to a table in the far corner. "We haven't seen you for a long time."

"I know that, Salvatore, but Mrs. Romano has been very ill."

Olive looked up and saw that Salvatore's face was desolate. "I hope she—"

Paulo cut him off quickly. "Tiresa died Wednesday morning."

Olive felt Salvatore's eyes on her and dropped her head. "Olive was with Mrs. Romano when she died. She was Mrs. Romano's closest friend and a great comfort to . . ." Paulo's voice faded. Olive looked up, startled by Paulo's words. But, suddenly

Salvatore's arms were around Paulo and Paulo's around Salvatore. Then she thought of what Tiresa had written in the journal about Sicilian faces. Salvatore's face had changed from desolate to tragic. They spoke in Sicilian and she knew they were speaking of Tiresa from their expressions and the tone of their voices. Then Salvatore lighted the red candle on the checked tablecloth. He stood back and looked at both Paulo and Olive. "You don't bother with order tonight. I bring you *caponata*, maybe? You like that?"

"No." Paulo shook his head. "Not tonight. Maybe fish—do you like fish, Olive? *Trance di Pesce alla Siciliana*."

Salvatore nodded. "*Insalata* . . ."

"*Cassata* for dessert." Paulo's hands gestured as he ordered.

"*Si, si,* and *vino*—I take care of everything."

"At first, Tirese never knew what was coming when I ordered in Sicilian, but she came to know as time went on. And Salvatore gave her some of his recipes."

Olive looked around the low-beamed room for the first time. Some fragrance of olive oil, tinctured with garlic and herbs, clung to the beams. Most of the candles on the tables were lit by now, and the faces around the tables, many of them Italian, took on a gentler cast. It was all very clean, very simple. Only the wine bottles ranged on the long dresser and the copper pitchers served for decoration. She turned to Paulo to ask what he had meant by . . .

"But, what you said about me being with her when . . . I thought you said—Bessie said she died early this morning?"

Paulo placed his hand on top of Olive's. "But, you said you felt her go from you there in her room . . ." Olive stared into Paulo's dark eyes, searching. His eyes reflected the wavering candlelight. "I guess Tiresa would say that was one of life's mysteries." He waved his hands as though the mysteries were just beyond their reach.

"And, what you said, Paulo, about me being—".

"Olive, I think you were her closest friend. A bit like the child we never—"

303

Olive's eyes filled with tears, "No, not me. You were . . ." Suddenly, Olive caught herself.

"I was what?" He leaned across the table.

Olive searched for words. "You—you were her closest friend."

"Oh, of course, but I think there are mysteries that perhaps only women share . . ." He smiled and patted Olive's hand.

For a moment, they sat in silence and watched the candle. Then Paulo took Olive's hand. "Now Olive, tell me about the journal."

"It's the one Tiresa kept in Sicily. Didn't you know she kept one?"

"No," he said slowly. "But she was always writing in notebooks. Do you have it?"

"I put it back in her drawer." She wondered uneasily if Tiresa perhaps didn't want him to know that she had thought of him as a child. Yet, he could see how she loved him. "I'll get it for you when we go back, Paulo. What a wonderful time you had."

"We did have. I took her to see where I was born and grew up. She fell a little in love with Sicily, I think. It's a beautiful land, you know."

Salvatore's father brought a tall-necked bottle of wine with a stained label and set it down in front of Paulo. He spoke in Italian, shaking his head sorrowfully. Then he pointed to the bottle. "For *Signora* Romano, '63 Soave." He opened it laboriously and poured a little in Paulo's glass, and at Paulo's nod, filled both glasses. Paulo sent him to get a glass for himself and they all drank to Tiresa. Olive saw the tears in Paulo's eyes.

"This is from Salvatore's very best," Paulo said. He lifted his glass so it caught the light. "Like Tirese, true and brilliant and beautiful." The sadness had crept back into his face, and they were silent over their soup. Paulo was looking at the bottle of wine, then he held it so Olive could see. The year is '63; that's the year we went to Sicily. And now you tell me there is a journal by Tirese." Excitement stirred in his eyes. "Tell me something more that is in the journal."

304

"You'll love it Paulo. Tiresa tells about both of you going to the old theater."

"Yes, we did that—our last afternoon there."

"Wednesday afternoon, when Tiresa woke up, she seemed—different. Well, you know how she sounded on the phone. After she talked with you she was a little confused and thought her hair was long again. She asked me to brush it and do it up on her head before you came. So I was brushing and talking about the journal, and I said I loved that time you were at the Greek theater, and quick as a flash, she said 'Greco-Roman.' So she wasn't really confused."

Paulo's face was intent and his black eyes glowed.

"And then I said you ran down front and leaned against a pillar and recited Greek. She didn't say anything for a moment, and then she said, you were Prometheus. Wasn't that amazing!"

Paulo nodded gravely and seemed to withdraw to think about it. The rest of their dinner came and Paulo ate only a little. He asked for coffee with the meal and sat drinking coffee more than eating. "And tonight you just happened to tell me about the journal because I said the door made Tirese think of one in Sicily," he said slowly. "What if we hadn't come here tonight?"

"You would have come across her journal anyway," Olive said.

Paulo looked up quickly. "But it's tonight that I need it." His hand beat against the table. "Don't you see? It means everything to have some words of Tiresa's—from a time when she was so well and happy."

Salvatore came over to see how they were doing but their silence and the sight of Paulo's hardly tasted food kept him from saying anything. He shook his head sorrowfully at Olive.

"Are you finished, sir?" the young waiter asked on his third visit to the table.

"Yes, you can take it," Paulo said. "Early in the winter, Tirese had me bring up the straw trunk we bought in Sicily, and she went over it. The journal must have been in there. I wonder what made her think of it." He went off into his own thoughts again. When the dessert came, he made a little effort. "You will like this, Olive. When I was a child, I thought this cake must be what they ate in Paradise." Now he was smiling at her, watching her reaction.

And then they were in the car on their way home. Olive wished they could have lingered longer in that cheerful place. But the apartment was easier to take when they came back; perhaps it was that Paulo was there, too, she thought. She got the journal and on an impulse stopped in her room to put the two snapshots back in it so Paulo would come on them.

He took the journal from her and held it in his hands, looking at it, but he didn't open it. "I'll read it later," he said, slipping it into his pocket. "Thank you, Olive. You'll be glad to get home to Johnny; this stay must have seemed long without him."

"You must see him soon, Paulo. Couldn't you come to New Jersey? Mother and Dad would love to have you stay with us overnight," she said, hoping they would.

He shook his head. "Thank you. I'd like to see them, but I haven't any plans beyond working and just trying to get through these next days, and weeks, and months."

A silence spread between them. Uncomfortably, Olive shifted and stared at the patterns on the carpet. The movement of her feet caught Paulo's eyes. He lifted his shoulders. "How selfish of me, Olive. You have been through so much with—"

"On, no," Olive interrupted him, "my troubles are nothing. I just wish I could do more—"

Paulo threw his arms around her, kissing her on each cheek. "Our child of joy. You have done so much, you will never know."

"Me? Oh, no. You and Tiresa . . ." her voice trailed off. They stood apart again.

"What are your plans now, Olive?"

Her own plans seemed so far removed, Olive hesitated.

"Come now, tell me," Paulo coaxed.

"I have been thinking about going back to graduate school," she said, almost shyly. "I have a friend, a room-mate from college, she's gone back and has been encouraging me to . . ."

Paulo's eyes sparkled. "Tiresa would like that! What will you study?"

"Marine Biology." Olive felt herself blush.

Paulo took her hands. "You are going into a unique field for a woman. Some time you must tell me what attracted you to that." He looked over at the clock on the mantle and grew silent again, almost as though the effort to speak had taken his last stores of strength.

Olive felt that Paulo wanted to be alone to read the journal. "I have to leave so early in the morning, I think I'll go to bed. Do you have an alarm clock, Paulo?"

"Yes, but I'll be up and call you. If we get up at six-thirty, we can have breakfast and get to the bus station in plenty of time. There won't be much traffic. And after the bus station, I'll drive straight up to the farm."

Once after she was in bed, Olive heard Paulo laugh in the other room. The sound seemed strange, but so good; she felt more cheerful herself. What had he read in the journal that made him laugh? Maybe over their first night in that villa. The laugh came again. She was so glad she had given him the journal, and she lay going over all that was in it. They were so happy in Sicily, that should be a comfort to him—or would it only make it harder for him? She hadn't heard him laugh again.

She thought of him driving up to the farm tomorrow and wished she were going with him. They would drive for miles without talking, and when they got there, the house would be empty and they'd miss Tiresa everywhere, but it would be better for Paulo to have someone with him. They could walk up to the cemetery together; she had never gone there. Or would he rather be alone . . . She fell asleep.

The sound that wakened her suddenly frightened her. She sat

up in bed listening. Paulo was groaning—no, he was sobbing. Now and then he said something in Italian. She heard the word "Tirese" and "No" repeated several times, and then the terrible sobs. He groaned again and the sound went through her. She slipped on her robe and went out to the living room as swiftly as she went to Johnny when he cried in the night.

The room was dark except for a line of light that came in from the outside, but she could make out Paulo sitting at the end of the couch, bent over in the contour of an old man, his head in his hands.

Olive sat by Paulo. "Don't cry like that, Paulo." Taking his hands, she searched for words, "It—it would hurt Tiresa."

Paulo's sobs stopped. Almost angrily, he burst out, "But Tiresa is gone. Nothing will ever hurt her again. Tirese's gone!"

"I know." She didn't try to say any more.

"Oh Tirese . . ." His sobs began again.

"Tiresa loved you so much, Paulo . . . you had something so special together. I could almost feel it," she murmured.

"But it was so short a time," he groaned. He lifted his head and she wiped his wet face with her hands. Olive patted his back and murmured the same soothing tones she used late at night when Johnny woke crying. Her mind drifted to what Tiresa had written in her journal and to how she had thought that Tiresa was crazy, that loving a man was nothing like loving a child. But maybe . . .

Paulo's sobs stopped and his sudden silence startled Olive from her thoughts. He was staring at her with a look she had never seen.

Awkwardly, Olive moved to the far corner of the couch. He was a stranger to her, hardly Paulo. They sat in silence. After an endless time, she started to get up, but Paulo caught hold of her hand.

"Stay, please. I am sorry. How selfish I am to—"

"Nonsense, Paulo, Tiresa would have wanted . . . No—" Olive caught herself. Was this what Tiresa had wanted all along?

What if . . . She looked over at Paulo and gripped his hand with her own. "No, no. I want to be here. I only wish I could—I could . . ." She hesitated. What?

Paulo's eyes held her own.

"Do you want me to go with you to the farm?"

Paulo dropped his eyes and was silent. After a time, he spoke. "No. You need to get back to Johnny." His hand fell from hers.

"Are you sure?"

"Yes." Paulo covered his head with his hands and turned from her.

She stood, frozen, for a moment. "Oh Paulo. I'll—I'll get you a glass of water."

As she came from the kitchen, Olive thought she heard him mumble. "Loneliness and discontent prove our separation . . ."

Paulo took a few sips of the water. "Thank you, Olive." He seemed more composed. She watched him and then looked across the room. A slow gray light of early morning was already crawling across the far wall. Paulo's eyes followed hers. They settled on the orange tree near the balcony. Paulo walked across the room. The gray shadows of the morning caught his figure as he poured the contents of his glass on the orange tree just the way Olive had seen Tiresa do so often.

"Tiresa gave this orange tree to me when we came back from Sicily so I wouldn't miss the orange groves too much." He was smiling as he said it. For some reason, Olive held back on reminding him that she knew, that Tiresa had told them that first day . . . Paulo turned, holding the empty glass in his hand, almost as though to give a toast. "I want you and Johnny to have this tree. You take it."

"Oh no, Paulo. Tiresa said it was yours. She bought it to remind you . . ."

"Yes, and it was mine, I suppose, so long as Tiresa was here, it was." Absently, Paulo rubbed the leaves between his fingers. "She always watered it; but now, I will forget to water it and—"

Olive interrupted him, "But you mustn't—you must—"

Paulo laughed, "Ah, youth, marvelous youth. Olive, you should take this tree and if my godson ever asks about it, maybe you can tell him."

Olive walked slowly to the balcony. Together, they stood and looked out over the dawn and watched as the lights from the streets faded, each lost in their own thoughts. Olive took Paulo's hand and held it between her own.

UNIVERSITY OF NEBRASKA PRESS

Other books by or about Mildred Walker:

Winter Wheat
By Mildred Walker
Introduction by James Welch

"You are either a Mildred Walker enthusiast or you are missing one of the best writers on the American scene."—*Philadelphia Inquirer.* "Describes a young woman's emotional and spiritual awakening as she confronts the disappointments and marvels of love. . . . Walker's heroine recognizes that love, like winter wheat, requires faith and deep roots to survive the many hardships that threaten its endurance"—*Belles Lettres.*

ISBN: 0-8032-9741-6; 978-0-8032-9741-8 (paper)

Light from Arcturus
By Mildred Walker
Introduction by Mary Swander

Stuck in the middle of Nebraska in the late nineteenth century, Julia Hauser felt restless. But what could she do? Married to a dull small-town merchant and soon confined by children, she lacked money and social position. *Light from Arcturus* shows how Julia stepped beyond sacrifice and duty, fed her spirit, and grew in dignity. Readers of Willa Cather's early prairie novels will recognize Walker's heroine.

ISBN: 0-8032-9769-6; 978-0-8032-9769-2 (paper)

Writing for Her Life
The Novelist Mildred Walker
By Ripley Hugo

Drawing on family memories, letters, diaries, reviews, and, in particular, the notebooks that Mildred Walker (1905–1998) kept for each of her novels, Hugo fashions an absorbing account of how her mother's characters emerged in the landscapes that she visited again and again. Alongside this developing picture of a writer at work, Hugo shows us the proper mother and social creature as carefully and consciously crafted; between the two lovingly detailed portrayals, we glimpse the depths of a life thus divided.

ISBN: 0-8032-2383-8; 978-0-8032-2383-7 (cloth)

Order online at www.nebraskapress.unl.edu
or call 1-800-755-1105.

Mention the code "BOFOX" to receive a 20% discount.